*Make time for friends. Make time for **Debbie Macomber**.*

CEDAR COVE
16 Lighthouse Road
204 Rosewood Lane
311 Pelican Court
44 Cranberry Point
50 Harbor Street
6 Rainier Drive
74 Seaside Avenue
8 Sandpiper Way
92 Pacific Boulevard

BLOSSOM STREET
The Shop on Blossom Street
A Good Yarn
Susannah's Garden
(previously published as Old Boyfriends)
Back on Blossom Street
(previously published as Wednesdays at Four)
Twenty Wishes
Summer on Blossom Street
Hannah's List
A Turn in the Road
Thursdays at Eight

Christmas in Seattle
Falling for Christmas
A Mother's Gift

Merry Christmas, Friends!

As you've probably already guessed, I love Christmas. And I have a special fondness for Christmas angels. After all, it was an angel who came to announce to Mary that she'd be giving birth. And later, when Jesus was born, it was angels who first told the shepherds watching over their flocks.

Shirley, Goodness and Mercy have proven to be three of my most popular story characters. Since they first appeared back in 1993, they've shown up periodically through the years. Last Christmas I was delighted to find huge wire angels strung with lights for sale in a local store. Naturally I purchased three and set them up in our front yard.

Wouldn't you know it, soon afterwards we had a snow-storm with blizzard-like conditions. When I woke the next morning, I was dismayed to find my precious angels face down in the snow. My clever husband smiled and said we had three fallen angels. What struck me, however, was that despite the horrific weather conditions, their lights continued to shine.

This Christmas they're shining again, my three angels —in our yard and in this two-story edition—and they're brighter than ever. I hope Shirley, Goodness and Mercy will bring you some Christmas joy and a smile or two. And you can bet that whatever comes their way—and ours—their lights will shine!

Have a wonderful Christmas. Remember there are angels among us…and sometimes we don't even know it.

Merry Christmas!

Debbie Macomber

Angels at Christmas

Debbie Macomber

MIRA

All the characters in this book have no existence outside the imagination of the author, and have no relation whatsoever to anyone bearing the same name or names. They are not even distantly inspired by any individual known or unknown to the author, and all the incidents are pure invention.

Published in Great Britain 2011
MIRA Books, an imprint of Harlequin (UK) Limited,
Eton House, 18-24 Paradise Road, Richmond, Surrey, TW9 1SR

ANGELS AT CHRISTMAS © Harlequin Books S.A. 2009

The publisher acknowledges the copyright holder of the individual works as follows:

Those Christmas Angels © Debbie Macomber 2003
Where Angels Go © Debbie Macomber 2007

ISBN 9781 848 45050 9

58-1111

MIRA's policy is to use papers that are natural, renewable and recyclable products and made from wood grown in sustainable forests. The logging and manufacturing processes conform to the legal environmental regulations of the country of origin.

Printed and bound by
CPI Group (UK) Ltd, Croydon, CR0 4YY

Debbie Macomber is a number one *New York Times* bestselling author. Her recent books include *44 Cranberry Point*, *50 Harbor Way*, *6 Rainier Drive* and *Hannah's List*. She has become a leading voice in women's fiction worldwide and her work has appeared on every major bestseller list. There are more than a hundred million copies of her books in print. For more information on Debbie and her books, visit www.Debbie Macomber.com.

CONTENTS

Those Christmas Angels

In memory of Sandy Canfield,
talented writer and dear friend.
And to Charles Canfield with affection and thanks
for the 38 years of love and support
he gave Sandy

One

Anne Fletcher pulled the last box of Christmas decorations from the closet in the spare bedroom. She loved Christmas—always had and always would, regardless of her circumstances. It was a bit early yet, a few days before Thanksgiving, but some Christmas cheer was exactly what she needed to get her mind off her problems. The grief that had been hounding her since the divorce five years ago... The financial uncertainty she now faced... The betrayal she still felt...

"No," she said aloud, refusing to allow herself to step closer to that swamp of regrets. It often happened like this. She'd start thinking about everything she'd lost, and before she knew it, she'd collapse emotionally, drowning in pain.

Carrying the plastic container down the hallway, she glanced inside her art room and let her gaze drift over to her easel and her latest project. The bold colors of the setting sun against the backdrop of the Pacific Ocean pleased her. Yes, she was divorced, but there'd been compensations, too. Her art had fulfilled her in ways she hadn't even realized were possible.

How different her life was at fifty-nine than she would've

imagined even five years ago—before the divorce. What
Burton had done was unforgivable. He'd hurt her, and he'd
cheated her out of funds that were rightfully hers.

Once again she stopped herself, not wanting to indulge
those bitter memories and regrets. She'd done plenty of that
in the beginning, when she'd first learned he'd found
someone else and wanted out of their thirty-year marriage.
It was a fling, or so she'd managed to convince herself. A
midlife crisis. Lots of men had them. Any day Burton would
come to his senses and see what he was doing to her and to
Roy, their son.

Only he hadn't, and Anne walked out of divorce court
numb with shock and disbelief. Not until the judge's gavel
echoed through the room had she fully believed her husband
was capable of such treachery. She should've known,
should've been prepared. Burton was a top-notch divorce
attorney, a persuasive man who knew all the ploys. But
despite everything, she'd trusted him....

Her friends had been stunned, too—less by Burton's de-
ception than by Anne's apparent acceptance of what he'd
done to her. It wasn't in her to fight, to drag her marriage
and her life through the courts. Burton had recommended
an attorney, whom she'd obediently retained, never suspecting that the man who'd represented her in court would apply
to Burton's law firm as soon as the divorce was final. Of
course, he'd been hired....

Burton had promised to treat her fairly. Because she was
convinced that he'd soon recognize what a terrible mistake
he was making, she'd blindly followed his lead. Without a
quibble and on her attorney's advice, she'd accepted the settlement offer—one that had turned out to be grossly unfair.
Although she hadn't been aware of it at the time, Anne was
cheated out of at least two hundred and fifty thousand
dollars' worth of assets.

Burton's ploy in this particular case had been simple: he'd strung her along. Twice he'd come to her in tears, begging her forgiveness, talking about reconciliation, and all the while he'd been shifting their assets to offshore accounts. All the while, he'd been lying, stealing and cheating. She'd loved him and she'd believed him, and so had taken her husband at his word. Never had she dreamed he could betray her like this. After thirty years, she'd walked away with only a pittance. And, needless to say, no alimony.

Yes, Anne could fight him, could take him back to court and expose him for the thief he was, but to what end? It was best, she'd decided long ago, to preserve her dignity. She'd always felt that life had a symmetry to it, a way of righting wrongs, and that somehow, eventually, God would restore to her the things she'd lost. It was this belief that had gotten her past the bitterness and indignation.

Admittedly she couldn't help lapsing sometimes, but Anne tried not to feel bitter. At this point, she couldn't see how anger, even righteous anger, could possibly benefit her. She'd adjusted. Taking the little she'd managed to salvage from her marriage, she'd purchased a small cottage on St. Gabriel, a tiny San Juan island in Puget Sound. In college all those years ago, when she'd met Burton, she'd been an art student. She had a flair for art and enjoyed it. Given the demands of being married to a prominent divorce lawyer, she'd put aside her own pursuits to assist Burton. Her husband's ambitions had become her own, and Anne was the perfect wife and hostess.

It'd been a disappointment to her to have only one child, a son they'd named after Anne's father. Young Roy was the light of her life, her ray of sunshine through the years. When she wasn't hostessing social events on her husband's behalf, Anne spent her time with Roy, raising him with limitless love and motherly devotion.

If she felt any bitterness about the way Burton had treated her, it was because of what he'd done to Roy. Unfortunately, Roy was the one who'd introduced Burton to Aimee. He'd never forgiven himself for that, despite Anne's reassurances. Still, Roy assumed responsibility for what had happened. He couldn't seem to forgive himself for his role in the divorce, no matter how innocent that role had been.

To complicate the situation even more, he refused to forgive his father, not only for betraying Anne but for stealing Aimee, the woman he himself had loved and planned to marry. Roy's anger was constantly with him. The anger had become part of him, tainting his life, as though he wore smudged, dark glasses that revealed a bleak, drab world. All Roy cared about now was his business, his drive for more and more, and while he'd achieved greater success than most men twice his age, Roy wasn't happy.

Her son's cynicism troubled Anne deeply—even more than the divorce itself. She'd put that behind her, as much as she was able, and built a comfortable life for herself, doing what she loved best—painting. Mainly through word of mouth, her work had begun to sell at the local farmers' market and then at a couple of galleries in the area; it now provided her with a small income.

Anne would've given anything to help her son. Regardless of how much money he made or how many accolades he received, he remained lonely and embittered. She desperately wanted him to find happiness.

In the five years since the divorce, Roy had not spoken to his father once, despite Burton's repeated efforts. Yet Roy was so like Burton. He shared his father's talents, his ambition. They shared another trait, too, the one that concerned Anne the most. He possessed his father's ability to be ruthless about marriage and relationships. He was thirty-three, and in Anne's view, he should get married. However, her son resolutely refused to discuss it. His attitude toward love and commitment had been completely warped. He no longer dated, no longer sought out relationships.

The only thing that mattered to Roy was the bottom line. He'd grown cold and uncaring; little outside of Fletcher Industries seemed to affect him. Anne realized her son was in trouble. He was hurting badly, although he seemed incapable of recognizing his own pain. Roy needed someone to teach him the power of forgiveness and love. She'd wanted to be that person, to show him that forgiveness was possible, but in his zeal to succeed, Roy had started to block her out of his life. It was unintentional, she knew, but nonetheless, it hurt.

Roy had established Fletcher Industries, his own computer security company, in Seattle, shortly after he graduated from college. His innovative, cutting-edge software led the competition in the field. Recent contracts with the government and several banks had given Fletcher Industries a solid position as one of the top companies of its type.

Those first years after he'd formed his business, Roy spent far too many hours at work. It wasn't uncommon for him to stay in the office for two or three days at a time, living on fast food and catnaps. That all changed after he met Aimee. Her son had fallen in love and he'd fallen hard. Anne had been thrilled and Burton was, too. Then Roy had brought Aimee to his parents' home in Southern California to introduce her...and all their lives had exploded.

Following his parents' divorce, Roy had quickly reverted to his old habit of working long hours. Only now a callousness had entered into his business dealings. Anne was aware of this, but she was helpless to change her son, and her heart ached with her inability to reach him. Time and again, she'd tried to tell him what he was doing to himself—that he was damaging his life and his future—but he couldn't or wouldn't hear.

The kettle whistled, and leaving the Christmas box in the hall, Anne moved into the kitchen. She took the blue ceramic teapot from the cupboard and filled it with boiling water, then added a tea bag—Earl Grey, her favorite—and left it to steep. After a moment, she poured herself a cup and took a first sip of the aromatic tea. She frowned, berating herself for allowing her thoughts to follow the path they'd taken. Just when she assumed she was free of Burton, she'd wallow in the pain all over again and realize how far she had yet to go. There was only one cure for this bout of self-pity and for the worry that consumed her. Setting down the china cup, Anne bowed her head and prayed. Sometimes it was difficult to find the words to express what was in her heart, but not today. The prayer flew from her lips.

"Dear Lord, send my son a woman to love. One who'll help him heal, who'll teach him about forgiveness. A woman who'll open his heart and wake him up to the kind of man he's becoming."

Slowly, as if weighed down by her doubts, Anne's prayer circled the room. Gradually it ascended, rising with the steam from the teapot, spiraling upward out of the simple cottage and toward the leaden sky. It rose higher and higher until it reached the clouds and then sped toward the heavens. There, it landed on the desk of the Archangel Gabriel, the same Archangel who'd delivered the good news of God's love to a humble Jewish maiden more than two thousand years ago.

Gabriel, however, was away from his desk.

Shirley, Goodness and Mercy, three Prayer Ambassadors who had a reputation for employing unorthodox means to achieve their ends, stood just inside the Archangel's quarters. Together the three of them watched as the prayer made its way onto his desk. Only the most difficult prayer requests went to the mighty Gabriel—the prayers that came from those who were most in need, from the desperate and discouraged.

"Don't read it," Shirley cried when Goodness, unable to resist, bent to pick up the wispy sheet.

"Why not?" Goodness had always had more curiosity than was good for her. She knew that peeking at a prayer request before Gabriel had a chance to view it was asking for trouble, but that didn't stop her. Mercy was the one most easily swayed by things on Earth, and Shirley, well, Shirley was nearly perfect. At one time she'd been a Guardian Angel but had transferred to the ranks of the Prayer Ambassadors. That had happened under suspicious circumstances, so Shirley's perfection was a little compromised. Shirley never mentioned the incident, though, and Goodness dared not inquire. She knew that some things were better left unknown—despite her desire to hear all the sordid details.

"Goodness," Shirley warned again.

"I'm just going to glance at the name," Goodness muttered, carefully lifting the edge of the folded sheet.

"Is it anyone we know?" Mercy demanded, drawing closer.

Goodness eyed Shirley, who was trying not to reveal her own interest. "Well, is it?" Shirley finally asked.

"No," Goodness said. "I've never heard of Anne Fletcher, have you?"

"Anne Fletcher?" Shirley echoed, and then as if her knees had gone out from under her, she sank into the chair reserved for Gabriel. "Anne Fletcher from California," the former Guardian Angel repeated slowly.

Goodness looked again, lifting the edge of the sheet just a bit higher this time. "Formerly of California," she said.

"Oh, no!" Shirley cried. "She moved. I wonder why. Tell me where she's gone."

"The San Juan Islands," Mercy said, leaning over Goodness to take a look for herself.

"She's in the Caribbean?" Shirley said, sounding distraught.

"No, in Puget Sound—Washington State," Goodness told her.

"I remember it well," Mercy said with a dreamy smile. "Don't you remember the Bremerton Shipyard? We had so much fun there."

"What I remember," Goodness informed her fellow angel, "was all the trouble *we* got in when *you* started shifting aircraft carriers and destroyers around."

"I don't know how many times you want me to apologize for that," Mercy muttered, crossing her arms defiantly. "It was a fluke. Nothing like that's happened since, and frankly I think you're…"

Her words faded as she saw Goodness studying Shirley. "How do you know Anne Fletcher?" Goodness asked softly.

"Poor, poor Anne," Shirley murmured, seemingly lost in thought. "I knew her mother—I was her Guardian Angel. I was with her mother, Beth, when she gave birth to Anne."

So Shirley had a connection to Anne Fletcher. "I didn't read the request," Goodness said, more eager than ever to throw caution to the winds and take a second, longer look.

"Maybe there's something we can do," Mercy said. It sounded as if she was encouraging Goodness to flout protocol, and Goodness was happy to go along with the implied suggestion. She quickly scooped up the prayer request, then almost dropped it when a voice boomed behind them.

"Do for whom?" it asked.

Gabriel. The Archangel Gabriel.

Goodness spun around and backed against the side of the

huge desk, crushing her wings in her attempt to hide. Oh, this wasn't good. Gabriel was their friend, but he wouldn't tolerate their snooping around his desk.

"Nothing." Mercy moved closer to Goodness until they stood shoulder to shoulder, wing to wing.

Shirley was lost in her own thoughts, sitting in Gabriel's chair, apparently oblivious to their dire circumstances.

"Do?" Goodness choked out. "Are we supposed to be doing something for someone?"

"It's Anne Fletcher," Shirley whispered, peering up at Gabriel, apparently still in a stupor. "We've got to help her."

"Anne Fletcher?" Gabriel's brow furrowed with concern.

"She's said a prayer for Roy," Goodness explained, and boldly handed Gabriel the request, as much as admitting it had been read. "She *wants* to believe. But she's worried about her son and has given up hope that anyone can reach him. We can't let her lose faith—we just can't!" She gazed up at Gabriel with large, pleading eyes. Her wings were folded back and she hung her head as though she felt the same sense of despair Anne Fletcher did.

Goodness had never seen Shirley so upset. Clearly this Anne person was someone she cared about.

Gabriel made a grumbling sound. Shirley glanced up and with a look of panic realized she was sitting in his chair. She bolted upright, then leaped to one side.

It was such a rare sight to see Shirley ruffled that, had she not felt so worried about her friend, Goodness would've been amused.

Once his chair was vacant, Gabriel sat down, ignoring the prayer request. Instead, he removed the massive book from the shelf behind him. With a soft grunt, he set it on his desk. He opened it to the section marked *F,* and ran his finger down a long list of names inscribed there.

Goodness wasn't going to risk standing on tiptoe and

taking a look. Even she understood when it was best to restrain her curiosity.

"Anne Fletcher," Gabriel said thoughtfully. "It's been five years since the divorce."

"Anne's divorced?" Shirley whispered. "Oh, my, I didn't know. How's she doing?"

"Actually, quite well," Gabriel told her. "She's adjusted far better than we'd expected." He nodded, smiling gently. "She's gone back to her art and that's helped her. It says here that she's living in Washington State, on a small island in Puget Sound."

"Burton always discounted her talent," Shirley said, and leaned on her palms against the desk, daring to read the huge volume that documented human lives. "She could've been a successful artist had she continued her studies."

"Still might," Goodness threw in, implying that she was in the know. She *hated* being left in the dark when it came to earthly matters. Humans intrigued her. They were the very pinnacle of God's creation, fearfully and wonderfully made, yet so obtuse. It was hard to believe free will could cause such problems.

"Anne Fletcher is indeed talented," Gabriel said, "but fame and fortune were never important to her. She's had to deal with various losses, but as you already know, for every loss there is an equal or greater gain. Often humans have to search for it, though."

Goodness nodded in full agreement, although she couldn't begin to guess what God had in store for the fifty-nine-year-old divorced woman. "God has another man for her, doesn't He?" she ventured.

Gabriel frowned as if Goodness's comments were starting to irritate him. "No, Goodness, not another man. Frankly, Anne isn't interested."

"I don't blame her for that," Mercy added. "After what

Burton did to her, she'd find it very difficult to trust again, and who could blame her?" She seemed to think that was all anyone needed to say on *that* subject.

"The prayer is for her son," Gabriel pointed out as he read the request.

"Roy," Shirley said. "You remember Roy, don't you?" she asked mournfully. "He was such a sweet child, so willing to please, so anxious to follow in his father's footsteps."

"Burton never forgave him for not pursuing a law degree," Gabriel commented absently. "Roy is gifted, but he works too hard."

"I'm sure Anne would like grandchildren," Shirley said, studying the prayer request.

"Of course she would," Mercy agreed.

For the first time since they'd entered the room, Shirley smiled. "God provides," she whispered, and then said in a louder voice, "Isn't that what you were just saying?"

Gabriel glanced up. "Roy isn't interested in marriage."

"Not now he isn't," Goodness chimed in. The possibility of romance rose before her—it was such fun to steer humans toward one another! Creating romance was by far her favorite duty on Earth. "We want in on this," she announced.

Gabriel leveled a fierce gaze on her, and she swallowed hard and took a step back.

"But only if you feel it's for the best," she mumbled.

"It's for Anne," Shirley pleaded. "Beth's little Annie."

"Are you saying the three of you want to return to Earth?"

Shirley, Goodness and Mercy all nodded simultaneously.

"I was afraid of that." Gabriel stroked his chin. "I'm not sure Earth has recovered from your last visit yet."

"We'll be exceptionally good this time," Mercy promised, folding her hands prayerfully. "I swear I won't even *think* about going near an escalator."

"It isn't moving staircases that worry me," Gabriel said. "It's everything else."

Goodness stepped forward again. She could tell by the look in his eyes that Gabriel was weakening. "We can help her, Gabe."

"Gabe?" he bellowed.

"Gabriel," she corrected swiftly. "I know we can. Besides, I have this romance thing down pat. Humans are eager to fall in love. All we have to do is lead them in the right dir—" She stopped when she saw Gabriel's expression.

For a moment, no one spoke and then in a low whisper, Shirley said, "Please?"

Gabriel took his time answering while Goodness waited, holding her breath in anticipation. She wanted to visit Earth again. They'd been away far too long—several Earth years at least.

Oh, Gabriel, make up your mind, she muttered to herself. *Say yes!*

Two

Roy Fletcher hated doing job interviews. He warily regarded the older man sitting on the other side of his desk. Dean Wilcoff had to be close to sixty and retirement. His thinning gray hair was brushed away from his face and his dark eyes met Roy's squarely. He was big, an inch or two over six feet, broad-shouldered and muscular. He'd obviously maintained himself physically, which was good. As head of building security, it was unlikely he'd be chasing intruders, but he should at least be capable of it if the need arose. Roy glanced over Wilcoff's résumé a second time. The man had an impressive work history.

"You were with Boeing's security force for twenty-six years."

"I was," Dean answered without elaborating. There'd been some downsizing at the airplane manufacturer, but Roy guessed that Dean Wilcoff had left or been let go for another reason. Still, his Human Resources department had selected this candidate for him to interview.

The dates on Wilcoff's résumé showed that he'd last worked nine months ago, yet Roy didn't sense any desperation in the man. Wilcoff should be worried. By now, his unemployment benefits would've expired and at his age, obtaining another job wouldn't be easy.

"What do you know about computers?"

For the first time Roy noticed hesitation in the other man. "Only enough to get around on the Internet. My daughter's been after me to take one of those courses, but frankly I don't see the need. I work security. It's what I know and what I do best. If you hire me, Mr. Fletcher, you can rest assured that no one's going to break into your offices, day or night."

Roy raised a skeptical eyebrow. Life didn't come with guarantees. Everything was suspect. Everything and everyone. This was a lesson he'd learned the hard way, but learn it he had.

"I'll get back to you," he said, dismissing the man. He'd finished the round of interviews and although all the candidates were qualified, there hadn't been a single one he especially liked. The day before, he'd talked to three applicants, and three more today. No one had really impressed him. Unfortunately he needed to make his decision soon if he didn't want hourly phone calls from his HR director. Well, fine. He'd put the names in a hat and simply draw one. At this point, that was as logical as anything else.

"How'd it go?" Julie Wilcoff asked her father as she set the salad on the dinner table. She hated to ask, but he hadn't exactly been free with details since his return from the long-awaited interview. Julie was afraid that meant bad news, and he'd already had enough disappointments. After nine months without a job, her father had grown restless and discouraged. She knew he was worried, especially with the holidays so close. He'd wanted to have a new job lined up by New Year's, and he'd had such hope for this one, which seemed perfect for him. Yet he'd barely said a word since he'd come home from the interview.

"Why hire an old man like me?" he muttered as he walked to the table.

"Because you're highly qualified, dependable and intelligent."

"I'm not even sure I want to work for Roy Fletcher," her father complained. He pulled out his chair and sat down.

Julie frowned. After weeks of searching, of making dozens of unsuccessful applications, after talking about this interview for days on end, his attitude came as a shock. But if her father, a man who never exaggerated or jumped to conclusions, made such a statement, there was a reason.

Roy Fletcher's name had appeared in the media for years. He was one of the geniuses in the security software business, the man entrusted by the government to keep out hackers. Fletcher Industries had prospered as doing business online had become increasingly prone to theft—of credit-card numbers, private information, financial records and more. Her father was in security, too, only a different kind. While Roy Fletcher made sure no one could break into computer files, her father prevented intruders from breaking into the doors and windows of buildings.

Julie sat down at the table and handed her father the meat loaf. It'd been her mother's recipe and was one of his favorite meals. Julie had hoped this would be a celebration dinner, but apparently not. Still, she wondered what had prompted her father's comment. "What's wrong with Mr. Fletcher?" she asked.

"I don't much care for him."

"Mr. Fletcher interviewed you himself?" Dad hadn't mentioned that earlier.

Her father nodded. "After I talked to a nice gal in what they call Human Resources." He paused a moment. "She sent me to see him." Another pause. "He isn't a pleasant man."

Julie scooped up a serving of scalloped potatoes and put

them on her plate. Toward the end of her mother's final bout with cancer, Julie had moved out of her apartment and back in with her parents. Her father had quit his job and stayed home to nurse her mother. His company benefits had paid most of the medical bills; Julie's salary as a junior-high physical-education teacher covered the rest. It had been a time of sacrifice for them all. Emily, Julie's fraternal twin, had helped, financially and emotionally, as much as possible, although she no longer lived in Seattle.

After six months of this arrangement, Julie's beautiful, petite mother had died. That was four months ago. From the beginning, the doctors had given them little hope. Julie, Emily and their father knew and were prepared for the eventuality of Darlene Wilcoff's death. Or so they'd assumed. What Julie had learned, and her sister, too, was that it didn't matter how ready you thought you were to face the death of a loved one; even when death is expected, it hits hard. Julie, her sister and their father had been left reeling. Julie felt her life would never be the same—and it wouldn't. The world had lost a graceful, charming soul; she and Emily had lost a loving mother; Dean had been deprived of the woman he adored.

Julie waited until their plates were filled before she questioned him again. "What didn't you like about Roy Fletcher?"

"He's cold." Dean hesitated and his brows drew together. "It's as if nothing touches him, nothing affects him. From what I've heard, people don't mean much to Fletcher. In fact, the whole time I was with him, I had the feeling there wasn't a single person in this world who meant a damn thing to him. I doubt he's an easy man to know."

"People usually have a reason for acting the way they do," Julie said, hoping that would encourage her father to continue the conversation. She couldn't help being curious. The job offered an employment package that was far above anything he would have received with another employer.

"Well, whatever the reason, I got the impression that Fletcher thinks everything comes down to money, but there are some things that can't be bought."

Julie nodded.

Her father sampled the meat loaf, then set down his fork. "It's time, you know."

Julie pretended she didn't understand, but this was a discussion they'd had more than once. Her father seemed to believe Julie should move back into an apartment of her own, now that her mother was gone. She disagreed. First, her father needed her. Oh, he'd muddle through with meals and housework; Julie wasn't concerned about that. But she knew he was lonely and struggling with an all-consuming grief. As well, finances were tight since he was on a significantly reduced pension, and it went against his pride to let someone, even his daughter, pay the bills.

What he didn't grasp—and she could find no way to explain—was how badly she needed to be with him. They'd suffered the biggest loss of their lives, and being together seemed to help. She wasn't ready to move out. Eventually she would, but not yet. For her, it was too soon.

"We've already been through this."

"And your point is?"

"Now, Dad, Emily and I think—"

"You should have your own life, instead of taking care of your old man."

"I do have my own life," she insisted. "I'll stay here until we're both back on our feet. Then you can kick me out."

"The thing is, I might never get back on my feet, especially financially," he said, his gaze dark and brooding. "It's time we faced facts here. I should sell the house."

"No!" Julie cried, the thought unbearable. Losing the family home so soon after her mother's death was more than she could cope with emotionally. Not if there was any way to stop it. "Emily and I refuse to let that happen."

Emily wanted to help more, but she was a young navy wife, living in Florida with two small children. Her husband was periodically at sea, sometimes for months at a time. Although twins, Julie and Emily were about as different as two sisters could be. Emily was like their mother, small and delicate, with blue eyes and wavy blond hair. A classic beauty. Julie took after her father's side of the family. Her hair and eyes were a deep shade of brown. Tall, strong and solidly built, she was a natural athlete. She'd played center in basketball, pitcher in softball and was a track star all through high school and college.

While boys had flocked around Emily, they'd mostly ignored her sister. Emily had brains, as well as looks, and although Julie had brains, too, she wasn't pretty the way her sister was. It had never bothered her until recently, when she'd turned thirty. Her sister was married, and so were most of her friends. Sure, she dated, but the number of eligible men had dwindled as the years went on. With her mother growing increasingly ill, Julie hadn't worried about it much. But now… She sighed. Like her father in his job search, Julie had given up hope of meeting the right man. For a woman over thirty, the pickings were slim.

The phone rang, and Julie and her father both turned to stare at it.

"Let the machine pick it up," he said. That had been a hard and fast rule during her teenage years—no telephone call was worth disrupting family time at the dinner table.

"You sure?" Julie asked.

Her father nodded and continued eating. "You did a good job on the meat loaf."

"It's Mom's recipe, remember?"

Her father grinned. "It might surprise you to learn she got it from a 'Dear Abby' column."

The phone rang again. "No way!" This was news to Julie.

Her father chuckled. "That broccoli salad I like came out of the paper, too."

Her mother had never told her this, but then it was Emily who usually hung around the kitchen. Julie was always at basketball practice or some sporting event. There'd been so many things her mother had never had the opportunity to tell her. Unimportant things, like this, and other things—revelations, advice—that really mattered. How Julie wished she could go back and recapture all those precious hours with her mother. If only she'd known...

The answering machine clicked on and they heard a disgruntled male voice. "This is Roy Fletcher."

Without thinking, Julie launched herself toward the phone, whipping the receiver off the cradle before Fletcher could end the call. "Hello," she gasped. "I assume you want to speak to my father?"

"Yes, if your father is Dean Wilcoff."

Her dad was right; the man's voice was devoid of the slightest warmth.

"Just a moment," she said, handing him the receiver.

"Dean Wilcoff," he said gruffly, frowning at Julie. His look said that if it'd been up to him, he would've left Roy Fletcher cooling his heels. Fortunately Julie had been closest to the phone.

She bit her lower lip as she studied her father. This *had* to be good news. Roy Fletcher wouldn't phone to tell a man he'd chosen another candidate for the job.

Her father's eyes widened. "Before I accept the position, I have a few questions."

Julie wanted to wave her arms over her head and scream. Her father needed this job and not only for financial reasons. *Oh, Dad, don't blow this now.* It was too important.

After what seemed like an hour but was probably five minutes, her father replaced the receiver.

Julie could barely contain her anxiety. "Well?"

"I'm seeing Mr. Fletcher in the morning to discuss my questions." The smallest hint of a smile touched his mouth. "For better or worse, it looks like I've got the job if I want it."

"Oh, Dad! That's terrific news."

"That, my dear Julie, remains to be seen."

Three

"Would you care to meet Anne Fletcher for yourselves?" Gabriel asked, eyeing the trio.

Goodness couldn't believe their good fortune. She nodded and smiled as Mercy eagerly agreed. It'd been so long since they'd visited Earth with its manifold delights. The place was definitely interesting—and appealing—but completely unlike Heaven. Earth was also dangerous, full of exotic allures and various temptations. Heaven, on the other hand...well, eyes hadn't seen or ears heard all that awaited those in glory.

Shirley's face brightened. "Could we visit Anne for just a little while? I haven't seen her in years."

"At one time she routinely prayed for her son," Gabriel explained as he guided them out of his quarters and to a convenient location to view Anne's little spot on Earth. "For quite a while after the divorce, she brought Roy's hardened heart to God's attention, but when she didn't see results, her faith weakened. Now only an infrequent prayer comes our way."

"That doesn't surprise me," Shirley whispered. "When I was assigned to her mother..." She paused and looked up guiltily, as if afraid she'd said more than permissible. "I'm sure all Anne really wants is for her son to be happy."

"But happiness is a condition of the mind, not of circumstances," Gabriel reminded them. "That appears to be a most difficult lesson for humans. They expect to find happiness in things, which we all know is impossible." Sadly he shook his head. "They repeatedly fail to see what should be perfectly logical."

"Humans require a lot of patience," Goodness said, trying hard to sound knowledgeable.

Gabriel studied the trio, as though gauging how much he could trust them if he did grant them passage back to Earth. Goodness did her utmost to look serene and confident. She fully intended to be good, but she couldn't count on Mercy. Shirley was iffy, too. Her friend seemed to have a special fondness for Anne, and there was no telling what she'd do once they arrived on Earth.

Goodness didn't begrudge Gabriel his doubts. The trio always left Heaven with the best intentions, but when they began to mingle with humans, their powers to resist grew increasingly weak. They found it impossible not to interfere in situations that hadn't been assigned to them—which inevitably got them into trouble.

Gabriel's gaze was drawn back to the big blue sphere, the view of Earth from Heaven.

Goodness peered closer but couldn't make out anything yet. Gabriel would need to bring everything into focus.

"Yes, I'm afraid that where her son is concerned, Anne's lost hope," the Archangel murmured sadly. "She doesn't understand that some things need to be believed in order to be seen."

Goodness was impressed. "That's so wise."

"Poor Anne," Shirley whispered, her brow wrinkled in worry.

"We can help her, I'm sure," Mercy insisted, sidling next to Shirley. "Anne needs us." She glanced from Gabriel to Shirley, looking for confirmation.

Goodness bit her tongue to keep from chastising her friend. They couldn't act too eager, otherwise Gabriel might become suspicious. He might wonder if they had ulterior motives for wanting to visit Earth. As unobtrusively as possible, she made a small waving motion with her hand, hoping Mercy would get the message.

"Of course," Mercy added with an exaggerated sigh, "there are any number of angels more qualified than the three of us."

"Yes, there are," Gabriel said bluntly.

"I thought you said we could see her from here," Shirley said, squinting through the thick cloud cover.

For a moment Gabriel seemed to be having second thoughts. His expression became more severe as he stared at them. Little wonder humans were terrified of Gabriel, Goodness reflected. His imposing stature was enough to intimidate the bravest men. That was one reason, she supposed, that he was only sent from Heaven on the most serious of missions.

Slowly he raised his massive arms and with one sweeping motion the clouds cleared and the mist gradually thinned, revealing the cottage surrounded by tall fir trees. Then Anne came into view. She stood in her art room, a paintbrush in her hand. A few Christmas decorations hung here and there, as if a halfhearted effort had been made to display them.

Once more Shirley leaned forward, peering downward. "Anne's painting," she said, and pointed to the scene below.

Once the mist faded completely, Goodness stepped closer to her friends to get a better look. Just as Shirley had declared, Anne Fletcher stood in front of an easel, apparently deep in thought.

Goodness examined the painting and was pleasantly surprised. Shirley had been right; the woman was a talented artist. She used bold, distinctive colors and strong, confident lines. But despite the beauty of her landscape, Anne was obviously dissatisfied. She seemed about to paint over the canvas and destroy her work. Instead, she set her brush and palette aside and slumped into a chair. Tilting her chin, Anne stared at the ceiling, blinking back tears.

"What's wrong?" Shirley asked, turning to Gabriel for an explanation. "She looks like she's going to cry."

"She's worrying about her son," Gabriel said. "She—"

"But she's prayed for him," Shirley broke in. "Anne knows to leave matters with God. Her mother taught her the importance of trusting in God," she said, adding, "But that was so long ago…."

"She spoke to her son a little while ago, and things are even worse than she realized. She's given up hope."

"But she *prayed*—how can you say that?" Shirley demanded. "After everything she's been through, after all she's suffered. Look," she cried, gesturing at the weeping woman, "there's no bitterness or hatred in her, no ill will toward Burton and his new wife."

"That's true," Gabriel agreed, and he seemed truly astonished by the simple human act of forgiveness. "Anne has forgiven her husband for what he did to her, but she feels helpless to influence her son."

"Why is God taking so long to answer?" Shirley asked, pacing restlessly.

"He has His reasons. It's not for us to second-guess the Creator of the Universe."

For an instant, Shirley seemed about to argue, but Goodness intervened. "Perhaps God knows that the right woman's going to come along. A woman who'll open Roy's eyes—and his heart. It can't be an ordinary woman, but one strong-willed enough to stand up to his arrogance."

"Who could that be?" Mercy asked, looking wide-eyed at Gabriel.

"This woman is waiting to be found, and I'm sending you to Earth to find her."

"We're going back?" Goodness hadn't been convinced that Gabriel would actually agree, since he so obviously had reservations about their dependability. She was thrilled. And just before Christmas, too! Oh yes, this was excellent news, the best yet.

"You may go," Gabriel said in a guarded voice, "but with a few stipulations. You have less than a month—the prayer request must be answered before Christmas Eve, and in the process your goal is to teach these humans a lesson. Can you do it?"

"We can," Shirley promised.

"We'll be better than ever," Mercy said.

"I'll keep an eye on them both," Goodness assured the Archangel.

"But who'll watch *you?*" he asked, cocking one dark brow.

Goodness sputtered, hardly knowing how to respond, then straightened. She recited her mission statement. "I...I will faithfully fulfill my duties as an Ambassador of the Almighty."

"Well said." Gabriel nodded with approval, but Goodness wasn't fooled. One wrong move, and they'd be immediately jerked back from Earth with its multitude of fascinating distractions.

A short while later, the three of them were gathered in Anne Fletcher's art room. It was a small area with plenty of light. Canvasses were stacked against the wall, some painted, others a pristine white, waiting to come to life. Anne sat near a phone, and after a long moment, picked it up.

"Who's she calling?" Mercy asked.

"Shh," Goodness warned. Thankfully, Anne wasn't aware of their presence nor could she hear their voices, unless special arrangements had been made well in advance. They

were required to go to Gabriel for permission to reveal themselves—not that there weren't inventive ways around that.

"Listen," Shirley said, hushing them all.

Anne punched out the private number to Roy's office.
There was no guarantee that he'd speak to her. She didn't
doubt that he loved her, but her son was avoiding her these
days. Anne wasn't fooled; she knew why he was doing this.
While she tried not to nag him, Anne realized she must
sound like a distant echo, repeating the same message over
and over. No wonder he looked for ways to sidetrack her—
or avoid her altogether.

"Roy Fletcher," came his gruff, disembodied voice.

"It's your mother," she said with a cheerful lilt. "I haven't
heard from you in ages." She wanted to bite her tongue. This
wasn't how she'd intended to start their conversation. Why,
oh, why had she said that? It must have seemed like a chastisement, and that was the last thing she wanted Roy to think.
"But I know how busy you are," she said, faltering a little.

"Do you need anything?" he asked, already sounding
bored. He'd be quick to write a check, and had on several
occasions, although she'd never cashed one. She wondered
if he'd noticed. It wasn't Roy's money she wanted, it was
his happiness. No amount of money he gave or received, no
matter how generous, could buy that.

"I'm fine, Roy. And you?"

"Busy."

"Are you telling me you can't talk now?" Or any other
time, she thought, disheartened.

He hesitated. "I have five minutes."

Anne almost had the feeling he was setting a timer. "I
called to tell you I'm coming into Seattle next Thursday." The
trip required a ferry crossing and a half-hour drive; it often took
a couple of hours to make the journey across Puget Sound.

"Any particular reason?"

"I'm meeting Marta Rosenberg for dinner."

"Should I know the name?" Roy asked.

Anne sighed, resigned now to his lack of interest and enthusiasm. Except for his work, everything in life seemed to be an effort for Roy.

"There's no reason you should remember the name," she told him. "Marta and I were good friends in college. We've kept in touch through the years—Christmas cards, that sort of thing. She's made a real name for herself in New York as an art dealer and gallery owner."

Surprisingly, that piqued his interest. "Is she going to sell your paintings?"

"Oh, hardly," Anne said, embarrassed at the idea. Anne would never approach her friend with such a request. Her paintings were amateurish compared to the work Marta sold, work by big names. Revered artists. "I was hoping you and I could meet beforehand," Anne suggested. She wanted to get to her main reason for calling before her allotted time elapsed.

"I have a half hour open at lunchtime," Roy murmured.

Anne's spirits lifted. "That would be lovely. I'm meeting Marta at seven and—"

"I'll pencil you in for noon. I have a meeting and I might be a few minutes late, so don't be upset if you're left twiddling your thumbs for a while."

"I was thinking I might decorate the windows at your office building before Christmas," she hurriedly added.

Her remark was followed by a lengthy pause. "You want to do what?"

"Paint your windows, you know, for Christmas."

"Is this a joke, Mother?"

"No, it'll give a festive air to the complex. I was thinking of those big windows in the front lobby. In case you hadn't noticed, 'tis the season, Roy. Don't you remember how we used to paint the windows at the house every year?"

Again his response was slow and edged with sadness. "Of course I remember, but I was a kid then. I've outgrown things like that."

Anne didn't feel that way in the least. She wanted to do whatever she could to resurrect happy memories for him. "You won't mind, though, will you?"

"If it pleases you, then by all means paint." His voice softened slightly. "I have to go."

"I know." Her five minutes was up.

"I can't promise you lunch, but I'll do my best to squeeze you in." With that, the phone line went dead.

Anne set the receiver back in its cradle as if it weighed thirty pounds.

"Squeeze her in!" Mercy cried, outraged. "This is worse than I thought. Anne's his *mother!* How are we ever going to find a woman willing to put up with that kind of behavior?"

Actually, Roy Fletcher was in worse shape than *anyone* had thought, Goodness mused. They had their work cut out for them.

"Oh, dear, look," Shirley whispered.

Anne Fletcher's hand remained on the telephone, as if she was trying to maintain an illusion of contact with her son. Her head fell forward and her shoulders slouched. Suddenly, before the other angels could react, Shirley slipped into the middle of the room.

"What are you doing?" Goodness asked, reaching out unsuccessfully to stop her.

"Anne needs encouragement," Shirley insisted. "She can't continue like this."

"You're going to get us pulled off this assignment,"

Mercy warned. "We haven't been on Earth five minutes. That's a record even for us."

"Don't you remember what Gabriel said?"

"Darn right I do! One wrong move and we're out of here."

"No," Shirley countered, "he said some things had to be *believed* in order to be *seen*."

"But he didn't say for us to leap in and do something we know isn't allowed."

Mercy's warning, however, went unheeded. "What's Shirley going to do?" she asked Goodness.

"I'm afraid to find out," Goodness replied.

"I'm going to prove to Anne that she *should* believe," Shirley announced grandly.

"But that's the opposite of what Gabriel meant," Mercy argued.

"I'm doing it," Shirley said.

Sure enough, she stepped through the thin layer of truth that separated angels from humans. For a moment she did nothing but soak in the earthly environment. Then, in a display of heavenly grace, the angel unfolded her wings, extending them to their complete and glorious length. With the full splendor of the Lord reflecting upon her, she revealed herself to Anne.

Anne Fletcher gasped and placed her hand over her mouth. To her credit, the human seemed suitably impressed. Slowly Anne dropped her hand and stared hard at Shirley, as if she expected her to disappear. She blinked once and then again, obviously testing to see if this could possibly be her imagination. Anne shaded her eyes from the light. Then, still staring, she reached for a pad and pencil and started to sketch.

"Oh, no."

Mercy looked around, certain they were about to lose all visitation rights until the next millennium. Nothing happened.

Seconds later, Shirley was back. Goodness forced herself

to keep quiet and not reprimand her friend. Mercy had no such restraint.

"How could you?" she wailed.

"Anne needed a sign," Shirley said, "and I gave it to her. God is working, and I wanted her to know that—to believe."

"But look what she's doing!" Mercy cried, watching as Anne worked on the sketch, her fingers moving at a furious pace as if she was struggling to get everything she'd seen down on paper before it faded from memory.

Goodness could hardly wait until Gabriel heard about *this*.

Four

Julie was proud of her father, and so pleased that he'd been granted this opportunity. Abraham Lincoln Junior High where she taught was only a short distance from Fletcher Industries. The first day he was scheduled to work, she suggested she ride in with him and then take her bike from the complex to the school. She planned to do the same thing in reverse every afternoon, unless there was a late meeting scheduled or one of her teams had a practice or a game. It was hard to find opportunities to exercise, and this seemed a good solution, in addition to giving her extra time with her father. Folding a change of clothes into her backpack, she dressed in her spandex pants and nylon shirt. She attached her bicycle to the carrier on the rear of the Ford, then joined her father in the front seat.

"Are you excited?" she asked. If he wasn't, *she* certainly was. Her father could use a psychological boost. It'd been a long dry spell for both of them.

He shrugged.

"Well, I am." It felt, in some strange, inexplicable way, as if they could finally begin to heal—as if their time of grieving was about to end. Not that either of them would forget Darlene Wilcoff. She was alive in their hearts and would forever remain a part of them. Now, four months following her death, this crisp, clear late-November morning seemed filled with renewed promise.

"You're sure about this bicycle business?" her father muttered as he started the engine. "I don't like the idea of you riding back in the dark."

"It's perfectly safe, Dad," she said, half-tempted to say that at thirty, she was well beyond the age of needing parental supervision. "I'm wearing a helmet and a vest that reflects in the dark, plus the bike has a flashing light in the front *and* the back."

He grunted, obviously still disapproving, but didn't argue further. As they reached Fletcher Industries, her father slowed. "You'll need to be here at five this afternoon."

"I will." That would allow her time to finish up some paperwork and cycle back to the complex. "Where would you like me to meet you?"

He frowned as if he hadn't considered this earlier. "In front of the building would probably be best. The parking lot is a secure area and I don't want you going in there without me."

"Okay. I'll see you at five."

Her father pulled up close to the tall office building and put his car in Park while Julie climbed out. Other cars had already started to arrive, and a delivery truck circled toward the back of the complex.

Julie walked to the rear of the Ford and removed her tenspeed. Her father drove off once he'd pointed out where they should meet. His taillights disappeared as he turned the corner and drove toward the employees' designated parking area, joining a line of other vehicles.

Julie had just finished snapping the helmet strap under her chin when a sharp male voice spoke from somewhere behind her. She whirled around.

"What's your business here?" Oh, great, her father's first day and she was going to have a confrontation with a security guard.

"Hello," she said, smiling warmly. "I'm Julie Wilcoff. My father—"

"I asked you to state your business."

The man was no guard, Julie could now see. He was tall, an inch or two more than her five foot eleven, and dressed in a dark suit, expensive, judging by the cut, although she didn't have a discerning eye when it came to fashion. He might have been handsome, but scowling as he was, he appeared intimidating and in no mood for excuses.

"I'm on my way to school."

His expression implied that she was lying.

"You're not a student."

"No, I'm a teacher. My father dropped me off here to show me where I should meet him tonight when he's finished work. Are you Roy Fletcher?" This could be the man her father had described; his attitude certainly resembled that of the company owner.

The man ignored her question. "Your father is Dean Wilcoff?"

"Yes." She had to bite back the urge to call him *sir.* It'd been a long time since any man had intimidated her, and she wasn't about to let it show. "I didn't realize there were rules against riding bicycles in this complex."

"There aren't. Be on your way," he ordered, starting toward the front door.

Julie planted one hand on her hip and glared at him. "I beg your pardon," she said in her best schoolteacher voice. How dare he speak to her like this!

He paused, and then with exaggerated patience, said, "You're free to go."

"In case you're unaware of it, I was entitled to do so

before." No wonder her father had taken a dislike to Mr. High-and-Mighty. He was, without exception, the most disagreeable person she'd ever met. His arrogance was absolutely staggering.

He turned his back on her and walked into the building.

Fuming, Julie climbed on her bike and locked her cleats into the pedals. She rode hard, her anger driving her faster and faster as she left the complex and then merged with traffic on the main thoroughfare outside Fletcher Industries. She arrived at Abraham Lincoln a good ten minutes earlier than she'd estimated. She parked her bicycle, still muttering to herself, and carefully took off her helmet.

"Mornin'," Penny Angelo, who taught English, said cheerfully as she passed the bicycle rack, briefcase in hand.

Julie managed a halfhearted greeting and then added, her outrage flaring back to life, "You wouldn't *believe* what just happened."

"Did you cross paths with a rude driver?" Penny guessed, eyeing her ten-speed.

"No, a tyrant!" Julie waited for her heart to stop pounding and exhaled slowly in an effort to regain perspective. She refused to let the encounter affect the rest of her day. "It's behind me now," she said, making a determined effort to put Roy Fletcher out of her mind. If it *had* been him. He hadn't answered her question, but from his demeanor and attitude she could only assume she'd run headlong into the company's owner.

Despite her rough start that morning, Julie had a good day. She enjoyed teaching; she was strict but fair, and her students understood that and respected her for it. After her last class, Julie changed out of her work clothes and back into her cycling gear and pedaled the five miles to Fletcher Industries.

Invigorated, she arrived at the spot her father had suggested. She hadn't been there more than a few minutes when a uniformed guard approached. It seemed she was destined for trouble. Probably Mr. Nose-in-the-Air had ordered him to chase her off. Well, if that was the case, she was ready. She had every right to be there, and she intended to point that out.

"Ms. Wilcoff?" the young man asked politely. His name tag read Jason.

She relaxed her stance. "Yes?"

"Your father said he'd be a bit late and asked that you meet him in his office."

"Oh, okay."

"I'll show you up."

What a difference from the way she'd been greeted that morning! The guard indicated where she could park her bike and then led her into the building. Entering the elevator, dressed as she was, Julie felt a bit self-conscious. She smiled shyly at a couple of women and decided that perhaps this bike-riding business wasn't the best idea, after all, especially if she was going to be meeting people. She'd give it a week and see how it went.

Her father's office was on the third floor. He looked up and smiled when she came into the room. "How was your day?"

"Great," she said, dropping into a chair. "How about yours?"

"Fine, fine. I won't be long." He returned to the computer screen, which he studied intently. "Just checking some employee records," he said. "I'm getting the hang of this computer stuff now."

"Take your time, I'm in no hurry."

"Wilcoff." The same unfriendly voice that had almost ruined her morning sounded from the doorway.

Julie turned her head to find the same unfriendly man— presumably Roy Fletcher. His eyes narrowed when he saw her.

"You again?" he said.

Her father rose and cast a glance from his employer to Julie. "This is my daughter, Julie. You've met?"

"I had the pleasure this morning." Fletcher held out his hand.

They exchanged brief handshakes. "Pleasure isn't exactly the word I'd use," Julie primly informed him.

"You teach English?"

"No," she said in a clipped voice. "Etiquette."

The merest hint of a smile touched his mouth. "I see."

"Julie teaches physical education, Mr. Fletcher," her father corrected, apparently surprised she'd claim otherwise.

Fletcher focused his attention on Dean. "I wanted to let you know my mother's stopping by in the next couple of weeks to paint a Christmas scene on the lobby windows." He frowned. "She seems to think some Christmas cheer will put me in the holiday mood," he said with heavy sarcasm.

Julie doubted he was interested in goodwill, now or at any other time of the year.

"I'll make sure no one bothers Mrs. Fletcher," her father assured him.

"I'd appreciate it." He turned to go, then changed his mind. "How was your first day?"

Her father hesitated. "Challenging."

"Good, glad to hear it." With that, Fletcher was gone as fast as he'd appeared.

"Good, glad to hear it," Julie repeated, and rolled her eyes. "Is that the most unpleasant man you've ever met in your life or what?"

"He's my employer, Julie, and he has more important matters on his mind than either you or me."

"How can you defend him?" she cried. "You said he was cold, but I had no idea he was *this* cold."

"He has a lot of responsibilities," her father said. "I've only been with the company one day, but I can see that people respect him, which says a great deal. There has to be a reason the staff feels like that about him."

If her father wanted to defend the tyrant, fine. She wasn't going to argue with him.

"I wonder what made him like this," she murmured while her father cleared off his desk. She didn't expect an answer and he didn't give her one. Perhaps eventually she'd learn more about Roy Fletcher. Then again, perhaps she wouldn't. Because Julie didn't care if she ever saw him again.

"It's her," Mercy shouted joyously, clapping her hands with delight. "She's the woman we've been sent to find for Anne's son."

"Who?" Shirley asked, looking around the empty office.

"Julie, of course," Mercy said irritably. "Dean Wilcoff's daughter." Mercy seemed disappointed that they didn't see things as plainly as she did.

"Julie? This Julie?" Goodness repeated, incredulous. "Get out of here!" Julie Wilcoff wasn't at all the kind of woman she had in mind. Besides, anyone could see those two had started off on the wrong foot. Julie openly disliked the man. Roy's feelings were harder to read, but she wouldn't be surprised if he'd had trouble remembering Julie's name two minutes after they'd met.

"Open your eyes," Mercy said, sitting on the file cabinet in Wilcoff's darkened office. "They're *perfect* for each other."

Shirley remained skeptical. "Sorry, I just can't picture it."

"Me, neither," Goodness concurred. She tried to imagine them as a couple. They didn't fit together, somehow. They both had strong personalities that would constantly collide. Goodness thought a gentle, loving woman would be better suited to the likes of Roy Fletcher. Someone soft and quiet. Someone less opinionated, more compromising. They hadn't found this paragon yet, but give them time and they would. Of course, they didn't *have* a lot of time. Their assignment on Earth was limited to a short three weeks.

"Am I the only one here with a brain?" Mercy groaned. "Julie's the right woman because she isn't going to let him intimidate her. She's got the strength of will to stand up to him, and he'll respect her for that."

"True," Shirley reluctantly agreed. "I don't mean to be unkind here, but have you noticed that…well, Julie's a very sweet girl, but…"

"She's a woman with all the right qualifications."

"Yes, of course, but, well, she's rather…large."

"I believe the term Shirley is looking for," Goodness said, stepping forward, "is big-boned."

"She's tall and she's…solid," Mercy said forcefully. "Don't forget, she played sports all those years. She's not some skinny little size-two model type."

"I know you mean well," Goodness said, not wanting any more distractions, "but Anne's son is handsome and wealthy, and frankly, he can have any woman he wants."

"He's well aware of that," Mercy declared, "and he doesn't care."

"Aimee was blond and beautiful," Shirley said.

"How do you know that?"

"I…peeked at the file on Gabriel's desk when no one was around."

"You did *what?*" Goodness burst out.

"It doesn't matter what Aimee looks like," Mercy insisted. "Okay, so she was blond and cute. Didn't work out, though, did it?"

"Obviously not," Goodness said grudgingly.

"Do you think he's still in love with her?" Shirley asked.

"I doubt it." Although Goodness couldn't know for sure, she suspected that Roy had put Aimee completely out of his mind—her and every other woman in the universe.

This was what made their mission so difficult. It was up to the three of them to find Roy a woman who would warm his cold, empty heart and teach him about love. No wonder Gabriel had warned them. This was perhaps their most difficult assignment to date.

"I like Julie," Mercy whispered.

"She's apple pandowdy and Fletcher wants cheesecake," Goodness said, proud of her analogy.

"He's had cheesecake." Shirley shot upward to join Mercy, crowding next to her on the filing cabinet. "I'm beginning to think Mercy's right. Roy's lost his taste for the exotic. He needs a woman with substance, a woman who's truly his equal."

Goodness thought perhaps her fellow Prayer Ambassadors had a point, but convincing Roy wouldn't be easy. "Just how are we going to persuade him to give Julie a second look?"

"And what about Julie?" Shirley demanded. "She didn't exactly fall for *him* at first sight."

"I think you're right," Goodness said. "Roy might need a bit of angelic assistance, but Julie's going to be even harder to convince."

"Oh, dear, I hadn't thought of that," Mercy muttered. "She's taken a rather keen dislike to him, hasn't she."

"That can be fixed, too."

Goodness and Mercy turned to look at their friend. "What do you mean?"

Shirley chortled happily. "Why don't I show you, instead?"

Five

"I hate the idea of you having to work on a Saturday," Julie said as her father prepared to walk out the door. He'd explained that it was because of the Thanksgiving holiday that had just passed.

"I don't mind. There's a lot to do." She watched him go and realized it'd been a very long time since she'd seen her father content. After only a few days, she was aware of what this new job had done for him. Once again, Julie was grateful that he'd been given this chance to prove himself. Despite her personal feelings about Fletcher, whom she considered both rude and egotistical, she appreciated the faith he'd placed in her father. Her sister agreed. They exchanged daily e-mails; Emily had told Julie she was encouraged by the changes she already saw in their father and suggested Julie make an effort to get along with the "big boss" if she saw him again—which she probably wouldn't.

Julie leaned against the door and sighed once her father had left for work. A sigh of relief, of satisfaction. Looking heavenward, she whispered, "We're going to be all right, Mom. We're moving ahead with our lives." Deep in her heart, she knew her mother heard her and approved.

The surprising thing Julie had learned in the past year was that life does go on. Despite her loss, despite her pain, she'd come to understand that. Clichéd though it sounded, it was true. Gradually, as she resumed her routines and her habits, it became easier. This didn't mean she missed her mother any less or had stopped thinking about her—that would've been impossible—but life continued.

After showering and doing a few housecleaning tasks, Julie tackled the kitchen. It was when she opened the refrigerator that she noticed her father's lunch. He'd forgotten it. Knowing he'd go without rather than pick up something at a restaurant, she called his work number. When he wasn't available, she asked the man who answered to please let her father know she'd deliver his lunch later that morning.

As she left the house, Julie decided this was the perfect opportunity to get in some exercise. Soon she'd start training for the STP, the annual two-hundred-mile bicycle ride between Seattle and Portland, Oregon. The two-day event was held every July and she'd participated faithfully until her mother's illness. Julie had skipped the past two years, but was eager to get back into a regular training program.

Dressed in her biking gear, she wheeled her ten-speed out of the garage and tucked her father's lunch in one of the paniers over the rear wheels. Then she headed for Fletcher Industries. It felt good to work hard, to pump her legs and exercise her lungs. At top speed she turned off the busy road and into the long driveway that led to the office complex. In the small mirror attached to her helmet, she saw a black sedan turning in behind her. The driveway was narrow and there wasn't room for her to move over or allow the vehicle to pass. Leaning forward as far as she could, her arms braced against the handlebars, Julie reached maximum speed, forcing her legs to pedal even faster.

Obviously the sedan's driver hadn't seen her. Julie gasped

as the black vehicle hit her rear tire. The collision sent her hurtling through the air, arms flailing. Her heart stopped when she realized there was no way to avoid missing a fir tree. A scream froze in her throat. If her head slammed against the tree at this speed, helmet or not, she'd be a goner. The last thought she had before impact was a fervent hope that her father not be the one to identify her body.

Then she landed.

It was as though she'd collided with a pile of pillows. Following impact with the tree, she fell on her backside with a solid thump. Too stunned to react, Julie sat there. By any law of nature, she should be badly injured.

Only, she wasn't. In fact, she seemed to be unscathed. Surely that was impossible!

"Are you all right?"

A pale, shaken Roy Fletcher stood above her. Equally shaken, Julie looked up at him and blinked several times, unable to find her tongue.

"I should be dead," she whispered, and thrust out her hand, assuming he'd help her up.

"You should be arrested for pulling a stunt like that," he said angrily, ignoring her hand. "Stay put until I can get an ambulance and the police." He took out his cell phone and started frantically punching numbers.

He wanted her arrested. Of all the nerve! "Listen here," she cried, still in a sitting position. "*You* were the one who ran into me."

"You're insane!" He was shouting now. "Not you," he said into the tiny cell phone and clicked it off. "I didn't touch you." He stared down at her, a puzzled look on his face. "I can't believe you're not hurt."

"I'm fine...I think."

"That was the most idiotic stunt I've ever seen. Why did you do it?"

"Me?" *He'd* run into her. And here he was yelling at her when the entire accident had been his fault. "Do you honestly think I voluntarily flew through the air and collided with a tree?"

He shook his head and rubbed his eyes as though to clear his vision. "I don't know what the hell happened, but I didn't hit you."

"Fine. Whatever. Just help me up." She extended her arm to him a second time. Unsteady as she felt, she needed the assistance.

"No!" He raised both hands. "Stay put," he said again. "You could've broken something and don't know it."

"I'd know it," she muttered. While she admitted to being shaken, she wasn't about to let him bully her. Although the trip to her feet lacked grace, she was soon upright.

"Don't move," he said. "Wait for the paramedics."

"I'm perfectly all right," she insisted, removing her helmet.

"You can't be sure of that. Now do as I say and stay where you are."

"Would you kindly be quiet and stop giving me orders?" Disgruntled, she brushed the dirt from her backside. So far, so good. Nothing even ached. She could see no scrapes or bruises.

Fletcher shook his head again, his expression one of hopelessness. "Are you always this unreasonable?"

Examining her ten-speed, Julie wanted to weep. It was ruined. "If you didn't hit me, how did *this* happen?" Maybe he planned to claim his car hadn't touched her bike, but she had evidence that said otherwise.

"If you hit that tree, why aren't you injured?" he snapped.

Julie didn't have an answer for him anymore than he did for her. They stood glaring at each other, both unwilling to back down, when the ambulance, siren blaring, rounded the corner.

Before she could protest, two paramedics had her

sitting down. While Fletcher explained what had happened, Julie, under protest, was placed on a stretcher. "Would someone please listen to me," she said as she struggled to sit up. "I'm fine. I don't even have any bruises. I'm not hurt."

The taller of the two paramedics picked up her dented helmet. "You hit that tree?" he asked incredulously.

"I saw it with my own eyes," Fletcher confirmed.

"He saw it because he ran into me," Julie immediately said. He wasn't an innocent bystander in this accident. He'd caused it.

"My car didn't touch her bike."

By this time, the police had arrived, and a cruiser pulled up behind the ambulance. Fletcher scowled at her as if to say this was all her fault, but *he'd* contacted the authorities. She hadn't wanted to. While the police officer talked to Fletcher, Julie answered the paramedics' questions. When they suggested she be checked out at the hospital, she refused.

"Look," she said, dismissing their concern, "I'm none the worse for wear." The last thing she wanted was to show up at the hospital in an ambulance when she wasn't even hurt.

"You'll have your own doctor examine you?" the second man asked.

"I will," she promised.

"I'll see that she does," Fletcher added.

The policeman knelt down in front of Fletcher's sedan. "I don't see any marks here."

Fletcher looked at Julie, his eyes full of suspicion. "I don't know how to explain what happened, but I swear I didn't hit you."

"Would you stop telling me how innocent you are?" Then it dawned on her that he was afraid she was going to sue him. As a man with deep pockets, he'd be worried about lawsuits.

"Nope, I don't see any evidence here at all," the police officer said, frowning in puzzlement.

Men always stick together, Julie thought irritably. Well, if that was what the police had decided, so be it.

"I'll leave it for you two to settle," the officer said.

"Thank you," Roy told him.

The paramedics climbed back into their vehicle and drove off, and shortly afterward the police car followed.

"Look at my bike!" Julie studied the damage to her ten-speed. The entire back wheel was bent and twisted; the frame had buckled beyond repair.

"I'll buy you another," Fletcher said as he loaded her crumpled bike into the trunk of his car.

"So you *are* admitting responsibility," she challenged, hands on her hips.

"No," he said in a flat, businesslike tone.

"You don't have to worry. I have no intention of suing you."

He didn't respond as he opened the passenger door. "Get in," he said curtly.

"Where are you taking me?"

"To my personal physician."

"I said I'm not hurt."

"I know what you said. Now are you going to do as I ask, or do I have to put you inside this car myself?"

Julie could see it was pointless to argue; he was determined to do things his way. "Oh, all right," she said with a complete lack of graciousness.

He slipped into the driver's seat and exhaled slowly. "Thank you."

Julie crossed her arms and tried to stifle a laugh.

"What's so funny?"

"Nothing." But then she couldn't help it and burst out laughing.

"What?"

"It's you," she said between peals of laughter. "You said 'thank you.' Were you thanking me for sparing you the effort of having to physically lift me?"

"No." He apparently lacked even the most rudimentary sense of humor. "I was thanking you for not putting up any more of a fuss than you already have."

He started the engine. "What are you doing here, anyway?"

Until he asked, she'd totally forgotten. "Dad's lunch. It's on the bike. He forgot it this morning and I was taking it to him." She turned around and looked behind her, wondering if his lunch had somehow survived the collision. "I need to get it to him."

"Your father can go without lunch—getting you to a doctor is more important at the moment."

She glared at him, and he groaned audibly.

"Oh, all right." Without her having to say another word, he drove up to the main entrance and parked. "Stay where you are," Fletcher ordered.

"I wouldn't dream of doing anything else," she said with exaggerated sweetness.

He looked as though he doubted her, then quickly leaped out of the car. Removing her sorely bent and abused ten-speed, he leaned it against the building. She couldn't see what he was doing, but a moment later, the side mirror on the passenger door gave her a brief view of him on his cell phone.

"Did you tell my dad I wasn't hurt?" she asked when he got back in the car.

"No, I was talking to Dr. Wilbur."

Great, just great. Her father would find her bike, a crumpled mess, and assume the worst. "Give me that phone."

He stared at her as if no one ever spoke to him like that. "Please," she added, realizing how rude she must sound. "I've got to tell Dad I'm all right. He won't know what to think if he finds that."

"By the way," he said wryly, "his lunch did not sustain any mishap. The sandwich isn't smashed at all. I thought you'd want to know." He reached inside his jacket and handed her the cell, which was the tiniest phone she'd ever seen. It took Julie a few minutes to figure out how it worked.

Her father was away from his desk and once again she had to leave a message with someone else. She explained the situation and said he should collect his lunch from her bike.

"Are you happy now?" Fletcher asked when she'd finished her call and returned his phone.

"Ecstatic."

"Good. Now sit back and relax."

"Don't be so bossy," she muttered.

"Don't be so stubborn."

"This really isn't necessary. I have no intention of suing," she said, not for the first time.

"Good thing, because you'd lose."

Julie thought she saw a hint of a smile. She looked again, certain she must be wrong. The high-and-mighty computer whiz was actually amused. Now *this* was something to write home about.

Anne Fletcher pulled the blanket around her shoulders as she attempted to fall to sleep. Opening one eye, she peered at the clock. Two in the morning. She should've been asleep hours ago. For no reason she could discern, she'd been having trouble sleeping. No matter what she did—read, drank warm milk, swallowed nighttime aspirin—she remained fully awake.

With a disgusted sigh, she tossed back the covers and reached for the switch on her lamp. She was wide-awake and any effort to sleep would be a waste of time. Her mind drifted to the memory of the angel who'd appeared to her. She leaned over to get her sketchbook from the bedside table and flipped the pages until she found what she wanted.

Anne was sure she'd imagined the visitation, and yet it had seemed so real. But none of this made sense. Why would an angel appear to *her?* Not a word had been spoken, not a sound uttered. But an angel had stood directly in front of her. So strong was the impression that even now Anne could feel the love emanating from the heavenly being.

To further confuse her, the image had lasted for several minutes, long enough for Anne to grab her sketchbook. Almost as if she was posing, the angel had stood perfectly still while Anne quickly outlined what was before her, unbelievable though it was.

"She was so beautiful," Anne whispered as she studied the drawing with fresh eyes.

The urge to paint the image onto canvas suddenly gripped her. After a long day in her studio, she should be exhausted; instead, she was filled with excitement. Anne got out of bed. Dressed in her nightgown and slippers, she decided she'd paint until she felt tired. She'd get started and see how things went.

The studio was cold and dark, and she turned on the light, then hurried into the kitchen to make a pot of tea. Taking a pristine canvas from the pile stacked against the wall, she set it on the easel and stepped back. No, bigger. The angel who'd visited her couldn't be displayed on such a small space. Searching through her supplies, Anne looked for the largest canvas she had.

She found one in a closet, bigger than anything she'd ever used before, and began to work. Thinking she'd soon grow tired, she didn't pause. She painted through the night and didn't stop until daylight. To her amazement, she noticed sunshine pouring in around her. She glanced at the clock on the wall. Almost eight! For the first time in her life she'd worked straight through the night.

"I'll just take a quick break," she told herself as she went back to bed. Exhausted, she climbed between the sheets and closed her eyes. Seven hours later, around three, she woke feeling refreshed and revitalized.

After showering and changing clothes, Anne resumed her painting. The next time she looked up, it was dark again. Shocked, she realized she hadn't eaten in nearly thirty hours. The refrigerator provided a chunk of cheddar and a small cluster of seedless grapes, which she munched on hungrily. She made another pot of tea. Then it was back to work.

When she'd finished the painting, she saw daylight again; for the second night in a row, she'd worked without sleep. Stepping back, Anne examined her creation with a critical eye.

"Yes," she whispered, awed by the painting before her.

This was her best work to date. She'd call it... *Visitation.* Smiling, she studied the painting from several angles.

The phone rang, startling her, and she hurried to answer it.

"Anne, it's Marta."

"Oh, Marta, hello." Her mind raced frantically as she tried to remember what day it was. Anne had a terrible feeling she'd missed their dinner appointment—not to mention her lunch with Roy—and sincerely hoped she hadn't. She thought for a minute; as far as she could calculate, it was Thursday morning. Never had she worked on a project in such a frenzied fashion—to the point that she no longer knew what day of the week it was.

"I just called to ask if you'd let me see one of your paintings."

"Oh, Marta, are you sure?" Anne would never presume to ask her friend for this kind of favor.

"I've been hearing good things about your landscapes. A colleague of mine was on the island last summer—Kathy Gruber—and met you. She saw your work at a local exhibit. You remember her, don't you?"

"Yes, of course."

"Since I'm in town this week, I'd like to take a look at some of your pieces."

Anne glanced at her angel. "I'll let you see one, but it isn't a landscape. As it happens, I just finished it." Eyeing the canvas, she frowned. The painting was too big; she couldn't bring it into town with her. "It won't fit in my car," she said.

"I can make a trip out to your place tomorrow, if that's convenient."

"Of course it is, but we're still meeting for dinner tonight, aren't we?"

"I wouldn't miss it for the world," Marta assured her.

"Me, neither," Anne said.

They spoke for a few minutes longer. When Anne replaced the receiver, she saw by the clock that she had just enough time for a short nap and a shower before heading into Seattle to meet her son.

Six

"Not bad," Goodness said as she studied the painting. She cocked her head to one side and decided that, as a portrait, it was uncannily accurate. "It certainly looks like Shirley."

"I had no idea I was so lovely," Shirley said, clasping her hands. "Is that truly the way Anne sees me?" She gazed expectantly at her two friends.

"So it seems," Goodness replied.

"What I want to know," Mercy began, making herself at home in Anne's studio, "is why we haven't been dragged back to Heaven in disgrace." She glanced pointedly at Shirley. "By all rights, we should be standing guard at the Pearly Gates after what *she* did."

Mercy was the one more accustomed to causing trouble on Earth. It used to be Shirley who made them tread the straight and narrow, but apparently the job had—unfairly—fallen to Goodness. For this assignment, anyway.

She couldn't give Mercy an answer. The Archangel clearly had his own reasons for keeping them on Earth.

"We have an important task," Shirley explained as if that should be obvious. "Anne and Roy need us."

"Seems to me Julie could use a hand, too," Goodness

muttered. She didn't want to be judgmental, but the woman Mercy considered the answer to Anne's prayer was being less than cooperative.

"What do you mean?" Mercy asked. "I thought the accident was a brilliant idea! It got Roy and Julie together, didn't it?"

"All they did was snipe at each other." Goodness wasn't disparaging her friend's effort, but it simply hadn't worked.

"I think I was more optimistic than I should've been," Mercy said when Shirley came and sat next to her.

"I thought everything went very well." Shirley seemed undeterred by Julie's lack of cooperation—or Roy's. She continued to stare at her portrait with an appreciative eye.

"How can you say that?" Goodness cried. In her opinion, Julie wasn't the only one who needed instruction in romance. It was evident that Shirley had difficulty recognizing what worked and what didn't. That staged accident certainly hadn't.

Shirley sighed. "I had real hope when Roy took her to his own physician."

"But then he dumped her there."

Mercy nodded vigorously. "The least he could've done was wait long enough to make sure she wasn't injured."

"He did pay for her taxi ride home," Shirley said. "They were getting along so well, too."

Goodness gaped at her friend and wondered if Shirley had lost all touch with reality. "They did nothing but argue!" She'd witnessed courtroom battles with less antagonism. Roy Fletcher and Julie Wilcoff were completely unsuited as a couple, but no one wanted to listen to *her*. As far as she could see, the two of them didn't even like each other.

Goodness might never have been in love—romance was for earthly beings—but she had an instinct for matchmaking, if she did say so herself. She'd successfully guided men and women toward each other a time or two, but none of that seemed to matter.

"Yes, they were arguing, but I was well aware even if you weren't that they like each other," Mercy insisted.

"I don't think so." Goodness hated to discourage her friends, but she didn't see it. The spark just wasn't there. She suspected Julie had become so discouraged about her prospects of finding a husband that she'd lost the ability to attract one. Goodness had wanted to shake the young woman for joking about her weight. A lady never discussed such things! Julie should know better. And Roy—he was one of the walking wounded. He didn't seem capable of feeling anything, except bitterness and cynicism.

"What are you suggesting?" Mercy asked.

Goodness knew it was one thing to criticize and another to offer an alternative. But she figured they'd better face up to the truth sooner rather than later. "We should give it up and search elsewhere."

Mercy folded her wings tightly, a sure sign she wasn't pleased.

"We did our part. Now it's up to the two of them. Agreed?" Goodness gave her friends a stern look.

"Just who do you think would interest Roy?" Shirley asked.

"Just who?" Mercy parroted.

They had Goodness there. "I don't know—yet," she said. "But we've done our part. Agreed?" she said again.

The other two nodded with unmistakable reluctance.

"Now I say we leave them alone, and if it's meant to be, it'll happen without any help from the three of us."

Mercy seemed about to argue, but then she sighed loudly. "Oh, all right, but I still have a strong feeling that Julie's the answer to Anne's prayer."

"Anne," Shirley whispered. As if she'd suddenly remembered something, the former Guardian Angel announced, "I'll be right back."

Goodness was having none of this. "Where are you going?"

Shirley glanced over her shoulder. "I'll only be a minute."

Goodness exchanged a look with Mercy and both of them followed Shirley. The other Ambassador didn't go far. She crept into Anne's bedroom and saw that the older woman was in bed, eyes closed.

"Is she asleep?" Mercy asked, floating above the bed.

"Not quite," Shirley answered with confidence.

Goodness peered closer, but couldn't tell. After working two consecutive nights on the portrait of Shirley, Anne must be exhausted.

"She's meeting her son later this morning," Mercy said. "She won't sleep long."

Goodness checked the clock radio. "The alarm is set."

"She thinks she only needs an hour or two."

"The poor thing," Shirley said. To Goodness's surprise, she moved to stand over the older woman. Gently pressing her hand to Anne's forehead, Shirley leaned forward to whisper, "You did a beautiful job." Then she lifted her hand and eased away.

"Look," Mercy said, pointing at Anne.

The softest of smiles touched the woman's lips, almost as if she'd heard Shirley speak.

"Roy?"

Roy glanced up at George Williams, his high-priced corporate attorney. "I'm sorry, did I miss something?" Judging by the pained expression on the other man's face, apparently he had. Williams had been discussing the profit-and-loss statement for Griffin Plastics, a company Roy was interested in purchasing. He'd half heard Williams drone on about "synergies"—which, as far as he could determine, just meant that Griffin would be able to make the cases for his security software. Sighing, he directed his attention to the papers on his desk. "Let me look these over and get back to you this afternoon."

The attorney frowned, gathered his files together and stuffed them in his briefcase.

"Before you leave I have a question," Roy said.

"About the Griffin figures?"

"No." Roy reached for a pen and made a few scribbles on a clean sheet of paper while he collected his thoughts. "Late last week, I had a minor...altercation with a bicycle rider."

"Altercation?" George Williams repeated.

"She fell—" he chose the word carefully "—off her ten-speed and hit a tree."

The attorney's eyes widened and he pulled a blank pad of paper toward him.

"She was unhurt," Roy rushed to add. "As an innocent by-stander, I immediately phoned the paramedics and notified the police."

"So, you're telling me that you were in no way responsible for her...fall?"

"That's correct."

"In other words, you happened along shortly after the accident, and out of consideration for this biker you stopped your vehicle and saw to her welfare?"

The attorney was describing a rather different scene than the one that had actually occurred, but Roy let him. "Yes," he said slowly, thoughtfully.

"Your concern is?" Williams asked.

"The woman claims I caused her accident." Just thinking about it irritated Roy. Although there was no evidence to validate her accusation, Julie Wilcoff had insisted he'd run into the rear of her bike. But he hadn't even seen her until the last second and had instantly slammed on his brakes. In mentally reviewing the incident, Roy had decided that the sound of his car behind her must have startled Julie; she'd lost focus and hit something in the road, which was the reason she'd catapulted off the bicycle and into the tree.

That, however, didn't explain the damage to her ten-speed. The bicycle clearly showed there'd been an impact from the rear. The back wheel was destroyed, the metal twisted and crumpled. Anyone looking at the bike would believe he'd hit Julie. But Roy knew otherwise, and there was no evidence on his car to suggest he'd collided with her.

"What injuries did she sustain?"

"None. She was unhurt. In fact, she refused medical treatment from the paramedics."

Williams frowned.

"I took her to my personal physician and he couldn't find any injuries, either."

The attorney scribbled furiously. "What have you heard from her since?"

"Nothing." That concerned him the most. With his name and his money, he was a natural target for frivolous lawsuits. However, any suit Julie filed might find a sympathetic jury. She could have a case, innocent though he was. It certainly wasn't unheard of for a jury to award a huge settlement for a minor infraction, depending on how effectively the case was presented.

"I did feel bad," Roy said cautiously. "The accident occurred on company property and I replaced her bicycle." The new one was twice the machine her old ten-speed had been.

Again Williams made a notation. Roy worried that replacing Julie's ten-speed might be seen as an acknowledgment of guilt. He should've thought of that earlier.

"Did she have a reason for being on company property?" Williams asked.

"I employ her father."

The frown was back, creasing his brow. "I see."

"Wilcoff was only recently hired." Roy had let chance make the decision. He'd studied the applications, chosen the top three and written the candidates' names on slips of paper, which he'd placed in an empty coffee mug. He'd drawn one name—Dean's. So perhaps all of this was fated....

"Have you spoken to the father since the incident?"

Roy hadn't. "Any suggestions on what I should do now?"

"I wish you'd said something sooner," the attorney murmured, his expression darkening.

Roy probably should have, but until now he hadn't seen the need. It hadn't been a serious accident. By her own admission and confirmed by his doctor, Julie was perfectly fine. This sort of situation had never occurred before. Williams was probably right; Roy should've consulted a lawyer immediately.

"Trouble?" he asked, unwilling to borrow any. He had problems enough.

Williams nodded abruptly. "Even if you haven't heard from this woman, that doesn't mean she isn't filing a lawsuit against you."

"She hasn't got a case," Roy argued. But she did have the damaged bicycle....

"You and I know that, but didn't you say she claims you were responsible for the accident?"

More times than Roy cared to count. Julie had accused him of running her down. It had become her mantra on their ride to Dr. Wilbur's.

"That tells me there's a good possibility of a nuisance suit."

Roy should have known, should have guessed. "What do you think I should do next?" he asked, tension tightening his jaw. The thought of paying this money-grubber a dime went against his principles.

"Offer her a settlement."

He didn't want to do that, not in the least, but he knew it was better to take care of such unpleasantness quickly. Otherwise he might end up dealing with her in court. She had the damaged bike in her possession. A long, drawn-out trial would drain him emotionally and threaten him financially. And, needless to say, it could destroy his reputation.

"How much?" he asked bluntly.

The attorney hesitated, then said, "My expertise is corporate law, so perhaps we should let a litigation expert answer that question."

Roy refused to waste another minute on this. "How much would *you* suggest?"

Williams shrugged. "Twenty-five thousand should more than compensate her for any pain and suffering."

As far as Roy was concerned, that was twenty-five thousand too much. But gritting his teeth, he agreed. He'd order the check cut right away.

"Anything else?" Williams asked, picking up his briefcase.

"No, that should be all."

The attorney gestured at the Griffin papers in front of Roy. "You'll get back to me this afternoon?"

Roy nodded. He'd read over the figures and make a decision by the end of the workday. He stood, and the two men shook hands. Williams saw himself out as Roy returned to his chair.

He leaned back and steepled his fingers, his mind spinning in various directions. Shaking his head, he opened the Griffin file. Try as he might to focus on the facts and figures regarding the buyout, his thoughts wandered to Julie Wilcoff. Part of him wanted to take her at her word—to believe she had no intention of suing him. But his experience with women said otherwise.

"You know by now you can't trust a woman." Until he heard the words, Roy didn't realize he'd spoken aloud.

Hoping to get a better feel for the situation, he called his executive assistant, Eleanor Johnson, and asked her to have Dean Wilcoff sent to his office. This potential lawsuit would bother him until he had some sense of what was likely to happen. The best way to find that out was through Julie's father.

Within minutes, his new head of security was shown into his office.

"Good morning, Dean." The older man stood by his desk, shoulders squared in military fashion.

"Sit down." Roy motioned toward the chair recently vacated by his attorney. "I asked to see you on a personal matter."

The other man didn't react at all. That was good. "I assume you heard about your daughter's bicycle accident."

Dean nodded. "She told me about it herself. I want you to know how much I appreciate the way you took care of her."

Roy dismissed his thanks. "She received the new ten-speed?" He'd had it delivered on Monday.

"She did, and I'm sure she'll want to thank you personally for your generosity."

"That isn't necessary." Roy paused, uncertain how to phrase the next question. "Uh, how is Julie?"

"How is she?" the other man repeated as if he didn't understand. "Oh, do you mean does she have any lingering aches and such from the fall?"

"Yes," Roy said without elaborating. He didn't want to tip Wilcoff off about his fear of a lawsuit. Sure as anything, Julie was talking to some fancy lawyer who'd promise her millions. Roy's millions. The tension gathered in his shoulder blades, tightening his muscles.

"Julie's tough," Dean answered, seeming to relax for the first time since entering the office. "As a kid, she had more scraped knees and bruises than any boy in the neighborhood. I will admit that when I saw her bike, I was a bit concerned, but she doesn't seem to have any ill effects from the accident."

"I'm glad to hear it."

"Like I said, Julie's tough."

"She's been able to work all week, then?" That was another important question. If she was badly hurt, as she might claim, her showing up at work would be evidence that those claims were only an effort to bilk him out of as much money as possible.

"Oh, sure. She went to school every day this week."

This was sounding better all the time, but it was no guarantee that she wasn't planning legal action at some later point. No, it was best to deal with this once and for all.

"Your daughter's convinced I caused the collision." There, he'd said it. He watched the other man closely, wondering how he'd respond.

Wilcoff dropped his gaze. "Yes, she did mention that."

Aha! Roy knew it. This was exactly what Williams had warned him about. Not hearing from Julie didn't mean he wasn't being set up for a multimillion-dollar lawsuit.

"I feel bad about the accident," he said, selecting his words with care. "While Julie and I have a disagreement as to the cause, I'd like to remind you she was riding on company grounds."

Wilcoff heard the censure in Roy's voice and reacted accordingly. "I'll make sure she doesn't do that again."

"I'd appreciate it." He shuddered at the thought of another accident on his property.

"Consider it done," Wilcoff said. He seemed eager to leave. "Was that all, Mr. Fletcher?"

"Actually, no," Roy said slowly. This next part nearly stuck in his throat, but he had no option. "I'd like to offer Julie a small settlement to compensate for her pain and suffering."

Shocked, his head of security held up both hands. "That isn't necessary. In fact, I think Julie would be upset—"

"I insist. I'll have my attorney draw up the papers and we'll consider the matter closed."

Wilcoff shook his head. "None of this is necessary. Anyway, you should talk to Julie about it, not me. But I know she'll feel the same way."

"Perhaps," Roy said, although he didn't believe it. He was a prime candidate for a lawsuit. He'd behaved stupidly in not getting his lawyer involved earlier. That oversight was a rarity for him; he hadn't come this far in the business world by ignoring the obvious.

"Whatever you decide, Mr. Fletcher, is between you and my daughter, but I'm certain Julie isn't interested in a settlement."

That's what they all say, Roy thought cynically. Julie Wilcoff was no different from any other woman he'd ever met—or any man in the same situation.

He was worried, but he didn't dare let it show.

Wilcoff left, and Roy started to read over the Griffin paperwork, but he still couldn't concentrate. The truth of it was, he'd quite enjoyed his exchanges with Julie Wilcoff. True, she wasn't the most attractive woman he'd encountered, but she possessed a quick wit and a quirky sense of humor. He couldn't recall the last time any woman had joked with him about her size or weight. He had to admit he found it refreshing.

His phone rang and he answered it. "I'm sorry to bother you, Mr. Fletcher," Eleanor Johnson said, "but your mother is here."

"My mother?" Oh, yes, now he remembered. He'd even put it in his daily planner. She'd asked about meeting him on Thursday and he'd suggested lunchtime. In his current frame of mind, he had no interest in food, but he couldn't slight his mother. He sighed, then said with obvious reluctance, "Send her in."

"Merry Christmas, Roy." Disregarding his mood, his mother came into the office and hugged him.

"How are you, Mother? And isn't it a little early for Christmas greetings?"

"Not at all," she said, smiling at him with sparkling blue eyes. "Once December arrives, it's never too early to say Merry Christmas." Roy smiled in return. He sincerely loved his mother. She often frustrated him, but he did love and admire her—although he didn't understand her. She'd allowed his father to swindle her out of a huge amount. Roy had wanted her to fight, had urged her to drag his father back into court and make him pay. Roy wanted his father's reputation destroyed, which was what Burton Fletcher deserved, but his mother had refused to do it. His father seemed to have some regrets, if his efforts to contact Roy were any indication, but so far Roy had adamantly rejected any kind of relationship.

Instead of fighting, his mother had apparently forgiven Burton and become a hermit, living in a ridiculously small cottage on a tiny San Juan island. What really upset him was that she claimed to be "reasonably happy." She'd been cheated, dumped and cast aside like yesterday's junk mail and she was *happy?* Roy just didn't get it.

"Are you ready for lunch?"

Roy couldn't think of a way to tell her he didn't feel like having lunch without disappointing her. He checked his watch.

"Is your meeting over?"

"Yup, I have half an hour." His problem was that he couldn't be around his mother and ignore the past. When he was with her, his heart ached for a life that was dead to him. He grieved for the innocents they'd once been, he and his mother. She'd taken one path since the divorce and he'd taken another. Hatred for his father and for Aimee consumed him. He wanted them to suffer, wanted them to rot in hell for all the pain they'd caused.

While his mother chose to forgive and forget, he chose

to remember every detail, every incident, every minute of their treachery. In retrospect, he realized Aimee had been interested in his father all along. He'd never been anything more than the means to an end.

"I'll take whatever time you have for me," his mother said in the complacent voice that always perturbed him. "Oh," she said, slipping her arm around his waist. "I have a painting I want you to look at one day soon."

"Another landscape?" Without her knowledge, he'd purchased several of her pieces, displayed under whatever name she used. Mary Something? He couldn't remember at the moment. She refused his financial help, but what she didn't know wouldn't hurt her.

"Not this time," she said, then softly added, "This time I painted something entirely different."

Seven

"You don't know how good it is to see you!" Marta Rosenberg greeted Anne, throwing her arms wide. The hotel foyer was dominated by a fifteen-foot-tall Christmas tree decorated with huge shiny red balls and large gold bows. Plush leather chairs and mahogany tables created an intimate atmosphere despite the openness of the room.

Anne hugged her friend. It'd been years since they'd last visited. Nearly ten if she recalled correctly. Burton had taken a business trip to New York and Anne had accompanied him. They'd gone to a show on Broadway, gotten together with old friends and strolled through Central Park holding hands. She and Marta had met for drinks one afternoon, gossiping and laughing like the college girls they'd once been. That was long before Aimee, long before the divorce.

A familiar ache stabbed Anne close to her heart. She made an effort to ignore it; she wouldn't allow her loss to taint this reunion.

"You look marvelous," Marta said, stepping back to get a better view. "What have you been up to?"

Anne laughed off her old friend's praise. "I spent most

of the afternoon buying Christmas cards and wrap—after I had lunch with Roy. I swear Scrooge has more Christmas spirit than my son." Her elegant white suit was left over from her old life. These days, she was most comfortable in jeans and an oil-smeared cotton shirt.

Marta was blond and tanned and she dressed strictly in black, no matter what the season. It was a New York thing, Anne figured. Her friend's hair haphazardly framed her face, but Anne knew there was nothing haphazard about it. She looked chic, rich, sophisticated, and her world seemed a million miles from the one that had become Anne's.

"Speaking of Roy," Marta said as she led the way into the dining room. "I understand he's making quite a name for himself."

"I'm very proud of what he's accomplished, but I worry about him." She didn't elaborate and thankfully Marta didn't question her. Despite her determination to enjoy this evening, Anne's thoughts went back to the lunch with Roy. He seemed preoccupied, but when she'd asked him about it, he'd brushed aside her concern. He so rarely permitted her any glimpses into his life; he'd closed himself off from her, the same way he'd shut out everyone else.

Marta announced her name to the maître d', and they were immediately seated. The man handed Anne a leather-encased menu, and with more ceremony than necessary, draped the white linen napkin on her lap.

A waiter came for their drink order, and both Anne and Marta requested a glass of white wine.

"What brings you to Seattle?" Anne asked her. "Business, I assume."

"What else? At one time I had a life, but now it's art. You wouldn't believe some of the pieces I've found. And—as I mentioned before—I really would like to see your work."

"I've only been painting for the last five years, Marta. My work is amateurish compared to the artists you represent."

"Let me decide that. You were the most talented girl in our class and I don't expect that's changed."

But it had. So much had changed in the forty years since Marta had first known her.

Their wine arrived, and they paused to sample it. Anne welcomed the break in conversation.

"Well," Marta said as she set her wineglass aside. "Let's get the subject of Burton out of the way. What happened?"

Anne gazed sightlessly into the distance. "What always happens?"

"Another woman." Marta scowled as she added, "Younger, no doubt."

Anne nodded. "Thirty years younger."

"I hope he paid through the nose for this."

Anne didn't answer. How could she? "Actually, no." The details weren't anyone's business but her own. "It depresses me to discuss it, so let's not, all right?"

"The jerk," Marta muttered, and said something else under her breath, something Anne wouldn't ask her to repeat.

"Shall we toast to independence?" Marta asked, tears filling her eyes.

"Marta?" Anne leaned forward and touched her friend's hand. "What's wrong?"

"What's always wrong?" she murmured, echoing Anne's earlier statement.

"Jack?"

Marta nodded, lowering her eyes. "He's got a girlfriend. Naturally, he still thinks I have no idea, but a blind woman could've figured it out."

So this was the reason Marta had sought her out. "What are you going to do?"

"Twenty-seven years with a man, and you assume you

know him. Silly me." She made a gallant effort to smile through her tears. Raising the wineglass to her lips, she took a long and appreciative swallow.

"You're considering a divorce?"

Marta shrugged. "I can't imagine the rest of my life without Jack, but I can't tolerate the thought of him with another woman—especially while he's married to me! I don't know what to do."

Anne noticed that her friend's hand trembled as she put down her wineglass. "Half the time I want to bash his head in for hurting me like this and the rest of the time I cry."

"You're sure he's having an affair?"

Marta reached for her wine and took another large swallow. "Very sure." Tears glistened in her eyes again. "All right, my wise friend, advise me."

Anne felt in no position to be giving her advice, although she supposed she could tell Marta what *not* to do. She'd been cheated and misled, and all because she'd been naive. The waiter appeared at their table, and Anne realized they hadn't even looked at their menus. They did so quickly, both deciding on the salmon entrée.

Resuming the conversation, Anne called on her own experience. The first thing she suggested was that Marta talk to an attorney, and not one her husband recommended. From this point forward, everything Jack said was suspect, since he'd lied to her already. Marta needed facts and information. Anne might have saved herself a lot of grief had she hired an attorney of her own choosing—and done so earlier.

Their dinners arrived. They chatted, they ate, they laughed and cried, and then laughed again.

"I can't tell you how wonderful it is to talk with someone openly and honestly," Marta said after their second glass of wine and two cups of strong coffee. "I didn't know where else to turn. Lots of our friends have split up over the years, but…this just can't be happening. Not to Jack and me, and yet it is, and I don't know what to do about it."

Anne squeezed Marta's hand. "I hoped Burton would come to his senses. I prayed and pleaded with God to give me my husband back. My entire identity was tied up with his."

Marta grew tearful again. "I'm beginning to wonder if God really answers our prayers."

Anne believed He did. "While it's true God didn't give me the answer I *wanted,* He did answer me."

"How do you mean?"

"I have my own identity now, and it isn't that of Burton's ex-wife. I'm Anne Fletcher—and I'm also Mary Fleming, artist."

"Why did you decide to use a pseudonym?"

It was a well-kept secret. Only a few people knew. Her fear was that friends, out of pity and concern, would purchase her landscapes in a desire to support her. Anne didn't want their sympathy. Come hell or high water, she was determined to make it on her own.

"Mary Fleming is business-savvy, smart and talented. Anne Fletcher is meek, mild and a victim, in the eyes of the world."

"I love it," Marta said, reaching for the tab and signing it to her room. "Speaking of Mary," she said, "I'm really looking forward to seeing her work."

Anne hesitated. "You're sure about this?"

"Is that Anne or Mary speaking?"

"Anne," she confessed with a laugh.

"That's what I thought."

"Okay, come to my car with me. I brought a sketch."

They left the hotel, and Anne handed the valet her claim check. He brought her car around, and at Anne's instruction, parked it by the outside curb to avoid delaying anyone who was pulling into the portico. The Cadillac was one of the few things she'd gotten as part of the divorce settlement. Roy said that was because Burton had wanted it to look as if he'd been fair.

"As I explained, this isn't one of my landscapes," Anne said, opening the door. Because of the size of the painting, she'd brought along her sketchbook. It lay on the passenger seat, and Anne picked it up and opened it to the sketch of the angel.

For a long moment Marta didn't say anything. "This is the sketch you painted from?"

"Yes, in a huge rush." She told her the size of the canvas. While on the ferry, she'd shaded in the sketch, using pencils. "Like I said this morning, I just finished the painting. I'm sure the oil is still wet." Then, because she regretted showing her art to such a renowned professional, Anne quickly added, "Listen, it's all right if you don't like it."

"Like it?" Marta said, meeting her gaze. "I *love* it. This is incredible. I realize it's only a sketch, but if the painting's anything like this, you have a real winner on your hands. Maybe it's my state of mind, I don't know," she said, staring down at the pad, "but I feel like…like I've been touched by God just looking at it."

Anne could hardly believe Marta had said that….

"I'm stopping by your place first thing tomorrow, and if this painting is half as good as I think it'll be, I'm taking it back to New York. Agreed?"

"I…of course."

"I can get eight or nine for this."

"Hundred?"

Marta grinned. "Thousand."

"Eight or nine thousand?" Anne knew she had to be dreaming.

"Maybe more. Now, I have to tell you that as the dealer, I take a percentage, but you could still end up with four or five thousand dollars."

Anne wanted to throw her arms in the air and scream for joy. Instead, she clasped both hands over her mouth and silently said a prayer of gratitude.

Eight

Now that her father was working, Julie always stopped at the mailbox on her way home. For obvious reasons, she no longer accompanied him or rode her bicycle—her brand-new bicycle—to and from school. As she strolled toward the house on Monday, she shuffled through the day's collection of bills, notices, Christmas cards and the usual junk mail—and paused at the thick manila envelope addressed to her. Julie hesitated in midstep. The return address was that of a well-known Seattle law firm.

Tearing it open, Julie juggled the house keys, the rest of the mail and her backpack as she extracted a letter and a thick wad of paper. Using her shoulder to open the door, she nearly fell into the house when she realized what she was reading.

A settlement offer.

From Roy Fletcher.

Julie scanned the details and by the time she'd finished she could hardly breathe. Mr. High-and-Mighty wanted to buy her off. He was willing to spend twenty-five thousand dollars to shut her up. Julie couldn't believe it, couldn't comprehend why anyone would go to such outlandish lengths to get rid of her, especially when she'd assured him she had no intention of suing.

She didn't want his money. She didn't want anything from him. His offer was the biggest insult of her life.

Pacing now, she stomped from one end of the living room to the other. She knew it wasn't a good idea to try to reason with Fletcher, especially when she felt like this, but she couldn't stand still and she couldn't stay home. She had to do *something* before she exploded with indignation. This pent-up energy had to go somewhere.

Her thoughts continued to churn as she tossed her car keys in the air and deftly caught them. Good idea or not, her mind was made up. She was going to tell Mr. Big Bucks exactly what he could do with his "settlement offer."

Julie was so angry she barely noticed the ten-mile drive in heavy traffic. Naturally there wasn't a single parking space available anywhere at Fletcher Industries. With no other option, she pulled into a handicapped spot.

Arms swinging at her sides, every step filled with determination, Julie headed for the company's headquarters. In the back of her mind a small voice whispered that this was probably a mistake. She didn't care. She was beyond caring.

She stormed into the building, past the security guard, a young man with impressive biceps. Jason, she recalled. She'd met him last week. "Miss," he said, stopping her. "You have to check in here first."

Julie waved her hand at him as he moved out from behind his desk. "You don't want to mess with me just now."

"Ma'am, I'm sorry, but I can't let you onto the elevator until you've been cleared by security."

"Hey, man, that's Mr. Wilcoff's daughter," a second guard said, coming around the corner. "How you doin'?" he asked, as if they were the best of friends.

Julie vaguely remembered him from the day of her

accident. Roy Fletcher had spoken to him briefly when he'd dropped off her bike at the office complex.

Julie smiled at the first guard. "You remember me, don't you, Jason?" she said. "I came here with my dad about a week ago. How's it going?"

"Okay, I guess," he said, eyeing her skeptically.

For once Julie was grateful for the family resemblance.

"Yeah, I remember you now," he said after a moment. "Do you have an appointment with your father?"

Julie smiled—and lied through her teeth. She had an appointment, all right, an appointment with justice. "I do. I apologize if I was rude earlier."

"No problem." Eager to please his boss, the guard returned to his desk and reached for his phone. "I'll let him know you're coming."

"Thanks," Julie said, and swallowed a plea not to call him, after all. She stopped briefly at the company directory to find the location of Fletcher's office. Just as she'd suspected—top floor. Rushing, she pressed the elevator button and glanced at her watch, trying to gauge how much time she had before she was found out. Once her father knew she was in the building, he'd wonder where she was—and what she was doing.

At the top floor she stepped out of the elevator and faced a large desk. An efficient-looking middle-aged woman glanced up, her expression surprised.

"May I help you?" she asked politely.

"I'm here to see Mr. Fletcher."

"Do you have an appointment?"

This paragon who guarded the lion's den knew exactly when Fletcher's appointments were scheduled, and Julie wasn't on any list.

"Oh, yes," she muttered, and without wasting another second, Julie bolted for the huge floor-to-ceiling double doors. Without bothering to knock, she turned the knob and barreled inside.

Fletcher was on the phone. Startled, he looked up. His gaze met hers and he didn't so much as blink. She gave him credit for that. Tall as she was, *angry* as she was, Julie knew she made an intimidating sight.

"I'll need to call you back," Fletcher said smoothly. "My office has been invaded and I have a feeling this is going to take longer than you'll want to wait."

"Mr. Fletcher, I'm sorry, she just…came in." Ms. Johnson entered the office seconds after Julie. The older woman was clearly flustered; presumably nothing like this had ever happened before. "I've contacted security—they're on their way up."

"Good plan." Fletcher rose from his seat, leaning forward on his desk, his eyes never leaving Julie.

"Should I stay with you?" his assistant asked nervously.

"I'll be fine, Ms. Johnson."

"I wouldn't count on that," Julie muttered.

Fletcher waved his assistant out of the room and returned his attention to Julie. "You had something you wanted to say?"

"Your settlement offer arrived!" she said. "Why would you do such a thing?"

"Why?" He cocked one brow as if to suggest it should be obvious.

"I told you I wasn't going to sue!"

He snickered.

"Are you so cynical that you don't trust *anyone?* So cynical you think you can buy your way out of everything?"

"Money is the universal language."

Julie folded her arms. "Listen to me, Fletcher, and listen hard. I don't want your money." She spoke slowly and emphatically so that even a man as emotionally obtuse as this one would get the point.

He angled his head sideways and stared at the ceiling. "Where have I heard that before?" Then, as though he was bored and ready to end the conversation, he said, "You want the money. Everyone wants the money. Just sign the agreement and cash the check. You can be outraged all over again—and twenty-five thousand dollars richer."

Julie's mouth sagged open. "You don't get it, do you? I'm not cashing the check. I'm not signing the settlement."

"Of course you're not signing the settlement," he snapped, his eyes so cold that for an instant she actually shivered.

She caught her breath and stepped back. "It isn't just me you distrust," she whispered. He wasn't capable of trusting a single, solitary person. Some elemental betrayal had waylaid him in the past, and he'd never recovered, never moved beyond it. She didn't know what had happened; in fact, she didn't want to know. But right now they were at an impasse unless she could think of some way to settle this, some way that suited them both.

"All right," Julie said. "Tell you what I'll do."

"Ah, the bargaining begins. Are you sure you don't want your attorney here?"

"I don't have an attorney. Now listen, because I'm only going to say this once."

"The schoolteacher speaks." He'd folded his arms and she relaxed hers.

"I'll sign your stupid agreement."

He flashed her a knowing, sarcastic grin. "I thought you'd come to your senses sooner or later."

"With one stipulation."

His smile vanished.

"I want a signed statement from you in which you concede that you caused the accident and—" she wagged her finger at his Cross pen "—I'd like a written apology."

His eyes narrowed and, if possible, grew even colder.

Hands pressed on the top of his desk, he leaned forward again. "I didn't cause the accident and there's no way I'll apologize for something I didn't do."

She'd figured that would make him mad. Good. Maybe he'd understand how *she* felt. "Explain the damage to my bike, then," she said, forcing her voice to remain calm.

His lips thinned. "I can't."

"What does it matter? You get what you want and I get what I want."

"What *exactly* do you want?" he demanded.

"I already told you. And I already stated that I was only saying it once."

"Good luck, sister, because you're not getting any apology from me."

"Okay," she said cheerfully, and then because she enjoyed riling him, she added, "Shall I have my attorney call yours?"

"I thought you didn't have an attorney," he challenged as if he'd welcome the opportunity to call her a bold-faced liar.

"I don't, at least not yet, but I imagine I won't have any problem finding one who'd be willing to take you to court."

"Julie..." Her father rushed into the room and stopped midway between Julie and Fletcher's desk. He spread his arms between the two of them, trying to assess the situation.

He looked at his boss first. "Mr. Fletcher, I apologize that my daughter burst into your office."

"Dad, you'd better hear me out before you apologize to that man." She gestured wildly at Fletcher. "He tried to buy me off with a settlement offer!"

"I know, honey."

"You know?"

Her father nodded. "Mr. Fletcher told me it was in the works, but it's none of my affair, so I didn't say anything."

"You involved my father in this?" Julie hissed at Fletcher.

"Sweetheart," her father said in the gentlest of tones, "perhaps it would be best if you left now."

"Not yet." Julie was going to stand her ground. As far as she was concerned, this conversation was a long way from over.

Her father glanced apologetically at his employer. "I'm afraid Julie's got a temper, sir."

"Dad!"

"She takes after her mother in that."

Julie was horrified to hear her father saying such a thing to a man who'd insulted her.

"I'm sorry, Jules," her father continued, "but you don't leave me any other choice." That said, he attempted to hoist her fireman-style over his shoulder and forcibly remove her from the office. Julie didn't try to fight him, but she was too heavy for him to carry. He did manage to lift her several inches off the ground.

"Dad! Put me down!"

Either she weighed more than he'd assumed or he was willing to listen, because he set her down on the carpet.

"Thank you," she whispered.

"Julie, get out of this office," he said in a low, irate voice. "*Now.*"

She could only imagine how amused Fletcher must be. "Not until this is settled," she said, glaring at her father's employer.

Suddenly her father walked behind her and wrapped his arms around her waist. The shock of it caught her unawares and she toppled back against him. Satisfied, he started to drag her out of the room, the heels of her shoes making tracks in the plush carpeting.

"Let me go!" she cried. When she looked up, she saw Roy Fletcher grinning widely. "Don't you *dare* laugh," she warned, stretching out her arm and pointing at him.

"Bye-bye, Ms. Wilcoff." He waved and had the audacity to laugh outright.

"We aren't finished!" she shouted. "Daddy, for the love of heaven, let go of me."

"Not until we're in the elevator," her father said. He dragged her through the large double doors.

Fletcher walked around his desk. Julie wanted it understood that he hadn't heard the last of her. "Furthermore, you owe me an apology!"

Fletcher's assistant stood at her own desk, eyes twinkling. "Nice to have met you, Ms. Wilcoff."

"You, too," Julie said, smiling weakly.

The elevator arrived. "This is your last chance, Fletcher!" she yelled.

"No, Julie," her father said as he entered the elevator car. The doors slid closed. "This is *your* last chance. I don't want you ever pulling anything like this again. Is that clear?"

She nodded. It was ridiculous to be chastised by her father at the age of thirty, but at the moment she felt more like twelve.

It seemed to take two lifetimes for the elevator to descend to the lobby. The silence was so tense it almost crackled—like static electricity. One glance at her father, who was the calmest man she'd ever known, told her he was furious.

"You will apologize," he said just before the doors slid open.

She'd need to think about that.

"Your car's going to be towed," he announced without inflection. "You took a handicapped parking space and you know better."

She resisted stamping her foot. Yes, she did know better.

"You can either wait for me to get off work to drive you home or you can take the bus. There's one every half hour."

Staying on Fletcher Industries property one second

longer was intolerable. "I'd rather walk," she muttered. It would help her work off some of her anger.

"I thought you might decide that."

"He's an unreasonable man, Dad."

Her father didn't answer. "Jason," he said to the guard who'd first questioned her. "Until you hear otherwise, my daughter is banned from the building."

Jason nodded grimly, as if to suggest she'd better not enter this lobby again, not on his watch. "Yes, sir!"

Great. If her father had anything to say about it, the next time she set foot on Fletcher property she'd likely be shot on sight.

Nine

Roy sat back down at his desk and for the first time in months—years—he burst out laughing. He laughed without restraint. Then he returned to work, stared at his computer screen and started to laugh all over again.

The phone rang and Ms. Johnson interrupted his laughfest. "Your mother's on line one."

His mother? Not until Roy picked up the receiver did he recall that he'd just seen her the week before. He generally heard from her once a month; any more often was unusual. She'd said something about wanting him to see one of her paintings, but he'd told her he'd do that on Christmas Day.

"Hello, Mom."

The line was silent.

"Mom?"

"Roy, is that you? You don't sound like yourself."

"It's me," he said. "What's up?"

"Are you…" She paused, apparently searching for the right word. "You're not laughing, are you?"

"Laughing?" he repeated, trying to sober his voice. "I was earlier."

"A joke?" she asked.

"Actually, it was a woman. Her father's employed here and she stormed into my office filled with righteous indignation about some nonsense or other. I have to tell you, I don't think I've ever seen anything funnier." Humor overtook him again and he burst into waves of laughter as he described Julie's outrage. Soon his mother was laughing, too. She seemed to find the scene as hilarious as he did.

"What can I do for you?" Roy asked as he wiped his eyes.

"I wanted to make arrangements to come and paint," she said.

"I thought you wanted me to come to your house—to look at one of your paintings."

She had him completely confused now. Did his mother believe he was going to let her do custodial work? "What do you want to paint?"

"The lobby windows," she said as if it should be perfectly obvious. "Remember? We talked about this a couple of weeks ago. I'm going to paint a holiday scene on the lobby windows."

In Roy's opinion, Christmas wasn't all that different from any other day of the year. He'd do his duty and spend it with his mother; they'd exchange gifts against a background of decorations that brought back painful memories for him— painful because they were good. The truth was, he no longer cared much for Christmas. The holidays didn't even resemble what he'd once known, those warm, happy times, joking with his parents, feeling their love for him and for each other. That had been a façade, he now realized. His father had become cynical and jaded as the years passed. Roy hadn't seen that until it was too late. Far too late.

"Oh, yes. Now that you've reminded me, I do remember. You can paint whatever you want, Mother," he told her. "I've already let the security people know."

"I have a wonderful idea."

She started to detail her plans—something about angels—but he cut her off. "Mother, this isn't the Sistine Chapel. Don't worry about it."

"I know, but…well, I was thinking I'd paint a religious scene with angels similar to the one in this painting I was telling you about. You wouldn't mind that, would you?"

There was no point in arguing with her even if he did object. "All right, paint your angels. I'll have the windows cleaned."

Her appreciative sigh came over the telephone line. "Thank you, Roy. I'll be there Wednesday."

"Fine."

"I'm not going to bother you," she assured him. "You won't even know I'm there."

This seemed to be his day for dealing with irrational women. He could hear the determination in his mother's voice. For whatever reason, she felt it was important to paint a Christmas scene, and not just any scene, either. But if painting angels on his windows made her happy, then he guessed there was no harm in it.

"Fine, Mother, come and do as you wish."

"I promise you're going to love my Christmas angels."

Roy rolled his eyes. "I'm sure I will, Mother."

She seemed to be in a chatty mood and went on about dinner with her college friend. "I'm not keeping you from anything, am I?" she asked after talking nonstop for several minutes. "I know how busy you are."

For the first time in a very long while, Roy found he actually liked speaking to his mother—as much as he was capable of liking anything other than business. "It's fine, Mom."

For some reason, she seemed to get choked up over that and quickly ended the conversation. He replaced the receiver and stared down at his phone, hardly knowing what to make of his mother. Women. He'd never understand them.

Roy worked for another half hour and then realized he wasn't in the mood. He wasn't sure *what* he wanted to do, but he was leaving the office. Any file he needed could be accessed from the computer at his condo—a sprawling five-thousand-square-foot penthouse suite overlooking Lake Washington.

As Roy left the elevator and walked into the lobby, he saw a truck towing a vehicle away from the handicapped parking slot.

Jason, the security guard, wore a satisfied grin. "Ms. Wilcoff's car," he said, answering Roy's unspoken question. "In her rush to get in to see you, she parked illegally. Her father wasn't willing to make allowances."

He was enjoying this more all the time. "Where is she?"

"Her father said she could either take the bus or wait until he was available to give her a ride. She decided to walk."

That was exactly what Roy would have expected. "Any idea how much of a hike that is?" he asked.

Jason nodded. Grinning, he glanced down at the polished marble floor. "I think it's about ten miles."

A smile tempted Roy. "I see."

"You can rest assured she won't make it past me a second time, Mr. Fletcher. Her father's banned her from the building, too, so you don't have anything to worry about."

"I appreciate that," Roy said, pushing through the glass doors, but as he walked out of the building, he realized that wasn't true. Despite everything, he'd enjoyed his encounter with Julie, reveled in it. He felt alive in ways he'd forgotten.

Roy turned back. "Do you know which direction she was headed?" he asked the guard.

Jason looked surprised. "North, I'd guess."

"Thanks." Roy was going south himself, but a small detour wouldn't be amiss. He didn't think she'd accept a ride, but he'd ask. Perhaps a brisk walk would help her vent her anger and make her a little more amenable to reaching some kind of agreement.

Roy drove a black Lincoln Continental with tinted glass. He could see out but no one could see in, which was precisely the way he wanted it. He exited onto the main street heading north and stayed in the right-hand lane. He drove a couple of miles, mildly impressed by how far she'd gotten. She'd made good time. Perhaps she'd grown tired and taken a bus. Or perhaps she'd hailed a taxi.

Then he saw her, walking at a quick pace, arms swinging at her sides. Roy reduced his speed to a crawl as he approached her. Traffic wove around him, some cars honking with irritation, but he ignored them and pulled up alongside Julie. With the touch of a button, the passenger-side window glided down.

She glanced in his direction and her eyes widened when she recognized him.

"Get in," he said.

"Why should I?"

Time to play nice, he figured. "Please."

She hesitated, then walked to the curb and leaned down to talk to him. "Give me one reason I should do anything you say."

"I'll drive you home."

That didn't appear to influence her. "I'm halfway there already."

Horns blared behind him. "If you don't hurry up and decide, I'll get a traffic ticket."

"Good. It's what you deserve."

"Julie, come on, be reasonable. I said please."

She looked away and then capitulated. "Oh, all right."

She certainly wasn't gracious about it, but he felt thankful that she opened the passenger door without further ado and slid into the car. As he hit the gas, she fastened her seat belt.

"Give me your address," he said.

Obediently she rattled off the street and house number.

Now that she was in the car, Roy couldn't think of the right conversational gambit. He had no intention of meeting her demands and she apparently wasn't interested in complying with his. Silly woman. With the stroke of a pen, she could be twenty-five thousand dollars richer, but she was too stubborn to do it. Perhaps she was looking for more.

"You don't have anything to say?" she asked him after a moment.

"Nope. What about you?"

"Not a thing," she returned testily.

He eased off the main thoroughfare and onto a quiet side street. It was a middle-class neighborhood of older homes, mostly small ramblers with a few brick houses interspersed among them, just enough to keep the neighborhood from being termed a development.

"Are you ready to listen to reason yet?" he asked as if he possessed limitless patience and was more than willing to wait her out.

"Are you ready to accept responsibility and write me an apology?"

"Not on your life."

"I'm not signing that settlement offer, either," she said, tossing him a saccharine smile. She exhaled sharply. "You can rest easy about one thing, however."

He looked away from the road to glance at her.

"I can't afford an attorney."

Far be it from Roy to point out that in liability cases lawyers were more than happy to accept a chunk of the settlement. Generally it was a big chunk. "Sorry to hear that."

"Yeah, I'll bet you are." She closed her eyes and leaned back.

Roy didn't completely understand why, but he found himself not wanting to drop her off at her house; he wanted to continue driving so they could talk. "We should discuss it further. Perhaps we could reach a compromise."

"Like what? I take twelve thousand five hundred dollars and you just apologize and don't accept responsibility?"

"Something like that. Why don't we have coffee and talk it over?"

Julie's head snapped up. "You're joking, right? Did I hear you invite me to coffee?"

"A gesture of peace and goodwill," he said in a conciliatory tone. "I hear this is the season for it."

"Oh, puh-leeze." She crossed her arms. "Thanks but no thanks."

Roy shrugged off her rejection, although he had to admit he was disappointed. "I was only trying to be helpful."

"Were you?" Her eyes narrowed with suspicion.

"It's no big deal."

"You're sincere?"

"Yes," he said simply. He felt her scrutiny as he drove.

"Fine," she agreed, "but I'd like to suggest we have coffee at my house."

Roy pulled to a stop in front of the address she'd given him. It was a small, well-kept house, probably two bedrooms. Green shutters bordered the windows and a rocking chair sat on the front porch. Christmas lights were strung along the roofline.

"You have coffee on?" he asked.

"No, but I'll make a pot."

"Why not a restaurant? Neutral territory."

"Because," she said, and sighed heavily. "I'd feel more comfortable on home turf."

He considered that. "Should I worry about being poisoned?"

"Hmm." A smile teased the edges of her mouth. "That's an interesting possibility."

"Perhaps we can use this as a lesson in compromise," he said.

"Compromise? How do you mean?"

"If I come onto your turf, we'll order dinner and I'll buy—"

Julie didn't allow him to finish. "Dinner? I thought we were having coffee."

"I'm hungry," he said. "And we'll eat in the security and comfort of your home."

For a moment he was sure she was going to reject the idea; then she turned to him with a tentative smile. "All right. We'll order pizza and I like anchovies."

"Pizza it is. I like anchovies, too." He'd never met a woman who did; once again she'd surprised him.

From the expression on her face, he wasn't convinced she believed him.

"I'm just a regular guy, Julie."

Muttering, "That's what Benedict Arnold used to say," she climbed out of the car and closed the door.

Roy joined her on the concrete walkway that led to the front steps. "I'm really not so bad, you know."

"That remains to be seen, doesn't it?"

He chuckled. "I guess it does. Friends?" He held out his hand.

She looked at his extended hand, sighed and gave him her own. "Don't think this means I'm going to change my mind about the settlement check."

"We'll see about that," he said as she inserted the key into the lock.

"Yes, we will," she responded with equal determination.

Roy grinned. This might not be so bad. A girl who liked anchovies on her pizza was obviously reasonable *some* of the time.

Ten

Exhausted, Mercy flung herself onto a passing cloud. "This romance business is hard work," she complained.

"But Julie's having dinner with him." For her part, Goodness felt encouraged. She had to give Dean Wilcoff's daughter credit; Julie had spunk, which was something Goodness admired.

The young woman hadn't been willing to accept Roy's settlement because money wasn't important to her. That was a rare human trait. The issue of earthly wealth confused Goodness. Money couldn't buy the things that were truly important. Roy owned a fabulous condo on prime waterfront real estate. The three of them had gone to it and investigated, needing to learn what they could about him. Goodness had hardly ever visited a more beautifully decorated place, but it wasn't a home. By the same token, Roy was surrounded by all kinds of people, employees and yes-men, but he had few friends. Those he'd once considered friends had drifted away out of neglect. While Roy was looked upon as rich, he was one of the poorest humans Goodness had ever seen.

"He likes Julie," Shirley said with a rather smug smile.

"She amuses him." Goodness wasn't fooled. Roy had no

real feelings for Julie. She wasn't typical of the women he'd known and he wasn't quite sure what to make of her. The laughter had been good for him. It had *felt* good, too, and that feeling had left him with the urge to laugh more. She suspected it was the reason he'd pursued Julie during her long walk home. Their shared pizza dinner had come about unexpectedly, and yet he was enjoying himself. They both were.

"Her stubbornness intrigues him," Goodness added. "He can't understand why she isn't interested in the settlement."

"Julie has principles," Shirley announced, "and Roy hasn't seen that in a woman in quite a while. Since before Aimee."

Mercy agreed. "What should happen next?"

The other angels looked at Goodness as if she was the one with the answers. "How should I know?" She shrugged, as much at a loss as her friends. This relationship was a fly-by-the-seat-of-your-pants affair. "I'm making this up as we go along."

"Yes, but you've done such good work so far."

"Me?" Goodness cried. "This is a team effort." She peered down through the cloud cover and stared into the house below. "They're eating their pizza now."

"And talking," Mercy noted with delight.

"No one seems to be yelling, either," Shirley said. "That's a good sign, don't you think?"

Goodness nodded. "He should ask her out next," she told the others, suddenly inspired. That seemed to be the most logical step. *Not* that she was convinced this relationship had much of a future.

"Out?" Mercy repeated. "You mean like on a date?"

"Yes, a date. He implied that he was interested in getting her on neutral turf, remember?" That was the way humans generally did those things, Goodness reasoned, because then no one had an unfair advantage. She gave a rueful grin. Humans tended to be so competitive....

"Roy doesn't date," Mercy pointed out. "Not in years. He's forgotten how. Besides, he's got this thing about women." From the exasperated look she wore, one might think Goodness had suggested Roy propose marriage as his next move.

"Then he has to believe it *isn't* a date." Goodness's head was spinning. Surely there was some social event he was obliged to attend. December was the month for that sort of function.

"Think," Mercy demanded.

Suddenly the air brightened and with a sound like thunder the Archangel Gabriel joined them. He held a massive volume in his hands. *The Book of Lives.* "How's it going, ladies?" he inquired.

The three of them rushed to give him brief updates. "Great," Goodness said cheerfully.

"Yes—very good," Mercy seconded.

"We think Julie Wilcoff is the answer to Anne's prayer," Shirley told him. "They're together now."

Gabriel seemed impressed. "And you three arranged that?"

Goodness swallowed hard. If she admitted their role in the bike accident, it could mean trouble. Much better if Gabriel didn't know about their little scheme. "Not entirely," she said— which was the truth. Still, it sounded becomingly modest.

"How's Anne?" Gabriel surprised her by asking.

Shirley, Goodness and Mercy froze. If he found out that Shirley had appeared to Anne, they could forget ever coming to Earth again. "Fine," Goodness said, and to her horror her voice squeaked. "She's painting Roy's office windows on Wednesday."

"An angel scene, if I remember correctly," Gabriel said, studying them carefully.

"What a nice idea." Mercy looked frantically to her friends for help.

"I can't imagine where she came up with *that* idea." Gabriel's eyes seemed to bore straight through them.

The three of them huddled close together. "It's that time of year, isn't it?" Goodness asked. "I mean, humans seem to associate Christmas with angels."

Mercy spread her wings and stepped forward. "Glory to God in the Highest," she said.

"Glory to God," Shirley echoed.

"Exactly," Goodness said. "We were there to announce the good news to the shepherds that night. Well, not us, exactly, but angels like us."

"I know all about that night, Goodness."

"Of course you do," she said.

"Now, back to the matter of Anne's prayer request."

"Yes, Your Archangelness," Mercy said.

Her friend didn't play the role of innocent well, Goodness thought. She resisted the urge to elbow Mercy, since she couldn't do it without being obvious.

"What are your plans?" Gabriel asked, scrutinizing them.

"Funny you should ask," Goodness said. "We were just discussing that. I don't think Roy's going to come right out and ask Julie for a date. He wouldn't be comfortable with such a direct approach."

"He enjoys watching the parade of boats," Gabriel said, flipping through the pages of the book. He looked up again. "Were you aware of that?"

It was all Goodness could do not to sidle over and take a peek.

Gabriel's attention returned to the page. "The last couple of Decembers, he's stood on his balcony alone and watched the decorated watercraft float by."

"And he's wished there was someone with him to share the experience," Shirley said. Goodness figured she was just guessing, but she'd probably guessed right.

Gabriel confirmed it. "That wish has been fleeting, but it *is* one he's entertained."

"Julie's so athletic, I'll bet she's a great sailor. She loves the water," Mercy ventured.

"So does Roy," Gabriel said. "Or he did at one time. Unfortunately, he hasn't sailed in years."

"Aimee used to sail with him, didn't she?" Goodness asked, although she was fairly sure she knew the answer.

"Roy sold his sailboat after they split up. He hasn't been out on Puget Sound since."

"How sad for him." Shirley sighed as she said it.

"Perhaps we could—"

"Carry on," Gabriel said. He seemed to be in a hurry now. "You're doing a fine job so far."

"We are?" Goodness couldn't keep herself from saying. "I mean, yes, I know. We're working very hard on this request."

"Good." Then as quickly as he'd come, the Archangel vanished.

Goodness relaxed. Gabriel had yet to recall them from an assignment, but there was always a chance he would, especially with Shirley disobeying the angels' number one rule: no revelations to humans.

Perhaps they were safe, for now anyway. She certainly hoped so.

Roy slept better on Monday night than he had in months. He always fell asleep easily enough but then he'd wake up two or three hours later. Often he roamed around his condo for much of the night, unable to get back to sleep. During the past few years, he'd tried any number of remedies, all of them useless.

As the alarm sounded, he rolled over and stared at the clock, astonished that he'd slept the entire night uninterrupted. That never happened, at least not anymore.

Roy felt rested and refreshed as he got into the shower. He stopped short when he realized he was humming a

Christmas carol. Christmas music? Him? Something was going on, and he wasn't sure what. Thrusting his face under the spray, he let the water hit him full force. It occurred to him that his good night's sleep was because of the evening spent with Julie. He liked her. Julie Wilcoff was different from any woman he'd ever known. His money didn't impress her, that was for sure. And she didn't seem to care about his position in the business world. If any other woman had behaved this way, he would've assumed she was pretending, but Julie was genuine. Even a cynic like him could recognize that much.

Roy had often been the target of women looking for a free ride. He saw himself as reasonably wealthy and reasonably attractive; he knew he could date just about anyone he wanted. However, the idea of dating any woman after Aimee had become repugnant to him. Until Julie. He wasn't convinced he liked this, wasn't convinced he was making the right move or that he was interested in making any move at all.

When Roy arrived at the office, it seemed his whole staff was watching him. He felt their eyes on him as he strode through the lobby and toward the elevator. People turned and stared, and he heard a few hushed and badly disguised whispers. He resisted the urge to stop and ask, "What?"

Once inside his office, he followed his normal routine. Ms. Johnson phoned to remind him of a meeting. The Griffin Plastics file was still on his desk and he picked it up reluctantly. He decided he needed more information before making a final decision.

"Could you ask Dean Wilcoff to be available after my meeting?" Roy asked. "I'd like to talk to him."

"I'll see to it right away."

"Thank you."

She hesitated as if she'd never heard him express his appreciation before. "Will that be all, Mr. Fletcher?"

"Yes." He hung up the phone and leaned back in his soft leather chair, folding his hands. Something was in the air, something he couldn't explain. He didn't know *what* was different, but there was definitely a change, and it wasn't just him.

The meeting, concerning the launch of a new line of security software for home computers, ran smoothly. Roy hurried back to his office when it ended, and Dean Wilcoff came a few minutes later. "You asked to see me?" the man said as Ms. Johnson showed him in. He certainly didn't waste any time, Roy observed. He got right to the point.

"I did. Sit down." Roy gestured to the chair across from his desk. He wanted to talk to Wilcoff, but the matter wasn't business-related. Julie had been on his mind from the moment he'd left her last night, and he realized he knew very little about her. They'd talked, but she wasn't one to dwell on herself, unlike a lot of women he'd known. Most wanted to impress him. Julie had surprised him in that way, too.

Dean sat close to the edge of the chair, apparently ill at ease.

"Did Julie mention we had dinner together last night?" Dean had called Julie to say he'd be home late, and Roy had left before Dean's return.

"She did," Roy's head of security answered stiffly.

"How old is Julie?" Roy had never thought to inquire, not that it was important.

Dean stiffened. "You should ask my daughter that, sir."

Ever respectful, Roy noted, and unwilling to mingle his personal life with his professional one. He tried another tactic. "While we were having pizza, Julie told me she's a twin."

Dean nodded but volunteered no additional information.

"I gave her a ride home from the office last night," Roy said, testing the waters, wading in a little deeper this time.

"So she said."

"I tried to get her to accept my settlement offer."

Dean didn't respond.

"She refused."

"My daughter's over twenty-one and makes her own decisions," Dean informed him.

"As she should," Roy murmured.

Dean met his eyes. "I've asked her to apologize for her behavior yesterday."

This should be interesting. "And she agreed?" Frankly, Roy would be surprised if she did. He'd tried to talk sense into her over pizza and she'd been as stubborn as ever. Judging by her dogged refusal, Roy didn't expect her to change her mind about his offer anytime soon.

"Julie said she'd give the matter of an apology some thought."

Roy smiled. So she hadn't ruled it out altogether. He admired her for that.

"Is there anything else?" Wilcoff asked, transparently eager to leave.

"Yes. Did I tell you my mother will be here at some point on Wednesday?"

"You did." Dean stood. "You said she'd be painting the lobby windows."

Roy stood, too. "I'll check in with you later about Julie."

"What about her?"

Roy saw that he'd spoken out of turn. "About...whether she decides to apologize or not."

"That's up to my daughter."

"Yes, of course. No reflection on your job performance, Dean, which to this point has been excellent."

"Thank you."

Roy nodded, dismissing the other man.

Dean moved to the door, then turned and met Roy's gaze. "Are you romantically interested in my daughter?"

Roy's throat went dry. Romantically interested in Julie?

Instinct told him to deny it immediately, but he wasn't sure. "Would it bother you if I was?"

"Again, that's my daughter's business. And yours."

"Yes, it is," Roy said. Theirs and nobody else's.

Shirley and Goodness, hovering above the office, nudged each other. Mercy gave them a thumbs-up and a big grin.

Kudos to Dean, they all decided, for having the nerve to ask. Romantically interested? Yes!

Eleven

Anne was enjoying herself. Paintbrush in hand, she stood in the large lobby of her son's office building and spread the bright colors across the smooth glass, creating a festive greeting for all to see. She'd drawn the outlines with a felt-tip pen and was now filling in the figures, using acrylic paints.

This was the first Christmas season since the divorce that she'd felt like celebrating. It wasn't an effort; nothing felt forced, least of all her happiness. She thanked the angel for that. The one who'd appeared to her. Everything had changed for the better that day. Her heart felt lighter, less burdened, and life suddenly seemed good and right again.

After all these years, her prayer request had apparently been heard. Even now, Anne couldn't get over the glorious, wonderful sound of her son's laughter. Such a minor joy had felt forever lost to both of them. Even more wonderful, a woman—the first one her son had mentioned in five years—had caused this spark of excitement.

"How does that look, Jason?" Anne asked the security guard. The young man certainly took his duties seriously. The entire time she'd been painting, Jason had watched her.

He must've been told that no one was to bother her, and he made sure no one did.

Jason didn't answer and Anne turned around to see him studying the parking lot.

"Trouble?" Anne asked.

"Perhaps it'd be best if you left the area, ma'am."

Anne peered outside; the only person she could see was a young woman wearing what appeared to be a soccer uniform. She was walking toward the building. "Who's that?" Anne asked.

"Julie Wilcoff," Jason answered in a low voice. He moved from behind the desk and stood directly in front of the glass doors, his posture a warning in itself.

Anne watched as the woman paused outside the door and smiled at the security guard. "Jason, I'm here to talk to my father."

"I'm not falling for that a second time," he said. "Your father told me to keep you out of this building and he hasn't told me anything different, so I'm keeping you out."

The woman glanced impatiently at Anne and then back at the security guard. "Jason, please."

"If you've got a problem with that," the guard said matter-of-factly, "then I suggest you take it up with your father."

Ms. Wilcoff promptly pulled a cell phone out of her pocket, punched a few numbers and held it to her ear.

Jason stood exactly where he was.

"Is this the girl who gave my son such a talking-to the other day?" Anne asked. If so, Anne was eager to meet her.

"Yes, ma'am."

"Her father banned her from the building?"

"I believe Mr. Fletcher gave his approval, ma'am."

Anne's spirits did an abrupt dive. "I'm sure he's had a change of heart," she said, praying she was right.

"Then he'll need to tell me that himself, ma'am." The guard wasn't budging, not an inch. That much was obvious.

Julie Wilcoff seemed to have difficulty reaching her father. With an air of frustration, she clicked off the cell phone. "My father isn't answering," she called from the other side of the door.

"That isn't my concern."

"He *asked* to see me," she insisted.

For a moment it seemed Jason might waver, but he held his ground. "He didn't say anything to me about that. I don't have any alternative but to do as I've been instructed. You aren't allowed in this building. I'm sorry, Ms. Wilcoff, but I have my orders."

Julie nodded. "I understand. Will you tell my father I was by?"

"If I see him," Jason said.

Julie nodded again and turned around. She started back toward the parking lot.

Anne refused to let this woman leave.

Jason moved from his post and Anne rushed to the door. "Ms. Wilcoff?" she called. "Julie?"

Julie glanced over her shoulder.

Anne stood in the doorway and gave her a quick wave. "I'm Anne Fletcher, Roy's mother."

"Oh, hi," she said. Turning again, she halted in her progress toward the visitors' parking lot. "It's a pleasure to meet you. I guess you heard about your son's and my disagreement." The wind whipped the hair about her face, and Julie swept it away with a stroke of her hand. "I actually came to see Roy, but I needed to talk to my dad first. I can see that's impossible."

"No, it isn't." Anne raised her index finger. "Wait just a minute." She closed the door and discovered Jason frowning at her. "I can't let her in here, Mrs. Fletcher," he said, "so don't go asking me to make allowances."

"I had no intention of doing that." She planned to take another approach altogether. "The best thing would be to contact my son and get this settled once and for all."

Jason said nothing.

"Can I use the phone on your desk?" She didn't have a cell phone; it was an expense she couldn't afford.

"Go ahead." He kept his gaze pinned to the door as if he half feared Julie might try to dash in while he wasn't looking.

Anne walked over to the desk and called Ms. Johnson, her son's assistant. "Hello, Eleanor," she said. "Could I speak to my son?"

The woman hesitated. "I'm sorry, Mrs. Fletcher, he's in a meeting."

"A meeting," Anne repeated. She'd long suspected that was the excuse Roy used when he wasn't in the mood to deal with her. "Did he ask you to say that?" she whispered.

"Not this time," his assistant admitted, confirming Anne's suspicions. "He actually *is* in a meeting."

"Oh, dear," Anne said, breathing a sigh.

"Is there anything I can do?"

Anne chewed her lip. "Do you happen to know Julie Wilcoff?"

"I do." Eleanor's voice grew warm and excited.

"She's here."

"In the building?"

"No, the security guard won't let her inside. Apparently there's some edict her father gave and she's forbidden to come in. Is that true?"

"I'm afraid it must be, but we all like Ms. Wilcoff."

Unfortunately, Jason hadn't gotten that memo. "Any idea on how we can get her inside to see my son?"

After another second's hesitation, Roy's assistant said, "I'll be down directly."

"Oh, thank you." Anne looked up and saw Jason

frowning at her. Julie hadn't moved from her position outside the doors.

"What did he say?"

"I didn't speak to my son, but Ms. Johnson is on her way down."

Jason frowned even more fiercely and shook his head. "That isn't good enough. It's got to be Mr. Wilcoff or Mr. Fletcher himself. No one else. As I explained earlier, I have my orders."

Anne ignored him and went back to the glass entrance doors. She opened one and said, "I phoned Roy, but he's in a meeting. His assistant is coming down to see what she can do."

"It's all right, Mrs. Fletcher. I'll just do this another time."

Anne shoved one arm out the door. "No! Stay where you are. I'll be right back." She turned away and then immediately turned around. "Promise me you won't leave!" If she was going to make a fool of herself, she wanted to be sure it was worth her while.

Julie grinned. "I won't."

"Thank you."

Anne addressed Jason next. "When Ms. Johnson arrives, tell her I've gone to get my son." She refused to let this opportunity—or this woman—disappear from Roy's life. With a determination that astonished even her, Anne marched over to the elevators and pushed the button. When a car didn't come fast enough to suit her, she pushed it again.

A high-tech buzzing finally announced an elevator. To her relief, it was empty, and she shot to the top floor in what felt like seconds. Stepping off, she hurried into the foyer, glancing around. Ms. Johnson, as Anne knew, wasn't at her desk. Anne thought she heard voices at the end of the hallway and headed in that direction.

Sure enough, there was a meeting taking place in the conference room. Anne remembered seeing it when Roy had given her a tour shortly after moving into the building.

She hated to barge in, but there was nothing else she could do. Knocking politely at the door, Anne walked inside, her smock smeared with paint and her hair a mess. The room, which had been lively with conversation, went silent. Twenty or so men and women, all important-looking, sat around a long, rectangular table. Every one of them turned to stare at her. Anne smiled weakly and noticed that Roy was standing at the front of the room.

"Mother?"

"Could I speak to you a moment?"

He raised his eyebrows. "Now?"

Anne held her breath. "Please."

Roy gestured apologetically at his associates. "If you'll excuse me?"

They all nodded and Roy walked to the back of the room. "What is it, Mother?"

From the way his eyes flared and the even, unemotional tone of his voice, Anne could tell he wasn't pleased. He guided her, none too gently, into the hallway.

"I'm so sorry to interrupt you," she said, clasping her hands tightly.

"If this has to do with the Christmas scene on the windows, then—"

"Oh, no," she insisted, "it's not about that." Her throat felt dry and it was difficult to concentrate. "This has to do with Jason…"

"And who is Jason?"

"The security guard downstairs. He tells me Julie Wilcoff has been banned from the building. I know it was her father's doing, but Jason seems to believe you supported that decision. Did you?"

His demeanor changed, and his mouth and eyes softened. "I might have. Why?"

"She's here."

"Now?"

Anne nodded. "Jason won't let her in to speak to you."

"She came to see me, did she?" He folded his arms and seemed to consider this information with some amusement. Then the humor left his eyes. "Did she give you any indication *why* she wanted to speak to me?"

Anne shook her head. "Not really."

His mouth twitched. Was that a smile trying to emerge? "Ms. Johnson did her best to talk Jason into letting her in, but he won't budge."

"I'll call him myself," Roy promised. "Go ahead and have Ms. Johnson bring Julie up to my office. Tell her I'll be there in fifteen minutes." He glanced at his watch. "Make that twenty."

"I hope I did the right thing," Anne said.

"You did exactly the right thing," he said, and to her complete shock, he took her by the shoulders and kissed her cheek.

Anne hurried downstairs. Jason was on the phone when she got off the elevator. He muttered something that sounded like "yessir," replaced the receiver and walked over to the glass door, holding it open for Julie.

"You can come in now," he told the young woman, who stood outside.

Julie walked into the building slowly, as if she expected alarms to ring the instant she stepped over the threshold.

"Thank you," she said to Anne.

"Mr. Fletcher would like you to wait in his office," Ms. Johnson told her.

"I'll be up in a moment," Julie said. She turned to Anne and the Christmas scene she'd started painting on the windows. "You painted these angels?"

"Oh…yes." Anne had almost forgotten the reason she was in the lobby at all. She'd painted three angels this time, floating on a cloud and looking down at Bethlehem and the manger scene. The angels dominated the painting, their joy at the Savior's birth evident.

"They're absolutely lovely," Julie said.

"Thank you."

"I had plenty of time to look at them while I was waiting, and they seem almost real to me."

Anne blushed with pleasure. "How kind you are."

"Roy said you were an artist. You're obviously very talented."

"Roy mentioned me?"

"Yes, although I don't know him well." Julie shrugged. "We definitely got off on the wrong foot. I'm here to talk to him and, well, I hope we can start again."

Anne clasped Julie's hand in both of hers. "I hope you can, too. Could—could you and I talk sometime?"

Julie smiled. "I'd like that very much."

"So would I," Anne said. "I'll be in touch."

Twelve

Julie was waiting in his office when Roy returned from the meeting, which he'd adjourned rather quickly. She sat in the chair across from his desk, looking unusually demure. His mood had improved from the moment he learned she'd come here to see him. He'd been thinking of her ever since their pizza dinner, and he'd wondered if he'd see her again soon. He had his answer now and frankly, it was one he liked.

"Julie." He greeted her warmly, walking over to his desk and sitting behind it. "This is a pleasant surprise."

"I hope I'm not disturbing you." She'd apparently come to his office immediately after school, not bothering to change into street clothes first. Despite the weather, she wore shorts and a sports jersey, and a whistle dangled like a long necklace around her neck.

"Not at all. What can I do for you?"

He assumed she was there to accept his settlement; she didn't need to show up in person, but he was delighted she had. So she *was* like everyone else—willing to take easy money. Yes, he was a little disillusioned, but he still liked her. He couldn't blame Julie Wilcoff for a quality shared by practically every other person on Earth. Greed was part of human nature, and he'd long since reconciled himself to that.

"I came to talk about what happened on Monday," she said simply. "My father felt I was out of line bursting in here the way I did."

"You were angry."

"Angry," she repeated, and with a soft chuckle added, "You have no idea. I don't think I've ever been more insulted than—" She bit off the rest of her thought. "At any rate, Dad's right. I should never have reacted like that. I made a fool of myself."

Roy was quite enjoying this. "So you've come around. Somehow, I knew you would."

"Come around? To what?"

He didn't know why she insisted on denying the obvious. Certainly, the settlement was foremost in her mind; it had to be. "I'm talking about the money."

Julie frowned and shook her head. "This has nothing to do with money. It has to do with an apology."

"You're *not* here because of the settlement?" He wasn't fooled, but decided to play along for the time being.

"I came to apologize for storming into your office and for the things I said. I'm not here about that stupid, insulting settlement offer, which I have repeatedly rejected. I'd think that by now you'd get the message." With a visible effort, she managed to keep her anger in check.

Roy's own anger was rising. "Everyone's interested in money, Julie, so don't even bother pretending otherwise. Let's both be honest, shall we? You aren't going to get a better offer, so just sign the papers my attorney mailed you and be done with it."

"I believe I already told you what I think of *that,*" she muttered. She slid closer to the edge of the upholstered chair. Soon she was barely perched on the cushion at all. He thought she might be in danger of slipping onto the floor.

"You're holding out for more money, aren't you?"

She bolted to her feet as if someone had pinched her. "You're impossible, you know that? I came here in good faith—"

"Good faith?" Roy didn't see it that way. Not when she said one thing and wanted another. But ultimately, human nature at its most basic couldn't be defeated.

"I thought we'd made some progress, you and I, and... well, I can see you're hopeless."

"Me?" he shouted. "*You're* the one who's got her eye on the almighty dollar."

"I don't want any of your stupid money! Why can't you get that through your head?"

"Because you're just like every other woman."

Her eyes seemed to grow wider. "Now you're insulting not only me but every woman alive."

"Yes, well, if the shoe fits."

Hands on her hips, Julie glared at him. "Then I guess you know what you can do with your shoe."

He glared right back. Standing, he reached for his phone and punched in the number for security. "Please send somebody to escort Ms. Wilcoff from the building."

Julie's mouth sagged open in what appeared to be shock. "Thank you very much, but I can see myself out." She started for the open door, every step filled with indignation. She got halfway across the room before she swung around and said, "I really tried, you know."

"Julie, just sign the settlement." They would put an end to this, once and for all. Then they could move on, maybe explore the possibilities between them. He'd be willing to overlook this flaw; no doubt he had flaws of his own. Naiveté about the motives of others didn't happen to be one of them. "Just sign, okay?" he said wearily.

"No!"

Well, that answered that.

"Furthermore, I think you're—"

"Uh-uh," Roy said, holding up his finger. "You don't want to say something you'll regret."

The elevator doors opened before Julie had a chance to insult him. Jason, the guard from downstairs, loomed in the doorway. "You asked for security, Mr. Fletcher?"

If looks could kill, Roy would be six feet under. As best he could, he ignored Julie's death-dealing glare. "I did."

Jason gripped Julie by the elbow. "Once she's gone, is she allowed back in the building?"

Julie closed her eyes. Roy looked at her curiously—was she grinding her teeth? For whatever reason, the anger seemed to drain from her.

"Let's play that by ear," Roy told the guard. When she saw that she had no choice but to sign, then and only then would Roy be willing to see her. He insisted on at least that much honesty.

Julie lifted her shoulders in a shrug. "I've destroyed the papers your attorney mailed, and I will destroy any replacement papers."

"This is my final offer."

She grinned. "I should hope so." Still in Jason's firm grip, she turned and walked away. "Goodbye," she said over her shoulder. "And I mean that."

"I'll see that she leaves the building," Jason told Roy as he hustled her out the door.

"Thank you." Roy reclaimed his chair. Their conversation hadn't gone the way he'd wanted. He'd hoped they could find some common ground. His problem was that he genuinely liked her. Okay, so Julie was a little stubborn and clearly unreasonable. But now he was afraid he might never see her again, judging by that final goodbye. She'd probably just mail the signed attorney's contract, disgruntled that her ploy to get more hadn't succeeded. She'd settle for twenty-five thousand and she'd avoid him from this moment on.

The thought depressed him. Besides, he was in the right. It was Julie who'd been unreasonable, not him.

He returned to a number of pressing business matters, determined to put Julie out of his mind. Fifteen minutes later, he began to pace, unable to concentrate. Fifteen minutes after that, he called Ms. Johnson into his office.

"Sit down," he instructed his assistant when she entered the room. "Please."

Watching him as he walked from one end of his office to the other, Ms. Johnson slowly lowered herself into the chair opposite his desk. "Is everything all right, Mr. Fletcher?"

"What makes you ask?" he muttered irritably.

She looked embarrassed now and her gaze followed him. "I don't think I've ever seen you so…agitated."

"I'm not agitated," he barked.

She dropped her eyes. "As you say."

Roy resisted the inclination to argue with her to prove his point. He sank down in his chair, tempted to explain that he was the same as ever. But why bother? Women always stuck together.

"You wanted to see me?" Ms. Johnson asked.

Roy nodded and steepled his fingers as he leaned forward, resting his elbows on his desk. "I have a question and I'd appreciate your honesty."

"Yes, sir."

Again Roy felt her hesitation. She probably wasn't the best person to ask, but his options were limited. "Am I an unreasonable man?" He didn't know why he was questioning his own behavior, his own perceptions. Was there the slightest chance he was wrong in his beliefs about Julie?

Ms. Johnson's shoulders rose and then fell in a soundless

sigh. "You can be at times," she said, obviously uncomfortable meeting his gaze.

"I see," he said. "Can you give me an example?"

She nodded. "Just now with Julie Wilcoff."

Roy was afraid she was going to say that. "You think *I'm* the unreasonable one?" *Women stick together,* he reminded himself.

"Mr. Fletcher, perhaps it would be better if you discussed this with someone else, someone more…appropriate."

Roy frowned, unable to imagine who else he could approach. "I asked you."

His assistant edged forward. "I had a chance to talk to Ms. Wilcoff while you were finishing up the Griffin meeting, and she seemed sincere to me. I know it was difficult for her to come, but out of respect for her father, she felt it was the right thing to do."

"She had a rotten attitude," he snapped.

"If you don't mind my saying so, it appears you're the one with the attitude problem."

His irritation flared briefly and then died.

"Not once did she mention the settlement," Ms. Johnson continued. "If I were to guess, I'd say she completely forgot about it. I believe she came here for precisely the reason she said—to apologize for bursting into the office. She admitted there were better ways of handling the situation and she felt badly about it. I think she was afraid she'd embarrassed her father."

"The only person she embarrassed was herself," Roy said.

"At least she was woman enough to admit it."

Roy looked thoughtfully at his executive assistant. She'd spoken frankly in a way he'd never expected. "What are you suggesting?"

"I'm saying that perhaps it's time…" She hesitated.

"Go on," he urged. He might as well hear it all.

"Perhaps," she said, "you should talk to Julie about this."
Roy nodded, swallowing hard. Perhaps she was right.

When she was this angry, the best thing for Julie to do
was run—as if a pack of wolves was after her. The minute
she got home, she tossed aside her shorts and changed into
running gear. After a few perfunctory warm-up exercises,
she took off. As her shoes hit the pavement, her thoughts
chased each other around and around. Six miles passed, six
pounding, breathless miles, before she found some measure
of serenity. By then, her calves ached and her lungs burned.
It was pitch-dark as she ran back to her neighborhood,
cheered by the bright display of Christmas lights on the
homes along her route.

As she rounded the corner to her house, she noticed a dark
sedan parked in front. Her father was home, too; she saw his
light blue car in the garage beside hers.

Instead of waiting for her inside the house, Roy Fletcher
sat on the top porch step. She came up the walkway, bent
over and braced her hands against her knees as she caught
her breath. "What are you doing here?" she asked between
gasps. If he wanted to resume their argument, she'd walk
into the house and slam the door.

Roy stood and brushed his hands against his sides. "I
don't know. It seemed like a nice afternoon for a drive."

"Sure it did," she said sarcastically, still breathing hard.

"Would you believe I just happened to be in the neighborhood?"

She shook her head.

"All right," he said. "Ms. Johnson suggested the two of
us talk."

"Talk…" Julie straightened, not hiding her shock. The
great Mr. Roy Fletcher was here to make peace.

"This time I was the one out of line." Apologies didn't

come naturally to this man; he seemed to have trouble saying the words.

Julie stared into his eyes to see if she could judge his sincerity. As far as she could tell, he meant it. She smiled and offered him her hand. He took it, then smiled back—a smile that was warm and lazy and completely sexy.

"Furthermore, I'm willing to make up for my rudeness," he told her.

"Really? And how do you intend to do that?"

"Dinner?"

"When?"

He pulled a BlackBerry out of his pocket and looked up, meeting her eyes. "What about tonight?"

Although tempted, Julie already had dinner in the Crock-Pot and test papers to grade. "Another night would be better."

He frowned, then suggested, "Friday? That works for me."

"Sorry, I've got a game."

"What sort of game?"

"I'm the girls' soccer coach."

"Oh." He scrolled down his appointment calendar. "Saturday evening is free from seven o'clock on."

"Yes, but…" Julie paused. "Isn't that the parade of ships?" This was one of her favorite Christmas traditions. Last year, she and her father had managed to get her mother down to the waterfront. It had been a highlight of the season for so many years, and she hated to miss it. Especially now, when the event held such a significant memory for her.

Roy glanced up. "Yes, I believe Saturday night is the annual Christmas parade of ships."

"I don't suppose you'd care to see that, would you?" she asked hesitantly.

"Actually I would. I have a good view of Lake Washington if you'd like to see it from my condo."

"Dinner, too?"

Grinning, he nodded.

"Wonderful." Julie was thrilled not only with the opportunity to view the boats festooned with their Christmas lights but to know Roy better. His coming here was encouraging. Then a thought sobered her. They continued to trip over the matter of that settlement again and again. "You have to agree to one thing first."

"Fine, let's hear it."

She threw back her shoulders. "If you say a word about the settlement or mention money even once, I'm out of there."

He seemed about to argue. "If you insist," he finally said.

"I do."

"Then I guess I have to agree."

"Good." She smiled and raised both hands, palms up. "See? That wasn't so hard now, was it?"

"As a matter of fact," he said with another grin, "it was."

Julie laughed, walking past him and into the house. She opened the front door and looked over her shoulder, silently inviting him inside. "I should ask my father to escort you from the house, just so you know how it feels."

"Yes, well—"

"Never mind." Her father sat in the living room reading the evening paper. He lowered it as Julie walked in, Roy Fletcher a few steps behind.

"Dad, make Mr. Fletcher welcome while I shower, okay?"

Her father's eyes widened. "What's this?"

"We made peace," Julie explained.

Dean turned to Julie and then his employer. "Somehow, I knew you would." He set his newspaper aside. "Do you play poker, Mr. Fletcher?"

"Now and then. I might be a little rusty."

"Oh, that's not a problem." Her father rubbed his hands together and gave a stagy wink. "I'll get a deck."

Thirteen

Anne couldn't stop smiling. Everything was working out so well between her son and Julie Wilcoff. With Eleanor Johnson, Roy's assistant, feeding her information, Anne had learned that he'd gone to Julie's yesterday afternoon—even though he'd thrown her out of his office. Her son had actually sought out this delightful and strong-willed young woman.

That alone was enough to make Anne weak with joy, but then she'd found out that Roy had gone a step further and asked Julie for a date. He'd invited her to his home on Saturday! Ms. Johnson was busy contacting caterers. He was having Julie over for dinner, and then they were going to watch the Christmas parade of ships.

This was almost more than Anne had dared to hope, the best early Christmas gift she could ever receive.

Although Anne had only met Julie briefly, she'd taken an instant liking to the young woman. Julie wasn't at all what she'd expected, although that didn't matter. Julie was nearly as tall as her son and solidly built, but as Anne had learned a long time ago, it was character and not appearance that counted. Roy had fallen for a pretty face and an empty heart once, and he'd suffered the consequences. So had Anne....

"Oh, my," she murmured aloud, irritated with herself. Describing Julie as "solid" made her sound dumpy and unattractive, and nothing could be further from the truth. She just wasn't Aimee, who was petite and blond and delicate. Julie was none of those things, and that was all to the good. Besides, *solid* applied to her character, solid and direct, unlike Aimee's wispy charm.

Anne had spent a second day at the office, finishing her angels. Home now, her spirits soaring, she stood barefoot in the kitchen chopping vegetables for a huge salad when the phone rang. She automatically checked her caller ID and noticed the New York area code.

It could only be Marta.

"Hello," Anne said, pleased to hear from her friend. The possibility that the angel painting might sell for an astronomical eight thousand dollars—or more—had set her heart racing with hope and excitement.

"Anne, it's Marta. How are you?"

"Fabulous! It was so nice to see you. I've been feeling great ever since."

"I'm glad," Marta said.

"How are you?" Anne was concerned about her friend's marital situation.

"I'm doing fine."

Somehow Anne doubted that. "And Jack?"

Marta hesitated. "He's still being Jack."

Anne knew then. Marta hadn't confronted her husband, because the potential aftermath of bringing the truth into the open outweighed the pain. Anne didn't blame Marta. Not so long ago she'd faced a similar situation; she understood and sympathized.

"I'm calling about the painting," Marta said brightly. A little too brightly.

Anne held her breath. "Did my angel sell?"

"It's not for sale," Marta said flatly.

Taken aback, Anne said nothing.

"Paintings are always more attractive when the artist refuses to sell, my dear."

"Oh." To Anne's way of thinking, that was dishonest.

"It *is* your personal favorite, isn't that correct?"

"Yes, but…" Four thousand dollars was half a year's worth of mortgage payments. Anne had begun to hope, to do something she'd told herself she never would, and that was to count on selling one of her paintings. "I *would* like to sell the angel…."

"But only if the price is right."

"Well, yes…"

"That's what I told her."

"Her?"

"Mrs. Gould. She's one of the Berkshire Goulds. She's got oodles and oodles of money."

"She likes my angel?" Anne was almost afraid to hope.

"Likes her?" Marta asked, laughing. "Evelyn is determined to have her, but I wouldn't sell. I explained the situation and told her I needed to discuss it with you first."

"Has she offered eight thousand dollars?"

"No."

Anne's heart fell. If an extremely wealthy woman hadn't offered that much for a painting she supposedly wanted, then perhaps she wasn't interested, after all.

"She offered more." Marta giggled.

"Ten thousand?" Anne whispered.

"More."

"And you turned her *down?*"

"Of course I did. I had to confer with you. Besides, if we cave too easily, she might suspect you really *want* to sell it."

"Oh, Marta, I don't know if we're doing the right thing."

"Trust me, Anne. I've been in this business for years. I

know how to work this buyer. Furthermore, my commission from this sale is my Christmas gift to you."

Anne was astonished. "I can't let you do that!"

"Yes, you can and you will."

"But I want to make it on my own, Marta." This was one of the very reasons Anne had chosen to paint under the name of Mary Fleming. She didn't want her friends' charity.

"If you knew Mrs. Gould, you'd know that she's—"

"I'm talking about the commission."

The line went quiet for a moment. "Actually," Marta confessed, "I might end up moving in with you at some point, and I was hoping to pave the way in case that happened."

"You're serious?" Sometimes with Marta it was hard to tell.

"Very."

"But you haven't confronted Jack?"

Anne heard Marta's sigh. "I've tried, and every time I broach the subject, it's as if Jack knows what's coming and starts talking about something else. Once he simply got up and left the room. I'm so emotional about it. All I seem to do is cry and then I get so angry with Jack and with myself that I'm a worthless mess."

"Of course you're emotional!" Anne said. "You have every right to be."

"I trusted Jack."

Anne had trusted Burton, too. Although she was reluctant to mention it, Anne felt she'd be doing her friend a disservice if she didn't share the painful lessons she'd learned. "Keep an eye on your finances." She hated to give her more to worry about, but this was the trap Anne had fallen into, at great cost to herself.

"Jack would never—"

"I said the same thing about Burton," Anne told her. "What you need to remember is that if Jack's untrustworthy in one area, he could be untrustworthy in others."

"Like Burton?"

Anne swallowed around the lump blocking her throat. "Like Burton," she repeated.

"How much did he cheat you out of?"

Anne didn't want to think about it, didn't want to confess how blind and foolish she'd been. "A quarter of a million dollars is my best estimate."

"Oh, my," Marta breathed. "That much?"

"I'm past the anger now."

"But how can you be?" she demanded, outraged on Anne's behalf.

"What else can I do? Hate him? Do you honestly think Burton cares how I feel about him?" Anne had gone through all of this after the divorce, gone through it over and over again. "It wouldn't matter. The only person I'd be hurting is myself."

"But you must've been an emotional wreck."

"Of course I was. In the beginning I was angry, and then I was so hurt I couldn't stop crying. For a while, I wondered if it was even worth living."

"Oh, Anne."

She'd never told anyone about those dark, ugly thoughts. Anne wondered if she should be confessing how bleak everything had seemed during those first dreadful months. When she'd discovered how bad her financial situation was, she'd sunk to her lowest depths. Once she'd learned she could cope with even that, her sense of self had begun to reassert itself.

"Frankly, I would've wanted to kill him."

Anne laughed. "I considered that, but I preferred not to spend the rest of my life in jail."

Marta laughed, too, but there was little humor in it.

"You want advice?" Anne had been in the same position Marta was now. She knew that her friend probably hadn't been ready to hear her suggestions when they'd spoken the week before. She also knew how difficult it was to make decisions and think clearly during any kind of crisis.

"Please." Marta's voice was as soft as a whisper.

"If I were going through it again, the first thing I'd do is see an attorney and have our joint assets frozen."

Marta's breath came in a rush. "You told me to see one when I met you in Seattle, but now? So soon?"

"The sooner the better."

"Okay," Marta said, her voice gaining conviction. "I can do that."

"A good one, but not one you both know."

"All right." Marta hesitated. "Should I tell Jack what I've done?"

To be fair to both parties, Anne felt she should. "I would. In your own time. It doesn't have to be confrontational."

"I should keep it simple, in other words, like…like, I know what you're doing and I've seen an attorney. Period. End of story."

"Something like that."

"I'll do it." Marta sounded determined now.

Anne longed to put her arms around her friend and offer her reassurance and comfort. Marta, so experienced and sophisticated, was as emotionally vulnerable as Anne had been.

"Call me the minute you know anything," Anne said, trying to encourage her.

"About the painting?"

Anne had forgotten about her angel. "That, too, but right now I'm more concerned that you take care of yourself."

"I…I think I'll wait until after the holidays," Marta said. "To see an attorney, I mean."

"Don't," Anne warned. "Do it today, before you lose your nerve."

"You're right, you're right. I will."

"And stay in touch," Anne said.

"I will," Marta promised.

Anne hoped she would. But there was nothing more she could say or do. It was Marta's decision.

Fourteen

Things were working out nicely, Goodness thought. Despite their differences, Julie and Roy had knocked down some of the roadblocks that stood between them. Although she hadn't admitted it yet, Julie was attracted to Roy. They were having their first official date on Saturday, and the relationship was starting to take shape. Mercy was right, after all. Goodness gave her friend credit; Julie might very well be the answer to Anne's prayer request for her son.

This was the second evening the three angels had hovered over the Wilcoffs' living room while Dean and Roy played two-handed poker. Granted, Dean and not Julie had invited him tonight, since they'd both enjoyed the previous poker game. But Julie hadn't objected. And she'd even made dinner again—black-bean soup, corn bread and a salad. Chatting as he dealt, Dean picked up his two cards for Texas Hold'em and set the deck on the coffee table between them.

Roy looked over his cards and quickly placed his bet. Mercy, a serious student of cards, peered down at his hand.

"Should I help him with the deal?" she whispered.

"No," Goodness cried. It was exactly this sort of intervention that got them in trouble. "Roy can win or lose this game on his own. Besides, I think it would do him good if Dean beat him again."

"Oh, come on," Mercy pleaded. "Don't be such a spoil-sport."

Shirley sat atop the light fixture and sighed expressively. "Have you ever noticed how the game of poker is a lot like Roy's life just now?"

Goodness and Mercy stared at her. Sometimes Shirley came up with the most bizarre pronouncements.

"In what way?" Goodness was already certain she was going to regret asking.

"Notice how willing Roy is to fold," Shirley said, pointing to the six and the three, one a spade and the other a heart.

"Well, yes, but if I was dealt those cards in Texas Hold'em, I'd fold, too," Mercy told her. "He doesn't have much opportunity to make anything of it, and Dean has something better."

"Roy's done the same in life," Shirley said. "He's cast his father and Aimee aside. His inability to forgive them, as Anne has done, is a blight on his soul." She shook her head. "Forgiveness is hard, and most people tend to hold on to their hurts, to take some kind of perverse satisfaction in them. I don't understand, but it's the way of humans."

"Roy needs more time," Goodness murmured. Angry and bitter as he was, any positive relationship with his father was impossible. Every effort Burton had made toward reconciliation with his son, Roy had rejected. He wasn't anywhere close to finding forgiveness for either his father or Aimee.

"Perhaps," Shirley agreed, but reluctantly.

"He'll get a better hand next time," Mercy said, watching as Roy shuffled the deck.

"He needs what humans call luck, and we both know there's no such thing as luck, only God," Goodness reminded them both, but no one seemed to be listening. Both her fellow Prayer Ambassadors were intent on the game.

"Roy needs all the help he can get," Shirley said. "That's why we're here."

"Did you lend him a little heavenly assistance?" Goodness asked when Roy came up with a pair of kings.

First Mercy and now Shirley. The two of them were out of control. Goodness was the only one with a sense of mission, a sense of purpose. They had important work to accomplish, and her fellow Ambassadors weren't taking it seriously. They seemed more interested in this card game. Not that Goodness was averse to poker, of course, but unlike her colleagues, she did have her priorities straight. Pouting, she folded her wings, crossed her arms and tapped her foot.

Mercy looked up, surprised at this uncharacteristic display of temper. "I didn't have anything to do with him getting that pair."

"Me, neither," Shirley said with an expression of such innocence that Goodness had no choice but to believe her. "I'm just saying Roy could do with a good turn of the cards, but I wasn't responsible for that one."

"Oh, all right," Goodness muttered. She was tired of policing her friends. And at least they seemed to be realigning their priorities....

The phone rang. "Who's that?" Mercy asked.

"Quiet," Goodness said. "Julie's answering it."

Both Shirley and Mercy flew around while Goodness hovered in the kitchen doorway, listening in on the conversation. "It's Anne," she said excitedly.

"How'd she get Julie's phone number?" Shirley asked.

"I don't know."

"Probably the phone book," Mercy suggested.

"What does she want?"

"Shh," Goodness cautioned. This was wonderful! She beamed at her friends. "Anne's inviting her to lunch."

"When?"

"Saturday."

"She's having dinner with Roy on Saturday," Mercy said with a worried frown.

Goodness motioned for them to be quiet, fast losing her patience. This was hard enough without the two of them pestering her. Mercy held both hands over her mouth, while Shirley whirled about the room like a hamster on a treadmill.

"Well?" Shirley said when Goodness left the kitchen doorway.

"They're meeting on the Seattle waterfront."

"I *love* the waterfront," Mercy said.

Goodness looked at her. "Promise me you won't start throwing those salmon again."

"I'm not making any such promise."

"Need I remind you that we're on a mission?"

Shirley nodded sternly. "A very important mission."

Goodness noticed how Mercy glanced longingly at the deck of cards and the piles of chips. She found it far too easy to get distracted. Maybe her priorities weren't quite in order yet.

Julie gathered the team of junior-high girls around her. Huddling close together to ward off the December-afternoon cold, her soccer team radiated energy and enthusiasm. Each girl thrust her right arm into the center of the huddle and gave a loud cheer.

The first string raced onto the field for the opening kick, and the others returned to the bench. As Julie started down the sideline, she glanced into the stadium. A number of parents had already arrived. More would come later in the game, depending on work schedules. The girls appreciated the support and so did Julie.

She had several talented players. Most of the girls had been involved with soccer from the age of five, and they knew how to play as a team. At halftime, they were ahead three to two.

Their audience had grown, Julie saw as she sent her girls back onto the field for the second half of the game. Darkness descended earlier and earlier these days, and the field lights came on automatically. As they did, she saw a lone figure standing by the chain-link fence at the far end of the field. *It couldn't be.* Roy Fletcher? Surely she was mistaken. Why would he attend one of her games?

Julie felt the blood rush to her face and then just as quickly drain away. He'd been to the house for dinner two nights in a row, and played cards with her father both times. He'd apparently enjoyed the meals, although she'd never thought of Roy Fletcher as the kind of man who'd appreciate a bowl of black-bean soup and buttery corn bread. He'd surprised her by accepting and then eating two big bowlfuls, all the while praising her cooking skills. He'd been equally enthusiastic about Wednesday's Crock-Pot stew. Now he'd shown up at her soccer game.

The two teams were tied in the third quarter, but Abraham Lincoln managed to pull off a win with a last-second goal, ending the match with a score of four to three. Julie went into the locker room with the team, but she didn't expect Roy to be waiting for her when she finished nearly an hour later, after the girls had showered, changed and cleaned up.

Locking the room, she carried the soccer balls to the equipment area, then headed toward the faculty parking lot. As she stepped from the building and into the darkness of late afternoon, she saw Roy silhouetted against one of the lights. He'd pulled his vehicle around to where she'd parked and leaned casually against the fender as if he had nothing better to do.

"I wondered if you'd gotten lost in there." He straightened as she approached and moved toward her.

"Hi." His being here flustered Julie. Roy Fletcher was a very important man, far too important to spend valuable time watching her coach a soccer game. "I thought I saw you." That wasn't the most intelligent comment she'd ever made, but she couldn't think of anything better.

"I didn't get here until halftime."

"You didn't need to come. I certainly didn't expect you to."

"I didn't expect to come, either," he confessed. His hands were plunged deep in his overcoat pockets. "It's been years since I attended a soccer match. This afternoon, a business associate sent me a report about our overseas sales, and I suddenly started thinking about European soccer."

"They take it very seriously over there."

"Seems to me your girls do, too."

"True." She nodded slowly. "My team works hard and winning is important, but it's about far more than that."

"I disagree," he countered. "Winning is everything."

"Perhaps in your line of work."

"In every line of work. In everything. Look at soccer. Each game counts and—"

Julie held up her hand. Life and business were intense for Roy. Or maybe life *was* business in his view. "Now isn't the time to be having this conversation," she said briskly. Julie was tired and cold and in no state to reason with Roy Fletcher. If he wanted to argue, she'd prefer to be at her best, and currently she was far from it.

"You're right," he murmured as he walked her to her car.

"You came, and I'd like to thank you for that," she said.

"That's the weird part," Roy went on. "I got sidetracked there for a moment. As I said, I was looking at European sales figures, and I started thinking about soccer. Then I remembered that you were coaching a game this afternoon and I had this strange urge to come and watch."

She noticed the urge hadn't been to come and see her. "Strange urge or not, I'm honored you were here." She told herself it was ludicrous to feel disappointed that *she* hadn't been the reason.

"It was an excellent game."

"Thank you on behalf of my team." She inserted the key into her lock, anxious now to get home and under a hot shower.

"And you're an excellent coach."

Again she smiled her appreciation. She tossed her backpack on the passenger seat. She didn't want to be rude by climbing into her car and driving away, but Roy didn't seem to have anything else to say.

As it turned out, Julie was wrong about that.

"Do you enjoy clam chowder?" he asked unexpectedly.

"Yes, I do." It was one of her favorite soups.

"There's a little hole-in-the-wall café not far from here. They used to serve the most incredible clam chowder. I don't even know if the café's still open. I haven't been there in years, but I'm willing to look if you are."

Julie wanted to be sure she understood what he was asking her. "Are you inviting me to dinner?" He seemed nervous about this, but she must be misreading him. Roy Fletcher had nothing to be nervous about.

"Yes, I guess I am asking you to dinner." He brushed a hand across his face. "Like I said, I don't know if the café's still open. I ate there in college quite a lot. The food was cheap and good."

Money certainly wasn't something he needed to worry about now.

The differences between them—between his fame and wealth and her middle-class obscurity—would probably be a factor if they were to continue seeing each other. In a flash Julie understood; it was more than dinner he was asking her about. He did want to see her, get to know her, and he was asking if she felt the same way about him.

The look in his eyes was intense. "I like what I know about you, Julie."

She was bewildered and a little shaken. Roy Fletcher was interested in dating *her,* a thirty-year-old teacher with few marriage prospects. "Other than your tendency to be arrogant, I like you, too."

He grinned. "You have your faults."

"Oh, yeah?"

"The word *stubborn* comes to mind."

"I'm stubborn when I happen to be right." She wasn't letting that one pass.

He smiled. "I think that's a conversation we should reserve for another time," he said, echoing her earlier remark. "Agreed?"

She nodded. "I can go to dinner dressed like this?" She had on a nylon blue-and-white running suit—the Abraham Lincoln school colors. Her name was printed across the back with the silkscreen of a wolf, the team symbol.

"Sure," he said. "Why don't you come with me and then I'll drive you back here to pick up your car when we're finished."

"Sounds good."

Once they were in the neighborhood, it took Roy fifteen minutes to find the café. The restaurant had moved in the eight years since he'd last eaten there. They sat in a booth in a far corner, ordered clam chowder and coffee and discussed movies, politics, the stock market, the state of the economy and a thousand other things. Before she realized it, the café was closing.

As Julie undressed for bed that night, she could hardly believe they'd had so much to talk about. For three hours, they'd chatted nonstop, as if they'd known each other their entire lives. She felt genuinely comfortable with him, enjoying his warmth and wit, qualities she wouldn't have guessed he had a couple of weeks ago. After a quick e-mail to Emily, she went to bed.

If anything surprised her, it was the fact that Roy didn't kiss her when he dropped her off at the school to get her car. He wanted to—she was sure of it—and she wanted him to, but...

"Are we still on for tomorrow night?" he'd asked.

Julie was looking forward to it more than ever. "Yes. As far as I'm concerned. What about you?"

"Oh, yes."

That was when she thought he might kiss her. He didn't, but she had the distinct impression he intended to make up for it while they watched the Christmas ships.

Fifteen

Anne Fletcher strolled leisurely along the Seattle waterfront on her way to Pike Place Market. Julie Wilcoff was meeting her at the seafood stand at noon. Christmas was only two weeks away, and the city was festive with holiday decorations and full of contagious excitement. Even the leaden sky couldn't dampen Anne's spirits. Despite being alone, she felt the goodwill and joy of others as they went about their business.

Walking up the tiered stairway called Hill Climb from the waterfront area to the market, Anne paused to look back over Elliot Bay, watching as the green-and-white Washington State Ferry glided toward the pier. On a clear day she'd be able to see the snow-crested tops of the Olympic Mountains to the west and the Cascade Mountains to the east. Until the divorce, California had been Anne's only home. She'd loved living on the ocean; her daily routine had included long walks on the beach. That was a habit she'd continued when she came to Washington.

The move north had been a financial necessity, as well as a practical choice. Roy lived close by, and while she treasured her independence, she needed the security of having her only child near at hand. It was a plus that property values in the more sparsely populated San Juan Islands were low enough to allow her to purchase a small cottage. The contentment she derived from her daily walks had rejuvenated her spirits and helped her recover in those first dreadful months after the divorce.

Seattle and the Puget Sound area were beginning to feel like home. Anne had told Roy she was reasonably happy, and it was true. She'd found satisfaction in her art, and seeing her son fall in love again brought renewed hope for the future.

As Anne made her way through the tide of shoppers and tourists, she discovered Julie waiting for her. The girl was as tall as her father, whom Anne had met the afternoon she'd painted the company window. She'd be a good match for Roy, physically and mentally. She smiled as she recalled her first meeting with Julie, a memory inextricably connected with her painting on the window. That painting had created something of a stir, according to Eleanor Johnson, Roy's assistant. Fletcher Industries employees had reacted to the angels over Bethlehem the same way Marta had responded to her portrait of the angel. Ms. Johnson claimed the artwork was the talk of the building. Everyone loved it, she said. Knowing her art pleased others filled Anne with a sense of joy.

"Merry Christmas, Mrs. Fletcher."

The greeting caught Anne unawares, involved in her thoughts as she was. "Julie, hello!" Anne leaned forward to kiss Julie on the cheek. "Call me Anne, please."

"All right."

She slipped her arm through Julie's, and they strolled into the market. "I can't resist taking a peek, can you?" The aisles between the vendors' stalls were crowded with customers buying seafood, vegetables and flowers, both fresh and dried. Arts and crafts shops were located downstairs.

"I love it here," Julie told her. "My mother used to bring my sister and me to the market on special occasions when we were little. She'd purchase a fresh salmon just so we could see the young men toss them back and forth."

"You must have a wonderful mother," Anne said.

"I did. She died earlier this year." Julie paused as though it was difficult to speak of her mother. "Dad and I miss her so much."

Anne gave the girl's arm a gentle squeeze. "It's harder around Christmas, isn't it? Especially the first Christmas."

Julie nodded. "Dad and I don't have the tree up yet. We just can't seem to muster the spirit. I'm hoping we can do it this weekend."

Anne tried to think of a way to introduce her son into the conversation. "Roy isn't much for celebrating Christmas. He'll come to my place for the day, but only because he knows I want him to. If it was up to him, he'd be just as happy to go to the office and appreciate the fact that he isn't likely to be interrupted." It hurt a little to admit that, but it was the truth.

"Ebenezer Scrooge, is he?"

Anne smiled and matched her steps to Julie's. "Yes, I do believe he is."

"Oh, my!" Julie exclaimed, stopping abruptly. "Did you see that?"

"See what?" Anne looked around and didn't see anything out of the ordinary.

"A fish just flew!"

"A fish flew," Anne repeated, certain she'd misunderstood. "These young men throw them back and forth," she reminded Julie.

"Yes, I know, but one just took off on its own—no one was standing next to it." She shook her head uncertainly. "I must've missed something. Oh, there goes another one!"

Anne looked at the fresh seafood nestled on a bed of crushed ice. Sure enough, a huge coho salmon was spread across a display of large prawns. Just as she noticed it was out of place, the salmon sprang straight up in the air and started to spin tail over fins, as if someone had caught it on a line. Anne rubbed her eyes, convinced she was hallucinating.

"Did you *see* that?" Julie whispered.

"I did," Anne said. "I think we should get out of here. There's something strange going on."

"I couldn't agree with you more."

Arms linked, the two women walked quickly out of the crowded market. Anne couldn't believe other people hadn't seen this startling phenomenon. But no one else had reacted at all, let alone with awe or astonishment.

Fifteen minutes later, they were in an Italian eatery off a side street. They sat at a small table with a red-checkered tablecloth; a half-melted candle stuck in an empty wine bottle served as the centerpiece. It reminded Anne of the inexpensive restaurants, usually situated in basements, that she and Burton used to frequent when he was in law school…. She cast off the nostalgia before it could trap her.

Anne and Julie both ordered a glass of Chianti with their spinach salads.

"I'm seeing Roy again tonight," Julie said after her first sip of wine. "We…had dinner last night."

"*And* on Wednesday and Thursday." Anne had found this out quite by accident when she'd phoned the house to arrange her luncheon date with Julie. It had given Anne such hope, such encouragement. Julie had made a point of letting her know that her father had invited him on Thursday—but that didn't explain Wednesday. Or Friday.

"We talked for a long time last night."

Anne noticed that Julie's hand tightened around the stem of her wineglass. She had to restrain herself from leaping up and shouting for joy. She wondered how much of their story Julie knew, so she asked, "Did he mention Aimee?"

Julie's eyes held hers. "No. Is she the reason you suggested lunch?"

"Not really." Anne shrugged. "I hope you don't think I'm a busybody."

"Of course not."

"I'm so glad Roy's finally met someone he can love." Julie abruptly dropped her gaze and Anne realized she'd spoken out of turn. "Oh, dear, forgive me. I shouldn't have said that."

"I don't know if Roy loves me—and it's far too soon to know how I feel about him."

"I'm so sorry. Please forget I said anything. I'm just a meddling mother who's eager for grandchildren." The instant those words were out, Anne realized she'd done it again.

"Grandchildren?" Julie's eyes grew huge.

"Oh, dear," Anne gasped. "I do seem to be having trouble keeping my foot out of my mouth." She set her wineglass down, determined not to take another sip until she'd fully recovered from whatever had loosened her tongue. Every word embarrassed her more.

"I take it Roy was once in love with Aimee," Julie said as the waiter brought their salads.

"He wanted to marry her, but she chose...someone else." Anne hoped to avoid the more sordid details.

"Seeing how successful Roy is now, I imagine she's sorry." Suddenly Julie looked chagrined and lowered her fork. "Forgive me. That was a dreadful thing to say."

Immersed in her own thoughts, Anne was confused. "Dreadful? How?"

"I didn't mean to imply that the only reason Aimee or any woman would love Roy is because he's successful."

"I know you didn't mean anything disparaging," Anne assured her. "Besides, you're wrong."

Julie looked puzzled, and Anne felt obliged to explain. "Aimee doesn't appear to have any regrets."

"Then she's happy?"

"I wouldn't know. You see—" Anne took a deep breath "—she's married to my husband." Although she tried hard to keep her emotions out of it, Anne heard the hint of bitterness in her voice. "I'm sorry, Julie, I meant my ex-husband."

The linen napkin on Julie's lap slipped unnoticed to the floor. "No wonder Roy has a problem with trust," she whispered. "His fiancée, his father…"

"Now you know," Anne said softly. "Roy wouldn't appreciate my telling you, though."

"I won't say anything."

Anne appreciated that. "Actually, digging up the skeletons in our family's sad history isn't why I asked you to lunch," she said. "I want to get to know you better."

"I feel the same way. I loved the picture you painted on the window. Dad says everyone's talking about it, and Roy speaks so fondly of you and—"

"What did he say?"

"Well," Julie said, beaming Anne a bright smile, "he brags about you."

"My son brags about me?" Anne hated to sound shocked—but she was. Half the time, she felt as though she was nothing more than an obligation in her son's life. He only tolerated her concern and seldom sought out her company.

"He's very impressed with your work. He told me about several of your pieces he's displayed in the building. He promised to show them to me on my next visit."

"If you can get in," Anne teased. It'd been a source of amusement, the trouble Julie had getting past the security guard.

"Ah, yes, Jason, protector of the gate." Julie rolled her eyes.

Anne had witnessed for herself how committed the young man was to keeping the poor girl on the other side of the company doors. She stabbed at a piece of spinach, suddenly realizing what Julie had said. "Let me make sure I understood you correctly. Did you really say Roy has my artwork hanging in his office building?"

"That's what he told me."

This was news.

"Five landscapes, I think he said. You didn't know that?"

Anne shook her head. "I never told him my pseudonym."

"He must've found it out on his own," Julie said evenly.

"I…I don't know what to say. Part of me is pleased and another part is irritated."

"But why? He's proud of your talent."

"I've told him a dozen times that I refuse to let him support me. I want my paintings to sell on their own merit. The last thing I want or need, especially from my own son, is charity."

"I doubt Roy would display work he didn't genuinely like."

Julie meant she was overreacting, Anne thought. "You're right of course." To cover her embarrassment, she dug into her salad.

Julie reached for a warm sourdough roll. "I'm glad you asked me to lunch."

"As I said, I want to get to know you—and I want to thank you for being so patient with my son."

Julie lowered her head and struggled to hide a grin. "We've certainly had our ups and downs. He's surprised me more than once."

Anne found this curious. "In what way?"

"Dinner on Thursday night—to take one example. I made a pot of black-bean soup and he seemed to really enjoy it. Plain ol' black-bean soup."

"You cook?"

Julie nodded. "A little. My twin sister is the real chef in the family, but I'm learning."

"Are you close to your sister?"

"Very. She lives in Florida, but we talk almost every day via e-mail. I've told her about Roy." Julie glanced down, as if she regretted telling Anne that.

Anne tried unsuccessfully to keep her tears at bay.

"Anne, is everything all right?" Julie leaned across the table and squeezed her hand.

"Of course it is," Anne whispered, smiling through her tears. "It's just that…I'd given up hope, you see. I'd convinced myself that Roy had completely closed himself off from love, and now he's met you and the whole world looks brighter. Thank you, Julie, thank you so much."

Julie shook her head. "You don't have anything to thank me for."

"But I do," Anne countered. "Don't you see, my dear Julie? You're the answer to my prayers."

Sixteen

The caterer's staff delivered dinner and skillfully set the dining room table in his condo, adding candles and flowers to create a romantic mood. Before they left, Roy paid them handsomely and inspected their work, admiring the small touches.

He'd been looking forward to this evening with Julie all day. He'd longed to kiss her the night before and hadn't. He berated himself for the missed opportunity. He'd sensed the disappointment in her and felt it himself.

He hadn't experienced these primal emotions, these deep erotic urges, in years. They were a distant memory now. But with Julie...

The table was covered with an off-white linen cloth that had elegant gold edging. It wouldn't have been his choice, but the caterer had brought it with her. A large candle inside a glass hurricane lamp, surrounded by poinsettias and sprigs of holly, adorned the center of the table. Again, that had been part of the dinner package. When he'd explained his requirements to Ms. Johnson and the caterer's staff, he'd been assured that they'd be able to create the mood he desired. His trust had been well-placed; his home had never looked better.

Everything about the condo spoke of romance. The lights

were dimmed and lit candles were arranged in strategic spots around the room. In the background, Christmas carols played softly. The stage was set. Roy, dressed in dark slacks and a gray cashmere sweater, checked his watch. Julie was due any minute.

While he waited, he poured himself a glass of chardonnay. To his surprise, he was nervous. He couldn't imagine why—or could he? His mind flitted from the past to the present and back again. The past was painful and the present was unpredictable...and the future? Well, who knew about the future?

Initially this relationship hadn't been too promising, but it had gained momentum in the last few days. Even now he wasn't entirely convinced that Julie was for real, that the settlement offer truly didn't interest her.

Gradually Roy could feel himself being drawn toward her, almost against his will. He'd decided never to fall in love again, but Julie Wilcoff made him crave the experience of love, the sensations and the feelings and the *hope*. This sense of wanting to be part of life again frightened him; so did the eagerness that surged through him at the prospect. Love eventually brought pain and betrayal. Yet all day he'd thought of little else but this dinner with Julie and the kisses they were bound to share.

His phone rang and he reached for the receiver, already knowing it was her. "Hello."

"I'm here." Even the sound of her voice was sultry.

He hit the numbers that automatically opened the electronic gates to grant her entrance. He couldn't resist taking his private elevator to the lobby so he could escort her up to his suite.

Standing by the glass doors that opened into the beautifully decorated lobby, Roy watched as Julie walked from her car to the building. Her head was bent against the cold. She had on a long wool coat, which she'd left unbuttoned.

Beneath it, he saw the sleek black skirt and matching jacket with a silky white blouse. He was struck by her loveliness. Every time he saw her, she seemed to look more beautiful. Was that just a matter of perception or was he finally seeing what had always been there?

He held the door and stepped back to let her enter. Once she was inside, he made a leisurely appraisal and sucked in his breath. He could think of only one word. "Wow!"

"You like?" Holding open her coat, she slowly pivoted to give him a better look.

"I like a lot."

"Don't act so surprised," she muttered. "I clean up good."

"I'll say." With his hand at her elbow, he steered her toward the elevator, which took them directly to the suite, the doors opening into his living room, with the large picture windows that overlooked Lake Washington. He'd grown accustomed to the spectacular sight and it no longer astonished him as it once had. But the view captured Julie's attention the instant she stepped out of the elevator. An uninterrupted panorama of Lake Washington and the sparkling Seattle lights stretched before her like some kind of Christmas fantasy.

"Oh, Roy," she whispered, "this takes my breath away."

"It's what sold me on the place." To his chagrin, she remained rooted to the spot. Seemingly without her noticing, he took off her coat, one sleeve at a time, and hung it in the hall closet. When he returned, she still hadn't moved.

"The parade of ships is supposed to start in less than thirty minutes."

She walked close to the window and, standing next to her, Roy pointed out some of the sights. "Naturally, the view is even more spectacular in daylight," he said.

"I can hardly imagine anything more beautiful than this." She hadn't even glanced around his condo, but Roy didn't care. Although it was a showpiece, he rarely had anyone up to visit. He'd heard that people were curious about his home, but Julie was obviously more intrigued by the view.

Without asking, Roy poured her a glass of wine. Joining her once again, he handed it to her. "Shall we have a drink before we eat?"

"Thank you." She accepted the glass, then turned back to stare out the window. "I can't bear to look away. This is just so beautiful."

He'd thought he'd wait to kiss her, but realized that delaying it another moment was beyond him. Taking the wineglass from her hand, placing it on the wide windowsill, he gently turned her toward him. "What you need is a distraction."

He didn't know a woman of thirty could blush, but blush she did. For long seconds her eyes searched his, telling him she wanted his kiss.

Bringing her into his arms, he watched as her eyes drifted closed and she leaned into his embrace. Then they were kissing with the familiarity and ease of longtime lovers. Roy felt a small tremor go through her, or perhaps he was the one who trembled; he no longer knew. What he did know was how *good* it felt to hold her.

She was taller than any other woman he'd kissed, broader through the shoulders, too, but he liked that. In fact, he liked everything about Julie. He immediately wanted to kiss her again. She opened to him a little more, parting her lips, as her arms slid upward and around his neck.

A voice in his mind started shouting that kissing her was too wonderful to continue without consequences. He hadn't intended to let things go this far, this fast, but there was no stopping either of them. Not yet. A few more kisses and then he'd pull away and they could go back to enjoying their wine.

Another kiss. Then he'd stop. Then he'd pause long enough to clear his head.

But already his hands, which had been innocently stroking her back, had worked their way down her waist. He loved the feel of her, loved the gentle contours of her utterly feminine body. As their kissing went on, it was hard to keep from touching more and more of her.

It'd been a long time since anything had felt so good.

"Nice," he whispered, reluctantly easing his mouth from hers. He could barely think, barely focus on anything but the woman in his arms.

"Very nice," she whispered.

Their eyes held. Her hands remained on his shoulders and his stayed on her waist. "Are you ready for dinner?"

She gave him the softest smile. "No." Her voice was a mere wisp of sound.

"Me, neither." He kissed her again, his mouth coaxing hers. Her lips were pliant, warm, moist. He didn't know how long they went on like that, lost in each other.

"Julie, listen…" Even to his own ears his voice was hoarse. He braced his forehead against hers.

"I'm listening."

"We're getting a little hot and heavy here."

"Yes…I'd noticed." She kissed the side of his neck and shivers raced down his spine.

"You don't have to be so agreeable."

He splayed his fingers through her hair, thinking that would bring her to her senses. In his experience, women didn't want their hair disheveled. Julie hardly seemed aware of it. He should have known….

He purposely pulled away, thinking that too much of a good thing would soon bore him. But he wasn't bored. In this, as in everything else, Julie had the opposite effect on him.

"We should have dinner now." With a superhuman effort he dropped his arms and took a step back. Julie reached for her wineglass and Roy saw that her hands trembled.

He spent a few moments regaining his composure in the kitchen. Dinner, a chicken dish—he couldn't remember what the caterer had called it—was warming in the oven. The salad sat on the top shelf of the refrigerator. Roy opened the door and stood directly in the blast of cold air with his eyes closed, hoping it would shock him into reality.

"It looks like the parade's about to start," Julie called from the other room.

Roy grinned. She was at the window again. "I'll be a couple of minutes."

"Don't rush on my account."

The meal now seemed a necessary nuisance. The truth was, Roy had no appetite for anything but Julie. For days he'd been conscious of how badly he wanted to kiss her, but he hadn't known what to expect once he did.

"Can I do anything to help?" Julie asked, coming into the kitchen. She sounded far more like herself.

"Not a thing. All I have to do is bring these dishes into the dining room." He carried the salad out and set it on the table.

Julie walked over to the fireplace and once again her back was to him. "Your home is lovely."

"Would you like a tour before we eat?"

She turned around, then surprised him by shaking her head. "I'm afraid we might not make it out of the bedroom."

Roy had always found her honesty refreshing and never more than at that moment. He chuckled. "I'm feeling the same way myself."

"I...we haven't known each other long enough for that kind of commitment."

Now, *that* was a word Roy tended to avoid. Instead of commenting, he chose to ignore it. "The salad is served." He stood behind her chair and held it for her.

Once Julie was seated, he took his own place across from her; they both had a full view of the parade of Christmas ships as they sailed or motored past. Julie remarked every now and then on a certain theme or design. After a second glass of wine, she declined another.

Rejecting caution, Roy poured himself a third. He needed something to fortify him if he was going to battle temptation. And Julie tempted him, all right. It wasn't easy to admit that, since Roy was a man who enjoyed being in control. And yet all through dinner—the chicken-and-mushroom dish, new potatoes and sautéed spinach—it wasn't the food so expertly prepared or even their conversation that engaged him. No, what was foremost in Roy's mind was the desire he felt for Julie. This weakness distressed him and yet…he hadn't felt so alive in years.

"Dessert?" Julie asked.

The question startled Roy and he suddenly realized she'd carried the dinner plates into the kitchen and returned with two dessert plates. Cheesecake, if he recalled correctly.

"No." For emphasis he shook his head. "On second thought…" He caught her around the waist and pulled her onto his lap.

She set the plates on the table, her face near his. Her eyes, dark and intense, were wide and so very expressive. They told him she wanted to kiss him again. Her throat was flushed, her skin warm. If *her* feelings were this easy to decipher, he could only imagine what she could read in *his* face.

"We're supposed to be watching the ships, remember?" Her voice trembled.

"I know."

She sighed and asked, "What's happening to us?"

Roy knew, but he didn't like the answer any more than he welcomed the question. "I don't think we need to figure that out just yet."

"My head's spinning—and it doesn't have anything to do with the wine."

"Mine, too," he told her. The alcohol was only partially responsible for the dizziness he was feeling.

"I…I saw a fish fly this afternoon," she whispered. Her mouth was close to his ear.

Roy frowned, not understanding.

"It's true," she said, her voice still low. "I was at the Pike Place Market, and it seemed to leap off the crushed ice and fly of its own accord."

"That isn't possible," Roy said impatiently. Either it was a trick of the eye or sleight of hand.

"That's what I thought," Julie told him. "Then it happened again and someone else saw it, too."

"My guess is there's a reason you're telling me this."

In response, she kissed the side of his neck. "The way I feel now is the same way I felt earlier when I saw that fish fly. I didn't believe it, although I saw it with my own eyes. I felt a little ridiculous. And I wanted to deny it, pretend it hadn't happened. Then, as I said, someone else confirmed what I'd seen and I realized I hadn't imagined it, after all."

"So…" Perhaps it was the scent of her perfume that clogged his brain. But for the life of him, Roy didn't know what she was talking about or where this rather unusual story was taking him.

"I left quickly because I had to get away to think about it."

Ah, Roy was beginning to understand, and his hold on her tightened. "You want to leave?"

"I should."

"What if I asked you to stay?" Now he was the one kissing her, dropping light kisses along the side of her neck, hoping to lure her into spending the night. They were both adults who knew what they wanted, and he wasn't interested in pretending otherwise.

Her answer was a long time in coming and held a pleading quality. "Don't ask."

"All right." Difficult as it was, he relaxed his grip.

She stood up from his lap and Roy immediately missed the closeness. He got to his feet, ready to protest when she retrieved her coat from the closet.

"I don't want you to go."

She smiled, walked over to where he stood and kissed him on the mouth. "I don't want to go, either."

"Then stay." He bit his tongue before he made the mistake of saying more. This decision had to be hers.

For just a moment, Roy thought he'd succeeded, but then he watched a renewed determination settle over her. "I can't. I just saw a fish fly through the air."

He didn't know what it was about that stupid fish, but it appeared to have some significance for her.

"I can't quite believe what's happened," she said, "but I'm afraid I'm falling in love with you."

Love? Roy's heart fell. That was the last thing he wanted to hear.

Seventeen

Julie stepped back from the freshly cut Christmas tree her father had grudgingly set up in a corner of the living room. This was probably the most difficult part of the Christmas season for him.

And for her.

Her mother had particularly loved their little tree-trimming ceremony. Just a year ago, the three of them had decorated the tree together. Andy Williams's Christmas album had played in the background and the smell of popped corn had permeated the air.

"It's perfect," Julie announced.

Her father shrugged. "If you say so. I brought the decorations up from the basement." He studied the tree, and Julie had the feeling that if she hadn't made the effort this year, he'd be willing to forgo Christmas altogether.

"Did you find the Christmas CDs?" she asked.

"Nope."

Julie suspected he hadn't looked. They were no doubt packed away with the decorations.

"I think I'll see how the Huskies are doing." He picked up the remote. The University of Washington football team was her father's favorite.

"You aren't going to help decorate?" Julie hated the thought of doing it all by herself, but she didn't want to force her father to participate. Lectures from her wouldn't do any good, as Emily's e-mail had reminded her that morning.

Her father's eyes grew sad. "I'm sorry, Kitten, but I just don't have the heart for it this year."

He hardly ever called her Kitten, a name from her childhood, and she blinked away tears. After everything they'd endured, Julie couldn't complain about his unwillingness to take part in an activity that brought back memories he might not be ready to face. "That's okay," she told him, although her heart was breaking. This was hard, so much harder than she'd realized it would be.

"I can do it," Julie said more to convince herself than her father. Maybe it wouldn't be as painful if he stayed in the room. "You can be my adviser."

He acquiesced with a reluctant nod. Settling down in his usual chair, he flipped through several channels, then found the Huskies game.

Humming "Deck the Halls" to herself, Julie located the string of lights and began to weave it around the base of the evergreen, working her way upward. This task had always been reserved for her father. Afterward, Julie and Emily—before her twin sister's marriage—along with their mother, took over the task of hanging the decorations. It had been an important tradition, representing a time of family fun, laughter and music. Now it seemed bleak and sad....

"Did you check those lights before you started putting them on the tree?" her father asked during the first commercial break.

"Uh…"

"I can see that you didn't." He clambered out of his chair. "Oh, all right, I'll do the lights, but that's it."

"Thanks, Dad!"

"I should've known," he muttered. "All you wanted me to do was put up the tree, you said. Well, I did that. Next thing you know, I'm stringing the lights. Are you plotting against me?"

"Would I do that?" she asked in a singsong voice that didn't conceal her amusement.

Since there wasn't much she could do while he strung the lights, Julie went into the kitchen and put a package of popcorn in the microwave. It was cheating, she supposed; her mother had done it the old-fashioned way. Still, popcorn was popcorn.

"If you're going to be popping corn, I want the buttered kind."

"Yes, Dad."

He was almost finished with the lights by the time she returned to the living room, carrying a large bowl filled to overflowing with popcorn. She set it in the center of the coffee table and got down on all fours to sort through the boxes he'd brought up from the basement. Pulling out the small stack of CDs held together by a rubber band, she placed it conspicuously beside the bowl.

"Oh, go ahead, then. Put one on."

She smiled and did exactly that, choosing a selection of instrumental Christmas classics.

Her father plugged in the lights. "I'll probably be hanging the ornaments, too," he grumbled. He paused long enough to grab a handful of popcorn. "Did I ever tell you about Christmas the first year your mother and I were married? We were too poor to afford a tree. A friend gave your mother a poinsettia, and we put our gifts under that." He smiled at the memory. "It was the most pitiful-looking thing, but you'd have thought it was as grand as a fifteen-foot tree."

Of all the gifts Julie had received through the years, perhaps the best was the fact that her parents had loved each other deeply.

"What I remember was all of us attending Christmas Eve services and then coming home and opening one gift each." Julie and Emily were eight years old before they realized that the one gift they were allowed to open always turned out to be pajamas.

"I'm going to miss Mom's turkey stuffing," Julie said, sitting back on her heels. For both Thanksgiving and Christmas, her mother had prepared the traditional turkey. Every year she fretted over her stuffing and every year she outdid herself.

"Yours wasn't bad," her father assured her.

Like her mother, Julie had worried excessively over her first attempt at cooking the Thanksgiving turkey. "Thanks, Dad. I guess I must've picked up something all those years I spent helping Mom." It felt good to be able to talk freely about her mother. Her father seemed to revel in it, too, although she knew he'd felt wary about reliving the past. Sharing memories made missing her less painful, and Julie knew that these memories would get them through the Christmas season. There would be poignant, tearful moments, but happy ones, too.

"Are you cooking a turkey for Christmas?" her father asked.

Julie hadn't given the matter much thought. Christmas was still two weeks away, and it seemed a bit early to be thinking about what she'd serve. "I suppose."

"Seems to me we had leftover turkey for at least a week after Thanksgiving."

Julie took out the ornaments, examining each one. "Would you rather I made something else?"

"No, no, I like my turkey. It just seems a waste to buy a big bird for the two of us."

"I could find a smaller one."

"Or…maybe we should invite a few guests."

"Guests? Who?" All their family was on the East Coast. Emily was in Florida, and longtime friends had their own families.

"What about Roy and his mother?"

He'd led into that suggestion with such ease Julie hadn't seen it coming. For a moment, she was too surprised to respond.

"What do you think?" he asked, watching her.

"Well," she said cautiously, "I don't know."

Her father brought the stepladder from the kitchen as he continued his task. "I met Anne this week, and she's a sensible woman."

Julie had liked Roy's mother immensely—and she'd been given real insight into Anne's son. On Saturday evening, she'd gone to his home with a new awareness of him, an appreciation for the man he was. Consequently her guard had been down. She'd felt as if her heart would shatter with joy when he kissed her. More than that, she'd sensed there could be a profound connection between them. But she had no way of knowing if Roy felt the same things she did. She *believed* he did, but that could be just wishful thinking.

"You're not saying anything." Her father frowned at her over the top of his reading glasses as he stood on the stepladder by the tree.

"That might be nice, but I'm not sure they'll accept."

"It won't do any harm to ask."

She agreed. This suggestion was unlike her father—but then it dawned on Julie that he might be saying something else. "You like Mrs. Fletcher, Dad?" It was logical; after all, he was alone, and so was Roy's mother.

Her father paused, the string of lights dangling between his hands. "I know what you're thinking, Julie."

"Dad, Mrs. Fletcher is a wonderful woman."

"I know she is, but I want to make something clear right now, and this is important. Anne Fletcher could never interest me romantically. No woman could replace your mother."

"Dad, I didn't mean—"

"I know you didn't," he said, cutting her off. "But it's

best to tell you that I don't plan to remarry, ever. I loved your mother, and frankly, there's no room in my heart for anyone else."

"You might feel differently down the road. Mom wouldn't want you to be lonely."

"I won't be. I have every intention of working as long as I can and living a productive life."

"I certainly hope so," she teased.

"But I'll live the rest of my life alone."

"That decision is yours."

"I appreciate your understanding, Julie. At some point, you and your sister might feel inclined to match me up, but it's not what I want."

"Okay, Dad."

He nodded, apparently relieved.

Julie scooped up a handful of popcorn and had just started to chew when her father glanced up again. "You were home earlier than I expected last night. Was everything okay between you and Roy?"

She swallowed quickly. "It went really well."

"Are you going out with him again?"

Roy hadn't asked, but she'd come to the conclusion that he would. "I think so," and then she added, because it was true, "I hope so. Does that bother you?"

Her father grinned. "It's a little late to be asking me that."

"Yeah, I suppose it is. I like him, Dad."

Her father's grin broadened. "I guessed as much. You've been walking on air for the last few days."

"Is it that noticeable?"

Her father chuckled and was about to say something else when the doorbell rang.

Julie stood, brushed off her jeans and hurried to the door. Roy Fletcher stood on the other side. She felt a surge of joy at the sight of him.

"Hi," he said a bit sheepishly.

"Hi, yourself."

"Doing anything special?"

She nodded and reached for his hand, pulling him into the foyer. "Want to help?"

"Maybe." He wrapped his arms around her waist. Nuzzling her neck with his cold nose, he whispered, "I woke up this morning and realized I missed you. By the way—" he dropped a kiss on her forehead "—I bought tickets for a Christmas concert, if you're interested."

"I'd love it." Happy chills raced down Julie's back and she sighed as he kissed her jaw, moving toward her lips. They were deeply involved in a kiss when Julie heard her father behind her.

"Yup," he said gleefully. "I'd say my Julie likes Mr. Roy Fletcher."

"I'd say she does, too," Mercy shouted, and exchanged a high five with Goodness. "Just look at the two of them."

Frowning, Shirley stood back, arms crossed. "It was too easy."

"What do you mean?" Mercy demanded. "I don't know about you, but I've been working hard to bring these two humans together. And I think I did a very good job."

Shirley shook her head. "There's trouble in the making, I can feel it. I'm telling you something's going to happen that none of us will like."

"Well, don't go looking for it," Goodness warned.

"I'm not," the oldest of the trio insisted, "but I can sense it coming."

"Don't say that," Mercy cried, covering both ears. "Roy and Julie are *perfect* together. They're falling in love, exactly like we planned."

"I wish I could agree," Shirley said. "But experience tells

me it was too easy. Mark my words, they're about to hit a major snag."

"You're just upset about that salmon," Mercy pouted.

Goodness wasn't thrilled about the fish free-for-all in Pike Place Market, but any chastisement would only encourage Mercy to misbehave. After Julie and Anne had left, Mercy had gone amok. Fish had been flying in all directions. Staff and customers were shouting and shrieking; chaos was rampant. It'd taken both Shirley and Goodness to get her out of the fish market.

"What could go wrong?" Goodness asked.

"Yes, just look at them," Mercy said. Roy and Julie had started to place the ornaments on the tree. Between each carefully hung bauble, they'd pause and exchange kisses and munch popcorn. "He's even telling her about Christmases he had as a boy. We all know he doesn't often talk about his parents."

"Speaking of parents," Goodness said, glancing around. "Where's Dean?"

"He made an excuse to leave and give them privacy."

"That's very considerate."

Shirley continued to frown. "I wish I had a better feeling about all of this."

So did Goodness, but she'd come to respect her friend's premonitions. She could only wonder what would happen next.

Eighteen

It was beginning to look and feel like Christmas, Anne thought as she walked out to her rural mailbox. The neighbors, whose house could barely be seen in the distance, had strung a multicolored strand of outside lights along their roofline. A six-foot-tall Frosty the Snowman stood forlornly in their front yard. Snow was a rare commodity in the Pacific Northwest, and a fake snowman was all there was likely to be.

As Anne strolled back up the meandering driveway that led to her cottage, she browsed through the assortment of holiday cards, bills and sale flyers. She'd been so busy with her artwork and traveling into Seattle that the mail had sat forgotten in her box for three days. Pouring herself a cup of tea, she settled at the small round table in her cozy kitchen and opened the top envelope.

It was clearly a Christmas card, an expensive one, judging by the large vellum envelope. Anne opened it and slid out the card. The scene was of snow and geese and a decorated Christmas tree in the middle of a pristine meadow. Curious now, she looked inside and gasped as she read the embossed name. A sharp pain slashed through her and she held her breath, closing her eyes at such blatant cruelty.

Burton and Aimee Fletcher

This Christmas card was obviously Burton's way of reminding Anne of what he'd done to her. Not that she needed reminders… She didn't know why her ex-husband hated her so much. Perhaps it was because, thanks to Aimee and the divorce, Burton had lost his son. Was he blaming *her* for that?

Refusing to dwell on the reasons for such unkindness, she tossed the card aside and reached for the rest of her mail. Her hands shook as she struggled to regain her composure. How sad that five years after their divorce, her ex-husband was still trying to upset her. Well, Anne wasn't going to let him. Then it occurred to her that perhaps it hadn't been Burton at all, but Aimee. If so, Anne couldn't begin to figure out why the other woman would want to hurt her.

Although she tried not to let the Christmas card bother her, Anne couldn't stop thinking about it. The fact that she hadn't recognized the return address told her Burton and Aimee had moved from the oceanfront home Anne had loved so much. She could just imagine the new house. No expense would have been spared; Burton was all too willing to spend his money on Aimee. It thrilled him to have a beautiful young woman on his arm. A woman dressed in designer clothes, wearing lavish jewelry that spoke of her husband's success. He'd done exceptionally well over the years. Twice now, she'd heard his name in conjunction with famous Hollywood stars and their very public divorces.

The phone rang. Anne wasn't in the mood to talk, and decided to let the answering machine pick up. Out of curiosity, she glanced at caller ID. When she saw it was Marta's New York number, she jerked up the receiver.

Anne had been waiting anxiously ever since their last conversation. The temptation to contact her had been almost overwhelming, but she hadn't given in. If Marta had sold the angel painting—or wanted to discuss her marriage—she would've called.

"Hi, Marta," Anne said, rushing her words together.

"Merry Christmas, Anne."

Anne so wanted this to be good news. She *needed* it after that dreadful Christmas card.

"How are you?" Anne asked.

Marta hesitated. "Okay, I think. Do you have a few minutes?"

"Of course I do." From the tone of her friend's voice Anne suspected the call had to do with Marta's husband and not the painting.

Marta sighed, a despairing sound. "I confronted Jack. I tried to follow your advice and casually mention that I knew about the affair. Unfortunately it didn't work. I came unglued."

"What happened?" Anne asked softly.

"You suggested I simply tell Jack I knew what he was doing and that I was protecting myself financially. That seemed so reasonable at the time, and I thought I could do it. I really did. But when the moment came, I burst into tears and called him every foul name in the book. I don't think I've ever been so angry. I've never been one to say those kinds of things."

"This is your life and your marriage, and your heart's breaking." Anne had struggled with this same vicious anger herself. Her self-esteem had been destroyed; she'd come to the end of her composure, no longer the complacent wife. Her self-recrimination had been as bitter as her resentment and her fury.

"I had no idea I was so furious."

"I didn't, either, when it happened to me," Anne consoled her. She hadn't turned on Burton, though. Instead, she'd wept until there were no more tears left and all that remained was her anger.

"On the other hand," Marta said with strained cheerfulness, "I took your advice and had everything planned before I spoke to him."

"Good!"

"I saw an attorney and had our joint assets frozen right away."

Anne approved. "That was smart—and practical."

"My attorney advised me to wait a week until he had everything in place. Then Jack came home smelling of her perfume and I went ballistic."

This was so unlike Marta that Anne could scarcely picture her friend in that kind of state. "How did he react?"

Marta's laugh was short. "Of course he denied everything."

Just like Burton had, accusing Anne of having a filthy mind, of being insecure and ridiculous. In the beginning, she'd felt dreadful for suspecting such terrible things about her husband. Burton had insisted on an apology and in her innocence, Anne had given him one. Her face burned with mortification at the memory.

"Burton denied everything, too."

"Then I told him about seeing an attorney," Marta said, her voice quavering, "and…and then I threw him out."

In every likelihood, Jack had immediately gone to the other woman, but Anne didn't mention that.

"He…he didn't want to leave. He kept trying to reason with me but I wouldn't listen. He said I was imagining things—and this is the crazy part—for a moment I actually believed him. Here he was, hours late, smelling of perfume and denying everything, and because I so badly wanted to believe him, I…I almost did."

"Of course you wanted to believe him. Jack's your husband."

Marta paused. "That first night was so dreadful. Jack called the apartment ten times. I wouldn't answer the phone and he left messages for me, pleading with me to hear him out." She released a soft hiccuping sob.

"When was that?"

"Three days ago."

"How long has it been since you talked to him?"

"Since that night… I just can't. I thought maybe I'd blown everything out of proportion and, Anne, I'm no longer sure what to believe. I know he's involved with someone else, but I so desperately want him back that I've decided I can't trust my own feelings. If I talk to him, I'm afraid he'll manage to convince me that this is all nonsense and I'll take him back."

"What are you going to do?"

"Right now, nothing. I've hired a private investigator. It sounds so stupid, so clichéd. You're the only person I'd admit this to, but I'm paying a man outrageous fees to follow my husband around and photograph him with another woman. Is that sick or what?"

"Oh, Marta. Of course it isn't. A detective might be the only means you have of learning the truth." Early on, before the breakup of her own marriage, Anne had considered the same thing. In retrospect she wished she'd done it. Photographic evidence might have opened her eyes to what Burton was doing.

"All I want is for this to go away. I think now I should've waited until after Christmas, but, Anne, I couldn't. I couldn't endure this for another second. I couldn't pretend and look the other way anymore."

"I'm so sorry, Marta," Anne told her friend. "I wouldn't have wished this on you for anything."

"Oh, Anne, I don't know what to do. Christmas is only a week away. I can't deal with this and the holidays, too. What am I going to tell our friends? How can I possibly face everyone?" The questions came between deep sobs.

"Oh, Marta, I'm so sorry," she said again.

"Why is this happening to me?"

Anne had asked herself the same question hundreds of times. "Would you like to fly out to Seattle? Stay with me and take a few days to collect your thoughts. Let your attorney know you're coming and just get on a plane."

"I can't believe you'd do that for me," Marta said, and continued to sob.

"I've walked in your shoes. I know how hard this is. What do you want to do?"

"Would you mind terribly coming to New York? I'd pay for your ticket. I just need someone with me—someone who understands."

"Of course I wouldn't mind! I'll check on flights the minute we get off the phone." Roy wouldn't care; Anne was sure of that. Her son would be just as happy to spend Christmas Day at Julie's. With Anne in New York, he'd be free to do so.

"Thank you. Oh, thank you, Anne. I'd fly out and join you, but I don't want to leave. There's no telling what Jack would do if I were to vacate the house."

Naturally her friend was right. "That's fine, Marta. I'll come to New York for Christmas and be your moral support."

"Thank you," her friend whispered again. "I don't know how I'd cope if it wasn't for you."

"We'll have a wonderful Christmas," Anne tried to assure her, although she knew what Marta was experiencing. The pain and shock...

"Oh, Anne, I'm just shocked that Jack would be so stupid."

"He might come to his senses yet."

"I'm not counting on it," Marta said. "He seemed so sincere, so horrified. He kept insisting I was wrong. I never knew he was capable of such lies."

It hurt just to listen to her friend's agony. Anne didn't have the heart to tell her that the pain, even when dulled by time, had a way of resurfacing when you least expected it. Anne had felt its sting only moments earlier when she'd opened her mail.

Marta grew quiet, as if she was composing herself. She took a deep, audible breath. "I've been so caught up in my own troubles I forgot to mention what's been going on with your painting."

Although she was dying to know, Anne was prepared to put it off. "That's not important now."

"But it is."

"Did Mrs. Gould decide against it?" Anne asked. She'd never been comfortable with letting the buyer assume she had no intention of selling her angel.

"No, she's more interested than ever, but now there's another prospective buyer."

"That's wonderful," Anne said excitedly.

"This one claims she'll match or beat anything Mrs. Gould offers."

"Are you saying that two customers have gotten into a bidding war?" Anne was almost afraid to guess what this could mean financially.

"That's exactly what I'm saying."

"How...how much?"

"Are you sure you want to know?"

"Yes!" she cried. "Tell me."

"Well, first of all," Marta teased, "I'm not positive the artist's willing to sell it."

"Oh, Marta." Anne couldn't help it; she giggled.

"It's an incredible painting, and everyone who sees it is drawn to it. Your angel has become the most talked-about piece in our gallery. She's aroused more interest than anything else on display, and of course, the fact that it's December is a plus. You couldn't have painted her at a more appropriate time."

Anne's heart swelled with pride. "Oh, you're making me feel so good!"

"That's what the painting does, you know. People look at your angel and they feel better about life."

"Has she helped you?" Anne asked.

"Oh, yes," Marta replied. "I don't know what it is, but there's a soothing quality about your angel. It's…almost as if I were standing close to God."

Anne regretted having given the angel up so quickly. Even now, she didn't know if she'd imagined the vision or it had actually happened. She chose to believe the angel had been real, but who was to know?

"Don't tell me you're having second thoughts."

"I…I'm not sure," Anne admitted.

"Well, let me know before I make a deal."

While Anne loved the angel, ten thousand dollars or more for one of her pieces would go a long way toward establishing her credibility in the art world—and paying her mortgage.

"I've been offered twenty-five thousand for it," Marta announced.

Anne felt faint. "How much?"

"You heard me right."

"I—I can't believe it! You've got to be making this up."

"No, and the bid is climbing."

"Marta, I have no idea what to say."

"Just call and tell me when your flight's coming in and I'll be there to pick you up, check in hand. We *do* want to sell this painting, don't we?"

Because she knew it was the right thing, Anne said, "Yes, we do." Burton would probably never hear about her success, but that didn't matter. Anne Fletcher was an artist and an unusual one at that. She could support herself with what she made on her paintings.

Nineteen

Roy caught himself whistling as he dressed for work Monday morning. He took a long look at himself in the mirror and saw something he hadn't seen in years. *Happiness.* It had sneaked up on him and could only be attributed to his relationship with Julie. He liked the way she made him feel, the way she challenged him and made him laugh. He liked her warmth and honesty. He'd discovered that he wanted to be with her more and more—all the time, in fact. And this had happened in only a few weeks. He often found himself impatient when they were apart, eager to be with her again. Suddenly he wanted—no, needed—to hear the sound of her voice.

Without further thought he picked up the phone.

Julie answered on the second ring.

"What are you doing?" he asked, keeping his voice low.

"Roy, it's six o'clock in the morning. I'm getting ready for school. What do you suppose I'm doing?"

"I was hoping you were thinking of me." He straddled a kitchen chair, grabbing his coffee mug. The best Colombian coffee and conversation with Julie—not a bad way to start his day.

"I *was* thinking of you," she admitted reluctantly.

"Will you have dinner with me tonight?"

"I've got a game."

"After the game?"

"I'd love to."

His heart soared at her excitement. Then again, it could be an echo of his own joy. He shook his head. This was crazy. He knew better than to let himself be swayed by feelings, especially feelings for a woman. Hadn't he learned that by now? Yet here he was, falling head over heels for Julie and he was doing it with his eyes wide open. A rational voice in his mind urged him to resist before he made another costly mistake. But a louder and more persistent voice promised him Julie was different....

"Where do you want to go?" he asked.

"Do we have to go anywhere?" she asked. "Dad's meeting some friends tonight. I can cook."

"After teaching all day and coaching a soccer game, you won't feel like cooking. Let me take you out."

"Nonsense. I'll start a stew in the Crock-Pot and it'll be ready when I get home from school."

Roy hadn't had regular home-cooked meals since he was a teenager. His mother, no matter how busy she was, had insisted on dinners together as a family. More often than not, his father had business to attend to, but Roy had always eaten with his mother, at least until he left for college in Seattle.

"Unless you don't want stew? I just thought it was a great wintertime meal and—"

"Your stew's wonderful," he assured her. She could serve dill pickles and he wouldn't have cared. All Roy wanted was to spend time with Julie. He had no idea where this was going and for the moment contented himself with the thrill of the ride.

They agreed to meet at her house at seven. Roy found

himself watching the clock all day. The morning seemed to crawl by, and his mind wasn't on his various meetings or the decisions he had to make. Even Ms. Johnson commented.

Roy brushed away her concern. He didn't admit it was Julie Wilcoff who occupied his thoughts, but he suspected Ms. Johnson had guessed as much.

That evening, at one minute to seven, Roy stood on Julie's front porch, clutching a bottle of excellent wine, and rang the doorbell. She answered immediately, her hair still wet from the shower. She'd combed it away from her face, and he noticed again how lovely she was, even without makeup. Her skin was smooth and healthy, her eyes bright, and her lips, with only the slightest color, looked as if they ached to be kissed. He knew *he* ached to kiss her. She wore slacks and a green sweater, and just seeing her turned his blood to steam. This was what he'd been fantasizing about all day, what he'd wanted from the moment he'd climbed out of bed that morning.

"You're right on time," she said, reaching for his free hand. With a slight tug she brought him into the house.

Roy saw that he'd been standing on the porch like a schoolboy, simply staring at her. He knew he should wait before he kissed her, but he couldn't stop himself. He set the wine on a hallway table crowded with gloves and unopened mail and, without removing his coat, brought her into his arms.

Julie went to him willingly and when their lips met, it was the first time that day he'd felt completely relaxed. She melted against him and he felt the soft fullness of her breasts against his chest. His head swam. The sensation their kisses evoked in him nearly sent him over the edge.

After several minutes, Julie pulled her mouth from his. "I…I've got bread under the broiler."

Only then did Roy smell the burning bread. He released her and, because his knees felt weak, walked into the living room and sat down. Shrugging off his coat, he struggled to regain his equilibrium. A minute later, he carried his overcoat to the hall closet and collected the wine, which he placed on the coffee table.

Julie returned just as he sat down again. "Thankfully I picked up two loaves," she said. Offering him a shy smile, she started to walk past him to the chair opposite his.

Roy grabbed her hand, weaving his fingers through hers. "I want to talk."

"All right." Her dark eyes were solemn.

He drew her into his lap and resumed the kissing they'd begun in the hallway. Cradling her, he slipped his hand beneath her sweater and groaned as he encountered her breasts. His kisses turned greedy and urgent and—

A loud *ding* startled him and he broke off the kiss.

"That's the oven timer," Julie explained, and gazed at him, her eyes warm. "Don't let it interrupt you." She frowned playfully. "On the other hand, I don't want to burn my last loaf of bread." She slid off his lap and hurried to the kitchen. "Hold that kiss—I mean thought," she called over her shoulder.

Roy grinned when she came back and returned to her position on his lap. "I was serious about wanting to talk," he said after a quick kiss.

"I can see that," she teased.

"The problem is, you're way too tempting."

She rolled her eyes, but the smile didn't leave her lips. "What do you want to talk about?"

"I can't think when we're this close."

"Would you like me to move?"

"No...yes."

She slid off his lap a second time and sat on the sofa across from him.

"How long do you intend to live with your father?" he asked, leaning forward.

The question appeared to surprise her. "I…I was thinking of renting an apartment after the first of the year."

"Don't," he said.

Her eyes narrowed. "Why not? Dad needs to make his own life now and—"

"Move in with me." He hadn't broached the subject with much finesse, but he saw no reason to wait.

Julie didn't answer and her silence unnerved him.

"I take it you're not looking for a roommate to share expenses," she finally said in what was presumably an effort at humor.

"We both know what I'm asking."

"Yes…well." She took a breath and then slowly exhaled. "We…only met a few weeks ago."

"We know how we feel—what we want."

She lowered her gaze rather than confess the truth.

"Julie," he said, "we're adults."

Slowly she raised her eyes to meet his, and he read her indecision. Hoping to persuade her, he stood up and crossed to the sofa, sitting beside her. Clasping Julie's hands, he brushed his mouth over hers. "We'd be good together," he whispered.

"I think so, too."

"Then why the hesitation?"

She shook her head.

"Come on," he urged. "Tell me."

"I'd hate to disappoint my father—I don't know how he'd feel about this."

Roy wanted to remind her that she was thirty years old and fully capable of making decisions without consulting her father. In any event, based on what he knew of Dean Wilcoff, the man wouldn't stand in their way.

"I'm afraid he'd do something rash," Julie said.

"Like what?" Roy couldn't imagine him doing any such thing. Dean was a sensible man. He wouldn't intrude on his daughter's life. He'd accept whatever Julie wanted and keep his mouth shut—as he should.

"He wouldn't approve."

"So?"

"So," she continued, "I suspect he'd quit his job."

"That decision is his, don't you think?"

"Yes," she agreed after a lengthy pause. "But he needs this job and for more than the money. It's been wonderful for him, Roy. I'm so grateful you gave Dad a chance to feel productive again. It's been exactly what he needed."

"Leave your father to me," he told her. Roy would square the situation with Dean and make sure he had no objections.

Still Julie hesitated.

"You don't need to decide right this minute. Take a few days, think it over. I'm not going to withdraw the offer."

A tremulous smile lifted the corners of her mouth. Roy was disappointed by her lack of excitement, although he wouldn't admit it. He'd hoped Julie would show as much enthusiasm for his idea as he felt himself.

Then it hit him. Naturally she was hesitant. She wanted it all, especially that ring on her finger, before she moved in with him.

"You want me to marry you first, don't you?"

"That's the way it's generally done," she said. "So...yes, I guess I do."

He appreciated her honesty and felt he couldn't be any less honest with her. "Sorry, Julie, it isn't going to happen. I'm not interested in marriage."

She took the news easily enough.

"Fine," she said, her voice just a bit unsteady. "But what *are* you offering me?"

Roy shrugged. "I'm offering you a place in my life and in my home. I'll be generous and attentive." He couldn't think of anything else she'd want. Although he hadn't spelled it out, he intended to give her all the things women craved. She could buy whatever she wanted: jewels, clothes, cars. It was up to her.

"I don't doubt that you'd be good to me."

"Then what's the problem?"

"For how long?"

His patience was slipping. "You want guarantees?"

"Six weeks? Three months? A year?"

"How am I supposed to know? For however long the two of us last." That should satisfy her. The way he felt just then, it could be a very long time, but she was right—maybe it wouldn't. Who could tell?

"You've done contracts with other businesses, haven't you?"

Roy had the feeling she was thinking out loud. "Yes—"

"You were ready to make a commitment to them, weren't you?"

"Yes—"

"But you aren't willing to make a commitment to me."

Ah, he was beginning to understand. "I can break a contract for a price. Is that what you're talking about?"

"Are you suggesting payment?"

He should have wised up by now, but she'd had him fooled. Still, he didn't care. He was a man accustomed to paying for what he wanted. At the moment that was Julie, and he wanted her badly.

"Fine," he said. "We can draw up a financial agreement."

She pulled her hands free of his. "That wasn't what I meant. I don't think you realize how insulting that is, Roy."

"Insulting? I thought it was what you wanted. Okay," he said, doing his best to figure her out. "Just tell me what it would take—other than marrying you—to get you to move in with me." He couldn't make it any plainer than that.

Aimee had moved in without a moment's hesitation. He couldn't understand why Julie needed all this discussion.

"I don't know… I want to think this through." As if in a daze, she stood and walked slowly back to the kitchen.

Roy followed her. This night wasn't going the way he'd anticipated. He'd never been much good with relationships, and his experience with Aimee hadn't helped.

"What about love?" she asked, suddenly turning around.

Roy had come to detest the word. He didn't know what it was anymore. "Julie, you're searching for an excuse, and I'm not going to give it to you. You're looking for ways to talk yourself out of something we both want. This would be an agreement between two mature people who are strongly attracted to each other. Nothing more and nothing less."

"What about your mother?"

"What about her? She'd be thrilled. She's been saying for a long time that I work too hard, and she's right. Knowing her, she'll kiss you on both cheeks and thank you."

Julie didn't seem to believe him.

"If it's any consolation, you should know I've only had one other woman live with me." Aimee. And whatever happened with Julie, it couldn't possibly end as badly as *that* relationship.

Taking two bowls and two wineglasses from the cupboard, Julie set them on the counter. "I want to think this through," she said again. She gave him a weak smile. "Like you said, this offer is good for more than twenty-four hours."

"Take all the time you need." But he wanted her in his home and in his bed. The sooner the better.

Twenty

"I don't know about anyone else," Goodness said, still in a huff, pacing inside Roy's office. "But I'm outraged." She fluttered her wings so her friends would know she wasn't kidding.

Papers slid off Roy's desk and he looked up, clearly puzzled by the sudden draft.

"Roy's a man," Mercy chided her, far too willing to overlook his weaknesses. "What do you expect?"

"And I'm an angel," Goodness said right back. "What do *you* expect?"

"These are human matters," Shirley insisted, lurking behind Roy's chair. "We can't interfere."

"Julie knows better. Mark my words—she'll refuse to do it."

Mercy sighed and sat on the corner of Roy's fancy desk, protecting his files from further disruption. "I wouldn't be so sure if I were you. She's tempted."

"Then we'll untempt her."

Shirley shook her head. "That's not our department. They send in the Warrior Angels to deal with temptations."

True, but Goodness had intense feelings when it came to the humans involved in her prayer requests. Shirley,

Goodness and Mercy had worked hard to bring these two together. She no longer felt any uncertainty about their choice; Julie was the woman Anne had prayed for. After all their efforts, the least Roy could do was marry her! Time was running out. They had to think of something quickly if he was going to propose by Christmas Eve. After that, they were off the case. Oh, dear, this could turn into a real disaster and of course Gabriel would blame the three of them.

"We've got to make Julie see sense," Goodness said urgently. If Mercy was right, then Julie might indeed give in to temptation. The prayer request was ambiguous; Anne hadn't stated that Roy needed to *marry* this woman, although it was implied.

"He hasn't heard from her in two days." Mercy flipped the pages of Roy's desktop calendar.

"Don't do that," Goodness cried, slapping Mercy's hand. "He might see you."

Mercy tilted her head and stared at Roy Fletcher. "He's deep in thought."

"He's wondering how long it'll take to hear from Julie," Shirley suggested. "He's growing impatient."

Goodness had noticed that, but she also knew he'd made no effort to get in touch with Julie. She suspected this was a ploy on his part—his way of telling Julie that if she chose to reject his offer, she wouldn't be hearing from him again. That was just plain wrong! Goodness intended to do everything within her power to make sure Roy's head was filled with thoughts of Julie every minute of every day. The man would be sorry he'd messed with the angels' plans to answer his mother's prayer.

"You know how cold he can be," Shirley commented, studying Roy intently. She shivered and wrapped her arms around herself.

"That's all an act," Goodness told them. "He loves his mother and Julie, only he's too stubborn to admit it."

"I say we get in there and do something," Mercy proclaimed.

"Like what?" Goodness was almost afraid to ask.

"What we always do." Mercy folded her hands prayerfully and fluttered her long, curly eyelashes.

"Heaven help us," Goodness muttered.

"No, you've got it all wrong," Mercy said. "*We're* the ones helping Heaven. Gabriel needs us. Otherwise, we'd be long gone by now. I for one feel that drastic times call for drastic measures."

"Drastic measures," Goodness repeated. "What—"

"Stand back everyone." Mercy threw open her wings.

"What's she going to do?" Goodness asked Shirley. "Toss a fish at him?"

Shirley giggled.

Just when Mercy was getting ready to make her move, Ms. Johnson entered Roy's office. The three angels glided out of the way as his assistant handed him a sheaf of papers that required his signature.

"Ms. Johnson," he said as the woman was about to leave, "would you mind if I asked you a couple of questions?"

"Are they personal questions?"

"Not exactly personal. Didn't you tell me you have a daughter in her twenties?"

"I do. Janice. She recently turned twenty-three. What makes you ask?"

"I was just wondering if—" He was interrupted by someone knocking on the partially opened door.

Shirley gasped.

"Who's *that?*" Goodness wanted to know.

"I think it might be Aimee," Mercy told her in a hushed whisper.

Indeed it was. The woman who'd dumped Roy for his father. She stepped into the office wearing a full-length mink coat and high-heel shoes. She was sleek, petite and very blond. They didn't call it *platinum* blond for nothing, Goodness thought spitefully.

"What's *she* doing here?" No one answered, and Goodness suspected her friends were as surprised as Roy obviously was.

He slowly stood. "That will be all, Ms. Johnson."

"Yes, sir." His assistant hurried out of the room.

"Hello, Roy." Aimee smiled seductively and walked up to his desk. "It's good to see you."

"How did you get into the building?"

"Oh, I have my ways."

Roy snickered. "I'll just bet you do." He made a mental note to talk to Dean Wilcoff about this.

"I think it's time we talked, don't you?" Without waiting for an invitation, she sat down and crossed her shapely legs.

Roy remained standing. "Actually, I think it's time you left."

Aimee sighed. "There's no need to be nasty."

"I mean it, Aimee."

She shook her head, her long, blond hair swinging softly from side to side. "Roy, this is ridiculous! You refuse to have anything to do with your father—"

"I have nothing to say to him *or* to you."

"That's sad, because we both want to reconcile with you."

His gaze narrowed. "I don't think I can bring myself to call you Mother."

She laughed, shrugging off his sarcasm. "I don't think you should. Tell me, how are you?"

"Fine. Now leave."

"I've come all this way, and I'm not going until you talk to me."

Roy lowered himself stiffly into his chair. "What do you want?"

Aimee's expression became petulant. "I always hated it when you used that tone of voice with me." As if she suddenly felt hot, she unfastened the buttons of her coat and slipped her arms free.

Roy stared at the mink and at the silk suit beneath, set off by a stunning emerald brooch. "I see Daddy's buying you lots of gifts."

Aimee raised one elegant shoulder. "You might not believe this, but I happen to love your father."

Roy raised his eyes to the ceiling. "Yeah, and I'll bet you love his bank balance even more." He'd understood long ago that Aimee had set her sights on his father from the beginning of their so-called relationship. He'd been used, and it wasn't going to happen again.

Her lips thinned. "You can insult me all you want, but I will not take offense. I came because I want to build a bridge between you and your father."

Roy laughed outright. "The woman who blew up the bridge now wants to build one? I find that interesting."

"It's true, Roy. It's been five years. Your father and I have a very good life, but he misses you." She pouted ever so slightly.

"Why am I having trouble believing that?"

"It's true," Aimee said a second time, even more insistently. "Talk to your father, okay? It's what he wants. Me, too. I'd like us all to be friends."

"I'd like world peace myself."

"Burton's your father!"

"He made his choice and I've made mine."

Aimee reached for her purse and removed a gold cigarette case. "Do you mind if I smoke?"

"I thought you quit."

"I am quitting."

"You were quitting five years ago."

She tapped the cigarette against the case, then inserted it between her lips. "It isn't easy," she muttered.

"Sorry, there's a no-smoking law."

"Whatever." She returned the cigarette to the case, which she thrust back in her purse.

"Just finish saying what you came to say and get out."

She looked hurt. "Burton wants to see you."

Roy didn't consider the request. "What for?" he asked scornfully.

"You're his son. He loves you."

Roy frowned. "He has a unique way of showing his love. Let me see… I love my son. I wonder how I can best show him that love? I know! I'll divorce my wife, destroy my family and steal his fiancée. That should do the trick. Well, guess what, it didn't work."

"Roy, don't you understand that what happened between me and your father just *happened?* Neither of us asked to fall in love with the other."

Roy's hand shot up. "Spare me. I don't buy that for a second. You no more love my father than you loved me. When I think of what a fool I was, I get sick to my stomach. It was never me you wanted. I see that now. You were always interested in my father and you used me to get to him."

Aimee flew to her feet. "That's where you're wrong. I *do* love Burton and he loves me. I love him enough to swallow my pride and approach you. Just talk to him, that's all I ask."

"Sorry, but I'm not interested."

"I'd hoped your mother—"

"Leave my mother out of this!"

"I sent her a Christmas card," Aimee said. "I thought the best way to reach you was through her."

Roy stood up and leaned against his desk. "You sent my mother a Christmas card? Why would you do such a thing? How was she supposed to take that?"

"I didn't write anything in it. I just wanted her to know I don't bear her any ill will."

Roy stared at Aimee, completely stupefied. "Did it ever occur to you that *she* might be the one who bears ill will?"

Aimee bit her pouting lower lip. Collagen injections? he wondered indifferently. "Not really."

"Thank God you never wanted to be *her* friend. I'd hate to think what you might have done if you'd actually liked her."

Aimee gave a little cry of dismay. "I didn't do anything to her!"

Despite his effort not to reveal his emotions, Roy felt himself clenching his jaw. "You stole her husband."

"I didn't," Aimee insisted. "Burton hadn't been happy in years."

Roy ignored that. "Then my father cheated my mother in the divorce settlement. He took what should've been hers by hiding the money in offshore accounts."

"Burton would never do that," Aimee said, shaking her head. The shimmering pale blond hair swung gently. Roy figured she was well aware of the effect.

"Stay married to him," he advised. "Now you know what he'll do if a younger, sexier replacement comes along."

"Burton and I are deeply in love," Aimee said. "Do you think it was easy coming here today? Well, it wasn't. I thought—I hoped you'd at least listen to me, but I can see I was wrong."

"You can tell my father one thing," Roy said angrily. "Tell him to—"

"I don't want to listen," Shirley cried, and covered both her ears.

"Me, neither." Goodness followed suit. She hummed a special hymn to blot out the terse, angry words. When she felt it was safe, she lifted her hands from her ears.

Mercy's eyes were wide. "That boy has quite the vocabulary."

"You listened?"

"Sure, why not? Aimee had it coming. That woman has some nerve, arriving out of the blue like that."

Shirley walked over to the door and peered out. "She's gone now."

"Good riddance."

"What a mess," Goodness said with a sigh. "I think she must genuinely love Roy's father, otherwise she'd never have shown up at the office."

"She lacks discretion," Shirley said sadly. "How could she possibly think that mailing Anne a Christmas card would help her cause?"

"She's feeling guilty."

"As well she should."

"We weren't sent here to deal with Aimee," Goodness reminded her friends. "That woman is going to require an entire legion of angels. Our concern is Roy."

"Oh, brother!" Mercy threw herself against the wall. "You won't believe this."

"What?" Shirley tried to peek but Mercy stopped her. "Oh, look at Roy."

Goodness studied him. Roy was in an agitated state, pacing back and forth across the room. Although she was unable to read his thoughts, one glance told her that those thoughts were dark and angry.

Mercy pointed toward the other room. "You'll never guess who just arrived."

"Not Anne," Shirley cried.

"No, worse," Mercy said. "It's Julie."

Twenty-One

Julie stepped off the elevator and strolled toward Ms. Johnson, the guardian of Roy's office. For two days, she'd wrestled with the question of what she should do. She dreaded giving him her answer, but now that she was here, she was more convinced than ever that she'd made the right decision.

Her natural inclination was to accept Roy's invitation and move in with him. He was correct about one thing: it was what they both wanted. Deep down, she clung to the hope that one day he'd love her. She suspected he already did, or had begun to, anyway, but refused to acknowledge his feelings. Moving in with him had been easy to rationalize. In the end, however, after a lengthy talk with her sister, Julie had to admit that she wanted more out of their relationship. The hard part would be convincing Roy that they both needed more time.

"Ms. Wilcoff." His assistant looked up, startled. "Did I know you were coming?"

"No, no, I stopped here on my way home from school. Is Roy busy?"

The woman, who was rarely flustered, seemed so now. "Let me check." Rather than use the intercom, she scurried away from her desk and disappeared behind Roy's office door.

When Jason, the downstairs security guard, had let Julie into the building without so much as a raised eyebrow, she should've realized there was a problem. The guard had worn a funny look, as if he knew something she didn't. Julie had wanted to ask him, but decided against it. Now Ms. Johnson was behaving in a peculiar manner, too.

A moment later, she reappeared. "He asked me to show you right in, but…"

"But?" Julie prompted when the woman hesitated. "Is Roy having a bad day?"

The older woman nodded. "You could say that. On second thought, seeing you might be exactly what he needs."

Now that Julie had arrived at her decision, she felt an urgency to get this conversation over with as quickly as possible. Delaying it might give her just enough time to change her mind.

Roy was sitting at his desk when she entered his office. He looked up and smiled, but she noticed that the warmth she'd grown to expect was missing.

"Should I come back later?" she asked uncertainly.

"No." He motioned for her to take a seat.

"I probably should've phoned first."

"Probably," he agreed. He relaxed in his chair and folded his hands over his stomach. And waited.

"I thought I should let you know what I've decided."

He nodded, his expression unchanged.

The tightness in Julie's throat increased. She leaned forward just a little and tucked her hands beneath her thighs, something she did when she was nervous. "I guess there's only one way to say this…"

"You're not accepting my invitation," he finished for her.

"Yes."

"Any particular reason?"

"Several, but I do want you to know how tempted I was."

"That's neither here nor there, is it?"

"Well, no—"

"Unless, of course, you're figuring I'll up the ante."

Anger flared instantly, but Julie mentally counted to ten before responding. "No, Roy, I'm not figuring you'll up the ante." She stood. "I think it'd be best if we talked about this another time."

"Now's as good as any," he said.

She leaned closer to his desk, desperately searching his face for the reason he'd changed. "What's wrong with you?"

"Me?" he demanded.

"You're looking at me like…like I've sprouted horns or something."

He laughed, but even his laughter sounded sarcastic. "All right, I'll play your little game. What would it take to get you into my condo? A monthly allowance? Jewelry? Just tell me and I'll arrange it."

"Don't insult me!"

"Is a thousand a week enough? You can quit teaching, live a life of luxury."

"I like my job!"

He snorted. "Don't give up teaching, then. Why should I care as long as you're there when I want you?"

Julie was beginning to feel sick. "I think I'd better leave."

"Don't go," he said, although he didn't offer her a reason to stay.

"What happened?" she asked, and made a sweeping gesture with her right arm. "Something must have happened."

"You mean other than an unexpected visit from my *step-mother?*" He dragged out the last word, as if even saying it was repugnant.

"Oh." He was talking about Aimee—which explained a great deal. "So you're back to that."

He arched one brow. "That?"

"All women are users and manipulators and not to be trusted, and therefore you ridicule every female you meet." She'd had enough. When Roy was in this frame of mind, there was no reasoning with him, as she knew from experience. She turned to leave.

Roy bolted out of his chair. "Where are you going?"

She ignored the question. "Perhaps we can talk when you're feeling less…angry."

"No, I want this settled today."

"Then it's settled. You have my answer." She started toward the door.

"I don't accept that."

Julie faced him and slowly shook her head. "You know what? There are some things you can't buy, and I'm one of them."

He scoffed. "You'll change your mind."

Rather than argue with him, she simply walked away. She was so furious her head felt about to explode. Mingled with the anger was a profound hurt. Roy didn't respect her, let alone love her. He viewed her as an object he could control—and then discard when he'd finished.

"Julie?" Ms. Johnson stood as Julie walked by.

Numb now, she only half heard the other woman. All Julie wanted was to escape. She hurried toward the elevators, hitting the down button.

"I shouldn't have let you see him," Ms. Johnson said anxiously. "He hasn't had a good afternoon."

"Don't make excuses for him," Julie told her, stepping into the elevator. As soon as the doors closed, she slumped against the wall. Everything had become clear. She knew that some people were unable to move past the pain inflicted by others. They carried it with them for the rest of their lives, and everyone they met, everything they accomplished, was blighted by that pain. Roy, sadly, was one of those people.

When the elevator reached the lobby, Julie straightened, eager to get away from Fletcher Industries—and Fletcher. When the doors slid open, Jason stood directly in front of her, legs braced apart, hands on his hips.

"Mr. Fletcher would like to see you," he announced.

"Tell him another time would be better," Julie said, attempting to get past him.

"He insisted. I'm sorry, Ms. Wilcoff, but I have my orders."

"Which are what? Shoot me on sight if I refuse to talk to your boss? This is illegal confinement, in case you weren't aware of it."

A smile cracked Jason's tight lips. "Just talk to him, all right?"

"I'm supposed to take the elevator up to his office?"

Jason nodded.

"I won't do that."

Jason's eyes pleaded with her. "As a personal favor to me, would you just do it?"

"Sorry, no."

"Ms. Wilcoff, he called down here himself and asked me to keep you in the building."

Despite her anguish, Julie laughed. "That's quite a contrast to his earlier commands, isn't it?"

"Can't help that." He shrugged. "I will say this—you've certainly made my job interesting."

Julie gave an exasperated sigh. Talking to Roy, especially now, wasn't going to solve anything. "I'm sorry, I can't." When it looked as if Jason was about to detain her, Julie leaped agilely to the right and then just as quickly to the left. To her astonishment, without the least bit of effort, she sprinted past the guard.

Jason appeared stunned. "How'd you do that?" he asked, chasing after her.

She was at the door, pushing it open, when he reached her.

He stretched out his arms, lunged forward—and froze in place. "I can't move," he cried. "Something's holding me back."

"Good try, Jason," she said as she walked outside, taking a moment to admire Anne's angel windows. Too bad Roy didn't understand the spirit of Christmas—or the nature of faith and love—the way his mother did.

"I'm not joking!"

The door closed behind her as she bolted toward the visitor parking lot. She glanced over her shoulder once to find Jason still in that odd position, one leg stretched out as if stepping forward to grab her. When he noticed her watching him, he called out for help. Smiling, Julie simply shook her head. He certainly had an inventive approach to getting her sympathy.

After she drove away from Fletcher Industries, Julie headed toward the school. It was almost dark now, but she needed to vent her frustration, so she changed into running gear and jogged toward the track. After doing a couple of quick laps, she left the field and took one of her usual routes in a friendly neighborhood near the school. Generally she avoided running in the dark, but her gear had reflective tape so she could be seen by oncoming traffic.

Her feet hit the pavement in a rhythm that matched the pounding of her heart. Her thoughts, however, flew at a far greater speed. Anger was soon replaced by sadness. Sadness became regret…and resignation. As she approached the five-mile marker, she became aware of a car driving behind her.

It could only be Roy.

He eased his car alongside her and lowered the passenger window. "You have a hard time following directions, don't you?"

"Not at all." She slowed to a clipped walk, her arms swinging. "Why would you say that?"

"What did you do to Jason?"

"I didn't do a thing to him."

Roy brought his sedan to a stop, parked it by the curb and then jumped out. Jogging around the front of the vehicle, he joined her. "That's not what he told me."

"Believe what you want." She tried to hide how hard she was breathing—and how pleased she was to see him. Because, in spite of everything, she was. But that wasn't going to change the situation.

"Come on, Julie, be reasonable. If you want an apology, you've got one. I was rude and arrogant." He paced his walk to hers.

"Yes, you were."

"Thank you for being so gracious," he muttered.

"I don't think we've got anything left to discuss. You have my answer."

"I want you to reconsider."

"It wouldn't work," she said, and she meant it. She stopped walking, and at the risk of letting down her guard, raised her hand to his cheek. "In the beginning, living together would've been wonderful—"

"It still can be."

"But it wouldn't last."

"Nothing lasts forever, and we'd be foolish to think otherwise."

"My parents' love for each other did."

"Mine didn't."

Julie shrugged. "I'm sorry for you, sorry for them, but I can't let what happened between your mother and father taint *my* life. I'm falling in love with you, Roy, and I want it all."

With an angry sigh of frustration, he threw back his head to stare at the dark sky. "Julie, come on! I'm willing to give you whatever you want."

"But that's just the point—you aren't."

He placed his hand over hers and brought it to his lips,

kissing the tender skin of her palm. "We could have something good. Who cares if it doesn't last a lifetime?"

"I care, Roy. I'm sorry, I really am. It would be so easy to let you persuade me, but in the end I'd have nothing left except a broken heart." He couldn't possibly know how much she already loved him.

Roy released her hand. "You're like all the rest, aren't you? You want to control me, get your hands on my success and make it your own. Naturally, your term for this is *love*. I'm supposed to marry you and promise to spend the rest of my life with you? Well, you can forget that."

"Oh, yeah, the old marriage trap. It's worked for thousands of years, but it's not good enough for you. Silly me— refusing to settle for anything less than love and commitment." She gestured wildly with one hand.

"I can't do it, Julie."

"I know."

"Then there's nothing more to say."

"Obviously not." Her throat constricted with sadness.

Neither moved. Neither wanted to be the first to turn away, Julie suspected, or to acknowledge that this relationship was over almost before it had begun.

Finally she was the one who turned and, with tears burning her eyes, ran in the opposite direction.

Twenty-Two

Saturday afternoon, Christmas music played softly in the background as Anne pulled her suitcase from the closet and laid it on her bed. She sang along with her favorite carols as she started to take sweaters from her dresser drawers. Since Marta had sent her the airline ticket online, she'd had two additional phone conversations with her. Things seemed to be looking up. Jack had made numerous attempts to speak to her and she'd agreed to meet with him—after she got the report from the private investigator. Needless to say, she didn't tell him that part; Jack had no idea his wife was having him followed. Their conversation would depend on what the investigator discovered. Still, Jack's willingness— indeed frantic desire—to get his wife back boded well, Anne thought. She was grateful Marta could benefit from her experience.

Marta hadn't given Anne any new details regarding the sale of her angel portrait. However, from everything her friend had told her, the news was good. The painting would definitely sell, and for a high price, too.

A noise in the living room startled Anne, and she paused to listen again. Someone was in her home. "Who's there?"

she called out, a little nervous. She tried to remember where she'd left her portable phone.

"Mother?"

"Roy?" She hurried out of the bedroom. "What are you doing here?" Her son's appearance shocked her. He hadn't shaved in a day or two and looked as if he'd slept in his clothes.

"Frankly, I don't know," he said, not meeting her eyes. "I started driving and then all of a sudden I was on a ferry, headed to your place. I guess I just need to talk."

"My goodness, what's happened?" she asked, resisting the urge to take him in her arms.

"I wasn't sure if you'd already left for New York or not."

"I fly out in the morning. Now, sit down and tell me what's wrong." For once he didn't argue. She directed him into her kitchen, sat him down at the small table and immediately started cooking. At times like this, food could be a wonderful comfort. She put on a pot of coffee, then took out a pan and set it on the stove. After that, she retrieved two eggs from the refrigerator. When she saw that she was paying more attention to creating the perfect omelet than to her son, she stopped. She pulled out a chair and sat across from Roy.

"What is it?" she asked gently.

"I asked Julie to move in with me," he mumbled.

Anne sighed heavily. That wasn't what she wanted for her son; in fact, she saw it as a mistake for both of them, but young people always thought they knew best.

"You don't approve. Julie knew her father wouldn't, either, not that it matters, anyway."

"She turned you down?"

"Lock, stock and barrel. I guess I should be grateful."

He certainly didn't *look* grateful. If anything, Roy seemed distraught. Immediate questions came to mind, but Anne avoided asking, knowing Roy would explain everything in his own time. "I'm sorry."

"So am I. Julie insists on what she calls love and, of course, marriage." He spit out the words as if they tasted foul.

"You've had setbacks before," Anne said, hardly able to credit this kind of reaction to a simple rejection. Privately Anne was cheering Julie for having the courage to hold out for what she wanted. It couldn't have been easy to turn him down. When Roy went after something, he did it with a determination that was difficult to ignore.

"This is more than a setback."

"How do you mean?"

Roy rubbed a hand tiredly down his face and shook his head. "I was foolish enough to believe she was different."

"Julie *is* different. She's special. I know you think every woman's like Aimee, but you're wrong."

"No, Mother, in Julie's case I'm right."

"Julie isn't anything like Aimee," she said adamantly.

"She just proved to me she is."

"What are you talking about?" He'd have to show her the evidence before Anne would believe him. Although she didn't know Julie well, Anne had sensed genuine goodness in her. She felt, too, that Julie had attained the spiritual and emotional insights that only someone who'd suffered could fully understand.

Roy reached inside his jacket and pulled out a wad of folded papers. "Read this."

Anne took the papers, opening them on the table. She put on her reading glasses and quickly scanned the contents. As far as she could see, it was a bunch of legal mumbo jumbo. "It's some sort of settlement offer," she said. "Oh, here's Julie's name."

"I know what it is," Roy barked, then cast her an apologetic glance. "Remember when I ran into her?"

"Yes, of course, your car collided with her bike. It's a miracle she wasn't hurt."

He gave an unpleasant laugh. "Correction, Mother. She was hurt twenty-five-thousand dollars' worth."

Anne snatched up the papers and skimmed them again.

"She signed the settlement offer," he pointed out. "A check's already been issued to her in the amount stated."

Anne knew that wasn't possible. Yet there was Julie's signature, plain as day.

Roy focused his gaze on the kitchen wall. "I pressured her at first, believing it was best to deal with the incident quickly rather than have her come back and bite me later. She repeatedly refused, and after a while I started to trust her.

"I finally decided she wasn't a gold digger. She had me convinced that money didn't mean a thing to her—and now this."

"Roy, I don't think—"

"You're holding the evidence in your hand," he countered, his voice raised in anger.

Only he wasn't really angry, Anne realized; he was hurt and disillusioned and growing more so by the minute. Oh, this was dreadful. It was as if God had broken a promise. Anne had felt so sure that Julie was the woman she'd been praying for all these years and now this…this betrayal.

"All along, Julie was holding out for more money." He rubbed his eyes as if he was exhausted. "I forgot about the settlement when we started dating." He expelled a shaky breath. "Then she declined to move in with me, and that was the end of our fine romance. Except that I remembered we hadn't settled her so-called accident and I contacted her again."

Anne didn't say anything, waiting for him to continue his story.

"She wouldn't talk to me about it."

Anne silently applauded; perhaps everything wasn't lost, after all.

"The thing is, Mother, I thought she was different, that I could trust her."

Anne reached across the table and patted his hand.

"Then she proved I can't."

"Roy, let's not be hasty here. Yes, it looks bad, but let's face it—if Julie was interested in your money, she would've moved in with you. Don't make the mistake of judging her too harshly."

"Harshly?" he snapped. "It isn't just about the money. I went over to her place to see her, to talk to her. I hoped we could find a way to compromise.... All I wanted was for the two of us to be together."

Anne bit her lower lip, afraid of what he'd say next.

"I told her if she didn't want to move in with me, I'd be willing to set her up in her own apartment."

After a moment, Anne managed to speak. "She wasn't interested in that, either, I take it."

"Not at all."

Anne smiled to herself. Perhaps, just perhaps, Julie was everything she'd hoped for. Surely God wouldn't be so cruel as to send another Aimee into Roy's life.

"I reminded her that I wasn't offering marriage, but she could have the next-best thing. I made it clear that this was my final offer. If she said no, I was walking out that door once and for all."

"She was willing to accept that?"

He hung his head. "Apparently so. Then I brought up the settlement. I told her I wasn't upping the ante. If she was going to get anything out of me, she'd better sign."

"You left the papers with her?"

"Yes," he said bitterly. "I had my attorney contact her. This afternoon I got the signed papers by messenger, with the attorney's notice that the check had been mailed."

Roy looked so disheartened Anne ached once again to take him in her arms the way she had when he was small. He'd come to her for solace, but there was nothing she could do or say to ease this pain. Julie hadn't turned out to be the woman Anne had hoped, after all.

"She has her money, then?"

He nodded. "It's what she always wanted. Twenty-five thousand—no strings. I'll say one thing for her," he muttered cynically. "She was good."

Anne's shoulders sagged with disappointment. "Live and learn," she said under her breath.

"She came in right after Aimee that afternoon," Roy said, speaking almost to himself.

Anne leaned closer, certain she'd misunderstood. "Aimee was five years ago."

"No, Aimee was three days ago."

Anne thought her heart had stopped beating. She needed a couple of minutes to calm herself before she asked, "Aimee came to see you? Recently?"

Roy's gaze darted to hers. "I didn't mean to say anything—I shouldn't have. I apologize, Mom, for bringing up unpleasant memories."

"Tell me," Anne insisted.

Roy tilted back his chair, staring at the ceiling. "She stopped by the office, unannounced and unwelcome."

"Whatever for?"

"Why does Aimee do anything?" Roy said sarcastically. "She wanted something."

"What?"

Roy shook his head as if to say he still didn't really believe it. "She came with some ridiculous story about my father loving me and wanting to see me again."

"I know Burton's tried to contact you," Anne said.

"Who told you that?"

She didn't want to get his assistant in trouble, but Ms. Johnson had volunteered the information. "It wouldn't do you any harm to talk to him, you know."

"I don't have anything to say to the man," Roy said bluntly.

Anne felt herself go rigid. "It's been five years since you last talked to your father. I know you don't want to hear this, but I think it's time you two called a truce." As difficult as it was, she gave Aimee credit for supporting Burton's desire to make peace with his son.

"We don't have anything in common."

"He's your *father*."

"He betrayed us both."

Anne didn't have a response to that. She wasn't in any position to defend Burton, and wouldn't. "At least Aimee tried to help."

Roy snickered. "Don't go painting her in any chivalrous light. She had her own agenda. She always has. I should've recognized it at the time, but fool that I am, I took her at face value."

"What do you mean?"

Roy looked away, as if he'd said more than he intended. "I called Dad."

"Oh, Roy, I'm so glad you did." Part of that was a lie, but for Roy's sake she was grateful. A son, no matter what his age, needed his father.

He shook his head. "The conversation didn't go well, but I did learn an important piece of information."

Anne waited for him to explain.

"Aimee wants something big and expensive for Christmas, and Dad told her if he was going to plunk down thousands of dollars, she could do something for him."

"I see."

"He got what *he* wanted," Roy murmured. "I phoned him, just like she knew I would."

Aimee's manipulativeness had left Roy deeply cynical toward women; Julie's actions, unfortunately, had only confirmed that cynicism.

"How is your father?" Anne asked despite herself.

"You honestly care?" Roy's eyes were skeptical. "The man betrayed you, cheated you, and now you're concerned about his well-being? Don't be, Mother. Dad is getting exactly what he deserves."

"And what's that?"

He laughed. "Aimee. She's spending money faster than he can earn it."

"I'm sorry to hear that."

He cast her a doubting look.

Anne grinned. "Okay, that's not entirely true. But I really don't harbor any ill will toward your father. I've gotten on with my life. After the divorce, I felt used up and old, but now…" She got to her feet, still talking, and poured them each a coffee. "Well, the thing is, I found a whole new part of myself. I believe that our world was created with a sense of order. For every loss, there's a gain. Sometimes we're so blinded by the loss that we don't see the gain, don't recognize the gift." She paused, handing him his cup. "There's a wonderful gift for you in Aimee's betrayal, and one day you'll discover it."

Roy gazed at her with puzzlement and what seemed to be renewed respect. "You're a better person than I'll ever be."

Anne hated to ask again, but she was curious about her ex-husband. "Is your father…well?"

"What you really mean is, does he have any regrets?" Roy supplied for her.

There was some truth in that. "I don't think your father would admit any regrets to you, would he?"

Roy agreed. "Not in so many words, but it was easy enough to read between the lines."

Anne held her breath. So often she'd speculated about Burton and his new life. "Other than financially, is everything as it should be?"

"I don't think so. My guess is that Dad's having trouble keeping up with Aimee, uh, physically. Now that he's in his sixties, his work pace is taking its toll. He didn't sound happy."

"How *did* he sound?"

"Tired, exasperated, overworked."

"I thought your father would've retired by now."

"He can't," Roy said, "not with the speed at which Aimee is spending his money, and that's only the half of it."

"What do you mean?"

Roy shrugged and she thought for a moment that he wasn't going to tell her. "It also seems that Aimee's taken a liking to some of his clients—men who are seeking comfort after their divorces."

Anne was shocked. "Your father actually told you that?"

"Not exactly, but close." He shook his head in disgust. "She spouted all these platitudes about loving my father and building a bridge between us, and it was all lies." A muscle leaped in the side of his jaw. "She came with a purpose, which she advanced with her lies. She wanted something from me, just the same as Julie did."

Obviously, it was Julie who was on his mind. "No matter what papers Julie signed," Anne said, "I still don't think she's anything like Aimee."

"I've been fooled before, and I'm not going to let it happen again."

"I know." It broke her heart to admit that. "I wish I wasn't leaving you over Christmas."

He frowned, and then smiled. "Do you honestly think it bothers me? Christmas doesn't mean a thing to me."

"But, Roy, it should." Her heart ached for her only child. Nothing had worked out as she'd hoped. Her prayers, like so many before, had gone unanswered. Roy would be alone on Christmas Day.

Twenty-Three

Three days before Christmas, Julie knew this was destined to be the worst one of her life. She was already dealing with the loss of her mother and now she'd lost Roy, too.

Even her twin sister's call hadn't raised her spirits. Julie ended the conversation and then wandered into the living room, where her father sat watching the evening news.

One look at her, and Dean grabbed the remote control and muted the volume. "That bad?"

"I feel just awful."

"Because of Fletcher?"

Slumping into the chair next to him, Julie nodded. "I don't know what happened. I went to see him on Wednesday afternoon, and it was as if he'd shut me out of his life." Julie still didn't understand it. He'd been so cold and defensive; nothing she said had reached him. And their second meeting, a day later, was even worse.

"Is it the settlement money?"

She shrugged. She'd never intended to accept a dime of that settlement, but Roy had angered her so much she'd agreed to his terms out of pure frustration. He seemed to believe all women were greedy for money and power.

"I was tired of fighting with him," she said in a subdued voice.

"I know. Fletcher's gone far in the business world by the sheer strength of his determination."

"Only in this instance, he's wrong."

"I know, Kitten."

Her last angry exchange with Roy lingered in her mind. Furious, she'd signed those stupid papers. It was what he'd expected, what he'd demanded she do—and so she had. But oh, how she regretted it. She hated to end their relationship on such a negative note, but what choice did she have? Roy had cast her from his life as if she meant nothing.

"I don't know if he's capable of love," she murmured, hoping her father had some consolation to offer.

"Every human has the capacity to love," he said with such confidence that her heart surged with hope. "But a person's ability to love is only equal to his or her openness in receiving it."

Julie valued her father's wisdom. He was right; nothing she could say or do at this point had the potential to reach Roy. He had certain beliefs about her and about all women, and he'd made certain assumptions as a result.

"I'd like one last opportunity to talk to him," she said. Not because she expected to change his mind. That seemed doubtful. All she wanted was an opportunity to undo the damage they'd inflicted on each other.

Her father seemed to weigh her words. "Do you think seeing him again is wise?"

"I…don't know. Probably not," she said, but the need still burned within her. "I just feel so bad about the way we ended everything…."

"Fletcher's been out of the office for a few days, but he's back now."

"It's almost Christmas and…in the spirit of the holidays I thought…"

"You thought he might listen?"

"At least long enough to understand my reasons."

"Do you want to do this for you or for Fletcher?" her father asked.

The question was a valid one. Julie mulled it over, then answered as honestly as she could. "I don't know. I guess it's for me. I don't feel right leaving things the way they are. I can't imagine he'll see me, but I have to try."

"Then write him a letter."

"A letter," Julie repeated. "I doubt he'd read it."

"Does that matter?" her father asked. "You'll have said what you feel is necessary. Then you can let him go."

"True," she admitted, the idea taking shape. The more she thought about it, the more she realized how much had been left unsaid.

"Whether Fletcher reads it or not is up to him," her father said. "When feelings run this strong, sometimes letters are the best form of communication. There's less room for misunderstanding or argument."

Julie immediately felt relieved. Writing Roy, explaining her thoughts and emotions, was a solution she hadn't considered before. She might never learn if he'd read her letter, but she'd have the satisfaction of knowing she'd done everything she could. If he responded, good; that would mean there was still a chance. If, as she expected, she never heard from him again, she could find peace in the knowledge that she'd tried.

"Oh, Dad, I don't think I appreciate you nearly enough."

Dean merely grinned and picked up the television remote.

Composing the letter took all evening. Julie read it over repeatedly before she was satisfied. In the first paragraph, she thanked Roy for the good times they'd shared, for opening his home and his life to her for even this short while.

That had been the easy part of the letter. More difficult was discussing his utter rejection of her. Then she related her father's observation, telling Roy he could only trust her as much as he allowed himself to trust. In the last third of the letter, she apologized for her own angry response to his lack of faith.

It was midnight when she finished. Although she'd had trouble sleeping since their breakup, she experienced no such difficulty that night. Once again, she marveled at her father's wisdom. It really didn't matter whether Roy ever read her letter. In the process of articulating her reactions she'd found the peace she sought.

The next morning, the last day of school before winter break, Julie took the letter with her, planning to drop it off at the post office. School ended at noon, but after she'd had a festive lunch with the other teachers and straightened up her classroom, it was nearly three. If she posted the letter as she'd originally intended, he might not receive it until after Christmas. She had no idea what his Christmas plans were; maybe he'd already left for a Caribbean cruise or a country inn in Vermont, she thought whimsically. At one time, she'd hoped to invite him and his mother to join her and her father. She hadn't even had a chance to broach the subject.

Nor had she spoken to his mother since Saturday. Anne hadn't called her, and Julie didn't feel comfortable putting his mother in the middle of this awkward situation.

Although it meant facing Jason, the guard at the entrance, she decided to deliver the letter personally.

Julie felt his gaze on her the moment she pulled into the parking lot. His eyes didn't leave her until she'd parked in an empty slot and then climbed out of her car. Julie half expected the security guard to block the entrance. But Jason sat at his desk, one hand on the phone, obviously ready to call for reinforcements.

He got warily to his feet when she walked in, but remained solidly behind his desk, as if it afforded him protection.

"Stay away from me," Jason warned.

Startled, Julie glanced over her shoulder. No one else was there. She couldn't imagine why the burly guard would be afraid of *her.*

"I don't know what you did to me, lady, but I don't want a repeat of it, understand?"

"Jason," she said in her most conciliatory voice, "what in heaven's name are you talking about?"

"You know." He gestured theatrically. "Just stay right where you are. You're not allowed in this building."

Actually she'd expected that. "Not to worry, I don't have any intention of storming into Mr. Fletcher's office. I have a letter for him." She advanced slowly toward Jason's desk, not wanting to intimidate him any more than she already had, although how she'd done that was a mystery.

He backed away until he bumped into the wall behind him.

"All I ask is that you give Mr. Fletcher this letter," she said, careful to enunciate every word. "You don't need to deliver it yourself," she assured him, in case it was the prospect of an encounter with Roy that had unsettled him. "I'm sure Ms. Johnson will be more than happy to see that Mr. Fletcher receives it."

Jason's eyes moved past her and a chagrined expression appeared on his face.

Julie looked over her shoulder again to find Roy standing there. He'd clearly just stepped out of the elevator. Her first instinct, absurdly enough, was to turn tail and run. A second later, she seemed completely incapable of moving. Or breathing. Or anything else.

"What's Ms. Wilcoff doing in the building?" Roy asked the security guard as if Julie wasn't standing directly in front of him.

"She has a letter for you."

"Yes. I wrote you a letter." She hated the way her voice trembled, but she hadn't been prepared to see Roy. It wasn't supposed to happen like this!

Jason handed Roy the envelope, which he reluctantly accepted.

Julie's heart pounded in her ears. She had to escape as quickly as possible. "I'll leave now," she said.

"That would be best," Jason boomed. With his employer close at hand, he'd apparently regained his nerve. He escorted Julie to the front door, going so far as to push it open for her.

Julie felt Roy's eyes burning holes in her back as she exited the building. She walked at twice her normal speed, intent on getting away.

Then she heard footsteps behind her.

"What's in the letter?" Roy demanded, following her into the parking lot.

Julie fumbled for her car keys. "I suggest you read it." She stood by the driver's door, while Roy waited at the rear bumper.

"I'll bet you declared your love and described how anguished you are by our parting."

Julie wasn't taking the bait. Everything she wanted to say was in the letter; she had no intention of repeating it and then arguing over the points she'd made.

"I'm not interested in the account of your undying love."

Her hand shook so badly she had trouble pressing the button to automatically unlock her car door.

"You're no different from Aimee." He seemed to want to provoke her into losing her temper. "What's the matter? Don't you have anything to say?"

A painful breath worked its way through her lungs. "Most everything is in the letter, Roy, but I realize now that there are a few things I left out."

"Good. You can say them to my face."

She studied him then, really looked at him, and saw how unhappy he was. This was the most joyous season of the year, and Roy was miserable.

"I didn't say I loved you," she said, her voice gaining strength and control. "As you'll discover if you read my letter."

He arched his brow in that all-too-familiar sarcastic way.

"But the truth is, I do."

"Spare me, please."

"It's foolish, I suppose, but I always did like a challenge, and you, Roy Fletcher, are definitely that." She even managed a brief smile.

Again the sardonic arched brow.

"The thing is," she continued, determined not to let his cynicism destroy her, "I do love you and it's up to you to accept that love or reject it."

He said nothing.

"We haven't known each other long, but in that time, I've learned a great deal about the kind of man you are. You have a tremendous capacity to give of yourself, a tremendous capacity to love." She thought of the fact that he'd hired her father and that, unknown to his mother, he'd bought her paintings. She recalled the afternoon he'd come to her soccer game—and so much more. His unpretentious enjoyment of her simple meals. The loyalty his staff felt toward him…

He held up his hand. "Not interested."

"I know, and that saddens me, because I'm going to get in my car and drive away. I didn't come here to argue with you—I didn't even expect to see you."

"It seems to me you planned it perfectly so you would."

Did he honestly believe she'd somehow manipulated their simultaneous presence in the company foyer? "I didn't. But whether I did or not is of little concern."

He shrugged. Julie knew he must have some feelings for her, otherwise he wouldn't be standing here now, wouldn't be listening to her. If this was her only chance to get through to him, then she might as well give it her best shot.

"You have the ability to decide what you want out of life, Roy. You can go on living behind your hard exterior, blocking out anyone who has the potential to teach you about love, or you can—"

"I already said I wasn't interested in love. I made that clear from the beginning," he snapped. "What is it with you? Every other word out of your mouth is something about love. Yeah, right! Well, I can't help wondering how much *love* you'd really feel if I wasn't who I am."

"Who are you, Roy?"

"You know what I mean." He gestured toward the building that stood as evidence of his prosperity.

"Are you the rich and successful entrepreneur?"

"You know what I mean," he said again.

"Unfortunately, I don't," she told him, opening her car door. "I thought I knew who you were, but I guess I was wrong."

"I thought I knew who *you* were," he retorted, his eyes blazing, "but you proved *me* wrong. All you care about is the size of my checking account and what you can get out of me."

She refused to listen to any more. With a heavy heart, she climbed inside the car.

"You're—"

She closed the door to drown out his words, then inserted the key into the ignition. When she glanced in her rearview mirror, Roy was gone.

Julie exited the parking lot, and as soon as she was out of sight, she pulled to the curb and wept tears of pain and grief.

Leaning her forehead against the steering wheel, she knew she'd never see Roy Fletcher again.

Twenty-Four

"This is absolutely terrible," Goodness lamented. All afternoon, they'd watched Julie put on a good front for her father's sake. She could just picture the scene in Heaven when they returned only seven hours from now. It was Christmas Eve, their deadline. Soon they'd be required to stand with the angelic host singing praises to the newborn King. Except this year, Shirley, Goodness and Mercy would arrive from Earth without having fulfilled their mission. Goodness wouldn't be able to look a single friend in the face. Well, she wasn't accepting defeat that easily.

"It can't get much worse," Mercy agreed.

"We've got to do something." Shirley was back to her pacing in front of the Wilcoffs' Christmas tree. The living room was empty, with Julie in her room and Dean overseeing a last-minute security check of the Fletcher building.

"This is your fault," Goodness said, glaring at Mercy. "If you hadn't been so busy tossing salmon in Pike Place Market and holding security guards by the knees, we might've made some headway."

"Give it up," Mercy growled. "Besides, we both know you had a hand on Jason, too. I couldn't have held him back all by myself. That guy has muscles."

"Stop." Shirley planted herself between the other two and shook her head. "We don't have time to play the blame game."

"You're telling me," Goodness moaned. "It's already five o'clock."

"That means we have seven paltry hours," Shirley said, glancing at the old-fashioned clock on the fireplace mantel.

"Woe is we." Goodness couldn't believe that a prayer request could go so wrong. They'd worked harder on this one than on any previous request. In years past, they'd each received separate assignments, but she'd assumed that with their combined efforts this one would've been simplicity itself. Not so. And if there was anything Goodness hated, it was having to admit she'd failed. "We've just *got* to do something." They had a few hours left. Just a few.

"But what?" Mercy cried.

"Think," Shirley ordered. "There's a way. There's always a way."

Defeated and depressed, Goodness walked into the darkened kitchen and threw open the refrigerator door. For a long moment, she studied the contents. It was easy to understand why so many humans turned to food for comfort. A pan of something dipped in chocolate was bound to improve any situation.

"I had hope until Roy threw out her letter," Mercy said. "Without reading it."

"How could he?" Shirley asked, although the question was rhetorical. "I thought humans were curious about things." That was a characteristic they shared with angels.

"I'm sure he was tempted," Shirley said, sadness weighting her words. "However, his fear was even stronger."

"He was afraid?" Goodness was unable to decipher human reasoning. "Of what?"

"Of changing his mind," Shirley explained. "He knew if he read Julie's letter, he might be swayed. He couldn't let that happen. He couldn't hold on to his anger if he allowed himself to feel her love."

"But love is what he needs!"

Goodness wanted to weep with frustration. Shirley was right. Roy had closed himself off from love, even though he needed it, even though he wanted it. He equated love with pain. Opening his heart made him vulnerable, and he couldn't risk that after what his father and Aimee had done.

"I'd so hoped for a better outcome," Shirley murmured forlornly, "especially for Anne's sake."

"Anne," Goodness repeated, remembering Shirley's previous connection to Roy's mother. She studied the former Guardian Angel and detected a suspicious smile in her eyes. Quickly Shirley looked away.

"Shirley," Goodness pressed, certain now that her friend was up to something, "you're holding out on us."

"Shirley?" Mercy joined in. "What did you do?"

A giggle escaped, followed by another. "I made a quick trip to New York, and…well, you'll see soon enough."

"Tell us!"

"And ruin the surprise?"

"Does it have to do with Roy and Julie?"

The laughter in Shirley's eyes faded. "Sorry, no."

"With Anne?"

The humor was back and she nodded. "All in good time, my friends, all in good time."

"But what are we going to do about Roy and Julie?" Even with the clock ticking away the last hours, Goodness refused to give up. Somehow or other, they *had* to accomplish their goal.

"That letter could always find its way back into his life," Goodness suggested. Of course, that might entail a bit of detective work…

"I will serve the Lord with my whole heart," Mercy said,

"but I am not digging around in someone's garbage. That just isn't me."

"You would if it meant we could answer this prayer request, wouldn't you?"

Mercy looked uncertain. With her arms crossed, she cocked her head to one side and shrugged. "Well…maybe."

"Then let's get to it," Goodness said with renewed hope. "We'll find the letter, *and* we'll make sure he reads it."

"How are we going to do that?" Shirley asked.

"We'll figure it out when the time comes," Mercy assured her. "You can't expect us to have all the answers, can you?"

"I don't expect all the answers," Goodness said, "but *one* answer would be nice."

"Why make things easy?" Mercy asked pertly.

"Right."

With renewed purpose the three hurried to Roy's condo. This was their last chance, and they had to make it work.

Roy picked up the remote control and automatically flipped through the channels. He didn't stay on any one for more than a few seconds. His patience was nonexistent, and his irritation mounted by the minute. Roy didn't understand why he felt like this. He should be thrilled. His company had just had its best year to date. When any number of dot-com businesses were fast becoming dot-gone businesses, his own was thriving. Money and happiness, however, didn't seem to be connected.

Roy had dreaded spending Christmas with his mother. Being continually reminded of everything she'd lost in the divorce was too much for him, especially during the holiday season. Pretending was beyond him. Now she was in New York with her college friend and he could do as he pleased.

Only nothing pleased him.

"What did you do in other years?" he asked himself out loud.

Work had dominated his life for so long that he had no idea how to relax. Christmas Eve should be special in some way, except it wasn't. If he was with Julie, it would be... He refused to think about Julie. She was out of his life and he was out of hers. Good. That was exactly how he wanted it.

With nothing on television to intrigue him, Roy sat down at his computer. Because he felt he should know what was going on in the world, he left the local news channel playing in the background. He decided to surf the Internet. Maybe he'd get so absorbed investigating Web sites that the evening would vanish without his realizing where all those hours had gone; it had happened often enough before. Then he could forget that it was Christmas Eve, forget he was alone.

That didn't seem to work, either.

No Web site interested him for more than a few minutes.

"A Christmas story of generosity that's guaranteed to touch everyone's heart," the newscaster said from behind him. "Details after a word from our sponsors."

Roy was in no mood to be cheered by anyone's generosity. He turned around to reach for the remote so he could switch off the TV. Love and goodwill were not in keeping with his current mood.

The remote was missing.

It had been on the coffee table just a moment ago and now it was nowhere in sight. He started lifting papers and cushions in his search, but he always kept it in the same place on the coffee table. It was gone.

A sentimental commercial about a college student arriving home on Christmas Eve began to play. It was a sappy ad, meant to tug at the heartstrings. Roy had never liked it. He groaned and renewed his search for the remote.

Then the female newscaster was back. "Tonight we have the story of a single gift of twenty-five thousand dollars donated anonymously at a Salvation Army bell station."

The scene changed to one outside a local shopping mall. Cars whizzed past as the camera zoomed toward a lone figure standing in front of a big red pot. Dressed in his overcoat and muffler, a scarf tied around his neck, the volunteer diligently rang his bell, reminding everyone that there were others less fortunate this Christmas.

Roy continued his search with one eye on the television screen. He knew he should simply lean over and hit the power switch, but for some reason, he didn't.

"An anonymous donor came up to Gary Wilson yesterday afternoon and slipped a cashier's check for twenty-five thousand dollars into his collection canister. This is the largest single donation a Salvation Army bell ringer has ever received in our area."

Roy froze, rooted to the spot, his quest for the TV remote forgotten.

"Gary, can you tell us anything about the person who gave you that check?" the reporter asked, shoving a microphone in front of the volunteer's face.

The poor man looked like a deer caught on the freeway, lights coming at him from every direction. "No," he finally blurted. "I didn't notice anyone who seemed rich enough to give away that kind of money."

The reporter spoke into the microphone again. "That money will go a long way toward making this Christmas a happy one for a lot of community families, won't it?" Once more she thrust the microphone at the Salvation Army volunteer.

"I think it was a woman," Gary Wilson said. "It was about the middle of my shift, I'd say. Things were moving pretty briskly and then this tall gal came up." He paused. "She said Merry Christmas, and she smiled. But I don't know if it was her or not. It could've been." He punctuated his comments with a shrug. "Or maybe not. Could've been that short fellow who wouldn't look me in the eye. Real short, he was."

"Elf-size?" the reporter asked with a grin.

Gary nodded. "Yup, elf-size."

"Well, it looks like Santa won't have to work nearly as hard in the Seattle area this year. Back to you, Jean."

"Thank you, Tracy," the female announcer said.

Roy sank onto the edge of his plush leather sofa. It was Julie; she *had* to be the "tall gal" the volunteer had mentioned. This was a calculated move on her part. She'd...

His thoughts ground to a halt. Julie hadn't done it for the publicity. With a cashier's check, she wasn't expecting to be honored for the donation. The truth was, Roy couldn't prove it'd been her. But it seemed more than a coincidence that the donation was the same amount as the check he'd given her.

Leaning back, he rubbed his face, then glanced at the coffee table. To his utter astonishment, there sat the remote control. He looked again, harder. Nah, couldn't be. He leaned forward again. It hadn't been there a moment ago. That wasn't the only thing on the coffee table, either.

Julie's letter lay there, right in front of him.

This was the envelope he'd recently discarded. The envelope with his name carefully written on the front in Julie's smooth and even cursive hand.

Roy gasped, leaped up and quickly looked around. Something very strange was happening.

He'd been working too hard, he decided, brushing the hair away from his forehead. He left his hand there as he tried to reason this out in his troubled mind.

The pressure had become too much for him. That was it. What hadn't made sense a few minutes ago now seemed perfectly logical.

The envelope almost glowed, daring him to open it. When he'd originally received the letter, the temptation to read it had been almost overwhelming. But instead, Roy had tossed it in the garbage as soon as he got home. Then, because he couldn't get it out of his mind, he'd carried the garbage from his kitchen to the chute in the utility room. The chute deposited all garbage in a Dumpster in the basement.

Yet here was the letter, back in his possession.

"Obviously I should read it," he muttered to himself, wondering if he should look for the phone number of a psychiatrist first. This couldn't be happening. But it was.

Sinking back onto the couch, he picked up the letter. He didn't *want* to read it, yet from the first word on, he felt compelled to continue. His cynicism gradually eroded as he recognized her sincerity with every sentence. He understood her exasperation with him and respected the honesty and integrity that underlined her actions, her beliefs. The most powerful of all the emotions that flowed through him as he read her letter was love. *Her* love.

Earlier, she'd told him she hadn't written that she loved him, but he felt it in every word.

After reading the letter once, he set it aside and tried to take in everything she'd said. Then he read it again, more slowly this time, sometimes rereading a sentence twice.

"She's right," he whispered. "She's so right." He'd been given this chance. The most wonderful gift of his life was within his grasp and he was rejecting it. He could allow what Aimee had done to taint the rest of his days, or he could move forward.

Christmas Eve, and he was alone. But he didn't have to be.

He could spend Christmas with Julie.

Christmas and every other day.

A surge of joy rushed through him. He wasn't waiting a moment longer.

Twenty-Five

For her father's sake, Julie was trying to make this first Christmas without her mother as cheerful as she could. For dinner on Christmas Eve, she served the meal Darlene had always prepared. A big pot of homemade clam chowder simmered on the stove and a loaf of freshly baked bread waited on the counter. Although she didn't have much of an appetite, Julie was determined to sit down, smile and enjoy their evening together. Emily had phoned earlier, and Julie had done her best to sound optimistic. She didn't know how well she'd succeeded.

"Something smells mighty good," her father said as he stepped into the kitchen. He lifted the lid from the large pot and gave Julie a smile. "Your mother's recipe?"

She nodded.

Her father closed his eyes and breathed in the scent of the chowder. "I feel that she's with us."

"I do, too, Dad."

"For the first time since she died, I feel her presence more profoundly than I do her absence. I'm sure it has to do with Christmas."

"I'm sure it does, too."

"She was such a Christmas person."

Her father wasn't telling Julie anything she didn't know. The house was always beautifully decorated for the holidays. Her mother spent endless hours seeing to every detail. Even her Christmas cards were special—because she wrote individual messages to each person. She baked and cooked for weeks beforehand, and every December she presented their neighbors with gifts of homemade cookies and candies. Julie had made an attempt to do the same, but she didn't have the time, the patience or the skill to match her mother's efforts. Her lone batch of fudge was a humbling experience and she ditched it before her father got home to see what a mess she'd made.

"Everything's ready," she announced. Instead of eating in the kitchen as they routinely did at night, they were using the dining room. After dinner and the dishes, they'd leave for Christmas Eve services at church.

"I'll bring out the chowder," her father said as the doorbell rang.

Julie frowned. "Are you expecting anyone?"

Her father shook his head. "I'll get it."

While her father dealt with whoever was at the door, Julie ladled soup into the tureen her mother had saved for special occasions. The bread, a recipe handed down for more than three generations, was a holiday tradition, too. Julie remembered how her mother had called Emily and Julie to the kitchen table and taught them the importance of kneading the dough. They'd loved doing it.

"It appears we have company," her father said from behind her.

Julie turned around. Had there been anything in her hands, it would have crashed to the floor.

Roy Fletcher stood beside her father, his arms full of gifts, which he arranged under the tree.

"I'll set an extra place at the table," Dean said as though it was a foregone conclusion that Roy would be joining them.

Julie was cemented to the floor. Had her life depended on it, she couldn't have moved. "What are you doing here?" she choked out.

"I read your letter."

Better late than never, she wanted to tell him, but speaking had become rather difficult.

"Oh."

"It was a beautiful letter."

Her father walked past Julie. "The two of you can sort everything out after dinner. You will stay, won't you, Roy?"

"Yes. Thank you, Dean…." He nodded, although the entire time he was speaking, his eyes were on Julie.

"Come on." Her father urged them toward the dining room.

As if in a dream, Julie left the kitchen. Roy held out her chair for her, and her father set the soup tureen in the middle of the table, moving aside the centerpiece of fir branches and silver bells Julie had created. He hurried back to the kitchen for the bread. When they were all gathered at the table, they joined hands for grace.

Julie bowed her head and closed her eyes. She'd prayed for this, prayed Roy would feel her love, prayed he'd know she was sincere. Still, there was a sense of unreality about tonight. Her father's words, asking God to bless their meal, barely registered in her mind. At the sound of his "Amen," she lifted her head to discover Roy watching her. Her breathing stopped at the unmistakable love she saw in his eyes. She didn't understand what had happened to him, but whatever it was had completely changed him. Or, more accurately, made him the person he was meant to be. The person he really was.

"Your coming by is a pleasant surprise," her father said conversationally as he stood and reached for Roy's bowl.

"I should've called first," Roy said, and his gaze, which had been on Julie, moved to her father. "I hope it isn't an imposition." His eyes returned to her.

"Not at all. Julie made plenty. You do like clam chowder, don't you?"

"Yes, very much." Again his eyes briefly left her. "Julie and I had clam chowder the first time we went to dinner."

"At an old college hangout of Roy's," she added.

Roy smiled.

"Julie baked the bread this evening," her father said proudly as he reached for Julie's soup bowl next. "It's her mother's recipe. She did an excellent job of it, too."

Julie passed the bread basket to Roy.

"It's an old German recipe. Her mother was of German ancestry," Dean went on to explain.

"I'm sure it's excellent."

"It is," her father said. "Julie's mother was an exceptional woman." He ladled soup into his own bowl and then sat down.

Her hands shaking, Julie offered Roy the butter.

Her father apparently wasn't finished. "Darlene used to say it was a couple's duty to keep their eyes open, their ears open, their hearts open and their mouths shut." He laughed robustly.

Roy grinned.

Julie was following that bit of advice at the moment. She couldn't possibly have carried on a civil conversation. All she could think about was the fact that Roy was in her home, having Christmas Eve dinner with her father and her. As far as she was concerned, this was nothing short of a miracle.

"I hope you'll attend church services with us later." Her father turned to Roy.

"I'd be delighted."

"My wife had a lot of wonderful sayings," he murmured, reverting to his previous topic. "She said interruptions were simply God's appointments."

"I interrupted you this evening," Roy said.

"Now, Dad…" All this talk about her mother and God would probably confuse Roy. Christmas Eve was not the time to eulogize her mother. Then it occurred to Julie that her father needed to do this, that he wanted to remember and honor her by sharing her favorite expressions.

"Please go on," Roy said. "I'd like to hear some of the other things your wife said."

Her father grinned and put down his spoon. "My wife firmly believed that God sends pain into our lives for a reason."

Roy frowned. "That's an interesting thought. Most people don't think of God in terms of pain."

"I know," Dean said. "Now, Roy, I realize from what Julie's told me that you've seen more than your fair share of emotional turmoil. I don't mean to discount that, but my wife always said we should lean into the pain, instead of running away from it."

"Like driving into a skid in order to correct it?" Roy suggested.

"Exactly," Dean crowed. "We have to *use* the experience. We can become either bitter or better."

Julie wasn't sure where her father was going with this conversation. "Daddy?"

"She only calls me that when she's upset."

"It's okay, Julie. I want to hear this," Roy said.

"Good, because I think it's something you need to hear." Her father had given up all pretense of eating. "Now it seems to me that you're interested in my little girl."

Julie knew her cheeks must be flaming. All this spiritual talk wasn't like her father, who kept his faith private. She couldn't imagine why he was saying the things he was.

"I care a great deal for Julie," Roy confessed.

Julie nearly dropped her spoon. As it was, the utensil clattered against the china bowl.

Roy glanced at her. "Unfortunately, it took me a while to understand what I was doing."

"So it seems." Her father gestured grandly with a piece of bread. "But all's well that ends well, right?"

"Right." He turned to meet Julie's eyes. "You're the one who anonymously donated that twenty-five thousand dollars to the Salvation Army, aren't you?"

Julie went very still. "Is that why you're here?"

"No, but it was a catalyst. The bell—so to speak—that woke me up."

"How did you know?" She'd done it anonymously for a reason.

"You haven't seen the news, have you?"

Julie was aghast. "It was on the evening news?"

"Channel Four."

"I watched Channel Four earlier and didn't see anything about it," her father said.

"It was there," Roy insisted. "They interviewed a man by the name of Gary Wilson, a volunteer stationed at the Alderwood Mall." He looked at Julie. "It *was* you who gave that check to the Salvation Army, wasn't it?"

For a second, she considered misleading him, then decided against it. "Would it matter?"

Roy thought for a moment, then shook his head. "No. I don't care what you did with the money because I know in my heart that you love me."

"Those are mighty sweet words," her father said, grinning from ear to ear.

"Dad!"

"Now, Roy, you say you care for Julie. Does that mean you love her?"

"Dad!" she cried again. She couldn't believe that her father would ask such a thing, especially with her sitting there.

"I love her."

"Good," her father said nonchalantly, as if men regularly talked this way at the dining room table.

Roy chuckled, but Julie spoke before he could say anything else. "Would you two kindly involve me in this conversation?"

"She's right," Roy said.

"Now *I'll* be the one to say those are some mighty sweet words," Julie muttered. It was the first time she could remember Roy admitting she was right about anything.

"I should warn you," her father said, leaning toward him. "She's got a stubborn streak."

"I know all about it," Roy whispered back.

Julie rolled her eyes. "Who are you calling stubborn?"

"Well," her father said. "Enough squabbling. Now if you two will excuse me, I'll get ready for church."

Julie didn't stop him although there was at least an hour before they needed to leave. She heard him turn on the radio in his room, presumably to give them greater privacy.

All of a sudden Julie and Roy were sitting at the dining room table alone. She wanted to remind him of his claim that he wasn't interested in love—and then remembered her mother's saying about keeping her ears open and her mouth shut. Good advice, and once again she planned on taking it.

"You don't have anything you want to say?" Roy asked, sounding uncharacteristically hesitant.

"I was about to ask you the same thing."

Roy took her hand and clasped it tightly. "This might not make a whole lot of sense, but I feel as though I got specific orders to come here tonight."

"Orders from whom? Your mother?"

"No… I have no idea who sent me, but I know beyond a doubt that I was supposed to be here."

Her heart began to beat faster. "Did you want to come?"

"More than anything, Julie, only I didn't realize it. I was doing what your mother said—running away from the pain."

"Oh, how I wish you'd known her."

"I think I already do," he said. "I know *you,* Julie, and I know your heart is good and that you have a gift for reaching out to others."

She looked away, uncomfortable with his compliments.

"I know you aren't influenced by money and that I can trust you with my heart."

"Your heart?" she repeated, her voice low and unsteady.

"I once asked you to move in with me."

Her throat started to close again, and she found it almost impossible to speak. "Is that why you're here?" she managed.

"No. I can say that was a mistake. I want to make you a permanent part of my life."

"Are…are you asking me to marry you?"

His fingers tightened around hers. "That would be a good place to start."

"You mean there's more?"

He chuckled. "About fifty years more, I'd say. Longer, if we're lucky. I'd like to begin our new life soon. Is that all right by you?"

"Children?"

He nodded. "A dozen, at least."

"Roy, be serious!"

"Okay, two or three, whatever we decide when the time comes. My mother's anxious for grandchildren and I wouldn't dream of disappointing her."

This was all happening so fast Julie couldn't keep up.

A strangled ringing sound startled her, and she looked around.

"It's my cell," Roy said, removing it from his pocket. He flipped the tiny phone open and glanced at the number. "My mother. I wonder why she's calling me so late. It's after eleven in New York."

"Answer it," Julie said. "We have some great news."

He looked at her expectantly.

Julie smiled. "You can tell her I've accepted your marriage proposal."

Roy's eyes were warm and loving as he reached for her with one hand, pushing the talk button on his cell phone with the other.

This was the most wonderful Christmas Eve of her life, and Julie gave silent thanks.

Was it a coincidence that "Hark the Herald Angels Sing" began to play on the radio at that very moment?

Twenty-Six

"Roy! Oh, Roy!" Anne was so excited she could hardly speak. "In a million years you won't believe what's happened."

"I have some pretty incredible news, too," he said.

Despite her preoccupation with her own joy, Anne could hear the happiness in her son's voice. "Tell me," she said.

"Julie has agreed to be my wife."

Tears of joy instantly pricked Anne's eyes. This was much more wonderful than she'd dared dream. "That's marvelous!"

"We haven't set a date, but I know it'll be soon. I've been waiting my entire life for her, Mom. I can't believe what a fool I was all this time. You must have wanted to throw up your hands."

"I prayed that God would send a special woman into your life," she whispered. Her prayer had been heartfelt, but she'd almost given up hope. Coping with her own problems, struggling to keep her head above water financially, Anne had tried hard to help her son. It had seemed hopeless for so long, she'd lost confidence that any woman was capable of touching his heart. And then he'd met Julie....

"Let me put her on the phone," Roy said.

"Yes, please." Anne felt so full of happiness she was practically overwhelmed. So much good news, and all at once.

"Anne…" Julie's tentative voice came over Anne's cell phone.

"Julie, Merry Christmas!" Anne burst out. "Roy gave me this phone for Christmas, and you're the first call I've made on it. I always thought of them as a nuisance, but tonight it's worth its weight in gold. I understand my son's finally come to his senses and asked you to marry him."

"He did and it didn't take me long to answer him, either."

"You're going to be a beautiful bride and exactly the wife he needs."

"Thank you—I certainly plan to try. I feel so blessed."

"Oh, me, too," Anne said fervently.

"I'll give the phone back to Roy now."

Anne could hear soft, loving sounds as the phone was transferred back to her son. "All right, Mother," Roy said, "I'm glad you're using your new cell. Now what's your news?"

"You won't believe this," she said again, and because she couldn't help it, she broke into giggles.

"Then tell me," Roy said.

"My painting of the angel sold."

"Congratulations! From the excitement in your voice, it must've been for a lot of money. The last I heard, you thought it might go for as much as twenty-five thousand."

"Try a hundred and fifty."

"What?"

"A bidding war drove up the price, but that's not the best part."

"What's the best part? What could possibly be better than that?"

"Oh, Roy, just you wait until I tell you *who* bought the painting." She paused, relishing the justice of it. "The check was written by Burton Fletcher. Your father."

Her announcement was followed by shocked silence.

"Why would Dad write you a check for that amount of money?" Roy finally asked.

"First," Anne explained, "he didn't know it was me."

"But—"

"Since I paint under the name of Mary Fleming, your father had no way of knowing that the woman who painted the angel was his ex-wife. Marta knew, of course, and she already had someone else interested, so she was able to use the other party to drive up the price."

"Go back to the beginning," Roy said.

"Marta—you remember my college friend who runs an art gallery here in New York?"

"Yes, yes, of course I remember her. You're staying at her place. Go on with your story."

"Well, when she shipped the painting to New York and hung it in the gallery, she put up a sign that said it wasn't for sale. But then Aimee came into the gallery and fell in love with it."

"Aimee," Roy repeated. "When she stopped by the office, she'd obviously been on a recent shopping spree. And, of course, there was her bargain with Dad—a phone call from me in exchange for…your painting, as it turns out."

"She wanted my angel in the worst way."

"And Dad actually forked out that kind of money to buy it for her."

"He did," Anne said, unable to keep the laughter from her voice. "But he had no idea he was giving me a big chunk of what I should've gotten in the first place. He cheated me with the divorce settlement and now…"

"You always did say that what goes around comes around," Roy said, sounding as satisfied as she was. "I think that painting must be very special."

"Thank you, Roy. I do, too, but I never *dreamed* it would sell for such an outrageous amount of money."

234   *Debbie Macomber*

"Does Dad know yet?" her son asked.

"I'm not telling him." Although it was tempting to do so, Anne had resisted. "I suspect that sooner or later he'll discover it on his own."

"Yes, I suppose he will. I'd love to be a fly on the wall when he figures it out."

"There's more good news," Anne said, unable to contain herself. "Marta said she could sell as many angel paintings as I want to paint. There seems to be a real demand for them now. I think I've finally found my niche."

"That's great, Mom."

Her son seemed genuinely pleased for her. "I'm planning to paint one for you and Julie as a wedding gift. It seems to me that we've all had angels watching over us."

"We'd like that very much."

"Marta and her husband—"

"I thought they'd separated."

Anne had nearly forgotten. With so much else going on, her friend's news had slipped her mind. "Jack and Marta are back together. Jack *was* seeing someone else, but apparently it wasn't as serious as Marta assumed. They're going to a counselor and are determined to work on their marriage."

"I'm glad for them."

"Life just seems to get better and better," Anne said, sighing softly, tired now and elated at the same time.

"Yes, it does," her son agreed. "Better and better."

"We did it!" Goodness was thrilled. Leaping up and down in the choir loft at the First Christian Church of North Seattle, she didn't even try to sit still. The church was rapidly filling as families streamed in from the vestibule.

Roy, Julie and Dean walked into the crowded sanctuary and found seats near the front. They were too late to find a pew in the back, where Dean preferred to sit.

"Isn't the altar lovely?" Shirley said with a sigh, pointing toward the poinsettias arranged around the table that held the Advent wreath. All four candles were lit, their flames flickering, little dances of delight.

"I wouldn't believe it if I hadn't seen Roy propose to Julie with my own eyes," Mercy said contentedly. "I have to tell you, scenes like this always get to me."

"Do they now," Gabriel said from behind them.

Shirley, Goodness and Mercy whirled around to face the Archangel. Goodness held her breath, convinced that Gabriel was going to chastise them for their earthly manipulations. They'd become far more involved in the things of the world than ever before, but surely Gabriel had made allowances on their behalf, knowing the challenge they'd had with Roy.

"Did you see Roy and Julie?" Goodness pointed. The proof of their success was sitting directly below.

"I did," Gabriel said, and nodded approvingly. "I must say you three used some unconventional methods to fulfill your mission. Tell me, what did Roy learn from all this?"

A prayer couldn't be answered unless there was a lesson learned.

"His lesson was about love," Shirley answered. "His mother's love touched him. Her prayers for her son were heard by all of Heaven, and God sent us to show Roy that he *could* find love."

"Very good," Gabriel said. "But then, you always knew that, didn't you, Shirley?"

The former Guardian Angel nodded. "I did. Anne was such a special child. I knew she'd grow up to be a special woman, and I was right."

"Can you give us a peek into the future?" Mercy asked, crowding between Goodness and Shirley in an effort to gain Gabriel's attention.

"Yes, please." Goodness added her request.

Only a few were granted the privilege of gazing into the future, and Gabriel was one.

"Tell me about Anne," Shirley pleaded.

"Your Anne will continue to paint for a number of productive years."

"Angels?"

"Yes, and landscapes. The fees she earns from the angel paintings will support her far and above what she ever imagined. She'll become well-known for her work. In the years ahead, she'll be recognized as a fine and talented artist. People will pay high prices to own one of Mary Fleming's paintings."

"I'm so pleased," Shirley said happily.

"And to think it all started with you," Goodness said to her. The instant the words were out, she realized what she'd done—alerted Gabriel to the fact that Shirley had appeared to Anne. She clapped both hands over her mouth.

Gabriel, fortunately, didn't seem to notice her slip.

"What about Burton and Aimee?" Mercy asked.

Gabriel's sigh was heavy. "They'll divorce in two years when she leaves him for another man. Burton will be stunned and hurt. He'll become something of a recluse after that. Over time, Roy and his father will reconcile and the greatest joy of his life will be his grandchildren."

"I'm so sorry to hear his marriage to Aimee didn't turn out the way he expected."

"Burton was a man who brokered misery," Gabriel reminded them. "He brought about his own unhappiness."

"He never gave Anne the credit she deserved," Shirley said. "How ironic that because of him, she'll become a famous artist."

"What about Roy and Julie? Will they be happy?" Goodness asked.

"Very much so," Gabriel said, brightening. "Their

marriage will be a good one. In the next five years, Julie will give birth to three children, two boys and a girl. All three will be athletic and intelligent. Their daughter, named Anne Darlene after her two grandmothers, will go on to be an Olympic swimmer. The boys will take after their father and eventually assume leadership of Fletcher Enterprises."

"What about Dean?"

"He'll retire soon, and then, at the age of eighty, he'll die peacefully in his sleep."

"So he'll be joining his wife in Heaven twenty Earth-years from now?"

"Yes," Gabriel replied. "Are you satisfied now?"

Shirley, Goodness and Mercy nodded.

"Ready?" he asked. In the distance, Goodness heard the strains of the heavenly choir as the angels gathered together to sing praise to the newborn King. But before she left Earth, Goodness had to know about Anne's mother. She just had to know.

Shirley stepped close to her side. "She was an artist, too, and a wonderful mother. I always had a soft spot in my heart for Anne and wanted to work with her after her mother's death. God had other purposes for me, but He allowed me back into Anne's life for just this short time. I'm very grateful."

So was Goodness.

The strains of the heavenly choir were richer and more distinct as the four of them drew closer. Ah, but this was a special night on Earth, one filled with glory and goodwill toward mankind. A night that came only once a year when God smiled down on those He loved and sent His angels to shout out the glad news.

* * * * *

Where Angels Go

For Debbie Sundberg
Who makes my Christmases beautiful

One

The sights and sounds of Christmas were all around him. At home, the scent of evergreen mingled with ginger and spice, and multicolored lights glittered throughout the house. This was Harry Alderwood's favorite time of year. He'd settled in Leavenworth, Washington, more than five decades ago, and he loved the way this town celebrated Christmas. Despite his eighty-six years and failing health, nothing could dampen his love of the season. Even sitting in Dr. Snellgrove's office, with its spindly artificial Christmas tree, waiting for what he was sure would be bad news, Harry didn't feel depressed. This appointment would probably drain him for the rest of the day, and yet it seemed pointless. He doubted there was anything left for Dr. Snellgrove to do. His heart was giving out; it was as simple as that.

Harry wasn't afraid of death. He often thought about it, especially with so many of his friends dying. He'd seen death, witnessed it countless times on the beaches of Normandy and the battlefields of Europe in World War II. He'd grieved when his own parents and his older brother, Ted, had passed away. He wasn't afraid, though. Maybe he should be, but why worry about the inevitable?

An exhausted young mother sat across the room, keeping her little girl entertained by reading to her. Looking at them, he found it hard to tell who needed the doctor most, mother or child. Both seemed to be suffering from bad colds. Harry was grateful for the distance between them, since his own immune system was so weak.

Harry knew this would almost certainly be his last Christmas, and that saddened him. He'd always been a man of faith, and that faith had grown stronger as he grew older. Which was a natural progression, he supposed. He wondered if the angels celebrated Christmas in Heaven; he suspected they did. Harry figured he'd find out soon enough. Meanwhile, he was determined to make his last Christmas on Earth as special as he could for Rosalie. Already he was thinking of what he might do to show his wife of sixty-five years how much he loved her. Leaving Rosalie. That was his one regret....

"Harry Alderwood."

He was caught up in his thoughts, and the nurse had to repeat his name before he heard her. She was a young woman named Kelly Shannon—or was it Shannon Kelly?—but he affectionately called her Nurse Ratched. She didn't seem to mind.

"Harry?"

"Coming." He needed a moment to clamber to his feet. Sometimes he forgot that his legs weren't as steady as they used to be. Not long ago, he didn't have a problem getting out of a chair, but these days he got so winded just standing, he could barely walk. Growing old wasn't for sissies, that was for sure.

Using his cane for leverage, he slowly pulled himself upright, smiled at the young mother across from him and carefully placed one foot in front of the other. More and more, walking even a few yards was a chore. Still, he waved off Nurse Ratched's offer of assistance. He took several deep breaths and winked as he walked past her. She smiled, adjusting the holly brooch she wore on her crisp white uniform.

He liked her attention to Christmas. And he was grateful that she didn't rush him. That was the problem with people these days. They all seemed to be in a hurry, stepping around him, practically pushing him aside, in an effort to get ahead in the grocery store or the parking lot. Didn't these folks realize he was moving as fast as he could? A few years ago, he used to be just like them, trying to get someplace quickly and then, once he arrived, wondering why he'd been in such a hurry.

"Your color's good this morning," Nurse Ratched said as she held open the door of the examining room and waited for Harry to move inside. "You must be feeling better."

Harry never did understand why other people made assumptions about how he felt. No one really wanted the truth. Well, okay…maybe doctors and nurses did. But when it came to friends and acquaintances, he wasn't interested in discussing his health. He accepted the likelihood of illness and the certainty of death, although he didn't want to get there any sooner than necessary.

"Have a chair." Dr. Snellgrove's nurse pointed to the one against the wall.

It took Harry a long time to reach that chair and sit down again.

The nurse, chattering in a friendly manner, checked his blood pressure, which was normal, took his temperature, which was also normal, and then after asking the usual questions, left the room, closing the door behind her.

Five minutes later, Dr. Snellgrove appeared. Harry still found it a bit disconcerting to have such a young doctor; Paul Snellgrove barely looked old enough to shave, let alone make life-and-death decisions. Harry had met a number of young physicians lately, both men and women. That was a good thing, in his opinion—even though their youth reminded Harry of his own age. But these newly minted doctors tended to be idealistic, which he approved of, and they were up on all the latest technology, treatments and medications. The only problem was that they could be a bit unrealistic, seeing death as the enemy when sometimes, at the end of a long life or debilitating illness, it was a friend. Dr. Snellgrove wasn't like that, though. Three or four years ago, he'd bought out Harry's longtime physician's practice. Harry admired the kid.

"What can I do for you?" Dr. Snellgrove asked, sitting on a stool and sliding it over so he was eye to eye with Harry.

Harry rested both hands on his cane, one on top of the other. "I'm having trouble breathing again." This wasn't a new complaint. It'd gotten worse, though. Twice in the past week, he'd woken in the middle of the night, unable to catch his breath. Both times he'd thought he was dying. He hoped to go gentle and easy, in his sleep or something like that, not sitting up in bed gasping for air and frightening poor Rosalie into a panic.

The young doctor asked him a few more questions. Harry already knew the problem. His heart was tired, which might not be medical terminology but seemed pretty accurate, and sometimes it just took a brief pause. The pacemaker was supposed to help and it'd worked fine for the most part…until recently.

"There's not much I can do for you, Mr. Alderwood, much as I hate to admit it," the physician told him. His eyes were serious as they met Harry's.

Harry appreciated that the other man didn't look away and was willing to tell him the truth. He was ready to release his hold on life. Almost ready. There was one thing he still had to accomplish, one arrangement he still had to make, and he needed enough time to do it. "No new pill?" He'd

swallowed an entire pharmacy full now. Twenty-six pre-
scriptions at last count—not all at once, of course. Thankfully, due to his years of military service, the government
helped pay the cost of those many expensive drugs.

"No, Harry, I'm sorry. No miracle pills this week."

Harry sighed. He hadn't really expected there would be.

"Your heart's failing," Dr. Snellgrove said. "You know
that." Then he frowned. "I see you're using the cane instead
of the walker."

Harry hated that blasted walker. "It's at the house."

"Harry, it's December." The physician looked exasperated. "The last thing you need is a fracture."

Harry dismissed Snellgrove's concern.

"I'm well aware that I'm dying," he said, leaning toward
the other man. "What I'd like is your best guess of how much
time I've got."

"Why is it so important to know?" the doctor asked.

"Because of Rosalie," Harry murmured. "She's forgetful
and gets confused now and then, and I don't think she'll do
well living on her own." Harry worried about his wife constantly. Even their children didn't realize how bad Rosalie's
memory had gotten in the last few years.

Paul Snellgrove reached for Harry's chart and glanced at
the top page. "You're still in your own home, right?"

Harry nodded. He and Rosalie had raised their two beautiful daughters in that house on Walnut Avenue. Lorraine and
Donna now lived and worked in Seattle and had raised their
families there. One or the other came home at least once a
month, sometimes more often; his sons-in-law were frequent
visitors, as well. Kenny, Lorraine's husband, had strung all
their Christmas lights last week and brought him and Rosalie
a tree. Oh, yes, Harry knew how fortunate he was in his
family, how blessed.

And his grandkids... The four grandkids were adults

themselves now and making their own way in life. Being around his grandchildren did Harry's heart more good than any of those pills he gulped down every morning.

"I want to move Rosalie into Liberty Orchard, that new assisted-living complex, before I die," he explained. "It's the best solution for her. For everyone."

The physician nodded. "Anything stopping you?"

"You mean other than Rosalie?" Harry joked. "I just need to convince her. That might take some doing, so I have to know how much time you think I've got."

The young physician calmly appraised him.

His daughters agreed their mother would need help sooner or later, but didn't feel the urgency Harry did. They didn't understand that he couldn't leave this life comfortably unless he knew Rosalie would be properly looked after.

"Tell me straight up," Harry insisted. "It shouldn't be that difficult to tell an old man how much time he's got left." He let the challenge hang between them.

The physician rolled the stool back a couple of inches and made a gesture that was more revealing than anything he might have said. "Harry, I'm not God, so I don't know for sure," he murmured, "but I'll be honest if that's what you want."

"I do," he confirmed.

Dr. Snellgrove slowly exhaled. "The truth is, you could go at any time."

The words rattled Harry. That wasn't what he'd expected to hear. He'd assumed he had a couple of months, possibly until spring. Maybe he'd even last until summer. He took a minute to absorb the reality of his situation, then nodded and said, "Okay."

As if he feared he might have said too much, the physician launched into a lengthy explanation of cardiac rhythms and stenosis and congestive heart failure.

Most of his words slid off Harry; instead, the thought of

dying reverberated in his head. When would it happen? Would he have time to arrange for Rosalie's care?

"Don't overtax yourself. Use your walker," Dr. Snellgrove was telling him.

"I will," Harry promised.

"Rest as much as you can," the doctor went on. "And, Mr. Alderwood—Harry—you'll have to stop driving. It's increasingly unsafe."

Harry nodded; he'd already accepted that. More arrangements to make…

No problem there. Harry didn't have the energy to do much more than take the simplest outing. Most days were spent in front of the television. He liked those court shows best, and the Weather Channel, too. The older he got, the more important the weather seemed to be.

In Leavenworth this time of year, it was mostly cold and snowy. The stores around town counted on that snow for their tourist business, especially this close to the holidays. The entire month of December was a Christmas extravaganza here. Every weekend, there was a parade featuring an old-fashioned Father Christmas, a chubby Santa and even the Grinch, followed by a tree-lighting ceremony.

"Is there anything else I can do for you?" the doctor asked as Harry rose awkwardly to his feet.

"You got a new heart for me?" Harry managed a grin.

The other man's face saddened. "Sorry."

Harry thrust out his hand. He wanted to convey his thanks for everything the doctor had done and for his honesty. "Merry Christmas, Doc. And in case I don't see you again, Happy New Year."

Snellgrove shook his hand warmly. "All the best, Harry. To you and your wife."

In the waiting area the nurse handed him his coat, which hung on a peg on the wall. He wrapped the scarf Rosalie had knit him twenty-five years ago around his neck. He still wore it every winter. Rosalie was no longer knitting, which was a shame; she'd been an accomplished knitter. Their kids and grandkids had been the recipients of sweaters and mittens and hats, all kinds of beautifully made things.

Time was… He paused and smiled as he placed his hat on his head. Time was… That phrase came to him more and more often these days. He waited a moment, then slipped his arms into the sleeves of his thick wool coat. It felt heavy on his shoulders, heavier than it had when he'd put it on earlier that morning.

He wished Nurse Ratched a courteous "Merry Christmas" and prepared to leave.

Leaning on his cane, he opened the door and steeled himself against the cold before he made the short trek to his car. Like the doctor, his daughters didn't want him driving anymore or going out on his own. They were right. He'd talk to them about selling the car; maybe he'd call them tonight. In the meanwhile, he'd drive very, very carefully.

The skies were dark and overcast, and the cold cut right through him. He climbed into the driver's seat, then started the engine. A blast of cold air hit him as he turned on the defroster. He shivered; it seemed he was always cold. According to the doctor, being cold indicated poor circulation. In other words, Harry's heart was giving out, and this was just another symptom.

With his gloved hands on the steering wheel, he waited for the windshield to defrost.

He could die anytime.

With that, another realization hit him. He had to convince Rosalie to move as soon as possible. But his wife could be a stubborn woman, and Harry knew he was going to need help.

Bowing his head, he closed his eyes. Harry believed more fervently now than ever, although he hadn't been as faithful about attending church and reading his Bible. But when he did go to Sunday services, he walked away with something he could use in his life—a sense of God's benevolence and a desire to be right-minded and honorable. The Bible was filled with wisdom—and some darn good stories, too. Rosalie generally went to services. The church was only a few blocks away, and every Sunday morning, his wife was there. Their next-door neighbor drove her or one of the girls did, if either happened to be visiting.

Another thing Harry didn't make a regular practice of was prayer. He regretted that because he believed God answered prayers. He didn't want to bother the Almighty with his own paltry concerns. Seeing that God was dealing with the big stuff like global warming and the problems in the Middle East, it didn't make sense to Harry that He'd have time to worry about one old man. An old man afraid of what would happen to his wife after he died... Only Harry didn't know where else to turn.

The inside of the car became his church. With his head bowed and his eyes closed, he whispered, "Okay, Lord, my time's getting short. I want you to know I accept that. I understand you've got much bigger problems on this earth than mine, and better things to do than listen to an old man like me. Nevertheless, I hope you won't mind if I ask for your help.

"It's about Rosalie, Lord. The house is too much for her all by herself. Without me there to look after her, I'm afraid she'll burn the place down because she'll forget to turn off a burner or start a flood because she forgot the bathwater was running. I know you love her even more than I do and that's a comfort. Show me how to convince her to move into that fancy new complex. Let me warn you, though, Lord, my Rosalie can be stubborn. But then, I guess you've noticed that.

"Lord, when I'm gone, you'll have to take care of her for me." He paused and decided he was taking up too much of God's time, so he added, "Amen."

When he glanced up, the cloud cover had broken and sunshine burst upon the snow, making it shimmer with light. Harry watched it for a long moment, feeling good. The problem now rested in God's hands.

Two

Harry's prayer rose upward, higher and higher through the snow-laden branches of the evergreens. His petition to God whisked its way past the thick white clouds, carried by the warm winds of his love to the very desk of the Archangel Gabriel. There it landed.

"Harry Alderwood," Gabriel muttered, turning the pages of the massive book that detailed the prayers and lives of the faithful. "Ah, yes, Harry." Gabriel remembered the older man. Harry didn't pray often and seemed to believe he shouldn't bother God with his petty concerns. Little did the old man know how much God liked to talk to His children, how He longed to listen to them.

Having the ear of God and sharing His love for humans, Gabriel felt tenderness for this man who was so close to making the journey from life into death. In many cases when death was imminent, the veil between Heaven and Earth was especially thin. Harry accepted that he was dying but he clung to life, fearful of leaving behind those he loved—especially his wife, Rosalie.

Harry's days were few, even fewer than the old man realized, and that brought a certain urgency to his prayer.

Unfortunately, Christmas was only eight days away, and Gabriel was swamped with requests.

Two prayers had now reached him, almost simultaneously, from the small Washington town of Leavenworth. The second was from Carter Jackson, a small boy who felt he could trust God more than Santa.

Carter's prayer wouldn't be any easier to answer than Harry Alderwood's. Requests like this got even more complicated at Christmastime. Heaven was busy, busy, busy. There was work to be done, prayers to be answered, angels to be assigned.

Gabriel studied the list of available Prayer Ambassadors and saw that his three favorite angels were indeed free. Shirley, Goodness and Mercy were close to his heart, but there'd been problems with them in the past.

Lots of problems.

Mercy, for example, tended to become too engrossed with the things of Earth. Gabriel shook his head in a mixture of amusement and irritation. No matter how short-handed he was, he dared not let those three visit Earth again. Giving Mercy the opportunity to be around forklifts and escalators was asking for trouble.

Not once could Gabriel remember assigning her a prayer request without regretting it afterward. Okay, perhaps *regret* was too strong a word. Mercy always managed to straighten everything out at the last second and he had to admit, she did make him laugh. But Mercy with Harry Alderwood...

"Poor Harry," Gabriel whispered.

"Harry," Mercy repeated from behind him.

She had a bad habit of sneaking up on him and Gabriel did his best not to leap back in surprise. Controlling his reaction, he turned to face the Prayer Ambassador. She was the picture of innocence, wide-eyed and hopeful.

"Did I hear you mention Harry Alderwood?" she asked,

as her wings made small rustling sounds. This happened whenever she was excited. The mere prospect of returning to Earth had Mercy nearly breathless with anticipation.

"You did," he said.

"If there's any way I could be of service," Mercy volunteered, "I'd be *more* than happy to help."

"I'm sure you would, but there's the small matter of—"

Mercy interrupted him, raising her hand. "If you're going to bring up that unfortunate incident with the aircraft carrier, I want to point out that I've repented."

"Actually," Gabriel said, clearing his throat. "I was thinking about the time you rerouted that 747."

"Oh."

Mercy's cheeks colored, as well they should. That had been the final straw as far as Gabriel was concerned. "I don't know if I can trust you back on Earth," he said pensively. But the number of available Prayer Ambassadors was limited....

"Please, please, please, give me another chance," Mercy begged, hands folded.

For all the trouble she caused, Mercy did have a certain knack for getting prayers answered. What humans didn't always grasp was that prayer requests usually required participation on their end. God liked it when His children trusted Him with their needs, but the Almighty Father welcomed human cooperation, too.

"Harry's prayer just arrived," Gabriel said with some hesitation. "He knows his remaining time on Earth is brief."

"Doesn't he realize he'll receive a new body once he gets to Heaven?" Mercy asked, seeming surprised by the older man's reluctance to leave Earth. "It's so much better here."

"He knows," Gabriel said. Perhaps it would be best if he allowed her a view of Harry and Rosalie. "Come and meet Harry," the Archangel invited and with one wide sweep of his arm, he whisked away the veil between Heaven and Earth. A moment later the two of them were able to look down upon the town of Leavenworth.

"Harry, is that you?" Rosalie called when he stepped into the house and closed the door against the bitter December wind.

"It's me," Harry replied in a strained voice. He felt short of breath, and his mind was full of what Dr. Snellgrove had told him. He knew Rosalie couldn't cope without him; he also knew he'd have to trust that God would answer his prayer.

"I have lunch ready," his wife said as he entered the kitchen.

He had little appetite, but Harry couldn't disappoint Rosalie, since she'd made the effort of preparing their meal. At this stage, she only remembered a few of her favorite recipes. Almost always, they had canned soup for dinner. No doubt that was what she'd made for lunch, too.

Food didn't interest Harry much anymore. He ate because it was necessary but without any real enjoyment.

Coming into the kitchen, he saw that he'd guessed correctly. Rosalie had heated up soup. Two steaming bowls filled with bright red tomato soup sat on the kitchen table. What was left in the small saucepan was boiling madly on the stove. When Rosalie turned her back to bring the silverware to the table, Harry reached over and switched off the burner.

Soon he joined his wife at the round oak table in the small alcove. They bowed their heads, and Harry murmured grace. When he finished, Rosalie smiled softly, her eyes brimming with love. "How did everything go at the doctor's, sweetheart?"

Rather than worry her, Harry simply nodded. "I'm as fit as can be expected for a man of my age."

Rosalie looked back at him with concern. She seemed about to ask him more but changed her mind. He'd told her what she wanted to hear.

"Is soup all right?" she asked.

"It's perfect." Not sure how to broach the subject of moving, Harry swallowed three spoonfuls of his lunch, then paused. This wouldn't be the first time he'd brought it up—far from it. He carefully set his spoon on the place mat.

"How's that nice Dr. Snellgrove?" Rosalie asked, shakily lifting a spoonful of soup to her mouth. She helped herself to crackers from the box and crumbled them in her bowl, one cracker at a time.

"I like him."

"I do, too. Did he give you another prescription?"

Harry shook his head. As it was, the visiting nurse, who stopped by the house every second day, had to use a chart to keep his medications straight.

"You're going to be fine, aren't you?" his wife asked.

Harry saw that her face had tightened with fear. "Of course I am. It's…it's just a matter of getting the proper rest."

She instantly relaxed. "Good. I don't know what I'd do without you."

Harry didn't, either. He sighed. Perhaps he should take this opportunity to introduce the subject—again. "I was thinking that the upkeep on the house is too much for me." Harry felt that if he described the idea of moving to assisted living as something *he* needed, he might have a better chance of convincing her.

Rosalie ignored the comment. Although her face had wrinkled with age, Harry saw her as he had that first time, sixty-six years ago. She'd worked at the lunch counter at a Woolworth's store in Seattle. Harry had gone over from Yakima to take a short training course, shortly after he'd gotten an underwriting position with the insurance company. He'd worked for the same company for more than forty years.

It had been his first trip to the big city, and the crowds and noise had overwhelmed him. A friend had suggested

Debbie Macomber

they stop at the lunch counter for a bite to eat. One look at Rosalie, and he was completely smitten. Until then, he would've scoffed at the very thought of love at first sight. He never did again. One look and he'd fallen head over heels for his beautiful Rosalie.

"Harry?"

He blinked, surprised at the way he'd become immersed in his memories.

"You're finished your lunch?" she asked.

"Yes," he murmured. "I'm not very hungry." She didn't seem to be eating much herself, he noticed.

"I'll fix you something later," Rosalie suggested.

"That would be good." He lingered at the table. "Dr. Snellgrove wants me to use my walker."

Rosalie pinched her lips together. "Haven't I been saying the same thing? If you fall down again, I won't be able to help you up, sweetheart."

This was a problem. A week ago, he'd fallen and, struggle as he might, he couldn't get back on his feet. Rosalie had tried to help and soon they were both exhausted. As a last resort, she'd phoned the fire station. They'd sent out an entire crew, embarrassing Harry no end, although the fire-fighters couldn't have been nicer. He purposely hadn't mentioned the incident to Dr. Snellgrove. No reason to. He was fine, a bit chagrined, but no worse for wear.

With careful movements, Harry shuffled into the family room and settled down in front of the television. Rosalie carried their soup bowls to the sink and after rinsing them out, sat in her own chair, beside his.

"*Oprah* will be on soon," she informed him.

This was her way of letting him know she'd be watching the talk show. Rosie liked Oprah and Dr. Phil, and while she'd grown forgetful in some areas, she had no trouble remembering when her favorite shows were on. Harry hated to admit it, but he'd come to enjoy them, too. The complete lack of common sense exhibited by some of the folks on those programs continued to astonish him, and he was always heartened by the occasional portrayals of heroism.

"We might think about visiting Liberty Orchard one of these days," he said, reclining in his chair. He reached for the afghan Rosalie had knit him years earlier and spread it on his lap. The cold never seemed to leave him.

"I don't see any rush, do you?" Rosalie asked.

Rather than go into what Dr. Snellgrove had told him, Harry said, "Like I was saying earlier, this house is too much for me now. I don't see any reason to delay. We could put our name in, anyway."

"We can, I suppose," Rosalie reluctantly agreed. "But I'd rather wait until summer."

He didn't want to alarm her and decided to put the discussion off until later. Perhaps after he'd rested...

Gabriel studied Mercy. Her deep-blue eyes brimmed with compassion as she turned to him. "He's very weak."

Gabriel nodded.

"How much longer does he have?" she asked, watching the tender look Rosalie sent her husband as she left her own recliner and walked over to where Harry slept. Rosalie gently tucked the hand-knit blanket around Harry's shoulders and pressed her lips against his brow.

"Not long," Gabriel responded.

"Surely God won't take him until after Christmas?"

"Unfortunately, Harry will leave Earth before then."

"Oh, dear. So his prayer request is urgent. Someone has to convince Rosalie to move, and quickly."

"Yes."

"But Christmas is only about a week away!"

No one needed to tell Gabriel that. "I know."

"Oh, my."

"Are you still interested in taking on this request?" he asked, certain she'd change her mind.

Mercy bit her lip, mulling over the situation. This was the most difficult request he'd ever proposed.

"There can be no shenanigans this time," he warned.

"None," she said solemnly. Her gaze remained on the old couple, and the warmth and love that flowed between them.

"Do you think you can help Harry?" Gabriel asked, still unsure. Mercy was so easily distracted....

"I can," she said confidently. She turned again to look at him and Gabriel was shocked to see tears in her eyes. Harry Alderwood had touched Mercy's heart. Gabriel couldn't hope for anything more. Mercy would do everything in her power to prepare both Harry and his wife for a life apart, for death.

Three

Beth Fischer couldn't wait to get home from her Seattle job as a paralegal for Barney, Blackburn and Buckley, one of the most prestigious law firms in the state.

The minute she walked into her small downtown condo, she logged on to the computer. As soon as she was on the Internet, she hit the key to bring up the computer game that had enthralled her for months. World of Warcraft had quickly become addictive. Six months ago, one of the attorneys at the office had casually mentioned it; he'd laughingly advised his colleagues to stay away from it because of its enticing qualities. Beth should've listened—but on the other hand, she was glad she hadn't.

While the game loaded, she hurriedly made herself a peanut-butter-and-jelly sandwich and carried it into the small office that served as a guest bedroom on rare occasions. Directly off her kitchen, it was a perfect computer room.

She sank into her comfortable office chair, tucked her shoeless feet beneath her and signed on. Her name was Borincana and she was a hunter. Her pet wolf was called Spot, not the most original name, but it had attracted the attention of a priest named Timixie, who had since teamed up with her. Both were Night Elves and together had risen to level forty.

They were unbeatable and unstoppable, a legend in the annals of online computer games—in their own minds, anyway. Both of them were addicted to the game and met every evening to play, sometimes for hours. They didn't need to be online at the same time but often were.

When Lloyd, the attorney, had commented on this game, Beth had been looking for a mindless way to fill her evenings. She needed something to relax her—and distract her from the fact that all her friends were getting married, one by one.

So far, Beth had served as a bridesmaid in ten weddings. *Ten.* Already three of her friends were parents, and another two were pregnant. If she'd enjoyed crafts, she would've learned to knit or crochet. The truth was, Beth couldn't bear the thought of spending her evenings sitting in front of the television, creating little blankets for all those babies, when the likelihood of her marrying and having a child of her own hovered around zero.

Marriage terrified her. Been there, done that—and failed miserably. Fortunately she was smart enough to realize her mistake. Some people were meant to fall in love, marry and produce the requisite two children, preferably a boy and a girl. Her younger sister, Angela, had done so in record time.

For a while, the pressure was off Beth. Recently, however, her mother had taken up the old refrain. "Meet someone. Try again." Joyce Fischer hadn't been subtle about it, either.

No, thank you, Mom. Beth wasn't interested and that was all there was to it.

The World of Warcraft was the best alternative she'd found to lonely nights—and the best diversion from talk of marriage and babies. She'd been grateful to find something that was so much fun and so involving. The bonus, of course, was Peter, her Internet partner—the priest Timixie. They chatted by instant message every now and then, congratulating each other on their successes. Like her, Peter seemed to make a point of avoiding relationships.

During the game they teamed up and traveled together, roaming the World of Warcraft landscape, and generally made a great couple—in strictly virtual terms, of course. As far as Beth was concerned, her relationship with Peter via the game was as close as she was willing to get to another man.

Just when life in the alternate universe was getting interesting and another battle seemed imminent, Beth's phone rang. Groaning, she glanced at caller ID and saw that it was her mother. She ignored it and after five rings, the machine picked up.

"Marybeth, I know you're there. Are you playing that blasted computer game again? This is important—we need to discuss Christmas. Call me back within the hour, otherwise I'll drive over to your condo and I don't want to have to do that."

Beth cringed at the sound of her name as much as the message. She'd grown up as Marybeth and had always hated it. For some reason, it reminded her of those girls on reruns of *Hee Haw*. Nevertheless, her mother refused to call her anything else. Beth could see she wouldn't be able to ignore the call. With a sigh, she started to log off.

Right away, Peter instant-messaged her. **Where are you going?**

She typed back. **Sorry. My mother phoned about Christmas and I need to be the dutiful daughter.**

Peter's reply came right away. **I hear you. I'm being pressured, too. My parents are after me to get a life.**

Beth read his comment and nearly laughed out loud. **My mother said almost exactly the same thing to me.**

Where do you live?

This was the most personal question he'd ever asked and she hesitated before replying. Seattle.

Get out of here! I do, too.

No way! It was hard to believe they'd been playing this game for nearly six months and yet they'd just discovered they lived in the same city. Gotta go, she typed quickly. I'll be back in half an hour.

See you then, Peter wrote.

Beth put Borincana and Spot, her animal companion, in hiding, where they'd be safe from attack, and reluctantly reached for the phone. Even as she punched the speed-dial button, she knew that the conversation would have little to do with Christmas. Her mother was trying to find out if Beth was seeing anyone.

As if she'd been sitting by the phone waiting for her call, Joyce answered on the first ring.

"No, Mother, I'm not dating." Beth figured she'd get to the point immediately. That way, she could bypass all the coy questions about coworkers.

"What makes you think I'd ask you something like that?" her mother returned, obviously offended by her directness.

"Because you always do," Beth countered. She loved her parents and envied them their marriage. If her own had gone half as well, she wouldn't be in this predicament. She and John, her college boyfriend, had been young, barely twenty-one, and immature. Everyone had advised them to wait, but they'd been too impatient, too much in love.

Within six months of the wedding, they'd hated each other. Beth couldn't leave fast enough, and John felt the same. He was as eager to escape their disaster of a marriage as she was.

It was supposed to be a painless and amicable divorce. Everything had gone smoothly; she'd filed because John seemed incapable of doing anything without her pestering him. If something needed to be done, she had to take responsibility because John was utterly helpless.

They couldn't afford attorneys, so they'd gone through the legal documents with the assistance of a law student on campus. They had no material goods to speak of. He'd kept the television and she took the bed. Still had it, in fact, but she'd purchased a new mattress a couple of years ago.

What surprised Beth, what had caught her completely unawares, was the unexpected pain caused by the divorce. This wasn't like breaking up with a boyfriend, which was how she'd assumed it would feel. This was failure with a capital *F.*

Following the divorce, she'd gone to see a counselor, who'd described her emotions as grief. At the time she'd scoffed. She was happy to be rid of John and the marriage, she'd said. Nonetheless, she *had* grieved and in some ways still did. It was perhaps the most intense pain she'd ever experienced. It'd left her emotionally depleted. Nine years later, she was unable to put her failed marriage behind her.

Twice during the divorce proceedings she'd hesitated. Twice she'd considered going to John and making one last effort to work it out. The problem wasn't that she'd found him in bed with another woman or that he'd been abusive, physically or mentally. He wasn't an addict or an alcoholic—just completely irresponsible and immature. She'd had enough, and in the end she'd walked away. Her failure to try again was one of the things that still haunted her.

"Marybeth, I was asking you about Christmas," her mother was saying.

"Oh, sorry, I wasn't paying attention."

"I noticed," Joyce said sarcastically. "Your father and I thought that instead of the big fancy dinner we do every year, we'd have a potluck."

A potluck on Christmas Day? Beth didn't like the sound of that, although she understood the reasoning. Her mother spent most of the day in the kitchen and that couldn't be much fun for her. Beth decided she'd do her share without begrudging the time or expense.

"Aren't you going to complain?" her mother asked as if taken aback by her lack of response.

"No. Actually I was thinking I'd bring the turkey and stuffing."

"You?"

"I can cook." Beth thought the question in her mother's voice bordered on insulting.

"Is that so?" Joyce Fischer asked. "When did you last eat anything that didn't come from a pizza delivery place or the frozen food section at the grocery store?"

Living alone, Beth didn't have much reason to stand over a stove. Not when it was convenient and easy to order takeout or grab something from the deli. Her microwave got far more use than her stove.

"Okay, okay, I'll order a cooked turkey. We *have* to have turkey, Mom. It's tradition."

"I'd like to begin a new tradition," her mother said. "I want to enjoy the day with my grandkids—speaking of which, when can I expect more?"

Beth was amused by the transition from dinner to her absent love life in one easy breath. "Probably never."

"Marybeth!" She seemed horrified at the prospect. "You're a beautiful woman. You need to put your divorce behind you and move on with your life. You know John has, and more power to him."

Mentioning the fact that her ex-husband had remarried was a low blow.

Lisa Carroll, a college friend of Beth's—correction, acquaintance, and an *un*friendly one at that—had gleefully shared the news of John's marriage a couple of summers ago. Beth had taken it hard, although they'd been divorced for seven years by then. John was perfectly free to try his hand at married life a second time. She was happy for him. Thrilled, even.

That was what she'd tried to tell herself, but it didn't explain the depression she'd sunk into afterward. For weeks she was weepy and miserable. In the back of her mind, she'd held out hope that one day John would return to her. It was an utterly outlandish notion, wholly unrealistic.

"I should never have told you John got married again," she said, unable to disguise the pain of her mother's words.

"I'm sorry, dear. But you do need to move on. I was in church this week and I lit a candle for you. I asked God to send someone special into your life and I feel sure He'll answer my prayer."

"You lit a candle on my behalf?"

"I always do when I have a special prayer."

Beth rolled her eyes. "You asked God to send me a husband?" She couldn't believe her mother would do this.

"Don't make it sound like I signed you up for a dating service."

"That's not what I meant."

"Isn't there *anyone* who interests you?" Joyce pleaded.

The desperation in her mother's voice made Beth uncomfortable. "Not really," she murmured.

"Someone at work?"

"No." Beth most emphatically did not want an office romance. She'd seen a couple of those go sour. After the last one, between a legal secretary and one of the partners, the law firm had set a policy against the practice of dating within the office. Which was fine with Beth, since she happened to enjoy her job and had no intention of risking dismissal.

Her gaze drifted toward the computer screen. "Well, there's someone I met recently...."

"There is?" Hope flared instantly.

You'd think Beth had just announced that she'd set her wedding date.

"We met on WoW."

"That ridiculous game?"

"Yes, Mom. I found out he lives in Seattle."

"What's his name?"

"Peter."

"Invite him to Christmas dinner," Joyce said promptly. "I'll do the full meal. Forget the potluck. I'll entice him with my cooking—and I promise to teach you how. You know what they say about the way to a man's heart."

"Mom!"

"I used to be scornful of those old wives' tales, too," her mother continued undaunted, "but so many of them are true. Now, don't worry, I'll downplay the fact that you don't cook. Leave everything to me." Her mother didn't even attempt to hide her delight.

"Mother, no!" Good grief, for all she knew, Peter was married. She didn't dare ask for fear he'd assume she was interested. All right, she *was* interested, but only because her mother had forced her into it.

"You've got one week to ask him."

"Mother!"

"I insist."

Beth closed her eyes and before she could protest further, Joyce disconnected the line. Sighing, Beth hung up the phone. It was either arrive on Christmas Day with a man or disappoint her mother. She sighed again as she recalled that Joyce had resorted to prayer in order to find her a husband.

Beth loved her sister and she treasured little James and Bella, her nephew and niece, but Angela hadn't done her any favors by marrying the exemplary Brian and then quickly producing two perfect grandchildren.

Trying to forget her woes, she logged back on to the

game and was pleased to see that her partner was still online. She joined Peter and soon afterward he sent her a message.

How'd the conversation with your mother go?

Okay. She wished she hadn't mentioned that she'd be talking to her family. She was more concerned with what had happened while she was Away From the Keyboard. **Did I miss anything exciting when I was AFK?**

Yeah. I teamed up with level 41 Dwarf Warrior and defeated the last two Warmongers to complete the Crushridge quest.

Beth sat up straighter. **Wow. Great going.**

You should've been here. I started pounding my chest.

You Tarzan? she joked.

Only if you're Jane, came his reply.

Beth read the line a second time. He almost seemed to be flirting with her. Nah, he was just teasing, which they often did, bantering back and forth and congratulating each other. It would be easy to misread his intentions, and she didn't want to make more of this than warranted.

When she didn't respond to his comment, they returned to the game. Only later, when she'd logged off and headed for the shower, did Beth pause to reconsider.

If Peter *had* been flirting, and that was a huge *if,* perhaps she should make an effort to learn more about him.

Beth turned on the shower. These were the thoughts of a desperate woman, she told herself grimly. Signs of someone who'd sunk to a new low—finding a date for Christmas Day through an online computer game.

Four

Gabriel gazed at Joyce Fischer's prayer request, which had appeared in the Book of Prayers a few days earlier. The book rested on his desk, spread open, filling up almost as quickly as he could make assignments. Joyce had prayed countless times that her daughter would finally meet the right man. Gabriel shook his head as he tapped his finger against the page. It would help if Beth was amenable to a new relationship. After her divorce, Joyce Fischer's daughter had completely closed herself off from men; this Peter, however, might be an interesting prospect.

"Gabriel?" He heard the timid voice of Goodness behind him. Gabriel knew the minute he'd assigned Mercy to Harry Alderwood's request, Mercy's usual companions wouldn't be far behind. It would be just like Shirley and Goodness to want a piece of the action, too. Far be it from them to remain in Heaven while Mercy got an assignment on Earth.

"About Beth?" Goodness pressed.

The Prayer Ambassador regarded him with imploring eyes. Eyes so blue they seemed to glow. Gabriel wasn't surprised to discover that Goodness had been reading over his shoulder. Apparently she was interested in the Beth Fischer assignment.

"What about her?" Gabriel asked, ignoring the plea in her eyes.

"She could use some help, don't you think?"

"All humans have fallen short," Gabriel explained, and while it was true, he took no pleasure in saying so.

"Which is why God assigned us to help."

He couldn't disagree with that.

"What's going on with Beth?" Goodness asked, stepping closer to Gabriel's desk and eyeing the huge Book of Prayers.

The Archangel stepped aside so Goodness could read Joyce Fischer's entire request. He pictured Joyce in St. Alphonsus Catholic Church, kneeling by the altar rail and lighting a candle as she bowed her head and prayed for her daughter. Although Joyce had referred to grandchildren, the real desire of her heart was to see Beth happy. Joyce believed that a relationship, a marriage and family, was the way to make that happen for her daughter. Gabriel felt reasonably sure she was right.

"What about Kevin Goodwin?" Goodness asked.

Gabriel was impressed. Clearly Goodness had already done her research on Beth.

"They work together. Kevin is unattached," Goodness continued.

"True," Gabriel murmured. He'd considered Kevin himself, but apparently God had other plans for the young attorney—plans that didn't include a relationship with Beth. Plus, there *was* the small matter of her company's policy on workplace romance, which created a further complication. "Personally, I like Peter," he said.

Goodness gave him an incredulous look. "From that computer game Beth's hooked on? *That* Peter?"

Gabriel nodded.

Goodness thought about it and when she spoke again, she betrayed her reservations. "He's a possibility, I guess."

Gabriel arched one of his heavy white brows. "You guess?" As endearing as Goodness was, he wouldn't accept insubordination from her or any of the other Prayer Ambassadors.

"Don't misunderstand me, I like Peter quite a bit," Goodness added hurriedly, obviously realizing she'd overstepped some invisible line. She should know by now, Gabriel grumbled to himself, that he took Prayer request protocol seriously.

"It's just that I'm afraid the only way they'll ever be able to communicate is as Night Elves," she said after a moment's pause.

This produced a smile. "Yes, well, the computer game's a concern, but a minor one."

"Beth likes Peter—doesn't she?" Goodness asked.

Gabriel had to reflect on that question carefully. "She's comfortable with him. With what she knows of him, anyway," he finally said.

"That's a start," Goodness murmured in an uncertain voice.

"You have a problem with it?" Gabriel asked, genuinely interested in her reply.

"Not a problem…" Goodness hesitated. "I think it's a sad state of affairs that humans are resorting to relationships through the computer. There's no real intimacy—but I could be wrong. I'll admit *that's* happened before."

Gabriel shrugged. "For some, it's simply an easier way to meet people. In fact, a person's character can be revealed in these role-playing games." He nodded sagely, pleased with his up-to-date observation. "The way Beth and Peter are able to work together as partners, for example."

"I suppose," Goodness agreed with evident reluctance. "I still think it's rather sad."

Gabriel studied her. With her current attitude, he had to wonder if Goodness was the right choice for Beth.

"How's she doing now?" Goodness asked.

"Shall we take a look?"

"Please." Goodness sidled closer to the Archangel. "You *are* going to send me to Earth, aren't you?"

Those same blue eyes gazed at him expectantly. Goodness wasn't his first choice and he feared this request was too difficult for her. Another Prayer Ambassador, one with a little more experience in complicated situations, might serve better. One who wouldn't be as tempted by things of the earth. Unfortunately—like Mercy—Goodness had a somewhat blemished reputation when it came to her prayer assignments. But even knowing that, Gabriel found he couldn't refuse her. "You can join Mercy."

"Oh, thank you," Goodness trilled, clasping her hands together. Her wings fluttered rapidly with excitement, dropping a feather or two. "I won't disappoint you, Gabriel. You have my word."

"I'm counting on that." He meant it, too. This was too important an assignment for her to bungle; it needed a delicate hand. He caught himself before warning Goodness. No, Gabriel decided, he'd let her unravel the revelations about Beth all on her own. This presented a growth opportunity for Goodness—and for Beth Fischer, too.

"What's she doing now?" Goodness asked, crowding close to Gabriel in her eagerness to see Beth.

"It's lunchtime," Gabriel said. "She's at a small waterfront restaurant with a friend." With one sweep of his arms, Gabriel parted the veil of clouds that obscured the Earth below. At first, the view was hazy, but a few seconds later, the air cleared. Then, as though they were gazing through glass, Gabriel and Goodness saw Beth. She and her friend were seated at a table in a busy restaurant. A wreath in the nearby window was decorated with sprigs of holly and red Christmas balls.

Beth's long dark hair was parted in the middle, and she wore a soft pink cashmere sweater with gray wool pants.

"She looks very pretty," Goodness whispered.

Gabriel could only agree.

"So, what are your plans for Christmas?" Heidi asked as she picked up half of the tuna-salad sandwich they were sharing.

"I'll spend it with my parents," Beth said without any real enthusiasm. Already she was worried. Her mother had suggested—no, insisted—that Beth invite Peter to join them on Christmas Day. It was an unlikely scenario. After six months of impersonal conversation, she had no idea how they were going to make the transition from being WoW partners to friends to…well, dating each other. Sort of. A Christmas Day blind date—with her family, yet. She grimaced.

How could she possibly convince someone she'd never even seen to accompany her to one of the most important holiday functions of the year? She might as well ask for a miracle.

"You've drifted off again."

Beth didn't need to ask what her friend meant. She often grew quiet when something troubled her. "Can I ask you a question?" Beth asked, setting down her sandwich and leaning toward Heidi.

"Sure, anything. You know that."

Beth considered the other woman one of her best friends. She'd been a member of Heidi's wedding party and was godmother to her son, Adam.

"When you first met Sam…" she began. Heidi and Sam had just begun seeing each other when Beth met her; they'd now been married four years.

"When I first met Sam," Heidi repeated. "Did I know I was going to fall in love with him? Is that what you want to ask?"

Beth blinked. That wasn't *exactly* it, but close enough. "Yes."

"The answer is no. In fact, I thought he was a total nerd.

I mean, could you imagine *me* married to an accountant? I found him so fussy and detail-oriented, I couldn't picture the two of us together."

It *was* remarkable. Heidi, her fun-loving, easygoing friend attracted to a bean counter. Yet as far as Beth could tell, they were completely happy in their relationship. They were so different; Heidi was slapdash and impulsive and, as she'd said, Sam was the opposite. But where it truly mattered—their feelings about marriage and family, for instance—their values were the same. Recently, with Heidi's encouragement, Sam had joined a couple of his friends in a new business venture. Their firm, specializing in forensic accounting, was doing well.

"It wasn't like that with John and me," Beth murmured. "When we first met, I was sure we were the perfect match." She swallowed hard. She didn't know why she continued to do this—torturing herself with the details of her failed marriage. All it did was remind her that she simply wasn't any good at relationships.

"John was a long time ago."

This was Heidi's gentle way of urging her to stop dragging the past into the present, and she was right. Sitting up straighter, Beth squared her shoulders. "I think I might have met someone."

That immediately sparked Heidi's interest. In the last five years, she'd frequently tried to introduce Beth to available men, mostly colleagues of Sam's. Beth had declined each and every time. "Who did you meet? Where? When?"

"We met online."

Her friend instantly brightened. "You signed up with one of those Internet dating services?" Heidi had suggested this approach months earlier—advice Beth had strongly rejected.

"No, we met... I mean, we haven't *really* met. We're partners in an online computer game."

"That war thing?" Heidi wrinkled her nose in distaste.

Beth nodded. "We teamed up in World of Warcraft last June. But I know next to nothing about him, other than the fact that he lives in Seattle." Even as she explained this, Beth realized it wasn't true. Peter was decisive, a characteristic she admired in a man. He was thoughtful, too. The two of them worked well together in the landscape of the game, anticipating and complementing each other's moves.

"Then find out more," Heidi urged. "Contact him outside the game. Meet him for coffee or something."

Beth shook her head. "I couldn't do that," she said automatically. And yet she had to, didn't she? Unless she was prepared to disappoint her mother for the thousandth time.

"Why couldn't you?" Heidi asked, genuinely perplexed. "You said you've been partners for…what? Six months. Make up an excuse. Tell him you want to discuss battle strategy and you'd prefer to do it in the real world."

"But…he might think I'm hitting on him."

Heidi smiled. "Well, aren't you?"

Her friend had a point. "Not really," Beth mumbled but it was a weak rejoinder.

"You want him to meet your family, don't you?"

That was a nerve-racking subject. She decided to tell Heidi the whole story, how all of this had started with her mother's phone call. As she spoke, she concluded hopelessly that inviting him to Christmas dinner was impossible. Actually *bringing* him would be worse. Then again…it might work if there was an understanding between them. But she couldn't figure out why Peter would agree to such an arrangement. He had his own family, his own obligations without taking on hers. No, she couldn't ask him.

On second thought, he *might* understand. He'd said his family was after him to get a life. Perhaps they could join forces the way they had in World of Warcraft. Combine their efforts.

Still…

"For all I know he could be fifty, living at home and unemployed." There, it was out—Beth's biggest fear. Of course, Peter could be wondering the same thing about her. "Or—" an even bigger fear "—he could be married."

Chewing her sandwich, Heidi didn't respond for a moment. "The only way to find out is to ask," she said reasonably.

"He might think I'm—"

"What? Available? Beth, you *are* available! Okay, so you made a mistake in judgment. It happens, it's too bad, but it isn't the end of the world!"

"Should I tell Peter right off?" she asked uncertainly. "About my divorce?" This was her other worry—how much to say and when. She was afraid that once they did talk, she'd compulsively blurt out her entire relationship history. After two minutes, her prospective Christmas date would flee for the border.

"Don't lie," Heidi advised.

"Should I be evasive?"

"Don't overload him with details in the beginning. That's all I'm saying."

"Right." It seemed ridiculous to be discussing this when Peter hadn't even agreed to meet her yet.

"You do like what you know about him, right?"

Beth considered the question, then nodded. "Yeah."

"That's the important thing," Heidi assured her.

Beth nodded again. All she needed to do now was take that first step.

Goodness sighed as the veil between Heaven and Earth slowly closed, blocking the angel's view. She turned to Gabriel, and he could see that she was waiting for him to comment.

"Beth's ready," he said emphatically.

"And Peter?"

"He's ready, too."

"He isn't fifty, living with his parents and unemployed, is he? Or…married?"

Gabriel shook his head. "No, he's single and he has a good position at the home office of Starbucks. He's doing well financially and is popular with his peers."

"Just like Beth."

"Beth's resisted opening herself to love," Gabriel said. As for this new relationship—well, there were a few facts yet to be uncovered, facts Goodness would have to learn on her own.

"Beth needs to be taught that she's capable of falling in love again," Goodness murmured.

"Yes," Gabriel said, encouraging her as much as he dared.

"Peter might not be the one, though."

He wasn't sure what Goodness had against the young man. "That's not up to us," he said sternly.

"Right." Goodness folded her hands. "I'll do my best to steer them toward each other. After that, they'll have to work it out for themselves."

Gabriel squinted at her. She sounded as though she was reciting something she'd memorized. "I'm relying on you," he reminded her. "You need to be very clear about your own boundaries. You're there to help them, Goodness, to give them a nudge—not to push them into each other's arms."

"I won't let you down," she promised.

Gabriel sincerely hoped that was true. Just as he was about to expand on his concerns, another urgent prayer request whisked past him, landing on his desk.

Gabriel sighed as he bent to read this one. It came from nine-year-old Carter Jackson. Ah, yes. This wasn't the first time he'd heard from the young man. Carter wanted a dog.

He decided to assign Shirley to this request, since she had a particular affinity for children.

Shirley, Goodness and Mercy back on Earth. If his hair wasn't already white, that would've done it.

Five

Carter Jackson pressed his ear as hard as he could against his bedroom door. If he shut his eyes and concentrated he could hear his parents' conversation.

"I'm sorry, honey. I know how much Carter wants a dog, but we can't afford one right now."

"But, David, we promised."

"I didn't promise him any such thing, Laurie. I said *maybe* he could have a dog for Christmas."

Carter's mother sounded sad. "It'll break his heart."

"Believe me, I know that. I don't like this any better than you do."

Although he was only nine, Carter understood that his father wanted him to have a dog, just as he had when he was Carter's age. Carter had already decided to give his dog the same name as his father's—Rusty. Rusty was a good name for a dog.

"We could get a dog from the shelter," his mom was saying. "A rescue."

"It's not the cost of the dog. It's the vet bills, the food, everything else."

His mother didn't respond.

"You looked at the budget, didn't you? If there was any

way we could make it happen, we would. But you know as well as I do that we can't afford a dog. We can barely afford a Christmas tree!"

Carter wasn't sure what a budget was, but he knew it must have something to do with money. Money always seemed to be a problem. His mother used to work at a dress shop in downtown Leavenworth, but the shop closed and she hadn't been able to find another job.

That was all right with Carter. He liked having her at home, and so did his little sister, Bailey. After school they both liked being able to go home rather than to the day care lady down the street. Their mother usually had a snack or a small surprise waiting for them. She seemed happier, too, not to be working such long hours, but Carter knew there were problems with the budget...whatever that was.

"Our health insurance rates just went up," his father said.

"I saw that," his mother murmured. Her voice was quiet, making it difficult for Carter to hear everything she said. "I try to keep the heat as low as I can while the kids are in school, not that it's helped all that much."

That explained why his mother was always wearing a sweater when Carter got home from school.

"The oil prices are killing us," his father said. He sounded angry.

"I know. I'm sorry." This came from his mother.

"It's not your fault, Laurie."

Carter risked opening the door a crack, to see what he could. It took a moment for his eyes to adjust to the light, but then he saw his parents. They sat on the sofa and his mother's head rested on his father's shoulder. His father had one arm around his mother, and they seemed to be leaning against each other.

"Should we tell Carter now or wait until Christmas morning?" she asked.

Carter bit his lip. They'd *promised* him a dog. His father said he hadn't, but he *had*. He just didn't remember. He'd said it this summer, and ever since then Carter had hung on to that promise—he could have a dog at Christmas.

It wasn't fair and he struggled not to break into tears. Turning his head, he buried his face in his arms and breathed deeply. He couldn't let them see him standing there—or hear him cry.

"I don't think we'll be able to buy the kids any gifts this year," his father continued.

"It's all right, honey," his mother reassured him. "There'll be plenty of presents from your parents and mine. The gifts from your family are already here. The kids will have something to open. Besides, we don't want to spoil Carter and Bailey. It's more important that they know the true meaning of Christmas."

His father seemed to agree.

Carter couldn't listen to any more of their conversation. His sister was sound asleep in the bed across from his own. Bailey was in first grade and he was in fourth. Bailey wanted her own room. But if he couldn't have a dog, then Bailey wasn't going to get a bedroom all to herself, either. That was what Bailey had asked Santa for in her letter.

The kids at school told Bailey she was stupid to believe in Santa. Carter didn't believe anymore, but he didn't want to say anything, especially to his little sister. She still believed. When he was her age, he'd wanted to believe, too.

Santa was like his grandparents who lived in Wenatchee. His mother's family didn't have a budget, or at least he didn't think so. It never seemed hard for them to buy presents the way it was for his parents. Maybe...

Carter decided he'd mention the possibility to his mother in the morning and see what she said. If his own mom and dad couldn't afford a dog, then maybe they'd let his grandparents buy him one. Or perhaps Grandma and Grandpa could pay the vet bills his dad was so worried about.

Feeling better now, Carter pulled back his sheets and slipped into bed. He'd just closed his eyes when a backup plan came to mind. Santa might be make-believe but God was real, and Christmas was Jesus's birthday. Remembering that, he got out of bed and knelt down. He'd already said his bedtime prayers, but this was extra. He hoped God wouldn't mind hearing from him again.

"Dear God," he whispered. "Thank You for Your birthday. I think it's great that because You were born we get presents. I'm really glad You arranged it like that. Um, God, I asked about getting a dog before and my parents said I had to wait. I waited. It was hard, too.

"They said I had to be nine years old before I was responsible enough to take care of a dog. Well, I'm nine and I do all my chores and I do my homework and I don't cheat on tests or anything."

He hesitated, thinking he'd better tell the whole truth. God knew anyway. "Sometimes Mom has to remind me about my chores. But I *try* to be good."

Carter paused, wondering if God might say something back. He listened intently, his eyes closed, but no matter how hard he concentrated he couldn't hear anything. That didn't mean God wasn't listening, though; Carter understood that.

"If You could find a way to get me a dog for Christmas, God, I'd really like it. I promise to take care of Rusty and train him right. I'll make sure he's loved. Thank you."

Finished now, Carter lowered his head and whispered, "Amen." He stayed on his knees a few minutes longer, in case God wanted to talk to him, after all. Eventually he climbed back into bed.

God had a dog for him, a special one. Carter was sure of it. He didn't know how the dog would arrive. Maybe his grandparents would give him one for Christmas, maybe not. He'd just wait and see. He might not believe in Santa anymore, but Carter believed God answered prayers. All he had to do now was be patient.

"You heard?" Gabriel asked Shirley. The Prayer Ambassador had once worked as a guardian angel and her love for children was the reason he usually assigned Shirley the prayer requests from boys and girls.

"A dog," Shirley repeated.

"There are more important requests, if you prefer," Gabriel said.

"No," came her immediate reply. "I want to help Carter get his dog."

"I thought you would."

"It's just that..."

"Yes?"

"It's just that I could probably take on two or three such requests while I'm on Earth," the angel said with utter confidence. "But I know why you haven't given me more than one."

"You do?" Gabriel asked. "And why would that be?"

"My *real* assignment is to keep watch over Goodness and Mercy. Heaven knows, and I don't mean that as a pun—" she paused and gave him a smug smile "—those two need looking after."

"Indeed they do," Gabriel agreed. "But it seems to me that you've taken part in their schemes a number of times."

"Under protest," Shirley rushed to explain. "I knew they were headed for trouble and I tried to warn them, but they wouldn't listen to me. So what choice did I have?" She shook her head ruefully. "You can't imagine the trouble I've saved you on other assignments. But I'm only one angel and there's only so much I can do on my own."

Gabriel didn't need a reminder of the problems these

three had caused. Yes, he did expect Shirley to be a supervisor of sorts for the other two, but as often as not they'd led *her* into temptation. Still…

"As the most responsible of the trio—"

"That would be me," Shirley said, cutting him off. She folded her wings close to her back without revealing any degree of eagerness as Goodness and Mercy had done. Shirley was the picture of calm serenity, of unquestionable confidence.

"Let me point out the time limitations involved," Gabriel said. "All three of you need to return to Heaven on Christmas Eve." This shouldn't come as any surprise, since it was one of the terms always set upon them during visits to Earth at this time of year.

A look of panic flashed into Shirley's eyes. "That means we have barely a week by the earthly calendar."

"Don't forget, we need you back for the festivities," Gabriel told her.

"Yes, of course." She did seem unusually concerned with the temporal constraints, which he found odd, considering that they'd answered prayer requests in less time than that.

"If there are problems, I can come directly to you?" Shirley asked.

It went without saying that with Goodness and Mercy, there were bound to be problems. "Of course."

On second thought, Gabriel wasn't so sure of that. He'd seen compassion and a new depth in Mercy; she understood the seriousness of her assignment. Harry Alderwood's days on Earth were few, and Mercy would have to convince Rosalie to move and at the same time prepare Harry for the crossing. Heaven awaited his arrival.

As far as Goodness went… That was an entirely different story. Beth Fischer had lessons to learn, obstacles to negotiate—obstacles of her own making. It might not be as easy as Goodness assumed to steer her toward the future. Gabriel would keep a close eye on this assignment.

And young Carter Jackson—this wasn't an easy prayer request, either, despite what Shirley seemed to think. She might be a relatively senior angel, but she had a few lessons to learn herself.

"Can I see Carter?" Shirley asked.

"Of course." As he'd done with the others, Gabriel parted the veil between the two realms and offered Shirley a chance to assess the situation.

Sitting at the breakfast table, Carter watched his parents closely.

"You remember this summer you said I could have a dog when I'm nine, Dad?" he asked, braving the subject dearest to his heart.

His dad exchanged a look with his mother. "I remember."

"I'm nine now."

His father put down his fork, and the careful way he laid it on the table told Carter this was going to be an important discussion. "Son, it hurts me to tell you this, but we can't afford a dog."

"Dad…"

"I'm sorry. I know you've been hoping to get a dog, but we can't manage it financially, Carter."

Despite his efforts, Carter's eyes filled with tears and everything in the room went blurry. His mother came to stand behind him. Embarrassed to be caught crying, Carter wiped his face with his sleeve and gulped several times.

"As soon as we can afford one, we'll get you a dog," she whispered, placing her hands on his shoulders. "We promise."

"But you promised *before*," Carter challenged. "You said I could have a dog when I turned nine. And then you said I had to wait until Christmas. And now…"

His father looked as sad as Carter had ever seen him. "I'm sorry, Carter. I'm doing the best I can, and so is your mother."

Bailey had started to cry, too. Carter tried to stop, but all he could do was sniffle back the tears. He felt like running away from the table. He couldn't eat.

"What about Grandma and Grandpa Parker?" he asked, clinging to the dream that his grandparents would give him the dog he so badly wanted.

"I've spoken to them," his father said.

Carter felt hope spring to life as he held his breath, waiting to hear the verdict.

"If your grandparents buy you a dog, that's just the beginning of what it'll cost. There's a whole lot more that goes along with owning a dog."

"He could eat my food," Carter insisted. He'd already considered this. "I don't mind sharing."

"Then there are shots."

"I'll take them," Carter said. It didn't matter how much they hurt, either.

"The shots are for the dog, Carter, and they're expensive."

"Oh."

"There's the license and obedience school and neutering and a dozen other costs. All of that would drain the family budget. It won't be long, though. Okay?"

Carter wasn't sure he should believe his father. "How long?"

"David." His mother's voice was soft and filled with warning, almost as if she feared his father would make another promise he couldn't keep.

"I don't know, but I promise that as soon as we can afford it, you'll get your dog."

That was the same thing his mother had said. Carter swallowed hard. He couldn't ask his father's parents. They lived back east and they mailed their gifts, which had arrived last week. The gaily wrapped presents were arranged on the coffee table with a miniature Christmas tree his mother had bought at the grocery store for five dollars. His one hope had been Grandma and Grandpa Parker—his mom's parents— and according to his father, it wasn't going to happen.

His last chance, his only chance now, was God. And with everything inside him, Carter believed God would send him a dog.

Six

Rosalie Alderwood was humming "O Come, All Ye Faithful" in the kitchen while Harry watched the news on TV. This was Wednesday, their traditional shopping day, and the advertised grocery specials were in the morning paper. Soup was on special, tomato, his favorite, two cans for a dollar. So was ice cream—three half-gallons for only six dollars. The brand wasn't his favorite but ice cream was ice cream, and Harry had always had a weakness for it. He didn't have much appetite anymore, but the thought of chocolate ice cream was appealing.

For years—ever since his retirement—Harry and Rosalie had done their grocery-shopping in the middle of the week.

"Should I get the car warmed up?" Harry asked. He'd put off the conversation with his daughters about selling it; maybe he'd call them tonight.

"Good idea." Rosalie came to stand in front of him, a dish towel in her hand, and glanced at the advertisements in the paper, spread out on the coffee table.

"You'll want to get a few cans of the tomato soup that's on special," he said.

"Yes," she agreed.

Because Rosalie had gotten so absentminded, Harry had begun compiling lists of items they needed to pick up at the store. This morning they were out of both milk and bread. He didn't want to miss that ice cream, either. He planned to arrive early enough to have his selection of fresh flowers, too. Maybe a potted poinsettia in honor of the season... His pleasures were few.

"I'll get my coat," Rosalie told him.

Harry nodded and reached for his car keys hanging on the peg by the door. She left, and knowing Rosalie, it would take her ten minutes to get ready. And that was *after* telling him to start the car. Early on in their marriage, that habit used to irritate him, but not anymore. This tendency to dawdle was part of Rosalie's personality and Harry had learned to accept it.

Before he went out to the car, he checked the refrigerator.

Another of Rosalie's longtime habits was her inability to discard things, even rotting food. He didn't understand it but had realized years ago that he was the one who'd have to toss the leftovers. Thankfully, with her cooking so little, there wasn't much. A quick inspection of the contents revealed several odd items. Frankly Harry had no idea why they needed anchovy paste or five varieties of mustard. Good grief, he hadn't even known they *made* that many.

Sure enough, it was ten minutes before Rosalie appeared. She'd put on fresh lipstick and combed her hair. "I'm ready, Harry."

"Me, too." Rosalie didn't drive. His own abilities were severely limited now and he took to the road only when necessary. In fact, he hadn't driven since he'd gone to see the doctor on Monday. The days of Sunday-afternoon excursions into the country had long since passed.

One of the advantages of shopping on Wednesday mornings was the lack of crowds. Mostly it was a few folks like Rosalie and him. Recently the store had gotten motorized carts for handicapped and elderly patrons, which made the whole experience a lot more pleasant.

Harry drove the motorized cart while his wife strolled by his side, filling the basket. Not once in the past year had Rosalie complained about the fact that he was the one who wrote their grocery lists, a chore she used to do.

They'd just turned down the soup and canned vegetable aisle when Lucy Menard entered from the other end. Her face brightened as soon as she saw them.

"Rosalie," Lucy called out. She left her own cart and hurried toward her friend, arms wide open.

The two women hugged for an extra-long moment. During World War II, after Rosalie and Harry were married and while he was off fighting in Europe, she and Lucy had roomed together while working in the Portland, Oregon, shipyards. At one time, they'd been as close as sisters. In fact, Lucy was godmother to their oldest daughter, Lorraine. Ever since Jake, Lucy's husband, had died, they hadn't seen much of her, which was sad. Mostly Harry blamed himself. Getting out and about was so difficult these days....

"I swear it's been a month of Sundays since I saw you two," Lucy said, stepping back. She looked good, better than the last time Harry had seen her, which was...well, no wonder. It'd been at Jake's funeral.

"I've been meaning to let you know I've moved," Lucy said excitedly.

"Moved?" Rosalie seemed to find that hard to believe.

Lucy beamed. "The kids finally convinced me that with Jake gone, I shouldn't be living on my own."

"I'm surprised you'd leave your home," Rosalie murmured. She glanced at Harry, then looked away. If it was up to Rosalie she'd delay moving as long as possible.

"I got a place at Liberty Orchard, the new assisted-living complex off Frontier Street."

That caught Harry's attention and he instantly straightened.

"Harry's been saying we need to do something like that, too, but I don't think I can," Rosalie admitted sheepishly.

"I said the same thing." Lucy nodded. "I figured after living in the same house for thirty years, I was too old to make that drastic a change. I told my children they were handing me a death sentence, moving me out of my home."

"That's how I feel," Rosalie said, once again avoiding Harry's gaze.

"But you did move," Harry broke in. "And you're happy now, right?"

"Oh, yes." Lucy smiled contentedly. "I always assumed it would take a forklift to get me out of that house. The thought of sorting through and packing up all those years of living just overwhelmed me."

Harry knew that was part of Rosalie's problem, too.

"Thank goodness the kids came in and made all the decisions for me. They went through each room, packing what I needed and dividing up what I didn't. One day I was in my home and the next I was making friends at Liberty Orchard. It's the best thing that's happened to me in ten years."

Frowning, Rosalie regarded her friend. "Don't they serve meals there?" she muttered. "Why are you shopping?"

"The meals are great, but a few times a week I don't feel like being sociable. That's my choice, you know. I fix myself something to eat. I've got my own refrigerator and microwave and that's all I need." She held up a box of microwave popcorn and giggled like a schoolgirl. "I love this stuff."

"It sounds like the ideal setup," Harry said.

"I'm not ready," his wife murmured.

Because Harry recognized her fears, he hoped to reassure her and gently urge her along. "Maybe Rosalie and I could come and see you at your new digs," he suggested jauntily, as though he was proposing a casual visit.

His hope was that once Rosalie saw the facilities for herself, she'd have a change of heart. If *he* couldn't get her to tour Liberty Orchard, perhaps Lucy could.

"How about tomorrow afternoon?" Lucy said. "Around three o'clock? We have a book club meeting at two and there's an exercise class before that. I wouldn't want to miss either one."

"They have exercise classes?" Rosalie sounded impressed.

"There's something to do every day. Before the move, it was a big deal just to step outside the house."

Rosalie shared a surprised glance with Harry. "I know what you mean. We'd love to come by, Lucy."

"I'll see you tomorrow, then," Lucy said, looking pleased.

She wasn't nearly as pleased as Harry, though. This couldn't have worked out better had he planned it. Lucy's opportune appearance had led to the next day's visit in the most natural possible way. It was exactly what he'd prayed would happen.

They finished collecting their purchases and by the time they returned to the house Harry needed a nap. The doc had insisted he couldn't carry anything heavier than five pounds, so his wife brought in the groceries from the garage. He made it to his recliner and was asleep almost before he elevated his feet.

Mercy was delighted at how well the meeting with Lucy Menard had gone. She sat in the motorized cart Harry had recently vacated, flushed with pleasure.

"How did you manage *that?*" Goodness asked, sitting on the handlebars of the same cart. "Did you know about Lucy?"

Hands behind her head, Mercy leaned back, gleeful with joy. "I did some research and discovered that Lucy and Rosalie had once been best friends. Then I noticed that she'd recently moved into Liberty Orchard. After that, all I had to do was arrange a coincidental meeting in the grocery."

"And, pray tell, how did this 'coincidental' meeting come about?"

"I simply absconded with her remaining package of microwave popcorn. I also shuffled around her collection of DVDs and put *It's a Wonderful Life* on top. Which reminded her it's time for her annual viewing—and that, of course, means she needs popcorn." Mercy chortled. "Piece of cake."

"Did someone mention the bakery?" Shirley asked, fluttering down from above, her wings stirring up flyers in the store's foyer. A youngster chased after them, then disappeared into the store.

When Shirley caught sight of Mercy on the motorized cart, her eyes widened. "Don't even think about it," she warned. "Gabriel asked me to keep an eye on the two of you. He knows, as I do, that you aren't to be trusted."

"I wasn't going to take the cart for a spin or anything," Mercy protested.

"But you *did* think about it."

Shirley knew her all too well. "I considered it." Mercy sighed heavily. "But I'm older and wiser now, and no longer given to flights of fancy." This thing was almost as good as a golf cart (there'd been that unfortunate incident at the Augusta golf course) but if Shirley wasn't going to say anything, Mercy certainly wouldn't, either.

"You're not to encourage her," Shirley warned Goodness.

"Moi?" The other angel brought her hand to her heart with an expression of pure innocence.

Shirley claimed the seat on a second cart. "I thought we should confer before we start our assignments," she said.

Mercy didn't know when Shirley had been put in charge or begun sounding so self-important. She obviously saw herself as their boss; this didn't sit right with Mercy, but she'd do whatever it took to finish her assignment.

"We each have an important task set before us," Shirley announced as if standing at a podium and addressing a huge crowd. She tilted her chin upward and spoke in deep, re-sounding tones. "This is our opportunity to prove ourselves once and for all to Gabriel and—" she paused, seemingly for effect "—to God."

"Gabriel and God," Mercy and Goodness dutifully repeated, their eyes meeting.

"It is our task," Shirley continued righteously, "no, our *duty,* to teach these humans a lesson from our heavenly Father before we answer their prayer requests."

"Our duty," Mercy and Goodness echoed.

At that point, Shirley deigned to actually face them. "You've got that look," she said.

"What look?" Mercy demanded.

"The guilty look that tells me you did something you shouldn't have."

"I haven't," Mercy insisted. "Not that it's any of your business."

"I'm working with Beth Fischer," Goodness said, getting in between the other two. "This isn't an easy assignment. I could use some advice."

"What's the problem?" Shirley's tone was, in Mercy's opinion, more than a bit condescending.

Goodness frowned meaningfully before she explained. "It appears that Beth's confidence in her ability to choose a life partner has been badly shaken. She doesn't trust her heart."

"Why is that?" Shirley asked.

"I don't know for sure. I've been watching and studying Beth, and she's a wonderful woman. It's just that…that…" She hesitated. "It's just that I'm afraid she's still in love with her ex-husband. How am I supposed to help her get over him and involved with someone else in only one week? It's *impossible.*"

Mercy could understand her friend's dilemma. "Didn't you tell me her ex has remarried?"

"Yes."

"Then you need to teach her to let go," Shirley said unequivocally. "This happens all the time. It's been almost ten years and she has to move on."

"I agree, but it's going to be difficult to convince Beth of that. Thanks for the advice, though." To Mercy's ear, Goodness sounded a little—just a little—sarcastic.

"I'll help you," Shirley said.

"No," Goodness returned immediately. "I appreciate the offer, but I can handle Beth on my own. She'll be in Leavenworth this weekend."

"Really?" Shirley moved her hand to her chin in a thoughtful gesture.

"Her friend Heidi invited her to come here for the Christmas festivities. No town does it better than Leavenworth—or so I've heard."

"What about your assignment?" Mercy asked, directing the question to Shirley.

For the first time, the other angel seemed unsettled. "Yes, well, my assignment is deceptively simple—on the outside."

"I don't believe you mentioned whose request you've been sent to answer."

"It's a boy named Carter," Shirley mumbled. "He wants a dog for Christmas."

Mercy swallowed a protest. *She* was dealing with a dying old man who had pressing concerns for his family. Goodness had to guide a young woman with a broken heart. And all Shirley had to do was find a little boy a dog! Talk about easy! Mercy could manage that with one wing tied behind her back.

"As I explained, my assignment is deceptively simple, but—"

"Yes, deceptively." Mercy looked at Goodness. "Listen, I'd love to stay and chat awhile, but I've got work to do."

"Me, too," Goodness said.

"Yes, well, Carter and his sister are in school, so I've got a few minutes to spare," Shirley informed her friends.

"I'm sure you do," Mercy said and promptly disappeared. Goodness followed, leaving Shirley sitting alone in the grocery foyer.

A minute later, Mercy returned, hovering behind Shirley, who hadn't moved from her position on the motorized grocery cart. Shirley seemed to assume the other two had left the premises, and Mercy let her think that. She studied the cart for a moment. These little numbers were a breeze to operate. Not that Shirley, so righteous and well-behaved, would know that…. With the lightest touch of her finger, Mercy fired the cart's engine to life.

Stunned, Shirley glanced around, obviously wondering what had changed and why. Mercy wasn't about to tell her. The cart took off into the store with Shirley on board.

Shoppers gasped and leaped out of the way. Several people reached for their cell phones to snap pictures of the runaway cart, careering through the store minus a rider.

Mercy covered her mouth to hold back a laugh. Goodness joined her, laughing, too. Shirley wasn't nearly so calm.

"Mercy!" she screamed. "Help! Do something."

"I believe she already did." Goodness chuckled and disappeared once again. Mercy did, too. Since Shirley had time on her hands, she could use it figuring out how to turn off the cart.

Seven

Beth wasn't imagining it. The relationship between her and Peter had shifted since the night of her mother's call. That'd been two days ago, and whenever they logged on to the game she lowered her guard a fraction more. So did Peter.

The biggest difference was that they chatted far more than strictly necessary. And their messaging didn't concern the game as much as it did each other.

You're right on time, I notice, he wrote when she logged on.

Beth kicked off her shoes as she settled into the chair by her desk. She set aside the soda she was drinking in order to respond. You're ahead of schedule.

I was anxious.

Beth read his words and leaned away from her desk. She wasn't sure how to decipher that comment. Did Peter mean he was anticipating her arrival? Or was he implying that he was worried she'd be late? It was hard to tell.

Anxious why? she asked, preferring the direct approach.

To talk to you.

Now that they'd reached level forty in World of Warcraft, the option to purchase a mount had been offered to them. It was a big advantage and one they'd been considering. Any particular reason? she asked, wondering if that was what he wanted to discuss.

Yeah.

That didn't tell her anything. Would you care to explain?

His reply didn't come for a couple of minutes, as if he needed to think about it first. So this obviously wasn't about the possibility of adding a mount to their list of resources.

We've been partners—how long? he asked instead.

Six months.

It seems longer.

Again Beth didn't know what to make of that. Really?

I trust you.

She laughed. As well you should. I've covered your butt often enough, oh mighty Timixie.

I've covered yours, too.

For which I'm most grateful.

That's only appropriate.

Beth laughed, enjoying the light, teasing quality of their exchange. She typed quickly. Are you going to chatter all night or are we going to play?

Can't we do both?

Beth felt a rush of warmth. It was a pleasant sensation and one she'd almost forgotten. Talking with the opposite sex was awkward for her, except in situations that didn't involve potentially romantic expectations—with family, for instance, or male colleagues or friends like Sam. She felt comfortable with Peter, at ease. Although they hadn't even spoken on the phone, let alone face-to-face, it was the first time she'd had that kind of reaction to a man since John.

Despite what her mother said, Beth *had* dated after her divorce; she just hadn't done it successfully. Most social conversations with men felt stilted. She struggled with how much to say or not to say.

Her record was three dates with the same man. Luke Whitcomb. He'd been a nice guy, entertaining and funny. His sense of humor had carried her for the three dates.

She probably would've accepted a fourth except that he'd admitted their relationship wasn't working for him. He'd been sincere when he said they should call it quits before either of them got hurt.

Well, surprise, surprise. Luke's rejection had cut deep and served, once again, to convince Beth that she was incapable of ever attracting another man. Afterward she'd steered away from dating at all and a couple of weeks later, she'd found the World of Warcraft and since then, almost her entire social life had been as a Night Elf and hunter.

Now there was Peter, a man she'd never actually met. His family had suggested he "get a life," so it was highly probably that he was single, too. Beth wanted to ask him, only she couldn't figure out how to do it without being obvious. A straightforward question about his marital status seemed out of line at this stage.

They'd been into the game for about ten minutes when Peter sent her another message. **This might be a stupid question but are you...single, married, whatever?**

He'd asked *her.*

Beth's relief was instantaneous. **Single.**

Me, too. Age?

Is this an interrogation? she typed back.

Sort of. Do you mind?

Not really. She didn't, because in the process she was learning more about him.

I'll tell if you will.

All right.

I'm edging toward thirty, he typed. **Which is one reason my family is after me to meet someone.**

Me, too. Her heart really started to pound then. Perhaps that candle her mother had lit in church was working. Perhaps, in some quirky way, her prayer had taken effect.

Peter was single; she was single.

He lived in Seattle and she lived in Seattle.

He was close to her age and a professional, just as she was. This almost sounded too good to be true.

My family says it's time I met someone, she typed next.

They do? He seemed as astonished as she felt—as if he, too, was finding this a bit too coincidental. Eerie, even.

A moment later, he typed, **What's wrong with you?**

Well, he was direct enough, but she'd been pretty honest with him, too. She toyed with the idea of telling him she'd been married and divorced, and then remembered Heidi's advice. It wasn't necessary to blurt out everything on the first date—even if this wasn't exactly a date.

I spend too much time playing computer games. She smiled as her fingers skipped effortlessly over the keyboard.

I've got the same problem, came his reply.

Silly though it was, Beth felt sure they were both smiling. Their conversation went on for another hour, and she was shocked to realize the game had become secondary.

That night when Beth crawled into bed and drew the blanket over her shoulders, she fell into an easy, peaceful sleep. She woke with a feeling of expectation, as if something wonderful was about to happen. Keeping her eyes closed, she tried to hang on to that sensation for as long as she could, afraid reality would chase it away.

The phone rang while she dressed for work. Call display told her it was her mother.

"Hi, Mom," she said, answering the phone while fastening an earring.

"You sound happy."

"I am—well, kind of."

Her mother's hesitation was brief. "Does this have anything to do with the man you met on that computer game you're always playing?"

Beth found it hard to believe she'd actually mentioned Peter to her mother. She'd done it on impulse—a bad impulse—hoping to shut down a barrage of veiled criticism and heavy-handed encouragement. Normally her mother would be the last person she'd tell. "We haven't even met, Mom," she finally confessed. "At least not in the flesh."

"What's the holdup?"

"He hasn't suggested we meet outside the game," Beth said, which in her opinion was a perfectly logical explanation. In her mother's generation, the men always did the asking. She figured this was an excuse even her marriage-obsessed mother would accept.

"Then *you* suggest it."

So much for that. "Mother!"

"I'm serious," Joyce said. "Why beat around the bush? You're a woman who knows what she wants. Now go and get it."

Beth thought about asking Peter. Why not? One of them had to break the ice. "I'd like to meet him but I don't want to appear forward."

"Marybeth, you don't have much time. Maybe he's shy. Maybe he's waiting for you to bring it up. Show a bit of initiative, will you? It's later than you think."

"Trust me, Mother, Peter isn't shy." She knew this from the way he attacked their enemies on WoW.

"Then why wait?"

Beth nibbled on her lower lip. "I don't want to rush into anything."

"But it's already December twentieth. Christmas is right around the corner."

This wasn't making sense. "Why is it so important that

Peter join us for Christmas?" Beth asked, beginning to have some suspicions.

"It isn't important… Well, in a manner of speaking it is. Your father and I have this wager."

"Mother!" Her parents constantly made small bets with each other. Most of the time Beth found this habit of theirs amusing. Not now, though. Not when their wager was about *her*. "You'd better tell me everything."

"Okay…" Her mother inhaled deeply. "Last Christmas, your father said that at the rate you were going you'd never remarry."

"And you disagreed with him."

"Of course I did! Marybeth, you have no idea what an attractive young woman you are. You should be happy."

"I am happy," she insisted.

"I disagree. You just think you are."

Beth rolled her eyes, knowing it wouldn't do any good to argue.

"You should be dating," her mother continued.

"And getting married and becoming a mother." The litany was a familiar one.

"Yes," Joyce Fischer said. "I hate the idea that you've got nothing more pressing to go home to than that darned computer game."

"You don't understand, Mom. Peter and I are at level forty and—" She stopped. There was no point in explaining further.

"I beg your pardon?"

"Never mind."

"Does this have anything to do with bringing Peter to dinner on Christmas Day?" her mother wanted to know.

"Nothing whatsoever."

"But that's the important thing here. Otherwise your father…"

"Yes?" Beth murmured.

"Otherwise I'll be hauling the garbage out to the curb every Wednesday for the next six months."

"A fate worse than death," Beth muttered sarcastically.

"It isn't that I mind dealing with the garbage," her mother went on, "but I do mind losing another bet to your father, especially when you're so close to actually having a date for Christmas."

Beth didn't consider herself close at all. In her desperation to win this bet, Joyce was being completely unreasonable.

"Promise me you'll ask Peter," her mother pleaded.

This had gone on long enough. "I'll do no such thing."

"If not for my sake, then your own, Marybeth."

"No!" That was final, too.

The silence that followed weakened her resolve. "Don't you realize how ridiculous you're being?" Beth said. "Peter's practically a stranger."

"Just meet him," Joyce wheedled. "That's all I ask. Whether he comes to Christmas dinner or not is entirely up to you. All I ask is that the two of you connect. Promise me that much."

While she'd never openly admit it, Beth was curious about her online partner. She couldn't help it. She wondered if he was being pressured by his family about meeting her, too. It was worth asking.

She ended the conversation with her mother by booking a lunch date for later in the week.

That evening, as soon as Beth got home from work, she logged on to the game. Peter came on ten minutes after that. The first thing he did was ask about the amount of gold they'd accumulated toward their purchase of a mount. The fact that he avoided the kind of personal comment they'd exchanged the night before was telling. She suspected he was uncomfortable with the way their conversation had turned toward the personal. It had unsettled her, too, and at the same time excited her.

Beth took his cue and simply answered his question.

They played for an hour, but neither one seemed focused on the game.

I need to leave early, she typed in.

Do you have a hot date?

It wasn't a date at all. Beth was meeting Heidi to go over the details of their weekend in Leavenworth. **An appointment,** she told him.

Business or pleasure?

He was getting mighty inquisitive. **Pleasure,** she answered.

There was a slight pause. **Have fun.**

You, too.

No problem meeting tomorrow night?

He'd never asked before. **None.**

Good. Talk to you then.

Beth put Borincana safely away and exited the game. The happy feeling that had greeted her that morning had completely evaporated. She didn't understand what had happened with Peter or why. Was he backing off, losing interest? He'd been eager to confirm that she'd be playing tomorrow, though, so he might just prefer his romance virtual. He might be afraid of taking their relationship into the realms of reality.

What a sorry lot they were, both of them more comfortable in the guise of a fantasy character than dealing with real life. They were two sad, lonely people reaching out at Christmas, wanting to connect and too afraid to try.

Eight

Carter waited at the bus stop with his sister and stamped his feet to ward off the cold. With only two school days—including today—left before winter break, everyone was talking about Christmas and what they expected to find under the tree. Carter knew that his parents couldn't afford gifts. Still, there were several wrapped ones from his grandparents that his mother had already set out. Their Christmas tree was pitiful, but he didn't care as long as there were presents. He just hoped all of his weren't socks or underwear.

As the big yellow bus belched to a stop, Carter grabbed his sister's hand. His mother had instructed him to look out for Bailey, and Carter took his duties seriously.

The bus doors slid open and Carter pushed Bailey ahead of him. As he climbed the steps and felt the warm air on his face, he pulled off his woolen mittens, stuffing them in his pockets. Bailey raced down the aisle toward her friend, Maddy. Ignoring her now, Carter took a seat next to his best friend, Timmy Anderson.

"Want to trade lunches?" Timmy asked. Carter tried to remember what his mother had packed in his *Pirates of the Caribbean* lunch pail. She'd baked cookies the night before and there was the usual peanut-butter-and-jelly sandwich, plus an apple. He had an apple every day, no matter what. Timmy did, too.

"What you got?" Carter asked.

Timmy opened his *Spider-Man* lunch box. "Potato chips, a Twinkie, a pudding cup and an apple."

"No sandwich?"

Timmy shook his head.

Timmy's lunch was filled with all the treats Carter only got if he traded. He loved Twinkies, but his mother baked really good chocolate chip cookies.

"Well?" Timmy pressed. "Wanna trade or not?"

"Okay."

The two boys switched lunch pails. Timmy seemed to like Carter's lunches better than his own. He wanted to trade almost every day.

The bus made another stop and three more students got on. Cameron and Isaiah Benedict came aboard, scrambling into the seat in front of Timmy and Carter.

Cameron twisted around and excitedly announced, "I'm getting an Xbox 360 for Christmas!"

"No way," Timmy said, eyes wide with envy and awe. "I put one on my list, but my parents said it was too expensive."

"Do you know for sure?" Carter asked. He'd thought he was getting a dog like his parents had promised, and that wasn't going to happen. He'd bet Cameron only *thought* he was getting the Xbox.

"Yeah, because Mom said if that's what I wanted, I wouldn't get anything else."

"And Cameron's just got one gift under the tree," his younger brother, Isaiah, explained.

"It could be underwear."

Cameron glared at Carter. "That's not funny."

"I'm getting a PSP," Timmy said.

Carter knew that was a PlayStation Portable, a handheld game everyone wanted. "That's great."

The other boys looked at Carter. "What are you getting for Christmas?"

He shrugged, reluctant to tell his friends that his parents had told him he couldn't have the one and only gift he'd ever truly wanted.

"Well, what did you ask for?" Isaiah leaned over the back of his seat.

Carter would've liked a computer and an Xbox, too, but his family couldn't afford those things. He hung his head and whispered, "I asked for a dog." Instantly a lump filled his throat.

"What kind of dog?"

Carter wasn't picky. "A red dog," he said. If he was going to name him Rusty, then he figured the dog should have reddish fur. "Medium size so he can run and fetch and do stuff like that."

His Grandma Parker had a small, yappy dog, a miniature poodle. Suzette was a good pet for his grandmother, but that wasn't the kind of dog Carter had in mind. His dog would play outside with him during the day, after school and on weekends. At night he could sleep in Carter's room on the rug next to his bed. That was what dogs did. They slept by their masters. Rusty would sleep in the very same spot where Carter had gotten down on his knees and prayed.

If he closed his eyes, Carter could picture his dog with big, floppy ears and a tongue that hung out the side of his mouth when he'd been running. Oh, and Carter wanted a boy dog. A girl dog would be all right, too, but he preferred a boy.

"Are you going to get one?" Cameron asked.

Carter hesitated. "I won't know until Christmas," he muttered.

"Your parents are gonna make you wait?"

He nodded rather than admit the truth.

"I wish I'd asked for a dog," Timmy said, sitting dejectedly back in his seat.

"I'll share Rusty with you," Carter offered, and then remembered there wasn't going to be a Rusty.

"You will?"

"Sure," Carter assured his friend.

Timmy gave Carter a gap-toothed grin, and when the bus arrived at school, the two boys hurried off together.

Their teacher stood in the hallway outside their classroom. As they approached, Timmy burst out, "Ms. Jensen, Ms. Jensen! Guess what? Carter's getting a dog for Christmas."

Their teacher's eyes lit up at the news. "Why, Carter, that's wonderful. Do you have a name for him yet?"

"Rusty."

She nodded approvingly. "That's a great name for a dog."

Carter tried to smile but a funny feeling in the pit of his stomach started to bother him. He didn't know what he was going to do once his friends discovered he didn't get Rusty, after all. He should never have said anything to Timmy.

"Carter said he'd let me play with his dog."

Ms. Jensen beamed at him. "It's good to share. I'm proud of you, Carter." With that, she turned into the classroom and left the two of them waiting in the hallway.

All during their arithmetic lesson, Carter's thoughts wandered to what his friends would say after Christmas when he didn't have his dog. He never should've lied. His stomach hurt the way it always did when he hadn't told the truth.

At recess, Carter walked up to his teacher's desk, holding his stomach. He rarely missed school. In fact, he hadn't stayed home a single day.

"Aren't you feeling well, Carter?" Ms. Jensen asked in a soft caring voice that reminded him of his mother's.

"I have a stomachache."

She pressed the back of her hand against his forehead, then took him down to the nurse's office. Mrs. Weaver was about the same age as his grandmother and had hair that was completely white. She spoke soothingly as she took his temperature. After she'd finished looking at the thermometer, she said he didn't have a fever and suggested he lie down on the couch for a little while.

Carter tried to sleep but he couldn't stop thinking. After a few minutes he sat up, gazing idly out the office window—and that was when he saw it.

A dog.

Outside in the schoolyard was a dog just like the one Carter had imagined. A dog with big, floppy ears. He was exactly the right size, and he jumped and leaped at the students and then chased after a ball. He was skinny and dirty, but Carter could tell that he was a good dog.

He was exactly the kind of dog Carter wanted, although this one didn't have red fur. It was dark and his plumy tail was clumped with mud, but that didn't stop him from wagging it furiously. Watching the other kids play with him made Carter's stomach stop hurting.

"I couldn't reach your mother," Mrs. Weaver told him when she returned.

"I feel better now," he murmured.

"Would you like to go back to your classroom?"

Carter nodded just as the bell ending recess rang. If the dog was still on the playground at lunchtime, Carter would play with him. A sense of exhilaration filled him and he could hardly wait for the midday break.

Carter ate his lunch in record time, then raced outside to the playground without bothering to button up his coat. He'd left Timmy discussing Christmas plans with Isaiah—and enjoying his chocolate chip cookies. The cold, sharp air hit him right in the face, but he didn't care. There weren't many kids outside, but the mutt was there, walking around the yard, sniffing, his nose to the ground. When he saw Carter, the dog instantly ran toward him, looking up with dark pleading eyes.

"Hi, boy," Carter said and dropped to one knee. He withdrew the Twinkie from his pocket, pulled it from its wrapper and fed it to the dog.

The mutt ate the Twinkie in two bites. The poor thing was starved. Now Carter wished he hadn't eaten any of his lunch. He wished he had more food to give his new friend. Thinking quickly, he hurried back into the school. His sister had complained that morning about *another* peanut-butter-and-jelly sandwich. If she didn't want it, Carter did. Not for himself but for the stray.

As he'd expected, his sister was with her friends. She'd eaten everything in her lunch but the sandwich.

"Bailey," he said, breathless now. "Can I have your sandwich?"

Bailey squinted up at him. "What did you do with yours?"

"I gave it to Timmy."

Bailey hesitated. "I was going to eat mine."

"No, you weren't. Come on, Bailey, I need that sandwich."

"What'll you trade me for it?" she asked.

Carter didn't have a lot of time. If he didn't hurry back outside, some other kid would make friends with the dog. He might even leave the schoolyard. "You can watch whatever you want on TV Saturday morning."

His sister's eyes widened. It was a generous offer and she knew it. They only had one television set and their mother made them take turns choosing what to see. Bailey liked sissy stuff, while Carter liked action heroes.

"*All* Saturday morning?"

Carter nodded. With a smug look, Bailey handed over her peanut-butter-and-jelly sandwich.

Grabbing it, Carter hurried back outside. The playground was crowded with kids by then, but as soon as the mutt saw Carter, he bounded across the playground toward him.

Once again, Carter got down on one knee. He wiped the muddy hair from the dog's eyes; his own hands got grimy in the process but Carter didn't care. Taking the sandwich out of his pocket, he tore off the plastic and held it out to the mutt. The bread disappeared as quickly as the Twinkie had.

"You shouldn't be feeding that dog."

Carter glanced up to find Mr. Nicholson, the sixth-grade teacher, who was on schoolyard duty during lunch, scowling down at him. "I've already called Animal Control about this dog once."

"No!" An automatic protest came from Carter. He didn't want this friendly dog to go to a shelter.

"He doesn't belong on the playground."

"He's a nice dog."

Mr. Nicholson didn't agree or disagree. "I don't want to see you feeding him again. Is that understood?"

Carter nodded. The teacher didn't exactly say Carter couldn't feed the stray. What he'd said was that he didn't want to *see* Carter do it.

The teacher went off to intervene in an argument between some sixth-grade kids, and Carter petted the dog's face. "It's all right, boy, I'll bring you food. Will you be here tomorrow?"

The mutt looked back at him with intense brown eyes, as if to say he'd be waiting for Carter.

On his way back to class, Carter washed his hands. He wondered how long the dog had been lost. He sure was dirty, and he seemed lonely, too. Carter's heart ached for him. What the stray needed was a good home and a family, just like everyone did. Carter hoped the Animal Control people didn't catch him before Carter figured out how to bring him to his house.

First he had to explain to his father that this dog wasn't a puppy but a grown-up dog that needed a home. This wasn't an expensive dog, either. He was a plain ordinary dog. He'd probably already had his shots.

That night Carter couldn't keep still at the dinner table. All he could think about was the dog in the schoolyard, out in the cold and dark by himself. He wanted to bring him home right then and there. He was worried the dog might not be safe, or that the people from Animal Control would take him to a shelter. That might not be such a bad thing, because he might be adopted by a family. Except that Carter wanted the dog for himself.

"Carter, eat your dinner," his father said.

Carter stared down at his plate. Spaghetti was one of his favorite meals. His mother had made it specially for him, and all he could do was swirl the noodles around with his fork. He needed to figure out how to smuggle the meatballs off his plate and hide them until morning.

"How were your classes?" his mother asked. It was the same question she asked every night.

"Good," Carter murmured. "I had a tummy ache but it went away."

"Carter fed a dog in the schoolyard and got in trouble." Bailey could hardly wait to tattle on him.

From across the table, Carter glared at his sister.

His father frowned. "Whose dog was it?"

Carter shrugged. "He doesn't belong to anyone."

"He's a stray?"

Carter stared at his plate again. "I guess so."

"He was real dirty and had mud all over him and Carter gave him a sandwich and petted him until Mr. Nicholson made him stop."

"Oh, Carter," his mother whispered.

His father shook his head. "I don't want you bringing that dog home, Carter. Is that understood?"

"Okay."

"I mean it," he said sternly.

Carter swallowed hard as he tried not to cry. "May I be excused, please?" he asked.

His mother gently rested her hand on his. "Yes, you may."

Carter went into the bedroom he shared with his sister and fell, fully dressed, across his bed. He buried his face in his pillow, praying the dog would still be there the following day.

Nine

Mercy regarded Shirley suspiciously, her arms folded, her foot tapping. "You brought that dog to the schoolyard, didn't you?" She pointed at the animal, who lay in the sandbox, head resting on his outstretched paws as he slept.

Shirley sat on the swing at the farthest reaches of the yard and shook her head adamantly. "I most certainly did not. I don't have a clue where that dog came from. Trust me, if I brought a dog into Carter's life, it wouldn't be *that* mangy mutt."

Mercy didn't believe her. "I, for one, find it mighty convenient that a stray dog should show up in the schoolyard today." And besides, she knew Shirley loved animals—despite the scornful way she'd spoken about this dog.

"I agree with Mercy." Goodness came to stand at her side, her foot tapping in an identical tempo.

"Stop looking at me like that," Shirley muttered. "Carter can't have a dog. That decision's already been made. You both know I can't interfere with the chain of command. Carter's father feels bad enough as it is, but he's said in no uncertain terms that his son can't have a dog. Why would I complicate matters?"

"Why would she?" Goodness turned to Mercy.

"I don't know, but like I said, I find this entire situation a little too convenient."

Shirley stepped free of the swing and brushed the snow from her hands. "Speaking of convenient, I think it's very interesting that Beth and Peter appear to be so well-matched."

Goodness raised both arms. "Don't look at me. I didn't have a thing to do with that. They met online six months ago, remember?"

"Quite right," Mercy confirmed. "And before you mention Harry and Rosalie running into Lucy Menard, I've explained that."

A wistful expression came over Goodness. "I do hope everything works out for Beth and Peter."

"Why shouldn't it?" Shirley asked.

"They're both so stubborn—and so scared. What they need is a good shove in the right direction."

"Goodness!" Shirley's expression was scandalized. "Don't even *think* like that. Our job is to teach these humans a lesson. They have to make their own decisions, find their own way."

"Find their own way?" Mercy didn't mean to sound sarcastic, but she couldn't help it. The evidence was overwhelming; humans were a pathetic bunch. "May I remind you that humans wandered in the desert for forty years on a trip that should've taken three months, tops?"

"Joshua had them march around Jericho seven times, looking for the main gate to the city," Goodness added, shaking her head.

Shirley frowned. "You both know there were very good reasons for those incidents."

"True, but you have to admit humans don't exactly have an impressive track record."

With a disgruntled look, Shirley was forced to admit the truth.

"Humans need help," Mercy reiterated.

"Our help."

Still Shirley didn't seem convinced. "But Gabriel—"

"Will never find out," Mercy assured her. "We won't be blatant about it—just a nudge or two where it's warranted. If Gabriel's going to place us under earthly time constraints, we need to be inventive."

"Inventive," Goodness echoed. "How do you mean?"

"Well, for one thing, it's obvious that you'll have to step in with Beth and Peter."

"I will?"

"Yes." Mercy didn't understand why *she* had to clarify everything for her fellow Prayer Ambassadors. "Didn't you tell me they still haven't set a time to meet?"

"Well, yes…"

"And the reason is?"

Goodness shifted uncomfortably. "Well, like I said, they're afraid…."

"Afraid of what?" Mercy asked. "Do you suppose maybe they're afraid of being disillusioned?"

"They could be," Goodness said. "And I agree—they need help. The last time I looked, Beth was depressed. Everything was going so well between her and Peter, and then he closed down for no apparent reason."

"Is there anything you can do about it?"

"I… Yes, of course there is." Her eyes darted from side to side. "Unfortunately, I can't think what it would be at this precise moment, but it'll come to me."

"Shirley." Mercy focused her gaze on the former guardian angel.

"Reporting for duty." She stood military straight, wings neatly folded, feet together. Mercy wondered if Shirley was making fun of her.

"How do you plan to help Carter?" she asked.

Shirley's shoulders sagged with defeat. "I'll make sure

the dog's nowhere to be seen when he arrives for school tomorrow."

"You're sure that's the right thing for Carter?" Mercy asked, her own heart aching for the little boy.

Reluctantly Shirley nodded. "His father said he couldn't have a dog, no matter what. I don't have any choice."

All three considered this unfortunate set of circumstances.

"Maybe I could steer Carter's father toward a better-paying job," Shirley suggested.

"That's an idea."

Goodness turned to her. "What's happening with Harry?" she asked.

Ah, yes, Harry and Rosalie. "They visited Lucy Menard earlier this afternoon and got a tour of the assisted-living complex."

"And what happened?" Shirley asked.

"Come with me and let's find out," Mercy invited. Together with her two friends, she descended on the house at 23 Walnut Avenue, where Rosalie and Harry sat across from each other at the dinner table.

"I was surprised at how many of our friends have moved to Liberty Orchard," Rosalie murmured, gazing down at her bowl of canned chicken stew.

She seemed deep in thought, and that encouraged Harry. The visit had gone even better than he could've expected. Rosalie had met three good friends she'd lost contact with in the last few years. Each one had urged them to make the change and become part of the community at Liberty Orchard.

"Did you notice how most people said they were sorry they hadn't moved into assisted living sooner?" Harry waited for his wife to protest. She hadn't wanted him to know, but he could see that she'd been impressed with the facility.

"What I liked was all the social activities," Rosalie murmured.

Harry agreed. He'd been impressed himself, glad, too, because he felt that after he died Rosalie would have the social contact she needed. A wave of sadness washed over him at the thought of leaving his wife behind. He tried not to dwell on the subject of death, but knowing it was imminent, he couldn't stop thinking about it.

Trying not to appear too enthusiastic about the assisted-living complex, Harry nodded.

"My goodness," Rosalie said happily, "those folks have something going on every day of the week."

Harry nodded again, taking a bite of his stew.

"Did you read the dinner menu?" Rosalie asked him. She'd found it posted outside the dining room and gone over it three or four times. She'd had all kinds of questions for Lucy, too. The midday meal was the main one of the day, with a lighter one served at about five. "Why, they had a choice of two soups *and* a salad, plus fish, chicken or meat loaf. And Lucy said it's different every day!"

"I took a look at it myself," Harry said gently. One thing was certain; the residents at Liberty Orchard weren't eating any of their meals out of a can—unless they chose to. He didn't need to point out the obvious, however.

His wife set down her spoon. "Harry," she began shyly, "I'm not sure if you've noticed, but I'm starting to forget things now and then." The admission came with some hesitation. "I've begun to wonder if one of the reasons is that my mind isn't as active as it used to be."

"Lucy said the same thing happened to her," Harry pointed out, reminding his wife of the conversation earlier in the day. "Do you recall how she said that as soon as she spent time with other people again, she wasn't nearly as forgetful?"

Rosalie thought about this for a moment. "She did, didn't she?"

Harry was cautious about saying too much too soon. Rosalie's eyes had been opened when she'd seen the facility, and it didn't hurt that a number of their friends had already made the move.

"Lucy also said the unit closest to hers is available." He said this casually and waited for a response. While his wife had been chatting with her friends, Harry had met with the administrator to see if they could secure that particular unit. Naturally, he wouldn't make a decision like this without discussing it with Rosalie first, but he was beginning to feel confident that she saw the wisdom of such a move.

Rosalie looked at him the same way she had all those years ago, when they'd considered purchasing this very house. She loved this place and Harry loved her. He would've moved heaven and earth to buy the house she wanted.

"Do you honestly think we should give up our home, Harry?"

He hated that it had come to this. "Like I said, this old place is getting to be too much for me."

Slowly Rosalie lowered her gaze and conceded. "And me."

This was the first time she'd been willing to admit that age had taken a toll on her, too. As far as Harry was concerned, it was a giant leap forward.

"We should ask the girls," she said tentatively.

"Good idea." Their youngest daughter was coming to spend Christmas with them, and Lorraine and family would arrive the day after. Both his daughters agreed with Harry. Like him, they recognized the necessity of this change, even if they hadn't quite grasped its urgency.

Harry knew that if Rosalie discussed the situation with either Lorraine or Donna, their daughters would reassure her in ways he couldn't. He felt it was only a matter of time. God willing, everything would fall into place....

"I don't want to discuss it again until after Christmas, though," Rosalie insisted. "I won't even talk about moving until the holidays are over."

"But, Rosalie, there's only the one unit," he blurted out. "Unless we give the administrator a security check, someone else might take it."

"Then so be it," she said, missing the point that he'd talked to the administrator without her knowledge.

"Mrs. Goldsmith told me there's another party interested." A sense of dread almost overwhelmed him. If they didn't act quickly, the unit would go to some other couple.

"Of course she told you that," Rosalie said with unshakable confidence. "That's what she's supposed to say. It's a tactic, Harry. You, of all people, should know the things people will say when they're after a sale."

Frustration beat hard against his chest. "But, Rosalie..."

"Harry, sweetheart, don't be so concerned. If we lose this unit, another will come up later."

Without telling her what Dr. Snellgrove had said, Harry had no choice but to agree. "Personally, I'd like this all settled *before* the holidays."

"Do you mind if we wait?" Rosalie asked. "It won't make any difference, will it?"

"I suppose you're right," he said reluctantly. "It doesn't really matter." Only it did, but Harry couldn't find it in his heart to tell her why.

Harry left the table and as much as he hated his walker, he reached for it. The damn thing was a nuisance, but at this stage it was a necessary one.

"The girls could help us move while they're here." He made the suggestion as he settled back into his recliner.

"Not over Christmas, Harry. Please, sweetheart, I don't want to ask that of them."

He nodded. He wouldn't mention it again. Not tonight.

"It doesn't look good," Shirley had the audacity to say.

"Rosalie wants to wait until after Christmas."

Mercy didn't know what to do. "That won't work."

"Why not?" Both her friends turned to face her.

Mercy sighed, more burdened now than ever. "Because Harry will be in Heaven by then."

Ten

J oyce Fischer had found a table at the ultra-busy Nordstrom Café by the time Beth got to the store. As soon as she appeared, her mother waved to catch her attention.

Beth felt wonderful and couldn't have disguised her mood had she tried.

"Hello, Mom," she said, giving her mother a quick hug.

"I took the liberty of ordering for you, dear. I just got two of what we usually order."

"That's fine." Beth only had an hour for lunch and although she would've liked to try something new rather than her standard soup du jour and turkey sandwich, she didn't object.

Taking off her coat, Beth draped it over her chair.

"You're positively glowing. What's going on?" Her mother looked like she was about to rub her hands together in glee. "Is it that young man from the computer game?"

"We're going to meet." Beth wasn't sure how and why the situation had changed. Just as she was losing hope that they'd ever take a chance, Peter had stepped forward. Without understanding why it had happened, she realized that a transformation had taken place.

They'd logged on to play World of Warcraft last night and after a while had started exchanging messages again. In the beginning it wasn't anything special, just their normal chitchat. Then out of the blue Peter had made a startling admission.

"He's divorced," Beth informed her mother.

"Well, dear, so are you."

"I know… That's not the point. Peter and I were talking."

"On the phone?"

"No, no, online. That's the only way we've communicated so far."

Her mother frowned, then decided not to make whatever comment hovered on the tip of her tongue. "Go on," she urged instead. "I want to hear everything."

"Well," Beth said, eager now. "He told me that it's taken him some time to get over the divorce, but he thinks he's ready to move on."

"How long has it been?" her mother asked. "I mean, since his divorce was final."

Beth frowned. Her mother was right; that was an important question. "I didn't ask him."

"You should, dear. If it's been less than a year, it might be best to move slowly and carefully in this relationship." Then, as if she regretted having given advice, she shook her head. "Follow your heart. Don't listen to a thing I say."

Beth thought cynically that this was all part of the wager her parents had. Her mother didn't care if Peter was the brother of Frankenstein's monster as long as he showed up. "You really want him there for Christmas, don't you?"

Her mother's eyes brightened. "Is there any possibility that might happen?"

Beth shrugged. Despite her mother's bet—and personally she felt Joyce deserved to lose—she'd like it if Peter could spend Christmas with her. She wanted to invite him, but it was a lot to ask of someone she hadn't even met. Everything depended on this weekend.

Her mother waved one hand impatiently. "So you told him you're divorced, too?"

"Yes, of course, and then we both started talking so fast it was hard for my fingers to keep up with my thoughts." Peter had been deeply hurt by his wife, who'd more or less kicked him out of the house and excluded him from her life. It'd been painful and harsh, and he'd taken the breakup of his marriage hard.

Beth understood. She'd experienced the same grief over the death of her own marriage. In the course of their conversation, they'd talked about regrets and all the things they might've done to save their marriages. Based on the few details Peter had divulged, Beth regarded his ex-wife as cold and calculating.

She talked about John in ways she never had with anyone else, including her parents. It was as though a festering blister had burst inside her and she spewed out the devastating pain of her own divorce.

The game was forgotten as they continued talking. It was after midnight when Peter reminded her that they both needed to be at work in the morning. Reluctantly Beth had signed off.

"What else did he say?" her mother asked. "Did you tell him your real name is Marybeth?"

"Hardly," she cried, annoyed that her mother would ask such an inane question. "And don't you tell him, either."

"So you did invite him for Christmas?" Her mother looked pleased beyond measure.

"No…not yet." The optimism Beth felt was a sign of her excitement about the way their relationship was developing. No man had interested her this much since college, when she'd first met John. Peter gave her hope. Maybe this wouldn't go anywhere, but at least she was finally taking a risk. Finally willing to try again.

The server brought their lunches, giving Beth a respite from her mother's relentless questioning. She tasted her cream of broccoli soup, and it took a few minutes for the conversation to return to Peter.

"You do expect to introduce him to your family, don't you?" Her mother smiled expectantly at Beth, the turkey sandwich poised in front of her mouth.

"If things go well." She nodded. "We have a lot in common, Peter and me."

"That's wonderful, dear."

Beth felt the giddy sensation of everything coming together at last. "I never dreamed that after all these months we'd connect the way we have."

"Well?" Her mother paused. "When are you going to meet?" Before Beth could answer, she added, "Soon, I hope."

"Is tomorrow soon enough for you?"

"Saturday? But I thought you were going to Leavenworth with Heidi."

"I am."

"You're meeting Peter there?"

Beth nodded. Peter seemed to be a closet romantic, although she suspected he'd never admit it. He was the one who'd wanted to have this initial meeting right away. He'd mentioned getting together on Saturday for lunch, and Beth had said she'd be in Leavenworth. Undeterred, Peter had suggested meeting there.

"But how will that work when you don't know what he looks like? Good grief, Beth, do you have any idea how crowded that town can get, especially this time of year?"

"We've got it all figured out. Heidi and Sam and I are taking the train with the kids and—"

"Peter will meet you on the train?" her mother broke in.

"Not exactly. The train sold out weeks ago, so Peter's taking the bus. We arrive at eleven and, depending on the weather, he should get in around noon."

"The train's always late."

"Oh, ye of little faith."

"I have a lot of faith," her mother said. "But I happen to be practical, too."

"We took that into consideration, Mother. The bus could be late, too, you know."

"Yes, of course."

"We're meeting by the gazebo in the center of town at four o'clock."

"Why not earlier?" her mother demanded.

Beth sighed. "I'm there to spend the day with Heidi, remember? Besides, if this doesn't work out…"

"Fine," Joyce said dismissively. "But how will you recognize each other?"

Beth described their plan. Peter would be carrying a single long-stemmed red rose and wearing a baseball cap with a Seahawks emblem. She, meanwhile, would be wearing a full-length navy wool coat and a red knit hat and muffler.

They should be able to find each other without difficulty. Then they'd watch the tree-lighting ceremony together. The train was scheduled to depart at six-thirty; his bus would leave shortly after that. They'd spend just a couple of hours in each other's company—a safe length of time whether the meeting went well or not. He hadn't said so, but Beth had the distinct feeling that if this meeting *did* go well, Peter would ask to see her again on Sunday.

"You sound so hopeful," her mother said.

"I am." Beth had a positive feeling about this.

"What if…what if Peter isn't as good-looking as you expect?" She seemed genuinely concerned that this might be a possibility.

"It doesn't matter." John had been drop-dead gorgeous. She'd been the envy of all her friends, and what she'd discovered was that good looks made very little difference. Most important was character. Moral fiber, sense of honor and kindness were far more compelling qualities in Beth's eyes.

"You say that now," her mother warned, "but you might change your mind once you meet him."

"Perhaps." But even as she said it, Beth was convinced that her feelings wouldn't change. If there was anything she'd learned from her divorce, it was that looks could be deceiving. John had been completely self-absorbed, selfish, irresponsible.... It was pointless to rehash his shortcomings, of which there'd been plenty.

They finished their lunch and because she had a few minutes to spare, Beth and her mother did some window-shopping. Seattle was a magical city at Christmastime. Beth loved the festive air—the decorations everywhere, the cheerful crowds, the music. Entertainers sang and played instruments. She and Joyce stopped to listen to a violinist whose rendition of "Silent Night" was exquisite as people bustled to and from stores with their bags and packages. The cold wind stung her face and she glanced up at the sky for any sign of snow. Her step was lighter and for the first time in years she felt a rush of joyful anticipation about Christmas.

Her mother wasn't the only one to notice her improved mood. Lloyd, the attorney who'd introduced her to the World of Warcraft, commented on it when she returned from lunch.

"You seem to be mighty happy about something," he said, smiling at her.

"I am," she responded cryptically.

At closing time, she hurried home. As soon as she was back in her condo, Beth logged online, hoping Peter would be there. He was.

Did you have a good day? he typed.

Great. What about you?

He didn't reply immediately. It couldn't have been better, he eventually wrote. Thank you for listening while I poured out my woes about my marriage last night. I don't often talk about it. I wouldn't have with you, but in all fairness I felt you needed to know.

Peter, thank you, she hurriedly typed back. I can't tell you how freeing it was for me to tell you about my divorce. It's not a subject I bring up lightly. I felt like such a failure when we split up and that feeling never went away.

I know. That's how I felt when my marriage ended, too.

It seems we have even more in common than we realized, she told him.

I was thinking the same thing.

They chatted for most of an hour until Beth's stomach growled, reminding her that she hadn't eaten dinner. Peter couldn't stay online long because he was seeing a friend, so they ended their conversation.

It was just as well, because Beth had to call Heidi and let her friend know there'd been a small change in plans.

After she reached her, Beth explained that she'd be seeing Peter in Leavenworth and said she hoped Heidi didn't mind.

"Mind? Of course I don't mind," Heidi told her. "I think it's so romantic that you two will meet up there. All we need now is some snow for the day to be absolutely perfect."

Snow in Santa's Village—that would indeed be marvelous.

"I wonder if I'm expecting too much," she said, suddenly anxious.

"How can you help it?" Heidi asked. "He does seem too good to be true."

No dating service could have set her up with a more suitable candidate. They agreed on practically everything they'd discussed. In the past week, Beth had learned that they both read the same books, liked the same kinds of food—Mexican and Chinese—and adored anchovies on Caesar salad but not pizza. Granted, those might be superficial similarities, but unlike John, Peter was responsible and dedicated, both qualities she admired. She knew this from his loyalty to his friends, his seriousness about his career—as a coffee buyer at Starbucks—his affection toward his parents and many other examples she'd gleaned.

Maybe he was too good to be true, as Heidi had said. But Beth's instincts told her that Peter was a man she wanted to know better, a man *worth* knowing better. Not that her instincts had been what you'd call reliable in the past. So, before things went any further, she had to learn if this could become a viable relationship—and there was only one way to find out.

In other words, Beth was counting on their face-to-face meeting to tell her whether these feelings for Peter were real—or just a fantasy concocted during their online adventures.

Eleven

Carter could hardly wait to get to school. As soon as the bus dropped him off he headed for the playground, instead of running into the classroom with Timmy and his other friends. Behind the building, he looked carefully around.

Rusty was nowhere to be seen. His heart sank.

"What are you doing out here?" Timmy asked, chasing after him.

"Nothing," Carter murmured, his shoulders slumping. All night he could barely sleep thinking about the stray. The more he thought about it, the more he realized this wasn't just any dog. This was *his* dog. His Rusty. God had sent him this dog. Rusty was the answer to Carter's prayer.

"Wanna play soccer?" Timmy asked. "I can get Cameron and Isaiah and—"

"No, thanks."

Timmy looked as dejected as Carter felt. "It's cold out here. Let's go inside."

"All right." Timmy followed him off the playground and into the building.

When classes started, he had trouble paying attention to Ms. Jensen. Carter kept wondering what had happened to

Rusty. He worried that Animal Control had picked him up, and then worried that they hadn't.

Deep down, Carter knew that if Rusty was at a shelter, he'd at least be out of the cold. And there'd be plenty of food for him. But Carter had brought an extra-big lunch today, just in case.

After the recess bell rang, his friends dashed out the door, eager to put on their winter clothes and get onto the playground.

"Carter." Ms. Jensen stopped him.

Carter trudged over to his teacher. "Yes, Ms. Jensen?" He thought about asking if she'd seen the stray dog recently, but then he remembered Mr. Nicholson's warning.

"Is everything all right?"

"Yes, Ms. Jensen."

"At home, I mean."

He nodded. He wanted to tell her that his family wasn't getting Christmas presents this year and that he'd lied to his friends. He still felt bad about misleading Timmy. But he didn't want the other kids to know that the only gift under the tree would be underwear from his grandmother.

"You don't seem yourself. Are you feeling well?"

"I'm fine, Ms. Jensen. Can I go outside now?"

"All right. Oh, and thank your mother for the cookies she sent me."

"I will," Carter promised.

As he hurried onto the playground, Carter noticed that his teacher was still watching him. No sooner was he outside with his friends than he saw Rusty. Carter could hardly breathe, he was so excited.

Rusty saw Carter, too, and even though one of the third-grade girls was offering him a cracker, the dog shot across the schoolyard. Carter knelt down to greet his friend. Rusty licked his face and seemed as happy to see Carter as Carter was to see him. Carter dug inside his pocket for a meatball he'd managed to smuggle out of the refrigerator early that morning. Rusty gobbled it up and looked to Carter for more.

"I'm sorry," Carter told him, and then because he was so ecstatic, he wrapped his arms around the dog. He didn't care that Rusty was filthy or that the sleeves of his winter jacket came away all muddy. His mother would be upset, but even her displeasure was worth the enjoyment Carter received from this special dog.

"We can't let Mr. Nicholson see you," Carter warned, then ran over to where his friends were playing.

Rusty followed Carter wherever he went. When Mr. Nicholson stepped into the yard, the stray quickly and quietly disappeared, just as if he understood.

Carter turned around and looked for him, but Rusty was nowhere in sight. Then he saw that the dog had gone into the trees that separated the schoolyard from the nearby houses.

"Good boy," Carter whispered. Rusty was no dummy. He knew who his friends were—and his enemies.

At lunchtime, Carter only ate his apple. The rest he saved for Rusty. Once again the mutt gobbled the food and gazed up at Carter with bright, shining eyes that revealed his gratitude.

Carter petted Rusty's head, although his hand got really dirty. What would happen to the dog over the holidays, when there was no one at the school? Who'd feed Rusty then? Who'd watch out for him? Carter already knew the answer. No one. After today, school was over for the year, and the yard would remain empty until the first week of January. Rusty could starve by then.

Holding the dog's muddy face between his hands, Carter peered into his deep brown eyes. Disregarding what his father had said, Carter whispered, "Rusty, listen, I need you to follow me home."

The dog blinked and stared back at him intently.

"I take bus number seven. Follow that bus, okay?"

Rusty cocked his head to one side.

Carter didn't know what more he could do. Disconsolate, he tried to accept that the dog wouldn't understand him, no matter how many times he repeated the information. After today, when the bus delivered Carter to his home, it was unlikely he'd ever see Rusty again. Carter couldn't bear to have that happen, but he had to prepare himself for disappointment.

Because it was the last day before winter break, school was dismissed an hour early. While Carter lined up with his friends for bus number seven, he scanned the area for Rusty. Again the dog was nowhere to be seen, and once again Carter's heart fell.

"You wanna come to my house and play video games?" Timmy asked, plopping down on the seat next to Carter.

"No, thanks."

His friend seemed dejected.

"Can I come on Monday?" Carter asked.

"Sure." Timmy perked up right away. "I'll show you all my presents under the tree."

"Okay." Carter tried to smile but it was hard. He was glad that his friend was getting lots of gifts. He wanted gifts, too—stacks and stacks of them. But Carter would give up every single one for Rusty.

God had answered his prayer, Carter told himself, struggling to believe. Rusty *would* find him. God had sent Rusty to that schoolyard and now God would figure out a way to bring him to Carter's house.

The bus stopped, and Cameron and Isaiah got off and ran to their home at the end of the street. Their house was the biggest and nicest in the neighborhood.

The next stop was for Carter and Bailey's block. Grabbing his backpack, Carter felt his heart beating hard. He hoped with all his might that Rusty would find his way.

Bus number seven. He'd told Rusty to follow bus number seven. Carter knew it would be a miracle if the dog had understood him, but God was in charge of miracles, and He'd already worked one. If He could do one miracle and send him a dog, then God should be able to accomplish *two*.

When the doors of the bus opened, Carter stepped down and looked in both directions. Rusty wasn't there. His heart felt about as heavy as…as a two-ton truck.

"Move," Bailey said, coming down the steps and shoving him in the back.

"Hey," Carter complained.

"You're blocking the exit," Bailey informed him in that prim tattletale voice she sometimes used.

Carter got completely off the bus then and started slowly down the sidewalk to their house. Bailey walked beside him.

"I saw you with that dog on the playground again," his sister said, matching her steps to his. She held her backpack with both hands, leaning into the cold wind.

"You're not gonna tell Mom and Dad, are you?"

"No. He's a nice dog."

Carter nodded. "He's smart, too." But not smart enough to follow bus seven. Not smart enough to know that winter break had begun and there'd be no one at the school to feed him or play with him or anything else. Sooner or later, he'd be picked up by Animal Control.

"You should wash off your coat before Mom sees it," his sister warned.

Carter had forgotten about the mud on his sleeves. "I will. You go in the house first, all right?"

"Okay."

True to her word, Bailey went into the house and while she distracted their mother, Carter removed his coat in their bedroom, then entered the kitchen.

"Ms. Jensen thanked you for the cookies," Carter told his

mother. She was folding towels fresh from the dryer on the kitchen table and nodded absently. "Your father's working late this evening," she said. "He's getting overtime pay, and that's good."

"Oh."

"He said we should have dinner without him."

"Can we have macaroni and cheese out of a box?" Carter asked. That was one of his favorites, and he knew it must not cost very much because his mother never objected when he asked for it.

"Okay," she said.

"I wanted hot dogs," Bailey whined.

His mother smiled. "We'll have both."

While his sister helped their mother put away the towels, Carter loped into the bathroom for a clean washcloth and soaked it. Then he wrung it out and took it into the bedroom where he'd put his coat. He wiped off the sleeves. The wash-cloth got muddy, but his coat looked a lot better.

"Mom said we could watch television," Bailey said, coming into the room.

Since his sister would choose sissy programs, Carter wasn't interested.

"I'm gonna go read."

That was an activity his parents always approved of. The only reason he decided on it now was that he didn't feel like doing anything else. He didn't want to visit his friends or watch television or even play with his toys. He just wanted to forget Rusty. Apparently God only did one miracle at a time. Carter had been wrong.

Slumping down on the floor, he opened his book, but he could hardly concentrate on the story. About fifteen minutes later, his sister barreled into the bedroom. "Carter, come and look!"

"At what?"

"Just come," she insisted, annoying him with every word.

"Oh, all right," he muttered.

She led him to the living room, where the television was situated. She pointed out the front window.

There was Rusty, walking up and down the sidewalk, looking this way and that.

Carter nearly screamed with happiness. "It's Rusty!"

"I know." His sister's eyes were huge.

Without bothering to get his coat, Carter burst out the door. "Rusty!" he cried. "Rusty."

As soon as the dog heard Carter, he turned and bolted toward him. Carter dared not hug him now because his mother would see all the mud. But how could she be angry? God had sent them this dog. Carter had proof that Rusty was the answer to his prayer.

"This way, boy," Carter said and led him to the back of the house. Because their mother had told them their dad would be late, Carter put Rusty in the garage. By the time he'd finished, his teeth were chattering with cold and excitement.

"Are you going to tell Mom?" Bailey asked, meeting him in the hallway.

"Not yet." A plan was taking shape in Carter's mind. "If Mom asks where I am, tell her I'm taking a bath."

"Are you?" Bailey wanted to know.

"No." He shouldn't have to spell *everything* out to his sister. "I'm going to give Rusty one. When he's all cleaned up, Mom will see what a good dog he is and talk Dad into letting me keep him."

Bailey's eyes widened and she nodded conspiratorially.

Carter filled the bathtub with warm water and then at an opportune moment, went into the garage and scooped up Rusty. He was heavier than Carter had thought but it was important that he not leave dog tracks on the floor. Once inside the house, Carter glanced around to make sure his mother wasn't looking. Then he hurried down the hall to the bathroom and shut the door with his foot. He gently set the dog in the bath, then turned quickly to lock the door.

It didn't take Carter long to make a startling discovery about Rusty. When he did, tears sprang to his eyes. Beneath all the caked mud and dirt, Rusty had auburn-colored fur. This really *was* the dog God had sent. He was perfect in every way.

Rusty loved the water. He stood still while Carter lathered him with the shampoo their mother had bought for him and Bailey. Then he rinsed him off with the cup that was by the sink. Rusty didn't bark even once. Using the towel still warm from the dryer, Carter had just lifted Rusty out of the tub to dry him when Rusty began to shake himself like crazy, spraying water in every direction.

"Rusty!" Carter protested, raising his hands to his face to wipe off the water.

"Carter," his mother called from the other side of the bathroom door. "Who's in there with you?"

He wanted to lie and answer *no one,* but he remembered what his stomach had felt like when he'd lied. "A friend," Carter called back. That was true. Rusty was his friend.

"What are you doing in there?"

"Ah…"

The door handle twisted and then his mother called again. "Carter, unlock the door this minute!"

Carter bit his lip as Rusty gazed back at him trustingly. "Okay, boy," he whispered. "It's showtime."

Carter unlatched the bathroom door and opened it for his mother. She stood there, hands on her hips. The moment she saw Rusty, her eyes went soft—and then immediately went hard again.

"Oh, Carter, a dog."

"But this is *my* dog, Rusty. God sent him."

"Carter…" His mother was almost crying. "Look at the

bathtub. It's filthy." Sure enough, there was dirt on the bottom of the tub and the ring around the sides was pretty bad, too.

"I'll clean it up," Carter promised. He would've done so earlier, but his mother had interrupted him.

"He's a really good dog, Mom," Carter felt obliged to tell her.

"I'm sure he is, honey. It's just that I don't know what we're going to tell your father."

Carter looked at Rusty and then at the worried expression on his mother's face. He didn't know what they'd tell his dad, either.

Twelve

Harry woke with a start. His eyes flew open as panic overtook him. He gasped for air, unable to get his breath. No matter how hard he struggled, he couldn't breathe. The pain intensified, suffocating him.

Blindly reaching for the small bottle he kept at his bedside, he popped a nitro pill under his tongue and waited. This had happened before in the early hours of the morning. It felt as though he was immersed in water and couldn't get any air.

Could this be his time?

It almost seemed that God intended to take him right then and there. Quelling the panic, Harry surrendered his life to God and then all at once, the ache lessened and his lungs filled with glorious air. The relief was instantaneous. He dragged in a second deep breath and realized he'd had a narrow escape yet again.

Wide awake now, Harry watched the jerky movements of the second hand on the old-fashioned alarm clock by his bedside. Rosalie had a clock radio, but he continued to use the one he'd always had. It needed winding every couple of days, but had served him well through the years and he could see no reason to change. The ticking was a familiar comfort.

Two minutes passed and he was still breathing normally.

His close call reminded him that he wouldn't be around for Rosalie much longer; naturally he wanted to get her settled before he left her. She was determined to spend Christmas in this old house. Harry couldn't deny his wife that. But while he sympathized with her feelings, Harry didn't have that kind of time. His fear was that when he was gone, Rosalie would just keep putting off the move. Harry couldn't let that happen.

First thing after New Year's, he'd make the arrangements, he decided, praying God would give him that long.

Harry sat up in bed.

"Harry?" Rosalie was instantly awake. The slightest movement on his part seemed to alert her. Similarly, when their girls were small, she'd wakened at the tiniest sound. Harry had never understood it because his wife was usually a sound sleeper. Not when their daughters were young, though, and not with him now.

He'd disturbed her sleep far too many times. After the full day they'd had touring the assisted-living complex Rosalie was exhausted, and Harry didn't want to interrupt her rest tonight.

"I'm fine, sweetheart," he whispered.

Her eyes drifted closed and she went back to sleep. Harry lay very still and listened to the regular cadence of her breathing. Twice his own went shallow and then regained an even consistency.

It went without saying that God had granted him yet another reprieve. Death would come. Not now, but soon— sooner than he would've liked.

When it became apparent that he wasn't going to fall asleep immediately, Harry slowly shifted the covers aside. He might as well empty his bladder, which he needed to do two or three times a night. Darn nuisance it was, but that was another symptom of age and his body's growing demands.

Once he'd finished, he started back to bed and remembered that he'd left his walker in the other room. Since he hated having to use the contraption, he sometimes forgot it. He knew he was in trouble; the short trip to the bathroom had depleted his strength and without the walker, he couldn't manage even the few steps back to his bed. Weak as he was, he leaned his shoulder against the wall, considering his options. There weren't any. He needed help and he needed it now.

"Rosalie," he called. His voice was barely a whisper. As soon as he'd reassured her that he was all right, she'd gone back to sleep. So much for the highly sensitized hearing he'd credited her with a few minutes earlier.

Despite all his resolve, all his determination, Harry began to slide toward the floor. Rosalie wasn't strong enough to help him up. If he fell, he'd stay that way until morning. If he survived until morning....

"Is this it?" Mercy cried, wringing her hands. "Is Harry going to die now?" She needed direction. Her initial response was to hold him upright, to help him. Angels routinely made physical appearances on Earth, but it was important to go through the proper channels, to get permission first. She didn't have time for that. She'd certainly bent the rules on occasion, but she couldn't risk interfering with God's plan for Harry.

"Gabriel," she shouted helplessly toward the heavens. "I don't know what to do."

A second later, the Archangel was at her side.

"Is it Harry's time to come to Heaven?" She pleaded for an answer before daring to take matters into her own hands.

The Archangel seemed strangely calm; Mercy was anything but. She hovered close to Harry, anxious to do what she could, awaiting word from Gabriel.

She could tell that Harry's strength was draining away.

As she watched, the old man's eyes widened and he placed one hand over his heart.

"Gabriel," Mercy shouted. *"Do something."* Hurriedly she revised her request. "Can I help Harry?" And because she'd come to genuinely love this old man, she added, "Please."

Gabriel nodded. "Take him back to bed."

"Thank you," Mercy whispered, greatly relieved.

Harry's eyes widened again. Only this time it wasn't his heart that worried him. Standing directly in front of him in plain view was a woman dressed in white. A woman with…wings. An angel? She regarded him with a gentle, loving look.

"I could use some help here," he said. In other circumstances Harry might think he'd died. The continuing ache in his chest told him otherwise. The pain intensified with every beat of his heart.

The beautiful angel stepped toward him and silently slipped her arm around his waist. She didn't seem to have any trouble handling his bulk. The next thing Harry knew, he was in bed and his rescuer was gone. Vanished. She'd disappeared as quickly as she'd come.

Grateful to have averted a catastrophe, or what had seemed like one a few minutes ago, Harry tried to figure out what had just happened. The angel might've been a figment of his imagination except for one thing. He'd been slumped against the wall with no strength left, no ability to stand upright. His walker rested next to his chest of drawers, where it had been all along. But now he was safely tucked into bed, next to Rosalie.

Harry blinked to clear his eyesight and picked up his glasses. Maybe then he'd be able to see the angel a second time. He peered into the darkness, resisting the urge to turn on the light.

She was gone. Truly gone.

Still, Harry was convinced she'd been there. She'd helped him back to bed. What a beauty she'd been, too. He'd always wondered about angels, and now he knew with certainty that they were real.

"Will he be all right now?" Mercy asked, leaning over the slumbering Harry.

"Harry will sleep comfortably for the rest of the night," Gabriel told her.

"In the morning will he remember any of this?" Part of her felt it might be best if the incident was erased from Harry's mind. Then again, she wanted him to know that God was looking down on him, and that he was deeply loved. The mighty angel Gabriel himself had come to Harry's aid.

"He'll remember. This close to death, the separation between Heaven and Earth is only partially veiled," Gabriel explained.

"It's almost as if Harry has one foot in Heaven and one still on Earth."

"Exactly." The Archangel began to leave, then paused. "I'm proud of you, Mercy," he said.

"You are?" She beamed, but she wasn't sure what she'd done to warrant such high praise. Gabriel didn't issue praise often. He was a strict taskmaster but a fair one.

Apparently reading her mind, Gabriel elaborated. "You didn't take it upon yourself to make a decision on the matter. You turned to Heaven and to me for help. That shows a new maturity."

Bubbling with pleasure at his words, Mercy fluttered her wings. Thankfully the Archangel hadn't been around when she'd sent Shirley scrambling in the electric cart.

"You did give me cause for concern at the Safeway store, however."

So Gabriel knew.

As if his words had summoned her, Shirley appeared.

"I *knew* Mercy was responsible for that unfortunate event," she cried, glaring at her friend.

"It w-was all in jest," Mercy stammered, embarrassed now. At times, especially while on Earth, she adopted a more human nature than an angelic one. As a human might have said, Shirley had been asking for it.

"Shall we discuss this elsewhere?" Gabriel said, gesturing down at the sleeping Harry and Rosalie.

"By all means."

The three of them moved to the living room. When they got there, Mercy saw Goodness on top of the Christmas tree Harry and Rosalie's son-in-law had set up in a corner of the living room.

"Actually, I'm glad to see you, Gabriel," Shirley said. "I'm having the worst time with my assignment."

"Are you, now?" Gabriel asked, eyebrows raised. Mercy and Goodness exchanged a sly glance. They had both agreed that Shirley's was by *far* the least complicated of the assignments.

"It's Carter," Shirley said after a moment's hesitation. "He's found a stray dog."

"And the problem is?"

Shirley shrugged uncomfortably. "The problem is that his father still insists the family can't afford a dog. I was trying to work around that."

"How?" Gabriel asked.

"His father worked overtime this evening and that money will come in handy for Christmas." Shirley rubbed her hands together nervously. "Only…"

"Yes?" Gabriel pressed.

Mercy had to admit she was curious, too, and apparently so was Goodness, because she'd left the Christmas tree to join them.

"Rusty, that's the dog, followed bus number seven home, just like Carter instructed him to."

Gabriel frowned. "Do earthly canines generally understand such detailed instructions?" he asked.

"No," Shirley cried. "That's just the point! I was afraid you'd think I had something to do with it and I promise you I didn't."

"You didn't?" Goodness asked skeptically.

"I'm innocent," Shirley said.

Actually, Mercy would've thought better of her friend if she *had* been involved.

"Every bit of information I've received indicates that Carter is not supposed to have this dog."

"You're sure about that?" Gabriel murmured, and his brow furrowed. "Where's the stray now?"

"This is another problem," Shirley said. "Carter and his mother have put Rusty in the laundry room. Like I told you, David—that's his father—worked late on Friday night and Carter convinced his mother to keep Rusty hidden until morning."

"So the dog's inside the house?"

"For now," Shirley said. "I didn't think Laurie would let him keep the dog for another minute but I was wrong." Shirley shook her head. "I don't know what to tell you about this dog. Not only is he able to read—"

"He *reads?*"

"He knew which bus was number seven, didn't he?"

"Don't you think he might have seen which bus Carter boarded?" Mercy suggested.

"May I please get on with my story?" Shirley asked in dignified tones.

"Don't let me stop you," Mercy muttered. Gabriel sent her a quelling look.

"Not only that, this dog instinctively seems to know

who's his friend and who isn't, and he has an uncanny way of making himself scarce when necessary. It's almost as if…as if he has heavenly qualities."

"I find that interesting," Gabriel murmured. "Report back to me on any further developments, will you?"

"Yes, of course."

"Goodness?" Gabriel said, turning to the third angel. "How are you doing?"

"Great! Beth and Peter are about to meet. Isn't it wonderful?"

"Excellent work." And with that, Gabriel returned to Heaven.

Harry woke and saw that Rosalie was awake. "The most astounding thing happened last night," he rushed to tell his wife.

Still sleepy, Rosalie blinked several times. "Did you have another of your attacks?"

"Yes, but that isn't what I want to tell you about."

His wife raised herself up on one elbow. "For heaven's sake, Harry, what's got you so excited?"

"I saw an angel!"

"Now, Harry…"

"I know what you're thinking, Rosalie, but it's true."

His wife frowned, and Harry sensed that she *wanted* to believe what he'd told her but had difficulty accepting it as the truth.

Later that morning, Harry heard his wife chatting on the phone with their youngest daughter. "I'm not sure what to think, Donna. Your father's telling me he saw… Well, he swears he saw an angel."

Harry was sorry now that he'd mentioned this event to Rosalie. She'd apparently concluded that he was losing his mind.

"Yes, yes, I agree," Rosalie said, keeping her voice low. "Please do."

A few minutes later, she hung up and then joined Harry in front of the television. "I was on the phone with Donna," she said conversationally, as if he hadn't noticed. Harry knew exactly who was on the other end of the line.

Nevertheless he didn't comment one way or the other.

"She's going to come early for Christmas. Isn't that nice?"

If the story about the angel had made his youngest daughter decide to come home early, then all the better. His angel had done him even more good than he'd realized.

Thirteen

Leavenworth was everything Beth had imagined it would be. When the train pulled in, the sun was shining, and the freshly fallen snow glistened brightly. The entire town was a Christmas wonderland, unlike anything she'd ever seen. Main Street was closed to cars, and in the center of the wide street, burn barrels had been set up, where people could gather to warm their hands. Children were sledding down the short slope next to the gazebo, while a group of costumed carolers entertained the crowd.

It was at this gazebo that Beth Fischer would be meeting Peter in a few hours.

Once they were off the train, Heidi, Sam, two-year-old Adam and Beth toured the area. Adam wanted to go sledding, so Sam quickly purchased a round plastic sled. Soon father and son were gliding down the incline while Heidi took photographs.

"I'll put one of these in our Christmas letter," she told Beth excitedly.

"Isn't it a little late to be mailing out cards?" Beth teased. Heidi was always late. In fact, last year's Christmas cards had arrived in mid-January. Heidi had said that

Beth should either consider them very late or exceptionally early.

Beth had been too nervous to eat all day and seeing a vendor selling roasted chestnuts, she purchased a small bag to share with her friend.

Heidi bit into one. "Hey, these aren't bad. They're kind of sweet."

Beth tried one, too, and then another. Now she could say she'd tasted chestnuts roasting on an open fire, just like the Christmas song said.

As they strolled down the street taking in the sights and smells and sounds of Christmas, Beth found herself studying faces. She wondered if Peter's bus had come in yet. Could that tall, handsome man be him? When a little girl leaped into his arms, Beth decided it probably wasn't.

"Are you sorry you agreed to meet Peter so late in the day?"

"Yes," she said tersely.

Soon after that, Sam caught up with them. Adam, bundled from head to foot, was asleep in his father's arms, exhausted from their outing in the snow.

"We were just talking about Beth's appointment," Heidi told her husband.

"I hope you and your WoW partner have a way to connect if something goes wrong," the ever-practical Sam said. "There must be a thousand people here this afternoon."

"Peter e-mailed me his cell phone number."

"Did you give him yours?" Heidi asked.

"No, I didn't think of it." That wasn't completely accurate. "Actually, I meant to, but we started talking and I forgot."

"That's not a good sign," Sam began. "What if—"

"Sam," Heidi interrupted. "Everything's going to work out fine."

Beth hoped her friend was right. "You'll come with me, won't you?" she asked Heidi. The time was growing closer.

At three o'clock, it started to snow. Clouds obscured the sky as dusk fell over the town; by four-thirty it would be completely dark.

"Come with you?" Heidi repeated. "You're kidding, aren't you?"

"Heidi, please. I'm so nervous I'm about to throw up."

"This should be interesting. All you've had to eat is a couple of roasted chestnuts."

"Don't joke," Beth muttered. "I'm serious."

"Okay," Heidi said. "I'll come if you really want me to, but I'm only going to stay long enough for the two of you to meet."

"What if we don't like each other?" Beth asked, feeling a sense of dread. She was bringing so many hopes, so much yearning, to this encounter that she was afraid she'd set herself up for failure.

The night before, as they exchanged instant messages, Peter was the one who'd seemed anxious.

They'd tried to reassure each other. That was when he'd given her his phone number. Online they had so much to talk about, and Beth sincerely hoped the chemistry that seemed to spark between them on the screen translated into real life.

At ten minutes to four, Beth and Heidi made their way toward the gazebo, where Peter would be waiting for her. She'd know him by the long-stemmed red rose and his Seahawks hat.

"This is the most romantic date I've ever heard about," Heidi said dreamily.

Beth slipped her arm through Heidi's. "I'm so grateful you're here."

They stood in the background because Beth was feeling shy and a bit shaky, which could've been low blood sugar, Heidi told her. In any event, her plan was to wait for him and then casually walk up and introduce herself.

"There he is!" Heidi said, pointing toward a cluster of people near the gazebo.

"Where? Where? I don't see him." And then she did.

"Beth, oh my goodness, look at him! He's *gorgeous.*"

Beth froze and her heart sank to her knees. Her stomach pitched wildly. "He's that, all right," she whispered numbly.

"How did you get so lucky?" Heidi was too excited to notice Beth's complete lack of enthusiasm.

"I don't know," Beth said, her voice low and emotionless.

Heidi turned to stare at her. "What's the matter with you? Peter looks like he stepped off the pages of a romance novel."

"He does, doesn't he?" Beth murmured. Then she covered her face with both hands and turned away. Whipping the red hat off her head, she quickly unwrapped the telltale scarf from around her neck, as well.

"Beth, what's wrong?" Heidi asked.

"What's wrong?" Beth repeated. "You want me to tell you what's wrong? That Peter is an imposter!"

"How can he be an imposter when you've never met him before?"

"His name isn't Peter," she choked out. "It's John Nicodemus and he's my ex-husband."

That news seemed to shock her friend. *"What?"*

"Let's get out of here before he sees me," Beth urged. Heidi couldn't possibly have known what John looked like, because she and Heidi hadn't met until five years ago—and she certainly didn't keep wedding photos at her desk or in her condo.

Together they hurried around the corner and Beth flattened herself against the side of a building.

"What are you going to do?" Heidi asked curiously.

Beth needed to think. At first she'd been numb with shock, but now she was angry. "He planned this. He knew all along."

"Beth, that's not fair. How could he have?"

"We never exchanged last names. And he changed his first name, didn't he? He tricked me."

Heidi shook her head. "Didn't you tell me you shortened your name to Beth after your divorce?"

"I did," she admitted. "I wanted to make a fresh start, so I decided that from then on, I'd just use Beth."

"Perhaps John did the same thing," Heidi suggested.

Beth wasn't willing to concede the point. "His middle name is Peter," she said grudgingly. "It never occured to me…"

"He *is* gorgeous, though."

"His good looks are the only thing he has going for him," Beth mumbled.

"That isn't what you told me earlier."

"What do you mean?" Heidi wasn't usually this argumentative. Clearly, she was taking Peter/John's side, and that infuriated Beth.

"Don't you remember what you said last week?" Heidi asked. "You told me Peter is everything your first husband wasn't."

"I said that?" What an idiot she'd been. What an imbecile. She'd allowed John to make a fool of her. He knew who she was. He *had* to have known. How could he not? But maybe…just maybe, he didn't. Could they have found each other online? No one would believe something this random could actually happen. It was more than bizarre. It was completely and totally implausible…wasn't it?

"You can't leave him standing there waiting for you like that," Heidi insisted. "That would be cruel."

Beth didn't respond, still trying to figure out how this had happened. It dawned on her that he *couldn't* have known, since he'd been the one to suggest she meet him outside the gazebo. If he'd known, he would never have given her the opportunity to see him first and then walk away. Unlikely though it seemed, she had to conclude that he was as much in the dark as she was.

"Did you hear me?" Heidi demanded. "You have to call him on his cell."

"No, you have to," Beth said frantically.

"I beg your pardon?" Heidi looked confused.

"Use my phone." She thrust it at her friend.

"Why me? Beth, you're the one who should talk to him, not me." She refused to accept the phone.

"I can't... He'll recognize my voice." He would, too. It might've been almost ten years since the divorce, but that wouldn't matter. John would know her voice the same way she would his.

"You don't want him to find out it's you?" Heidi asked, sounding even more confused.

"No. Not yet. I need to think." This awkward situation had to be handled delicately or John might assume she'd tricked him—which was what *she'd* suspected about him.

"Here—I'll do it," Heidi said and snatched the phone away from her. "What should I tell him?"

Beth hadn't thought that far ahead. "I—I'm not sure."

"Should I say something came up at the last minute and you had to leave?"

"But if he asks what it is..." Beth was growing desperate.

"He won't," Heidi said. "Anyway, something did come up, so it isn't like you're lying."

Beth shrugged helplessly.

"Give me his cell phone number." Heidi held out her hand.

Digging through her purse, Beth nearly dumped the entire contents in the snow.

"Relax," Heidi said in an annoyingly calm voice. "Re-e-lax."

Beth scowled at her, and as soon as she found the crumpled slip of paper with his phone number, she slapped it in Heidi's hand.

Heidi punched out the number, holding the phone close to Beth's ear.

Peter/John answered on the first ring. "Hello."

"Is this Peter?"

"Beth? Where are you?"

Heidi glanced at Beth, who gestured for her to continue speaking. "I'm so sorry, Peter, but I can't make it. Something, uh, came up—at the last minute and I can't keep our appointment. I'm *so* disappointed." This last part was said with feeling.

"I am, too," Peter responded. "I didn't know what to think when you didn't show up at four."

"I'd like to meet you. I really would—just not now. Can we arrange another time?"

Beth glared at her friend. She made a frenzied cutting motion with one hand but Heidi ignored her, turning her back on Beth.

Beth hurried around in order to face her. Once more, she made exaggerated cutting motions, using both hands to emphasize the point.

"Next Friday, after Christmas, would be perfect," Heidi went on to say. "Since I was the one who let you down, please come to my place. Yes, yes, I'm sure."

Beth's mouth fell open. Her friend had really crossed the line with that one. Before she could stop her, Heidi rattled off Beth's address.

A moment later, Heidi clicked the cell phone shut and returned it to Beth.

"Have you gone insane?" Beth cried. "You gave him my address!"

"Well, yes, that's what you wanted me to do, isn't it?"

"No…yes. Oh, I don't know." Beth's ears felt frozen and she covered them with her hands. She didn't dare put on her hat until they were far from the gazebo.

"That gives you six days to prepare him."

"You're worried about *John?*" Some friend Heidi had turned out to be!

"Not John," Heidi explained patiently. "I'm concerned about Peter, the man you fell in love with over the last six months."

Then it hit Beth, something she'd completely forgotten. "He's married."

"What do you mean, he's married?"

"A friend told me she'd heard John remarried and if that's the case, he's either divorced a second time or cheating on his wife." A sick feeling attacked her stomach.

"My guess is that your friend was talking about some other John."

"It can't be..." Or could it? Beth no longer knew. All she did know was that she had six days to sort this out before she confronted Peter/John with the truth.

Fourteen

Early Saturday morning, Carter tiptoed down to the laundry room as quietly as he could. After working late at the pizza place he managed, his father hadn't come home until way past Carter's bedtime. Carter had lain awake, worrying that his father would somehow discover Rusty in the house. If he did, he just might take the dog away in the middle of the night.

When Carter heard the garage door close, he'd prayed really hard that Rusty wouldn't bark at the strange noise. The dog seemed to have a sixth sense about things like that, because he stayed quiet all night.

Carter could hear his parents talking, and even though he'd had his ear against the door, he couldn't make out their words. All he knew was that after about ten minutes they went to bed. Then and only then was Carter able to sleep.

In the morning, he sneaked down the hallway and freed Rusty from the laundry room. Rusty wanted outside, and Carter let him into the backyard to do his business. As soon as he'd finished, Rusty hurried back onto the porch, where Carter waited for him.

"Are you hungry, boy?" Carter asked softly. No one else

in the house was awake. He bent down and stroked the rich auburn fur of his new best friend. Then he led Rusty back into the laundry room and filled his water dish. He gave him a bowl of Wheaties with milk because they didn't have any dog food.

Rusty seemed to like the cereal and when he'd licked the bowl clean, Carter returned to his bedroom. The dog walked politely beside him. Without being asked, Carter made his bed, dressed and brushed his teeth, too. All the while, Rusty lay on his bedroom rug, his eyes never leaving Carter.

When he heard his parents stir, Carter was ready. He knew it would take a lot of fast talking to convince his father to let him keep Rusty. His one hope was that once he heard Rusty had followed him home, he'd understand that this was a special dog. This was the dog God had sent Carter.

Through his partially open door, he could hear his father step into the kitchen and immediately start making coffee. Rusty dashed out of the bedroom before Carter could stop him. He raced after the dog but it was too late. Rusty skidded into the kitchen, his long tail wagging excitedly.

His father caught sight of Rusty and bent down to pet him. "Where did you come from, boy?" he asked.

"Hi, Dad," Carter said tentatively.

"Do you have a friend spending the night?" David asked, glancing at his son.

Carter swallowed hard. "Rusty's my friend."

"Rusty?" his father repeated.

"I named him after the dog you had when you were a kid. You told me about him, remember?"

Slowly his father nodded. "Where did you get the dog, Carter?"

Carter's mother came into the kitchen just then, tying the sash on her housecoat. She looked uneasily from Carter to his father. "I meant to tell you about Rusty last night, David," she said, pouring them each a cup of coffee.

"I suppose it slipped your mind," David commented, frowning.

"No. I decided you were too tired and didn't need to deal with another problem. We couldn't do anything until morning anyway."

His father turned to Carter. "Where did you get the dog?" he asked a second time.

"He was in the schoolyard, but Dad, this is a *special* dog. Really special. Out of all the kids there, Rusty came to me."

"Did you feed him?"

"He was starving, Dad! And his coat was all muddy and…he needs a family."

"You gave him something to eat, didn't you?"

"Yes." Carter bit his lip. "I fed him a Twinkie and then Bailey let me have her peanut-butter-and-jelly sandwich." Because he wanted his father to know his sister hadn't willingly donated her sandwich, he explained. "I traded my Saturday TV privileges, though, so Bailey would give me her sandwich."

"Carter," his father said gently. "Rusty came to you because he thought you'd feed him."

"Not at first," Carter insisted. "He didn't know about the Twinkie."

"He could probably smell it in your pocket. Dogs have a keen sense of smell."

"Oh."

"As for him following you home?"

"Yes, he…Rusty's not just any dog. He's smart and he listens and he understands, too."

His father crouched down so they were eye to eye. "Did you encourage him to follow you?" he asked.

"He followed the bus! I told you, Dad—he's smart."

Reaching out, his father rested a hand on Carter's shoulder. "Rusty could see that you liked him."

"It's more than that!" Carter cried. "I prayed really hard

and God sent me Rusty. He was so muddy I...I didn't even know his fur was red until I gave him a bath."

"In our tub?" his father asked.

Carter nodded reluctantly.

His father stood and cast him a disapproving look.

"Did he make a mess?" The question was directed at Carter's mother.

"I cleaned it up," Carter inserted. "Tell him, Mom, tell Dad that I washed out the bathtub and everything."

"He did," she confirmed, handing his father a mug of fresh coffee.

David accepted it, closing his eyes as he took his first sip. "I'm glad you cleaned up after the dog."

Relieved, Carter offered his father a hopeful smile. "It was like God was telling me this dog was for me because he had red fur."

A pained look appeared on his father's face. "Did you stop to think that Rusty might belong to another little boy?"

The thought had never entered Carter's mind. "Rusty might have another family?"

His father set the mug aside and put his hand on Carter's shoulder once again. "There could be a little boy out there who's lost his dog."

"Not Rusty," Carter said with certainty.

"We can't be sure of anything when it comes to a stray."

Carter shook his head. "Rusty needs a family," he stated boldly. "*Our* family. He adopted us."

The same sad look came over his father. "I wish we could keep him. He seems like a nice dog."

"He's a *wonderful* dog, and he's housebroken and he doesn't eat much. He can have my food."

David drew one hand across his face. "If it was just a matter of food, we could deal with that, but it isn't. I already explained this to you, Carter. There are the vet's fees for one thing. Since Rusty's been on the streets for a while, he should be checked out by a veterinarian."

"I'll pay for it with my allowance," Carter said. "I have thirty dollars and seventy-six cents."

"David," his mother murmured in a soft, pleading voice.

"That wouldn't begin to cover the cost of a checkup and shots. And what if he needs some kind of treatment? Then there's the license and heaven knows what else. We can't keep him, Carter. I don't want to sound heartless but we'd be doing Rusty a disservice, too."

Carter didn't want to cry but his eyes filled with tears before he could hold them back.

His mother wrapped her arms around him and held him close. "I'm so sorry, honey," she whispered.

"Where will you take him?" Carter sobbed, looking up at his father.

"He'll have to go to the animal shelter."

"No, Daddy, *please!*" Bailey came into the kitchen, dragging her stuffed Winnie the Pooh bear on the linoleum. She was still in her pajamas and her hair was all frizzy because she'd gone to bed with it wet.

"Can't Rusty stay until Christmas?" Carter begged.

"That'll just make it harder to give him up," his father said. "Besides, we don't know if he's picked up any parasites, and the sooner he's checked out, the better."

Rusty lay down on the small rug in front of the kitchen sink and rested his head on his paws. Bailey sat on the floor next to him.

"Get up, Bailey. He probably has fleas."

"No, he doesn't, Dad," Carter said. "I washed him real good. Ask Mom."

"We'll take him down to the shelter this afternoon," his father said, not waiting to see if Bailey obeyed him. He walked out of the kitchen.

"Mom?" Carter could feel the tears running down his face.

"You heard your father." She looked like she wanted to cry, too.

"But…"

"Remember what Dad said about some other little boy losing Rusty? Can you imagine how happy he'll be to find him?"

Carter tried to imagine what it would be like to lose his dog and how awful he'd feel. Sniffling, he wiped his cheeks with one sleeve.

"If we take Rusty to the animal shelter, that little boy will get him back," his mother went on in a reassuring voice.

Being brave was hard, but Carter did his best. His lower lip quivered and he sat down on the floor and buried his face in the dog's fur. Bailey sat on Rusty's other side, clutching her bear and murmuring sweetly. As if seeking a way to comfort him, Rusty licked Carter's hand.

"You might have another family that loves you even more than I do." Carter's voice broke as he spoke to the dog.

"Carter," his mother said softly. "As soon as we can afford it, you'll have your dog. I talked to Mrs. Smith at the school, and she said there'll be an opening at the cafeteria in February. I'm going to apply for it and if I get the job, then you can have a dog."

Hope flared and then just as quickly died. "But it won't be Rusty."

"No," his mother agreed, "it won't be Rusty."

"I don't want any dog except Rusty."

"Oh, Carter."

"I mean it, Mom. Rusty's the only dog I want."

"I should never have let you bring him in the house," his mother said, and she sounded angry with herself. "It just makes this more difficult. I'm so sorry, honey, but your dad's right. We can't give Rusty the kind of home he needs."

"Rusty is Carter's dog," Bailey wailed. She held her Pooh bear tight against her chest, as if she was afraid their father would take her stuffed friend to the animal shelter, too.

"Can I call Grandma?" Carter asked. His grandparents were his last hope. If he explained everything to them, maybe they'd be willing to pay for the checkup, the dog license and whatever else Rusty needed.

"Your grandparents are gone this weekend," his mother said.

"I can't call them?"

"No, Carter, they're visiting friends in Seattle."

"Oh."

Carter knew he didn't have any choice. He had to give up his dog. He spent all morning with Rusty, talking to him. Bailey used her own hairbrush to comb the dog's fur until it was shiny and bright. Rusty stood still and even seemed to enjoy Bailey's ministrations.

Midafternoon, his father came into Carter and Bailey's bedroom. "You ready, son?" he asked.

Carter wouldn't ever be ready. He hugged Rusty around the neck, face buried in his fur, and nodded.

"You don't have to come with me."

"I want to," Carter said stubbornly.

His father sighed. "Okay, then. Let's go."

Rusty seemed to think they were going to a fun place, because the instant David opened the car door, he leaped inside and lay down in the backseat next to Carter.

His father didn't say a single word on the ride to the shelter in Wenatchee.

Neither did Carter. He stroked Rusty's head and struggled not to cry.

The county animal shelter was busy. Lots of people had come by to choose dogs and cats during the Christmas holidays. Some other family would be getting Rusty. Some other little boy would get Carter's special dog.

"You can stay in the car if you want," his father told him.

"No." Carter was determined to be with his dog as long as he possibly could.

His father went inside the shelter and came back with a woman who was carrying a collar and leash. Carter listened as his father spoke to the lady.

"My son found Rusty in the schoolyard, and the dog followed him home. According to my wife, the poor thing was caked in mud. He seems to be a gentle dog, and he's obviously had some training, so I assume he's lost."

His father opened the passenger door and Rusty raised his head expectantly.

The woman reached into the car and stroked Rusty's head. "Oh, what an attractive dog he is. Probably part Irish setter—they're a nice breed. We could've adopted him out a dozen times over earlier in the day."

This wasn't news Carter wanted to hear. "What about his other family? My dad said there might be other people who owned Rusty." That was his one comfort—that bringing Rusty to the shelter might help the dog locate his original owner.

The lady from the shelter sighed. "His other family didn't take very good care of him, though, did they?" she said. "Rusty didn't have any identification on him, did he?"

"No," Carter admitted.

She examined the insides of Rusty's ears. "No tattoos, either."

"How will you figure out who owns him, then?" Carter asked.

"We can check for a microchip, but I doubt we'll find one. Without that, there's no way of knowing where his family is," she explained. "Still, this is the best time of year to guarantee him a good home. I'm sure he'll be adopted quickly. That's what you want for him, isn't it?" She looked directly at Carter.

Hard though it was to agree, Carter nodded. With his heart breaking, he threw his arms around Rusty for one last hug.

Fifteen

All day Rosalie had been fluttering about the house, getting ready for their daughters' arrival. Harry was exhausted by all the activity around him. She'd changed the sheets on the beds and while he wanted to help her with the guest room, he couldn't. Without his saying a word, his wife seemed to realize how much he hated his physical limitations. Twice she made a special trip into the family room, where Harry sat watching television, to give him a kiss on the forehead.

"Donna will get here tomorrow afternoon," Rosalie announced for about the tenth time that morning. "Donna and Richard are coming first, and Lorraine and Kenny will drive over on Christmas Eve. The grandkids are coming then, too. Did I tell you that already?"

He nodded. Her memory wasn't the problem in this instance; Rosalie was just plain excited. Chattering incessantly was something Rosalie did when she was happy. And although Harry wasn't constantly talking about his daughters' visit, he felt the same joy. It'd been a lot of years since their two girls had spent Christmas with them. The whole family would be together. According to Dr. Snellgrove, this would be his last Christmas on Earth, and for Rosalie's sake, he wanted it to be a good one; having their daughters with them would ensure that.

"The girls don't want you to worry about cooking," Harry reminded his wife. There'd been two or three conversations that very day between his daughters and Rosalie. Lorraine had insisted on ordering a special ham for their Christmas dinner and would be bringing it with her. Donna had a scalloped potato recipe she planned to make. As for the other side dishes, apparently their daughters were taking care of those, as well. And Rosalie was baking the family's favorite pie for Christmas Day dessert.

Although the menu had long been determined, his wife spent hours poring over cookbooks. Harry didn't know why. But seeing her this involved raised his own spirits.

She hadn't mentioned the appearance of the angel. Not since he'd told her about it. Afterward, Harry had done quite a bit of thinking. That angel had been real. As real as Rosalie. Most important, she'd been there, at his side. Harry would never have made it back to bed without her.

That led him to remember again what the young doctor had told him. Anytime, Dr. Snellgrove had said. Death was getting close. Harry could feel it. Every day he seemed to grow weaker. Every day it became more difficult to accomplish even the simplest and most mundane tasks, such as dressing and shaving. When he'd finished brushing his teeth, he was nearly too weak to stand.

"I thought I'd bake cinnamon rolls for breakfast Christmas morning," Rosalie was saying as she stalked through the family room, a feather duster in one hand. She swiped the thing every which way, swirling up dust left and right.

"Rosalie," Harry protested.

"Sorry, sweetheart, but I want the house to look its best for the girls."

In a blur, his wife dashed past him and into the next

room. Where she found the energy, Harry couldn't even imagine. Next he caught sight of her fluffing up the sofa pillow, squeezing it hard, then pounding it into place. Harry couldn't help smiling.

"Rosalie," he called out. "Sit down a minute, would you? I'm getting tired just watching you."

"I don't have time to sit."

"I need to talk to you."

"All right, all right." The way she breezed into the room reminded him of Loretta Young's entrance on her television show in the fifties. He'd seen that moment hundreds of times, and it lingered in his mind to this day. Rosalie had been every bit as beautiful as Loretta Young back then. Still was, in his opinion.

"Sit." Harry pointed to her chair, which stood next to his own. They shared an end table and a lamp.

"Yes, sweetheart?" She sat on the very edge of her seat, signaling her impatience to get on with her work.

"I was thinking we should talk about Liberty Orchard."

"Harry Alderwood, I told you—I don't have time to talk about this now."

"Please?" he asked quietly. It had been weighing on him all day.

Rosalie released a gusty sigh that the neighbors could probably have heard if they'd been listening. "*Must* we?"

"It would put my mind at rest," he told her.

She sighed again, accepting that he wasn't going to let this drop. "Fine. If you feel it's that important, then let's talk."

Harry was grateful. If possible, he'd like Rosalie's future settled before the girls arrived. He knew it was necessary to set things in motion, which meant they had to secure the unit. Harry felt an urgency that his recent heavenly visitation had only heightened. He might have mere days to live. Mere days to arrange all of this.

"You said you didn't want to think about moving until after the holidays," he began, "but—"

"I don't," Rosalie broke in. "I've got enough to do with the girls and their husbands coming here for Christmas."

"I agree."

She seemed surprised by that.

"But," he added before she could crow at her apparent victory, "I'd be more comfortable if we told the administrator we've decided to take the unit."

Rosalie hesitated. "Do you really think a few more days will make that much difference?"

"Yes," Harry said firmly. "It'd give me peace of mind."

Rosalie folded her hands in her lap. "I don't know, Harry…"

"What's to know?" Dear heaven, Rosalie couldn't have changed her mind already, could she?

"Harry, we've been in this house for so many years. To give it up like this… I don't think I'm ready."

"You said—"

She held up her hand. "I *know* what I said. Yes, we had a good time at Liberty Orchard. Lucy's always been a persuasive person. And at first I was excited to see my friends again, but now…" She let the words fade and refused to meet his eyes.

"But now?" Harry prodded.

"Now I'm not sure we should be in such a rush. Let's talk to the girls about it some more."

"They'll agree with me."

"I agree with you, too, Harry. But why do we have to do it right this minute? It's going to be hard on me to leave this house, you know."

"I know. For me, too." It would be even harder for him to leave Rosalie and his family.

"I'm going to call the administrator," he said.

"Harry!" Rosalie gasped.

"If we change our minds, we'll only be out a few hundred dollars." Despite what Rosalie thought, Harry was convinced Mrs. Goldsmith hadn't been lying. He believed someone else *was* interested in that unit. So he wanted to make the deposit immediately.

"A few hundred dollars?" Rosalie repeated in a stunned voice. "Since when have we ever had money to burn, Harry Alderwood?"

As children of the Depression, Harry and Rosalie had lived frugally. They'd budgeted their entire lives and saved ten percent of every dollar earned. Neither one wasted anything. Rosalie even kept those plastic bags from the grocery store. Young people these days didn't know the value of a dollar. And credit cards! He'd seen more people get into financial trouble because of those cards.

"This will be money well invested," Harry assured his wife.

Rosalie continued to look uncertain. "If you're positive this is what you want—"

"It is," Harry said, cutting her off. "You know, Rosalie, that angel was real."

She frowned.

"I needed help. I collapsed and I couldn't get up. I wouldn't have managed without her."

Her frown deepened. "You're on a lot of medication."

He realized this was the rationale Donna must have offered her mother when he'd heard the two of them discussing the incident. In fact, that conversation was what had prompted his youngest daughter to visit a day early. "All I know is that I was in trouble and I didn't have my walker and then…I was back in bed."

"Why didn't you call me? If you needed help, I would've come right away."

"I would have if I'd had the strength." As he recalled, Harry had made an effort to rouse his wife, to no avail. Not that she could've helped him up or supported him on the walk into the bedroom.

Rosalie got to her feet. "I can see you're determined, so go ahead and make that phone call," she said. "We'll both adjust. You're right, Harry. If it was up to me, I'd put off the move indefinitely. We need to start making plans."

Relief washed over him. As soon as his wife went back to her fussing and cleaning, Harry removed his wallet from his hip pocket—a procedure that left him short of breath—and took out the business card the administrator had given him.

Elizabeth Goldsmith.

He reached for the portable phone. They had three phones in the house, thanks to Lorraine. One in the bedroom, another in the kitchen and the third next to his recliner on the small end table.

Although it was a Saturday, the administrator had promised him she'd be available.

A woman with a pleasant voice answered the phone. "Liberty Orchard," she said brightly. "How might I direct your call?"

"I'd like to speak with Elizabeth Goldsmith."

"One moment, please."

"Thank you." Harry closed his eyes, afraid that if Rosalie looked his way, she might try to talk him into waiting, despite the fact that he'd made the best decision. The only decision.

"Elizabeth Goldsmith," he heard half a minute later.

"Harry Alderwood," he returned. He didn't understand why people felt they had to announce their names when they answered the phone. He knew whom he'd called and presumably Elizabeth knew who she was. He'd noticed that it had become a common business practice in the last few years.

"Ah, yes, we spoke recently, didn't we?" Elizabeth said.

"My wife, Rosalie, and I were by to see the facility a few days ago."

"Ah, yes. You're friends of Lucy Menard's, aren't you?"

"Yes."

Harry got right to the point. "When we spoke, you confirmed that you had one unit open."

"Yes." Elizabeth paused. "But—"

He continued to speak, eager to get this done. "We discussed my giving you a check to secure that unit," he said.

"Yes, I do recall that I urged you to make the deposit right away."

He was well aware of that and had thought of little else since their meeting.

"I mentioned that there was only one unit open, didn't I?" she went on.

"Yes." Harry was beginning to worry just a bit.

"And I did mention that someone else had shown an interest?"

"Yes, you did."

"Well, I'm afraid, Mr. Alderwood, that the first party came back the following day with a check."

"You mean...the unit's already been taken?" He could hear the stunned disbelief in his own voice.

"I'm afraid so. And unfortunately there was only the one."

He wished she'd quit reminding him of that.

"How soon will you have another unit available?" Harry asked, still in shock.

Elizabeth considered her answer. "That's difficult to say. It could be three months but it might be as long as six."

"Oh."

"I'm sorry, Mr. Alderwood."

"No...no, I'm the one who's sorry. You suggested we decide quickly and I thought we had."

"If there's anything else I can do for you, please let me know. Oh, and in the meantime, Merry Christmas."

"Thank you. Merry Christmas to you." He put back the

phone and released a deep sigh of regret, knowing he should have taken action that very day.

Now it was too late.

Too late for him.

In three months' time he wouldn't be here. In three months' time Rosalie would be a widow.

Sixteen

Beth slept fitfully all night. She couldn't escape the thoughts tumbling crazily through her mind, but every once in a while exhaustion overtook her, and she'd slip into a light sleep. Then she'd dream—dreams filled with John. And the shock of what she'd discovered would jerk her awake. Before long, the whole process would start all over again.

In the morning, she was blurry-eyed and her temples were throbbing with the beginnings of a headache. Despite how she felt, she had no choice but to attend Mass. James and Bella, her nephew and niece, were participating in a special Christmas program. Not to show up would disappoint them. Besides, her entire family would be there; it was easier to make the effort and go now than to offer excuses later.

Before she left, Beth swallowed two aspirin with a glass of orange juice. Her mother had planned a large brunch afterward.

By the time Beth arrived at the church, the parking lot was almost full. She hoped her mother had saved her a place.

Joyce was lying in wait just inside the church vestibule, which meant she had something on her mind—and Beth could easily guess what it was.

"You're late and it's time for Mass," her mother said, slipping her arm around Beth, as if she was afraid her daughter might make a run for it at the last minute. "Your father saved us two places, but I don't think he'll be able to hold on to them much longer."

"Sorry, Mom, I got a slow start."

"I want to hear every detail about Leavenworth." Joyce narrowed her eyes. "*Every* detail," she repeated ominously.

"Yes, well… I'll explain later." She wouldn't tell her family everything, though. She felt overwhelmed by the events of the day before. Heidi's arrangement with Peter—John—on her behalf was a further complication, one she didn't need. But the immediate problem was how much to say to her parents.

As soon as Mass began, Beth's problems seemed to lift from her shoulders. The beauty of the church, with its decorations of poinsettia and evergreen boughs, the joyful music and the sermon's message—about forgiving yourself and not allowing past mistakes to hold you back—seemed to be just for her. The Christmas pageant was delightful and when she joined in the carol-singing, her heart felt free.

That morning, her entire life had felt like a disaster. By the end of Mass, Beth had begun to feel a new sense of hope. Maybe this bizarre coincidence involving John was meant to be. Maybe…maybe they'd have a second chance, despite all the bitterness and grief.

The family brunch at her parents' home was her only remaining hurdle today. Everyone wanted to know about Peter.

"Don't keep us in suspense," her mother said as she passed the platter of scrambled eggs to Beth.

"Mom, please." Foolishly she'd hoped to avoid lengthy explanations and at first she'd thought that might actually happen, since everyone's attention was focused on her niece and nephew, who'd played minor roles in today's program.

But she should've known it wouldn't be that easy. At Joyce's comment, everyone stopped eating and stared at Beth.

"We're just curious," her sister added. "If you tell us to mind our own business, we will."

"Angela," their mother said. "Don't even suggest Marybeth keep this to herself!"

Groaning, Beth could see that it was useless to resist. Her mother felt entitled to an answer—and it had better be the right answer, too. Joyce had lit a candle, after all.

"Yesterday I—" Beth thought about telling the truth. The direct approach had its benefits. But the thought of explaining that Peter wasn't Peter but John Nicodemus, her ex-husband, was more than she could handle. As her mental debate continued, Beth hesitated, leaving her sentence unfinished.

"Marybeth, *please,*" her mother implored.

"We didn't meet," she blurted out.

"You didn't meet?" The question echoed around the table.

"Don't tell me you chickened out," her mother cried. The horrified look was back, as if Beth had, once again, been a disappointment to the family.

She couldn't tell them the real reason she hadn't met Peter, so she just sat and gazed blankly at the wall.

After a moment, her parents' eyes met. Her father cleared his throat. "Actually, your mother and I suspected this might happen. We feel it's time, Beth, for you to consider counseling."

"What?" Beth couldn't believe what she was hearing.

"Your father and I are willing to pay for it," her mother put in.

There was no point in arguing. Beth could see they weren't going to budge from their decision. "I don't object to counseling," she murmured. "In theory, that is. I just don't think I need it."

"You need it," her mother said grimly.

"Can we talk about this after Christmas?" Beth asked, wanting to delay any further discussion until she'd had time to analyze her own reactions to the Peter/John confusion.

"Of course we can," her sister assured her sympathetically.

So her sister was in on this, as well. That loving, compassionate look was a dead giveaway.

Beth left her parents' home shortly after the brunch dishes had been washed and put away. As she drove back to her own place, she deliberated on what to say to Peter. Despite the fact that he was really John, she'd come to think of him as Peter—a new man. A *different* man.

Once home, she shed her coat and purse and logged on to the Internet. The moment she did, Peter sent her an instant message.

I wondered when you'd get here.

His comment indicated that he'd been waiting for her to come online.

I'm here now, she typed back. I want to talk to you about meeting later this week.

Are you having second thoughts?

She mulled over her answer. Yes. You see, I've already made one disastrous mistake in my life when it comes to relationships and I'm not eager to make another.

In other words, you're gun-shy.

Frankly, yes.

This might surprise you, Peter wrote back, but I am, too.

Really? Then because she couldn't resist, she asked, Was your marriage that horrible?

I guess not. We were both young and immature.

Beth couldn't leave it at that. This was a perfect opportunity to discover exactly what Peter thought of her. Do you have any regrets?

He didn't reply right away. Some.

Me, too, she told him. More than I realized.

Has your ex remarried? Peter typed.

This was a tricky question. I heard he did.

So you don't keep tabs on him?

No. What about your ex-wife?

I have no idea. We went our separate ways. I don't harbor any ill will toward her. I couldn't tell you if she's remarried or not.

Did you love her? For one long heartbeat, Beth's finger was poised above the key that would submit her question. Her mind raced; she was afraid this was one she shouldn't be asking. She sent it anyway.

His answer came in the form of another question. Did you love your ex?

Her reply was simple. Yes. I guess I still do in some ways. And you?

Yes. A short pause and then he added, Is that the real problem? Are you so in love with your ex that you aren't ready to fall in love a second time?

Peter deserved the truth—but not yet. He admitted he'd loved her once, maybe still did, but preferred not to discuss her.

What Peter couldn't know was that she had information he didn't....

Listen, let's put the matter of our former marriages to rest. His next words flashed across the screen. My wife and I behaved badly. We were both at fault and I've accepted that our problems were complex. I've moved on and apparently so has she. Although painful, the divorce was for the best.

The best? Beth read those words and her throat tightened.

I wish her well and I'm sure you don't begrudge your ex-husband happiness. Am I right?

Yes, she typed back.

Good. Then let's drop the subject. Agreed?

Beth read his words, then pressed her fingers to her lips

as she wondered how to respond. **Agreed...only I'm not sure the timing is right for the two of us.**

In what way?

It's Christmas, and I have enough family pressures without worrying about what will happen once we meet.

I know what you mean.

Shall we put this off? she asked.

For how long?

Why don't we wait until after New Year's.

Okay.

His clipped reply implied that he was disappointed. Well, she was, too, but she couldn't spring the news on Peter like this, two days before the biggest holiday of the year.

You aren't going to duck out on me again, are you? Peter asked.

Beth appreciated his directness. **No,** she typed. **I'd just like a little more time.**

Whatever you say. But I believe it's important for both of us to put the past behind us.

"Behind us," Beth repeated aloud. Little did Peter know how impossible that would be.

"After New Year's?" Goodness gasped, leaning over Beth's shoulder to read her messages.

"What's wrong?" Mercy asked.

As far as Goodness was concerned, *everything* was wrong. Nothing was going the way she'd planned. She'd worked so hard, too, trying to bring these two lonely humans together.

"They *have* to meet before Christmas Eve," she muttered.

Mercy nodded. "So what are you going to do about it?"

Goodness smiled; a plan was already taking shape in her mind. She didn't want to intervene in human events; strictly speaking, that was against the rules. However, Beth and Peter weren't giving her much of an alternative. Either she acted on their behalf or Gabriel would have to report that she'd failed. No one would blame her for a small intervention, least of all Gabriel, but so far her track record had been exceptional—if she did say so herself—and she wanted to keep it that way.

Everyone in Heaven knew that humans were difficult subjects. At times they required a clear and unambiguous sign, or a bit of coaxing. Or both. And some people needed more help than others. In Goodness's opinion, Beth was one of those.

"Well, you have to admit we all had a shock," Mercy said, reminding Goodness of the scene in Leavenworth the day before.

"I agree." Goodness frowned as she contemplated her next move. Letting Peter and Beth stumble into each other on the street would be too convenient—and too subtle. No, whatever Goodness arranged would have to be dramatic. Personally she'd prefer a car crash, involving a massive explosion—no deaths, of course. The possibility of a SWAT team thrilled her and if she could manage it, a helicopter rescue. That would make her day. Those boys in black always did get her adrenaline going.

"Goodness," Mercy prodded gently. "I recognize that look in your eyes and I don't like the way your wings are fluttering."

"I think it might be best if you left now," she said primly.

"Goodness!"

"I don't want you to get in trouble, too."

Mercy's wings lifted her off the ground. "*What* are you going to do?"

Goodness pressed her lips together and shook her head. "It's better for you not to know."

That was when Shirley arrived. "What's going on here?" she demanded.

"I've got a few problems," Goodness said.

"You do?" Shirley muttered. "Well, you aren't the only one. My assignment's not working out the way it's supposed to."

Mercy frowned, and her gaze swung back to Goodness and then to Shirley again. "Do either of you have the feeling we might've been set up?"

Goodness sent her a puzzled glance. "What do you mean?"

"Think about it," Mercy said. "Shirley gets what would usually be a dream assignment. Just how hard can it be to give a boy a dog?"

"Well, actually, this prayer request is one of the most difficult ones I've ever received." She sighed. "Not only do we have the issue with Carter's father, there's this one dog that refuses to go away."

"I see."

"But under normal conditions, it wouldn't be difficult, would it?"

Shirley lifted one shoulder in a halfhearted shrug. "Not really. The thing that troubles me most is this dog. He doesn't seem…ordinary. And he simply won't leave. I think that problem's finally been solved, though. He's at the animal shelter and he'll probably be adopted soon."

"Good."

Shirley wore a sad frown. "Well, there's nothing I can do right now, so I've put the matter out of my mind. I'm here to help you two."

Mercy looked crestfallen. "My assignment's also failing."

"You don't happen to need a SWAT team, do you?" Goodness asked excitedly. It seemed a shame not to call out the big guns when they might be able to help her friends, too.

Mercy's expression was horrified. "Goodness, what are you thinking?"

She held up her hands. "Imagine this: helicopters descending, ropes dropping to the ground and men—young, handsome men—sliding down to the rooftops."

"To do what?" Mercy cried. "You'll ruin everything. I've got enough troubles with Harry and Rosalie as it is. I don't need *that* kind of help. Just the sound of those helicopters would send him into cardiac arrest."

"So what *can* we do?" Goodness asked. "We've got three unfinished assignments on our hands."

"At this point," Mercy suggested, "maybe we should let these situations play out and see what happens."

It seemed so little. But perhaps Mercy and Shirley were right. She'd done her best to bring Peter and Beth together, and her efforts, such as they were, had resulted in shock and confusion. Perhaps she should step aside and see what these humans could figure out for themselves.

Still, she *was* disappointed.

Seventeen

Carter had been weepy and sad ever since his father had driven him to the animal shelter where they'd left Rusty. All night long, he'd lain awake, thinking about his dog. He knew how bad his parents felt, so Carter tried not to show how miserable he was.

He realized his parents didn't have any extra money, and even the allowance he'd saved up wasn't enough.

"Carter," his mother called from the living room. "Come and see what your father brought home."

Hoping against hope that it was Rusty, Carter ran into the room. It wasn't. Instead, his mother stood in front of an artificial Christmas tree. The tree they had was dinky. So small, in fact, that it sat on the coffee table. It was in a flower pot and it was decorated with tiny glass balls. This one was real. Well, not exactly real because he could tell that the branches weren't like those of a live tree and it didn't have that nice Christmas smell. But it was real in size. And it came complete with strings of lights.

"A Christmas tree," his sister squealed with delight as she joined him in the living room. "Where did you get it?"

"Your father found it," his mother said. "On his way to

work this morning, he caught a glimpse of something in an alley. He stopped, and there was the tree. Someone must've gotten a new tree because this one was propped up against a Dumpster. So your father brought it home for us."

That explained why Carter had heard his father return to the house shortly after he'd left for work.

Bailey clapped her hands. Even Carter smiled. It was an old Christmas tree, a little worn and raggedy, but a whole lot better than the miniature one they had now. *That* one was more like a plant than a tree.

His first thought was that he wanted to show it to Rusty, except he couldn't because Rusty wasn't with him anymore. It hurt to remember his dog, but Carter couldn't think about anything else. He hoped Rusty would go to a good home and that someone in his new family would love him as much as Carter did.

"Do the lights work?" Bailey asked.

"We'll have to see," his mother said. She got down on the floor, crawled behind the tree and plugged in the cord. The lights flickered for a moment and then went out.

"That's probably why it was in the garbage," Carter told his mother.

"It's just a pretend tree," Bailey whined.

"It's pathetic-looking," Carter muttered. "But…it's okay." He tried to pretend he was happy about the Christmas tree, and he was, only…only it was old and the lights didn't work and no one else wanted it. That made him think of Rusty again. No one else had wanted him, either, but Carter did, in the worst way.

"We can make it look pretty," Bailey said, rebounding from her disappointment. "I have some colored paper from school and I could make an angel for the top," she said excitedly.

"We could string popcorn and cranberries, too," their mother suggested.

Carter didn't say anything for a long time. "I know how to cut out snowflakes," he finally told her.

"Thank you, Carter." As if recognizing how much effort it had taken him to offer, his mother hugged him tightly.

Carter tried to squirm out of her embrace. He was too big to have his mother hug him, but at the same time he kind of liked it. He didn't want his friends to know about it, though.

"We'll have the tree decorated when your father gets home from work," his mother said.

"Okay." Carter was willing to do his share.

Soon the aroma of popping corn filled the house. Carter sat at the kitchen table and patiently pierced the kernels with one of his mother's big sewing needles. He strung twenty-five kernels, then added a cranberry. Bailey decided to string her own and followed his pattern.

"Make it your own way," he snapped at his sister. "You don't have to do everything like me, you know."

"Carter," his mother said. "She just wants her string to match yours."

"Why can't she do her own design?"

"Because you're her big brother and she looks up to you."

Carter wanted to be angry, but he wasn't. His sister had helped him with Rusty and had loved the stray, too.

"What do you think Rusty's doing right now?" he asked his mother. "Will he remember me?"

"Of course he will," his mother said. "Rusty will always remember the boy who brought him food and washed the mud off his fur."

"And played catch with him."

Carter thought he might cry, but instead he smiled. Thinking about all the things he'd done with Rusty seemed to ease the ache in his heart.

The phone rang and his mother answered it quickly. "Hi, honey."

That meant it was his father.

"We're decorating the tree," his mother continued.

His father must've said something else because his mother went quiet.

Then she said, "Of course. He's right here." Placing her hand over the mouthpiece, she turned to Carter. "Your dad said he'd like to talk to you."

"Okay." Scooting off the chair, Carter took the phone. "Hi, Dad."

"How's it going?"

Carter shrugged. "All right, I guess."

"What do you think of the Christmas tree I found?"

"The lights don't work," he murmured.

"I'll take a look at those when I get home."

It was unusual for his father to work on Sundays. But he must've been putting in overtime at the restaurant. Christmas was a busy season and his father said they could use the money, so he worked as many overtime hours as he could get.

Carter wished his father was home the way he was almost every Sunday. Usually they watched football together. If he'd been able to keep Rusty, then his dog would've joined them. Carter was sure Rusty would enjoy football as much as he did.

"You still feel bad about Rusty?"

"Yeah."

"So do I," his father admitted.

"I know."

"He's going to a good family and they'll love Rusty, too."

But Carter didn't want any other family to love Rusty. He wanted Rusty to be *his*. He hung his head. "When will you be home?" he asked, his voice cracking.

"I'll get there as soon as I can."

"Bye, Dad."

"Bye, son."

Carter handed the phone back to his mother; before she hung up, their father spoke to Bailey, too.

Then he heard it.

A dog barking.

It sounded as if Rusty was right outside the door. That wasn't possible, but it sure *sounded* like his dog.

"What's that noise?" his mother asked, frowning in his direction. She walked to the back door and opened it.

As Carter held his breath, he heard his mother cry out.

"Rusty!" Bailey shrieked.

"Rusty." Carter flew out of his chair so fast it went crashing backward onto the kitchen floor.

His mother opened the screen door and Rusty ran in, leaping up on his hind legs and dashing around in a circle and then jumping straight up in the air.

A moment later Rusty was licking Carter's face, yelping with joy. He flopped down on his belly, right in front of Carter, tail waving madly.

When Carter looked up at his mother, he saw that she had tears in her eyes. Soon she was down on the floor with him, hugging Rusty, too, along with Bailey. Even his sister was crying.

"How did he ever get here?" His mother stared at Carter.

He didn't have an answer for her. All he knew was that the animal shelter wasn't close by. It was miles and miles away.

Carter got a dish and filled it with water. Rusty lapped that up and ate every bit of popcorn on the floor.

"I'm not sure if popcorn's good for him or not," his mother warned.

Carter went to the cupboard for the cereal he'd fed him the day before. He prepared another large bowlful, with plenty of milk. His dog certainly wasn't a picky eater.

"Oh, Carter." His mother sighed deeply. "I don't know what your father's going to say about this."

"Don't call him at work," Carter pleaded. He was afraid his father would come home and take Rusty back to the shelter that very minute. He didn't want that to happen. Not yet. Not ever. Still, he realized his father wouldn't let Rusty stay, and he wanted to keep his dog with him as long as he could.

They finished stringing the popcorn and draping the strands on the tree. When Carter crawled underneath, Rusty came with him. With the dog at his side, Carter plugged the electrical cord in the socket again. This time the lights went on—and stayed on.

"Cool," his sister cried and clapped her hands.

"It's magic," Carter said. "Rusty brought it with him."

When they crawled out from under the tree, Rusty lay down on the carpet and rested his head on his paws. He looked about as tired as Carter felt, and he wondered if Rusty had stayed awake all night, thinking about Carter, the way Carter had about him. Unable to stop himself, Carter yawned.

"Why don't we all lie down for a bit," his mother suggested, eyeing him. It was almost as if she knew he'd hardly slept the night before.

"I don't take naps," Carter said indignantly. Bailey sometimes did. When she got cranky, their mother would send her into their bedroom. Bailey always fell asleep.

"It looks like Rusty's tired," his mother suggested. "I just thought you might want to keep him company."

"Oh."

Rusty followed Carter into his bedroom and lay on the rug beside his bed. Instead of climbing onto the mattress, Carter got down on the floor next to his dog. He flung his arm over Rusty and drifted off.

The next thing Carter heard was the sound of his father's voice.

"How is this possible?" his father was asking.

"Dad!" Carter leaped to his feet and tore into the kitchen, Rusty at his heels. "Did you hear?"

"Yes," his father said. "What I don't understand is how he found the house."

"But he did."

Rusty approached his father and gazed up at him.

His father bent down to pet Rusty's thick fur. "Well, my son said you were a special dog."

"Not only that," Carter rushed to tell his father, "when we first plugged in the tree, the lights only flickered and then they went out."

"And after Rusty got here, Carter plugged in the lights and they worked," Bailey said, so happy and excited that her words ran together.

Carter frowned at his sister. "*I* wanted to tell Dad that."

"Can he stay?" Ignoring him, Bailey turned to her father, eyes wide.

"I'm sorry, kids, we've already been through this."

"David, here's the number for the shelter," his mother said as she came into the room.

"I'm going to call and find out what happened." His father took the slip of paper and reached for the telephone. Carter stood by his side. He wanted to learn what had happened, too.

His father seemed to wait for a long time. Carter could hear the phone ringing. Holding the receiver away from his mouth, his dad muttered, "The shelter must be closed for the night."

Hope flared to life inside Carter. Maybe they'd have to keep Rusty overnight. Maybe—

"Hello," his father said, dashing Carter's hopes. "Yes, I understand the shelter's closed." He seemed to be listening. "We're the family who brought Rusty. He's the reddish stray that showed up in the schoolyard and followed my son home. I dropped Rusty off at the shelter yesterday afternoon. Well, Rusty's now here."

This announcement was followed by a short silence. Carter's father was shaking his head, as if the person on the other end of the line was arguing with him.

"I assure you he's here."

Another silence.

"Well, you might want to go and check his cage."

The person from the shelter must've said something else, because his father grew quiet once more. "He's going to check the cage where Rusty was put earlier," he told Carter.

The shelter employee was obviously back on the phone.

"Yes, he's here," his father explained for the third time. "I don't have a clue how he escaped or how he managed to get back to this house, but somehow or other, he did."

"Can he stay the night?" Carter pleaded. "Just one more night. Please, Dad, please."

"Yes, I'll bring him back in the morning," his father was saying.

Carter wrapped his arms around Rusty's neck. He had no idea how the dog had found his way across miles and miles of snow-covered roads to their house—but he'd always known Rusty possessed special powers.

His father hung up the phone. "He can only stay until morning, Carter."

Carter nodded. It wasn't long enough, but for this one last night, Rusty was his.

Eighteen

"They're here!" Rosalie shouted from the living room. Her voice rose with excitement. She'd gone to look out the window every few minutes, waiting for their daughter and her husband.

"Is it Donna?" Harry asked. He was no less excited than his wife.

"Yes," Rosalie said, letting the curtain fall back into place.

Harry struggled to get to his feet, and instantly Rosalie was at his side. She brought him the walker he hated and then slid her arm around his waist, guiding him into the hall.

"How do I look?" she asked.

Harry pretended to study her, noting her carefully combed hair, a soft lovely gray, and the antique cameo she wore with her dark green dress. "You couldn't be more beautiful if you'd tried."

"Oh, Harry."

At his words, Harry could see the blush of pleasure that crept across her cheeks.

The door opened and in breezed his daughter, with Richard, their son-in-law, both of them laden with parcels and bags. Soon everyone was kissing and hugging. Rosalie had tears in her eyes and, for that matter, so did Harry. Seeing his daughter renewed his waning strength.

All their married life, Rosalie had been a gracious hostess, and as soon as Donna and Richard had taken their coats off, she led them to the formal living room and brought out a tray of coffee and cookies.

Donna helped serve, and before long they were all sitting together, chatting and catching up. Harry watched his daughter's animated gestures, and his heart swelled with love. In appearance, Donna resembled Rosalie's family, with her dark brown hair and eyes. Her personality, though, was all his. She was practical but enjoyed taking a risk now and then.

Donna was a teacher and had taught kindergarten and first grade for nearly thirty years. She was close to retirement, as was Richard. They'd met in college and married soon after. They'd presented him with two wonderful grandsons, two years apart.

"Tell me about Scotty," Rosalie said, eager for news of their youngest grandson. In a recent conversation, Donna had hinted that she had something special to share.

Donna and Richard smiled at each other, and Richard reached for his wife's hand.

"Scott's engaged!" Donna said happily.

"Is it Lana?" Harry asked. Their grandson had stopped by to visit in September and had brought a young woman to meet them. Harry recognized the look in his eyes. The boy was in love.

"Yes. Everyone likes Lana," Donna said. "We're all so pleased. Rich and I recently met her parents, and they're just as thrilled as we are."

"When's the wedding?" Rosalie asked.

"February," Donna told her mother.

"So soon!" his wife trilled, her eyes glowing. "Oh, I'm so glad."

"Lana wanted to wait for June," Donna said, "but Scott said a Valentine wedding was more romantic."

"Who would've guessed that about Scott?" Richard asked.

Rosalie glanced at Harry and they exchanged a smile. "He gets his romantic heart from his grandfather."

"Dad?" Donna did an exaggerated double take.

"Your father's sent me flowers every Valentine's Day since the year we met. Even during the war." Her eyes filled with tears as she looked at him. Pulling her lace-edged handkerchief from her sleeve, she dabbed her cheeks. "This is such good news, isn't it, dear?"

Harry nodded. All his grandchildren would be married now. Although Harry had only met Lana that one time, he believed the young woman was a good match for his youngest grandson.

"That's not our only news," Donna said. Once again she smiled at Richard. "Phillip called last week and Tiffany's pregnant."

Rosalie squealed with delight.

"Rich and I are going to be grandparents."

"Oh, my goodness," Rosalie said, clasping her hands. "That means Harry and I will be *great*-grandparents."

"You're much too young to be a great-grandmother," Harry teased, just so he could watch Rosalie blush once more.

"Nonsense," his wife countered. "Some of our friends are great-grandparents several times over."

That was true, and Harry didn't bother to comment. He'd hoped to live long enough to meet his first great-grandchild but that wasn't to be.

Richard helped himself to another cookie. Rosalie had picked them up at the bakery on Saturday, and although he wouldn't tell her this, Harry thought they were as good as any she might have baked. Actually, he wouldn't mind a second one himself. As soon as he stretched out his arm, Rosalie immediately lifted the platter and offered it to him.

Donna was still talking about the baby. She'd be the perfect grandmother, Harry knew. She'd been an excellent mother, and after all those years spent teaching six- and seven-year-olds, she had a real way with kids. Donna's students loved her; it wasn't unusual for teenagers and adults to come and see her—people, who at one time, had been in her class.

"When's Tiffany due?" Rosalie asked.

"July," Donna said. "We don't know if it's a boy or a girl, although I don't think anyone really cares. The timing is certainly good."

Richard smiled. "Phillip's out of graduate school now and the job he got with Microsoft seems secure. Or as secure as any corporate job is these days." He turned to Harry, who nodded. Over the years, they'd often discussed the economy and related issues.

"Phillip does a bit more traveling than either of them would like," Donna added, "but he's in training, so that goes with the territory."

Richard sipped his coffee. "I understand the two of you are planning to sell the house," he said.

Rosalie sighed and aimed a sad smile at Harry.

"Unfortunately we had some bad news regarding Liberty Orchard," Harry told him. In retrospect he'd give just about anything to have handed the administrator a check for the deposit the day they'd toured the facility. "Apparently the only available unit has already been taken."

Donna leaned forward. "That's what Mom said, so I phoned Liberty Orchard and talked to Elizabeth Goldsmith myself."

"She can't wave a magic wand and make another unit appear." Harry didn't want to admit how much the news depressed him. This was to be his last gift to Rosalie before he died, and now it wasn't going to happen.

"When I phoned," Donna went on to say, "Ms. Goldsmith said she was just about to contact you."

"The unit's available?" Harry felt a surge of hope.

"Not the one you originally saw, but another one."

"Did someone die?" Rosalie asked, frowning.

"No, it belonged to a couple. Perhaps you met them. Ralph and Daisy—I can't remember their last name."

"McDonald," Harry supplied. He remembered talking with the two and had quite liked them. Their children both lived in Chicago. "Are they moving closer to their son and daughter?"

"Yes."

"When?" Rosalie asked.

"They hope to be out by the fifth of January. It'll take a couple of days to give the unit a thorough cleaning and then it'll be ready for you and Dad by the tenth."

"I'll get them a check right after Christmas," Harry said, unable to hide his pleasure.

"It's all taken care of, Dad," Donna said. "I knew you'd want the unit, so Rich and I put it on our credit card."

"I'll get the check to you then. Immediately." The fact that they'd used credit bothered him; he couldn't help it.

Donna gestured magnanimously. "Consider it your Christmas gift."

Harry wouldn't allow his daughter to do that; still, the certainty of acquiring the unit afforded him real peace of mind.

"That's wonderful news," Rosalie agreed, nodding vigorously.

"It's even better than you realize," Donna said. "I'll be here the entire time to help you move."

"What about school?" Harry asked.

Donna smiled. "That's my other surprise. I'm retiring. As of now."

Harry stared at her. "But…it's the middle of the school year."

"Actually, this is a good news/bad news situation," Rich explained. "Donna needs knee-replacement surgery."

Their daughter nodded. "I guess that's what I get from all those years of crawling around on the floor with my kindergarten classes. It isn't extensive surgery, but it'll require several weeks of rehab. I'd already decided to retire at the end of this school year. But with the wedding, the surgery and the baby, Rich and I felt it made more sense to do it now."

"I think this is wonderful," Rosalie said again.

Rosalie had always supported their children's decisions, even when they gave Harry pause. She was loyal to a fault; he loved that about her.

"The paperwork's been turned in and everything's a go."

"You should've told us," Rosalie chastised.

"I couldn't until I got the final word. I didn't mean to hide it from you, Mom, but I know how you worry."

While Donna claimed it was the surgery, the wedding and the baby, Harry suspected there was another reason his daughter had chosen to retire early. "So you'll help us pack up the house," he said.

"Absolutely. Lorraine, too."

This was welcome news to Harry. His prayer had been answered—they had a place at Liberty Orchard now. And his daughters would both be here. If God should choose to bring him home, Harry could be assured that Rosalie would be well looked after.

This was going to be the best Christmas of his life. And the last…

Nineteen

Beth yawned. It'd been a long day, beginning with church that morning and then brunch with her family. Now, at almost ten, she was tired and ready for bed. She'd logged on to World of Warcraft a little while ago and was disappointed to discover that Peter wasn't online. Still, she felt relieved that they'd decided to postpone their meeting until after New Year's. That gave her time to make a few decisions, time to assess the situation and consider how to deal with what she'd learned.

The doorbell chimed. Beth frowned, wondering who'd stop by this late at night.

When she checked the peephole, she saw a lovely woman standing in the hallway. Whoever it was had the most incredible blue eyes. Beth didn't recognize her. But even though she didn't know who this woman was, she unlatched the door and opened it.

Instead of the woman she'd seen through the peephole, a man stood there in front of her. Not just any man. John Nicodemus, her ex-husband.

Peter.

If Beth was shocked, it was nothing compared to the look on Peter's face.

"Marybeth?" he whispered as if he couldn't seem to find his voice. "What are you doing here?"

"I live here."

"No, you don't," he argued.

"Are you looking for Borincana?" she asked.

Peter went pale.

"You're Timixie," she added. It was obvious that they both needed to sit down, so she stepped out of the doorway and waved him inside.

Peter moved into the living room and sank heavily onto the sofa. Elbows balanced on his knees, he thrust his fingers through his hair and stared down at the floor.

Beth understood exactly how he felt because she'd experienced the very same mix of emotions when she'd seen him in Leavenworth. It had felt as if the sidewalk had started to crumble beneath her feet. The shock had been followed by anger and disbelief.

Yesterday in Leavenworth, she'd suspected him of somehow arranging this. As she watched his face, she could see that he was feeling doubt, incredulity, suspicion—just as she had.

"How can this be?" he murmured after several minutes.

"I asked myself that, too."

His eyes narrowed. "How long have you known?"

She wanted it understood that she hadn't arranged this, any more than he had. "Since Leavenworth."

His mouth tightened. "You were there?"

Beth nodded. "You were standing by the gazebo, exactly as we'd agreed. Then I saw that red rose and I nearly fainted."

"Who was on the phone?" he demanded. "I would've recognized your voice."

"My friend Heidi. She's a new friend—you never met her."

He straightened, then leaned back against the sofa as he absorbed her words.

"Why are you here?" she asked. Beth studied him carefully. He was even more attractive than she remembered. The years had matured him, and his features had lost their boyish quality. He looked more serious now, more...adult. They'd both been so juvenile and irrational, so quick to get out of the relationship. Beth had felt blindsided by the pain of it and she thought that John...Peter might have been, too. Certainly, his online confidences suggested as much.

"I shouldn't have come," he muttered. "The whole time I was driving here, I couldn't figure out why I was doing this."

Beth didn't understand it, either. They'd already said they'd wait until after New Year's.

He closed his eyes for a few seconds, then opened them again and looked directly at her. "This afternoon we made our plans but all of a sudden that wasn't good enough. I couldn't stop thinking about you. I was afraid that if we delayed meeting again, neither of us would ever be ready. It was just too easy to keep putting it off."

Beth could see that was true.

"Once I made the decision, waiting even an hour seemed intolerable. I had your address from the phone call in Leavenworth—thanks to your friend, as it turns out. I decided to meet you and I didn't care that it was after nine at night and I was coming uninvited."

"Only you *had* met me."

"Well, I could hardly know that, could I?" he snapped, then seemed to regret his outburst. "How did something like this happen?" he asked helplessly.

She responded with a question of her own. "When did John become Peter?"

"When I began working in the corporate office at Starbucks. There were four Johns, so I decided to use my middle name and I just got used to it. The only people who call me John these days are my parents."

In other words, his name change had come about in a perfectly rational way—it was certainly no attempt at subterfuge.

"What about you, Mary*beth?*"

"Marybeth became Beth after the divorce."

He regarded her skeptically. "Any particular reason?"

"I wanted a new start, and Marybeth sounded so childish and outdated to me, so I shortened it to Beth. The only people who still call me Marybeth are my family."

"I see." He rubbed his face. "I don't mean to be forward here, but I could use a cup of coffee."

"Of course. I'm sorry, I should've asked." She stood and took two steps toward the kitchen before abruptly turning back. "How'd you do that, by the way?"

"Do what?"

"I checked the peephole in my door before I unlocked it and there was a woman on the other side."

"A woman?" He wore a puzzled frown.

"She was attractive and had blond hair and striking blue eyes."

"It wasn't me."

"Obviously."

He met her gaze head-on. "I was the only one there, Beth. Maybe you should have your eyesight examined."

"Maybe you should—" She clamped her mouth shut. They had too many other things to discuss. An argument would be pointless; it didn't matter what or whom she'd seen—or *thought* she'd seen. "Give me a minute to make that coffee."

Unexpectedly, Peter followed her into the kitchen. "What just happened back there?" he asked with obvious surprise.

"What do you mean?" She efficiently measured the grounds and poured water into the coffeemaker.

"You dropped the discussion."

Confused, Beth glanced over at him. "What discussion?"

"It used to be that you absolutely *had* to be right," he told her. "You'd go ten miles out of your way to prove how right you were and how wrong I was."

"I did?" Beth didn't remember it like that.

"You always had a point to prove."

"Yes, well, people change."

Peter didn't speak for some time. "I've changed, too."

"I'm sure we both have." For the better, although she didn't say that. After six months of being his partner on WoW, she knew this man, knew important things about his character, and he wasn't like her ex-husband at all.

The coffee started to drip and Beth got two mugs from the cupboard. Staring down at the kitchen counter, she gathered her courage to ask him a question.

"Did you mean what you said this afternoon about...still loving me?" The words seemed to stick in her throat.

"Yes."

She wished he'd elaborate—and a moment later he did.

"I never stopped loving you, Marybeth. That was one of the problems. For years, the people closest to me have encouraged me to find someone else and remarry. I tried."

She jerked up her head. "So it's true?" Abruptly her heart sank, and she actually felt ill. "You did marry again."

"No," he returned vehemently. "Who told you that?"

"A friend. Well, sort of a friend. Lisa Carroll. Remember her?"

"Yeah." Peter frowned. "She told you that?" When Beth nodded, he pressed his palms on the kitchen counter. "That isn't even *close* to being true. Why would she do that?" He paused. "What about you? Have you...did you find someone else?"

Beth shrugged, unwilling to disclose that she'd been practically a hermit in the dating world. "I went out some. No one for long."

"I occasionally dated, too," he confessed. "Including Lisa," he added in a low voice. "For about two weeks."

Well, that explains it, Beth thought—but didn't say.

"No one clicked with me," she said after a brief silence.

He offered her a sad smile. "No one clicked with me, either."

"Mostly I was afraid." Because she needed something to do with her hands, she filled the two mugs with coffee, welcoming the distraction.

Peter reached for his mug and she automatically opened her refrigerator and took out the milk.

He smiled. "You remember that I take milk in my coffee."

"How could I forget?" she asked, a smile tugging at the corners of her own mouth. "Don't you remember we had that huge fight over milk? I'd forgotten to pick some up on my way home."

Peter threw back his head and stared at the ceiling. "I was pretty unreasonable back then."

She'd thought the same thing. He'd accused her of intentionally forgetting the milk, apparently convinced that she'd done it in retaliation, since he'd been right in a silly argument they'd had the day before. It'd all been so stupid, so adolescent.

Peter poured a dollop of milk into his coffee, then returned the carton to the refrigerator. Beth watched in amazement. While they were married, he'd driven her to the brink of insanity by leaving everything out. He left drawers open, newspapers on the floor, dirty dishes everywhere.

When she complained, he'd accused her of being too fastidious and a "neat freak." Beth hadn't seen herself as either; however she'd considered him lazy and disorganized—and had told him so.

They both sipped their coffee for a couple of minutes, leaning casually against the kitchen counters. Despite her relaxed pose, Beth felt anything but.

"Did you mean what *you* said?" Peter gazed at her over the top of his mug.

She knew what he was asking. "I always loved you. Even when I filed for divorce, I loved you. I couldn't live with you, but that didn't change how I felt about you."

He chuckled softly and nodded. "It was the same with me. You were driving me crazy."

"We did it to each other." Beth set her mug on the counter. "So," she said, sighing. "This afternoon you said you don't want to look back and that it's time to move forward."

He nodded again. "It's time for *both* of us to let go of the past, Marybeth."

"And...what about the future?"

He didn't answer right away. He glanced at her, his eyes uncertain, then looked away. "In other words, you're asking where we go from here."

"It's a fair question, don't you think?"

"I agree. Only I'm not sure what to say. Is it just a coincidence that we've been online together for the past six months and neither of us realized it?"

"I never dreamed it could be you," she said. "I didn't set this up... I wouldn't know how."

"I believe you. I couldn't have, either."

Suddenly she recalled the conversation she'd had with her mother and the fact that Joyce had even lit a candle in church on her behalf. She took a deep breath. "It seems to me that we were brought back together for a reason."

"Yes."

Beth's heart pounded frantically as Peter put down his mug and walked around the counter to stand in front of her. He settled his hands on her shoulders and stared into her eyes.

"If you're willing to give us another chance, I think we should do it," he said in an urgent voice.

Beth gave him a tentative smile. "I'm willing."

That was when he kissed her. As he lowered his mouth to hers, Beth closed her eyes and slipped her arms around him. His lips were soft, pliable, warm. The years fell away, and it was as if they were college students again, hungry for each other, desperately in love and ready to take on dragons and warriors and despots and worse.

Beth eased her mouth from his. "Do you want to spend Christmas with me and my family?" she asked, smiling up at him.

Peter laughed. "If you'll spend New Year's with mine."

"Very clever, Goodness," Mercy said, sitting on the counter in Beth Fischer's kitchen, swinging her feet.

"I had to do something," Goodness told her. "Peter and Beth were content to delay their meeting, so I had to put an end to *that*." She turned to Mercy and smiled. "I've learned men are much more suggestible than women."

"I've discovered the same thing," Shirley said, joining them. "That wasn't all, though. Stepping in front of Peter when he arrived at Beth's so she saw your face instead of his was brilliant."

"Tricky, too." Mercy's voice was admiring. Goodness had to reveal herself to Beth, yet remain hidden from Peter. Not an easy task and if Gabriel ever found out, she'd never hear the end of it.

"Gabriel will be pleased when he learns Beth and Peter are together again."

"I think he will, too," Goodness said.

Her mission had been completed.

The candle Joyce Fischer had lit in the church flickered one last time and then went out.

Twenty

That night, knowing Rusty would have to go back to the animal shelter, Carter settled the dog on his bed. Placing both arms around him, Carter spoke softly in his ear.

"You're the best dog any kid could have," he whispered.

As if he understood the words, Rusty licked Carter's face. He seemed to be saying that Carter was the best friend he'd ever have, too.

"I'd do anything to keep you. Well…almost anything." After his father had come home from work and explained that they'd be taking Rusty back to the shelter in the morning, Carter had seriously considered running away.

If his mom and dad weren't going to let him have Rusty, then Carter decided he no longer wanted to be part of this family. He'd find another family, one that could afford a dog and kept promises.

He had over thirty dollars saved from his allowance, which should be enough to get him to his grandparents' house in Wenatchee. He was sure that if they knew about Rusty, Grandma and Grandpa Parker would pay whatever it cost to keep him.

But in the end, Carter couldn't do it. He couldn't run

away. He loved his mother and father and even his little sister, although she was a pest most of the time.

"I'll go back to the shelter with you," Carter assured his friend. In the morning he'd ride down with his father. He was determined to speak to the lady who'd taken Rusty before.

Carter wanted to make *sure* his dog went to a good home. Not just a regular home, either. The very best.

Carter had prayed for a dog and he'd prayed hard. Although he loved Rusty, maybe—despite everything—this wasn't the dog God meant for him.

Tears welled up in his eyes and he tried to hold back a sniffle. He didn't want his sister to hear him crying, so he buried his face in the dog's fur.

"I want to keep Rusty, too," Bailey whispered from the other side of the room.

Carter pretended not to hear.

"I love Rusty just as much as you do," she said, only louder this time.

"I know."

She sniffled once and then Carter did, too. "Go to sleep," he said.

Bailey didn't answer, and Carter suspected she felt as sad as he did. Even if Rusty belonged to him, he was willing to share his dog with Bailey. Not every day; just some of the time—once a week or so.

Except that Rusty wouldn't be his to share. His friend would be with him for only a few more hours. The realization was crushing.

"Go to sleep," he repeated and hugged Rusty closer.

"This is a fine mess you've gotten yourself into," Mercy muttered, glaring at Shirley. They were both inside the children's bedroom. Shirley sat on the foot of the bed, where Rusty lay tightly curled up next to Carter's feet.

"Me?" Shirley wore a look of innocence as she continued to pet the dog.

"Yes, you." Mercy pointed an accusing finger at her fellow Prayer Ambassador. Then she crossed her arms as she surveyed the sleeping children, lost in their dreams.

"How could you have let this happen?" Mercy asked.

Shirley straightened defensively.

Mercy wasn't fooled. "*You're* the one who stopped by the animal shelter and conveniently opened the cage and set Rusty free."

"Ah…"

"That wasn't the only door you opened, either." Mercy was on to her friend's antics and she wasn't going to let Shirley squirm out of this one.

"Well…" Shirley shifted uncomfortably. As though aware of their presence, Rusty lifted his head and looked around.

"It's all right, boy," Shirley whispered, reassuring the dog.

Rusty put his head down on his paws and closed his eyes once more.

"Don't bother to deny that you're the one who set him free," Mercy said in a stern voice.

"All right," Shirley confessed. "That was me—"

"I thought so."

"I couldn't help it! Carter loves that dog, and Rusty loves him. The two of them are *meant* to be together."

"Not according to what you first said." Although she made it sound like a complaint, Mercy was actually delighted with her friend. In the past, Shirley had been a real stickler for protocol during their earthly visitations. The former guardian angel always took on the role of supervisor, policing Goodness and Mercy as if that was her right. She found it gratifying that, for once, Shirley had broken the rules herself.

"Just look at Carter and Rusty," Shirley urged. "How can anyone take that dog away from that little boy?"

Mercy gazed down at the sleeping figures. Rusty slept peacefully close to Carter and Mercy was moved almost to tears by their mutual devotion.

"What's going to happen now?" Mercy asked.

"I don't know." Shirley shook her head. "I pleaded Carter's case to Gabriel. That's all I can do."

"You did?" Many a time Mercy had done the same, but to no avail. She didn't think Shirley had gone to the Archangel even once to request assistance. Until now.

"What did he say?"

Shirley cleared her throat. "He said I'd already interfered where I shouldn't have. That God has everything under control."

"So he knew what you'd done." This shouldn't surprise Mercy. Gabriel always seemed to be aware of their every move.

"I'm to butt out." She sounded a little affronted, and Mercy couldn't blame her.

"Gabriel told you that?"

"In exactly those words, too. He warned me that I'm not to involve myself in any way from this point forward. He did ask me to stick around, though."

"I should hope so."

Shirley glanced down at the floor. "Gabriel wasn't happy with me."

Mercy shrugged, as if to imply that should be expected. "Don't worry about it. Gabriel knew what he was doing when he sent us back to Earth."

Shirley nodded morosely.

Seeing that her friend felt bad, Mercy decided to inject a bit of entertainment into their visit to Leavenworth. "Want to have some fun?"

As little as a week ago, Shirley would have sharply chastised Mercy for even suggesting such a thing. This time she simply gazed at her. "What do you have in mind?"

"Have you noticed the ornaments hanging from the street-lamps?" Actually, they were pretty hard to miss. The town council had hung large wreaths, candy canes and candles, interspersed with a few unrealistic-looking angels.

"I was thinking," Mercy went on, "of rearranging the ornaments, mixing things up a bit."

"We could make all the ornaments that aren't angels disappear," Shirley said tentatively, entering into the spirit of the enterprise.

"I like it," Mercy said excitedly.

"Let's contact Goodness and get started."

Tonight was December twenty-third, and they had one last day on Earth. Christmas Eve, they'd have to return to Heaven for the celebration. Only one day left, and Mercy intended to make the most of it.

Carter was tucked warmly in his bed when Rusty began to bark. The barking became louder and more frantic and it didn't stop. At first Carter ignored it, trying to sleep. But when he finally forced open his eyes, he couldn't see. The entire bedroom was filled with fog. There was a horrible smell. Like something burning.

The fog was so thick he couldn't even see his sister's bed. He choked. Taking a breath was painful.

Completely disoriented, he sat up.

"Bailey?"

His sister didn't answer.

"Bailey!" He tried again.

All at once, the bedroom door burst open and was shut with a bang. Out of the fog, his father emerged with his hand cupped over his nose and mouth.

"Dad? What's happening?"

"Fire," his father said tersely. It wasn't fog then, but smoke. Carter's dad swooped him off the bed and into his arms. He stumbled across the room, carrying Carter, then set him down and reached for Bailey. Jerking open the bedroom window, he gently dropped her, bare feet and all, into the snow.

"Get away from the house as fast as you can," he said. "Your mother's out front waiting for you."

Carter watched his sister race through the snow.

The smoke that was now pouring out of the bedroom window made Carter's eyes smart. He was next. His father lowered him carefully into the snow, then looked over his shoulder and leaped out himself.

Father and son ran hand in hand around the side of the house.

In the distance, Carter heard the wail of a fire engine, the alarm piercing the night.

His house was on fire.

His mother cried out with relief when she saw Carter and his father. Sobbing, she held out her arms. She swept Carter into her embrace and started kissing him. He hugged her tight and felt the tears on her cheeks.

The fire truck arrived and suddenly there were all kinds of people in front of the house. The paramedic put Carter and his family inside the aid car and checked their vital signs. His father had to breathe into an oxygen mask for a few minutes.

When Carter looked out the back of the aid car, he saw flames shooting up through the roof. The firefighters had the hoses going, and there seemed to be a dozen men and women at work.

"What woke you up?" The question came from the man who'd given his father the mask.

Carter answered. "Rusty." All of a sudden he realized he didn't know where his dog was. Bolting to his feet, Carter screamed, "Where's Rusty?" even though it hurt his throat to do that.

His father removed the mask. "My son's dog was barking," he said hoarsely. "If it hadn't been for Rusty, I would never have been able to get my family out of that house."

"Where's Rusty? Where's Rusty?" Carter cried, looking frantically in all directions. The thought of his dog still inside terrified him.

Then the sound of Rusty's bark cut through the night.

"Rusty!" Carter jumped out of the aid car as the dog raced across the neighbor's yard toward him. Getting down on one knee in the snow, Carter wrapped his arms around the dog's neck and hugged him. "You saved us. You saved us," he whispered again and again.

His father joined Carter and knelt down next to him and the dog.

"Well, boy," David said and his voice was shaking. "We still can't afford a dog, but you've earned your way into our home for the rest of your life."

"Do you mean it, Dad?"

"Every word."

"Rusty," Carter choked out. Rusty *was* his dog, just the way he'd always hoped, just the way he wanted. Tears fell from his eyes and Rusty repeatedly licked his face.

"All I can say," the man inside the aid car told them, "is that you're mighty lucky you had that dog."

"It wasn't luck," Carter insisted. "Rusty's the dog God sent me."

The medic nodded. "You've got all the proof you need of that."

Twenty-One

Lorraine and her husband, Kenny, had arrived early on Christmas Eve. Now it was two o'clock, and Rosalie was busy in the kitchen with her daughters, getting everything ready for dinner that evening. Richard and Ken sat with Harry in the family room, watching a football game on television. Two of the grandchildren would come later that afternoon.

This was all the Christmas Harry needed. With his children and two of his four grandchildren close, he was at peace.

Rising from his chair was difficult, and embarrassed by his need for it, Harry groped for the walker.

"You need any help with that, Dad?" Richard asked.

"No, I'm fine. A little slow, but fine." A bit wobbly on his feet, he glanced over at the two men who'd married his daughters. He loved them as much as he did Lorraine and Donna. They were the sons he'd never had. It was through their children that Harry and Rosalie would live on.

"Where are you going, Dad?" Lorraine asked, stepping out of the kitchen, wiping her hands on a dish towel. Harry didn't know what they were cooking in there, but it sure smelled good.

"I thought I'd rest for a while before dinner."

She put her arm around his waist and walked him down the hallway to the master bedroom.

Inside the room, Harry sat on the edge of his bed and Lorraine placed the walker where he could reach it once he awoke.

"I'm grateful to have this moment alone with you," he said to his oldest daughter.

"What is it, Dad?" She sat on the bed beside him.

"After I'm gone, I'll need you to look after your mother. You and Donna."

"You know we will." Tears filled her eyes.

Harry took her hand and squeezed it. "I don't want there to be tears when I pass, understand?"

"Oh, Dad, of course there'll be tears. You have no idea how much you're loved. You're the very heart of our family."

Harry sighed, knowing their sadness couldn't be avoided. Death for him, though, would be freeing. "Donna will be here to help your mother with the move."

"Kenny and I plan to come, as well."

"Thank you." Harry wasn't sure he'd still be around by then. But everything had been set in motion, and that brought him a sense of peace. "I think I'd better rest for a while."

"Good idea." When he lay down on the quilt, she kissed him on the cheek, then rearranged his pillows.

He'd just closed his eyes when Rosalie came into the room. "How are you feeling, sweetheart?" she asked.

"I'm tired, that's all."

She picked up the afghan at the foot of the bed and covered him gently. "Rest now, and I'll wake you in time for dinner."

Harry nodded, and then, as his wife of sixty-six years was about to leave the room, he reached for her hand.

Rosalie turned back expectantly.

"I've always loved you, my Rose."

She smiled softly. "I know, Harry. And you're the love of my life."

"This life and the next."

Rosalie bent down to kiss his cheek, and Harry closed his eyes.

"Harry," Mercy whispered.

Harry Alderwood's eyes flickered open and he stared at her in astonishment. "Am I dead? In Heaven?"

Mercy nodded. "Look," she said, with a gesture that swept from his head to his feet. "You're not old anymore. You're young again."

"Rosalie?"

"You'll see her soon," Mercy promised him. "And when she gets here, she'll be the young woman you met all those years ago."

"I saw you before," Harry said, pointing at Mercy. "That night I forgot my walker."

Mercy smiled. "That was me."

"You helped me, and I'm most appreciative."

Shirley, Goodness and Mercy surrounded Harry. "Come with us," Mercy said. "Your parents and your brother are waiting for you."

"Mom and Dad?" he asked excitedly. "And Ted, too?"

Mercy smiled again. "Everyone. All of Heaven has been waiting for your arrival. We're celebrating Christmas and you'll see—it's nothing like it is on Earth."

Gabriel appeared before them. "Harry Alderwood?"

Harry, young and handsome, nodded.

"Welcome to Paradise," Gabriel said. "I'll take over from here." The Archangel looked at the three Prayer Ambassadors, dismissing them. "I'll be joining you shortly."

* * *

Shirley, Goodness and Mercy stood in the choir loft at Leavenworth First Christian Church for the seven o'clock Christmas Eve service. Once they were finished here, they'd join Beth and her family at Midnight Mass in Seattle.

As the organ music swelled with the opening strains of "O Holy Night," Goodness leaned over to her friends. "Just wait until these humans hear the music in Heaven. Boy, are they in for a surprise."

"Like Harry," Mercy said. She'd served God as a Prayer Ambassador but she'd never assisted in the crossing before now. Watching as the frail body of Harry Alderwood was transformed into that of a young man had been a moving experience. His spirit had been set free from his weak and failing heart, free from his pain and free from the restraints of the world.

"Like Harry," Gabriel agreed, suddenly standing beside them. He focused his attention on Mercy. "You did well."

"Thank you," she said humbly. "I'm glad I was there to escort him to Heaven."

"How's his family doing?" Mercy asked, concerned for Rosalie and Harry's daughters. She couldn't imagine what it must've been like for Rosalie to come into the bedroom and find that her husband had died in his sleep.

"It's never easy for those on Earth to lose a loved one," Gabriel told them.

"They don't understand, do they?"

"Not yet," Gabriel said. "For now, they're looking through a dim glass. Soon, each one will know, each one will have his or her own experience and understand that death is not just an end but a beginning. A true beginning."

"How's Rosalie?"

"At the moment, she's overwhelmed by grief. Her

daughters are with her, though, and their love will sustain her. One or both of them will stay here until she's settled in Liberty Orchard."

That reassured Mercy.

The music came to a halt and the minister, Pastor Williams, stepped over to the podium in the front of the church.

"I have two announcements to make before we proceed with the Christmas program," he said. "I've received word that Harry Alderwood passed away this afternoon. I ask that we keep Rosalie and her family in our prayers."

Hushed murmurs rippled through the congregation.

"Also, as many of you know, the Jacksons lost their home in a fire last night. Fortunately, they have insurance. However, all their belongings have been destroyed. They're staying with relatives in Wenatchee right now, but if the people of our community could open their hearts to this young family, I know you will be blessed."

"That's Carter's family," Shirley said, glancing at her friends.

"Ah, yes, Carter," Gabriel muttered, turning a suspicious look on Shirley.

"I promise you I didn't have anything to do with the house fire," she said, holding up her hands.

"I know—because the three of you were out rearranging the street displays."

"Ah…" Mercy stared down at her feet. It was just a little thing, something they'd done for enjoyment. Surely Gabriel wouldn't mind. The residents didn't seem to.

"You knew about the fire?" Shirley asked the Archangel.

"I did."

"What happened?" Clearly, curiosity was getting the better of her. "How did it start?"

Gabriel leaned against the railing in the choir loft. "You remember that Christmas tree David Jackson found by the Dumpster?" he asked.

"Yes..."

"There was a reason it'd been thrown away."

"It shorted out?"

Gabriel nodded. "Carter's mother didn't turn off the lights when they went to bed because she was afraid that once she did, they wouldn't come back on." He sighed. "Foolishly they hadn't checked the batteries in their smoke alarm."

"Oh, dear."

"The fire, while devastating, will work out well for the family. The insurance will take care of replacing their earthly possessions. David, Carter's father, will soon be offered a new job at higher pay."

"And his mother?"

"She'll get that job with the school district and the family will be able to afford Rusty without a problem."

"That's wonderful news," Goodness said.

"What about Rusty?" Shirley asked.

"He'll live a good life and a long one. Rusty will be Carter's constant companion. They'll remain close until Rusty dies when he's sixteen human years old."

"Oh-h-h," all three of them breathed.

"Carter will remember his dog for the rest of his life." Gabriel touched Shirley's arm. "Well done."

Shirley beamed at his praise.

"Tell us about Beth Fischer," Goodness said.

"Ah, yes, Beth and Peter. They're going to step into church right now." In the blink of an eye, it was almost midnight. The three Prayer Ambassadors and Gabriel made the transition from Leavenworth First Christian to St. Alphonsus Catholic Church in Seattle.

The loft was crowded with members of the choir, resplendent in their long red robes. The music had just begun when Goodness saw Beth walking into the church with Peter at her side. A smile came over her as Beth and Peter entered the pew where the Fischer family was sitting.

Even from this distance, Goodness could see the surprise on Joyce Fischer's face as Beth gestured toward Peter. Soon Joyce and Peter were hugging.

"What'll happen with them?" Goodness asked. "Do they remarry?"

Gabriel grinned. "Yes, they'll wed just a few weeks from now. They've both learned from their mistakes."

"They'll have children, won't they?"

"Three," Gabriel said. "Two boys and a girl."

"Please tell me they won't name their children after their characters from World of Warcraft." Goodness grimaced and shook her head.

Gabriel laughed. "Don't worry. The oldest boy will be John, the daughter Mary and the youngest boy's going to be named Tim."

"For Timixie?"

"You'll have to ask them."

"I can?" Goodness squealed excitedly.

"Not for many years but in time, yes, you'll have that opportunity."

Goodness couldn't possibly have looked more pleased.

"I believe we're late," Gabriel said, ushering the three toward Heaven.

"Silent Night" played softly at the church as Gabriel, along with Shirley, Goodness and Mercy, returned to Heaven, where the joyous celebration of the Savior's birth was about to take place.

"Peace on Earth," Gabriel murmured as they ascended.

"And goodwill to all mankind," Shirley added. "Dogs, too."

Goodness and Mercy laughed as the gates of Heaven opened to bring them home.

* * * * *

Read on for a sneak preview of Debbie's next book
SILVER BELLS, part of Christmas anthology

THAT CHRISTMAS FEELING,

out next month!

"She's pretty, isn't she, Dad?"

Philip Lark glanced up. He sat at the kitchen table, filling out an expense report. His daughter sat across from him, smiling warmly. The way her eyes focused on him told him she was up to *something*.

"Who?" he asked, wondering if it was wise to inquire.

"Carrie Weston." At his blank look, she elaborated. "The woman we met in the elevator. We talked this afternoon." Mackenzie rested her chin in her hands and continued to gaze at him adoringly.

Philip's eyes reverted to the row of figures on the single sheet. His daughter waited patiently until he was finished. Patience wasn't a trait he was accustomed to seeing in Mackenzie. She usually complained when he brought work home, acting as though it was a personal affront. He cleared his mind, attempting to remember her question. Oh, yes, she wanted to know what he thought of Carrie Weston. For the life of him, he couldn't remember what the woman looked like. His impression of her remained vague, but he hadn't found anything to object to.

"You like her, do you?" he asked instead, although he wasn't convinced that pandering to Mackenzie's moods was a smart thing to do. She'd been impossible lately. Moody and unreasonable. Okay, okay, he realized the move had been hard on her; it hadn't been all that easy on him, either. But they'd be here for only six to eight weeks. He'd assumed she was mature enough to handle the situation. Evidently, he'd been wrong.

Mackenzie's moods weren't all he'd miscalculated. Philip used to think they were close, but for the past few months she'd been a constant source of frustration.

Overnight his sane, sensible daughter had turned into Sarah Bernhardt—or, more appropriately, Sarah Heartburn! She hadn't whined this much since she was three. Frankly, Philip didn't understand it. Even her mother's defection hadn't caused this much drama.

"Carrie's great, really great."

Philip was pleased Mackenzie had made a new friend, although he would have been more pleased if it was someone closer to her own age. Still, as he kept reminding her, the situation was temporary. Gene Tarkington, a friend of his who owned this apartment building, had offered the furnished two-bedroom rental to him for as long as it'd take to complete construction on his Lake Washington house. The apartment wasn't the Ritz, but he hadn't been expecting any luxury digs. Nor, truth be told, had he expected the cavalcade of characters who populated the building, although the woman with the crystal ball looked fairly harmless. And the muscle-bound sixty-year-old who walked around shirtless, carrying hand weights, appeared innocuous, too. He wasn't as certain about some of the others, but then he didn't plan on sticking around long enough to form friendships with this group of oddballs.

"Dad," Mackenzie began in a wistful voice, "have you ever thought of remarrying?"

"No," he answered emphatically, shocked by the question. He'd made one mistake; he wasn't willing to risk another. Laura and the twelve years they were together had taught him everything he cared to know about marriage.

"You sound mad."

"I'm not," he said, thrusting the expense report back inside his briefcase, "just determined."

"It's because of Mom, isn't it?"

"Why would I want to remarry?" he asked, hoping to put an end to this conversation.

"You might want a son someday."

"Why would I want a son when I have you?"

She grinned broadly, obviously approving his response. "Madame Frederick looked into her crystal ball and said she sees another woman in your life."

Philip laughed at the sheer ridiculousness of that. Remarry? Him? He'd rather dine on crushed glass. Wade through an alligator-infested swamp. Or jump off the Space Needle. No, he wasn't interested in remarrying. Not him. Not in this lifetime.

"Carrie's a lot like me."

So *this* was what the conversation was all about. Carrie and him. Well, he'd put a stop to that right now. "Hey." He raised his hand, palm out. "I guess I'm a little slow on the uptake here, but the fog is beginning to lift. You're playing matchmaker with me and this—" person he couldn't recall a single thing about "—neighbor."

"Woman, Dad. Carrie's young, attractive, smart and funny."

"She is?" He hadn't noticed that earlier, but then how could he? They'd met for about a minute in the elevator. "She's perfect for you."

Four characters, four lives, one unforgettable story

Every Thursday at eight, four women meet to talk
and share their lives. As one life-changing year
unfolds, it becomes a true celebration of friends
helping each other through the tough times.

**Make time for friends.
Make time for Debbie Macomber.**

www.mirabooks.co.uk

From the bestselling author of *Thursdays at Eight*

When eighteen-year-old Susannah Nelson
was sent to school abroad, she never
saw her boyfriend, Jake, again.

Years later, Susannah finds herself regretting the
paths not taken. Returning to her parents' house
and to the past, she discovers that things are
not always as they once seemed…

**Make time for friends.
Make time for Debbie Macomber.**

www.mirabooks.co.uk

MIRA

A time for sharing...

Every Wednesday a group of four women meet,
each with her own share of worries and troubles.

As friendships deepen, these women start to
confide in each other, but will listening and
sharing be enough for them to move
forward, leaving their pasts behind?

Make time for friends.
Make time for Debbie Macomber.

www.mirabooks.co.uk

What do you want most in the world?

Recently widowed bookshop owner Anne Marie Roche wants to find happiness again. When Anne Marie and several other widows get together, each begins a list of twenty things they always wanted to do but never did.

As Anne Marie works her way through her wishes, she learns that dreams can come true—but not necessarily in the way you expect.

Make time for friends.
Make time for Debbie Macomber.

www.mirabooks.co.uk